The door swung op̶e̶ ̶ ̶ ̶ ̶ ̶ ̶ ̶ ̶ ̶ ̶ ̶t.

The living room was quiet, a black lacquered lamp lay on the carpet, the shade tumbled askew. Geraint's nerves began to jangle. People who live in places like this didn't leave their doors open.

Francesca looked puzzled, dumb, as if trying to focus on the scene. "Where's Annie?" she mumbled.

"Don't know. This seems a bit odd, but I'm sure there's nothing to . . ." His voice trailed away as he stepped farther in and saw the hint of a stain in front of the door to his left. He couldn't be sure, it might be no more than spilled wine, but his guts were beginning to churn and he was afraid.

"Fran, why don't you just sit, uh, down there and I'll call down to security?" He steered her to a plush chair facing away from the far door, and reached for the telecom on the table beside it. That way he could open the bedroom door and peek in unobtrusively while making the call.

Geraint would never have believed a body had so much blood in it.

SHADOWRUN 8: STREETS OF BLOOD

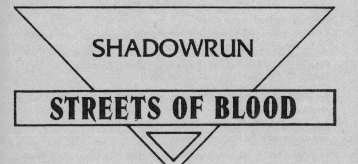

SHADOWRUN

STREETS OF BLOOD

CARL SARGENT
&
MARC GASCOIGNE

A ROC BOOK

ROC
Published by the Penguin Group
Penguin Books USA Inc., 375 Hudson Street,
New York, New York 10014, U.S.A.
Penguin Books Ltd, 27 Wrights Lane, London W8 5TZ England
Penguin Books Australia Ltd, Ringwood, Victoria, Australia
Penguin Books Canada Ltd, 10 Alcorn Avenue,
Toronto, Canada, Canada M4V 3B2
Penguin Books (N.Z) Ltd, 182–190 Wairau Road,
Auckland 10, New Zealand

Penguin Books Ltd, Registered Offices:
Harmondsworth, Middlesex, England

First published by Roc, an imprint of New American Library, a division
of Penguin Books USA Inc.

First Printing December, 1992
10 9 8 7 6 5 4 3 2 1

Series Editor: Donna Ippolito
Cover: Keith Birdsong
Interior Illustrations: Larry MacDougall

R&C   REGISTERED TRADEMARK—MARCA REGISTRADA
SHADOWRUN, FASA, and the distinctive SHADOWRUN and FASA lo-
gos are trademarks of the FASA Corporation, 1026 W. Van Buren, Chi-
cago, Illinois 60507.

Printed in the United States of America.

BRITAIN 2051: ZONAL MAP

1

The first gleam of blood-red light arced across the cabin just as the massive tires of the suborbital Ghost shuttle screamed on first contact with Runway 11 of the world's busiest airport. The mage's mind was elsewhere, and the rough impact jolted him back into the real world of Heathrow's dazzling lights and concourses.

The call had come just when Serrin thought he'd almost gotten used to Seattle, even begun to feel slightly at home there, his suitcases slouched against the wall of a cheap hotel for more than the usual week or two. He'd been wary of the offer made by the suit with the impossibly even tone of voice, but the nuyen glowing on his credstick was no lie and money enough to bring him to London as requested.

Perhaps the corporation that wanted to hire him couldn't find a registered British mage to do the job for them. That was plausible enough, considering the way the Lord Protector's offices had nearly every British mage tied up good and safe in red tape. Every practitioner of magic had to pay a hefty fee and submit a DNA sample to be registered by the Lord Protector's office. A foreigner trying to register could wait weeks, or even months, just for the processing of his or her application. Serrin had bypassed the usual difficulties and delays—and possible refusal of his application—because the powerful Renraku Corporation had owed him a few favors. Thanks to them Serrin's carefully coded DNA sample was properly filed in one of the huge basement complexes of the Temple District. Gently, without admitting it, they had pointed him in the direction of the right people, which was the least they could do to make up for his leg turned to mincemeat while doing some work for them.

"We'd like you to sign this disclaimer of responsibility, however," the jittery accountant had muttered, all the while avoiding his gaze. "It'll, ah, tie up any loose ends. Just protocol." Maybe a leg turned to mincemeat was just protocol after all.

The magnetic seatbelt unclipped and Serrin got slowly to his feet, reaching up to open the overhead compartment. He pulled out his pigskin bag, then instinctively clutched it to his chest as if protecting some intimate part of himself. He edged forward along the aisle behind a snot-nosed child, who whined in protest as a blotchy-faced woman dragged him along toward Customs. For a split-second, the elf had a feeling of pure absurdity, a sensation of unreality, of being almost out of his own body. He grabbed at the papers inside his shabby jacket as if for support. With a shake of his head, he focused on the passport, the visa, the medical documents, the permits, and the licenses. Damn the British love of bureaucracy! Getting through Customs and Immigration in London was like having to read a long letter very slowly to a very deaf, half-senile great-aunt who, even in her rare moments of lucidity, willfully feigned a lack of comprehension.

Standing at the head of a stairway leading to British tarmac, Serrin shivered. It was one-fifteen in the morning, early November, the temperature hovering around zero Celsius and a dismal filmy drizzle of rain coating his skin with grime from the London skies. So much for the year 2054 and the city's miracle weather-control dome!

He descended the steps slowly and a little painfully, his usual fine tremor become a veritable tremble. Coughing into a balled fist, he made his way gratefully to the warmth of the passenger coach waiting to deliver him unto British officialdom. I hate London, he thought, but at least you can get a decent malt whiskey here. Comforting himself with that prospect, he ducked his cropped

gray head into the coach doorway and found himself sitting next to a pile of duty-free items and another sniveling child. The tall, gangling elf gave the boy a sinister look that made the youngster shrink back in alarm. Good, thought Serrin wearily, that should keep him quiet for a while.

* * *

At the moment Serrin was closing his eyes for a bit of rest, somewhere in London's East End, blood was dripping down onto the floorboards of a nondescript apartment in the neighborhood known as Whitechapel. The knife had done its work and now was the time for greater precision.

In Chelsea, yet another part of the city, a nobleman was turning his gaze from the flickering computer screen to the elegantly fluted bottle resting in a monogrammed silver ice bucket. Geraint drew the bottle toward him, wrapped a linen cloth around the cork, and pulled it out so carefully that the hiss of escaping gas was barely audible. She hadn't heard; she would be deeply asleep by now. Dom Ruisse '38 would have been wasted on the girl—one of Geraint's rare lapses of taste.

He clipped the rubber seal over the bottle and depressed the silver hooks to keep the chilled champagne fresh. The wine tasted good, and he contemplated the pleasure of it as he idly swirled the bubbles in his glass. Then his gaze traveled, almost involuntarily, past the row of financial yearbooks and references by his work station to the mahogany box etched with images of dragons. He hesitated for only the briefest instant, then flipped the gold catch and drew out the black silk bundle containing his deck of cards. He cleared a space on the cool white surface of the table, pushed his glass to one side, then expertly shuffled the unwieldy deck several times. He sat for several long moments, mentally aligning himself with the Tarot. Feeling the rapport established, he lit a cigarette and left it to spiral blue smoke from the marbled ashtray.

With a sudden motion he reached out to cut the deck

with a single, decisive sweep, then flicked over the top card.

The Magician.

Geraint was startled, not expecting this after so many years. The signal from a card of the Major Arcana was quite unequivocal: Serrin!

The Magician is here, he thought. The deck was telling him, and he felt it in his gut. He pursed his lips with his fingers, forgetting everything else around him, intent only on the extraordinary image of the snake-crowned juggler smiling at him. More than a century ago, the artist had given the Magician card the distinctly pointed ears of an elf; what had she and the designer of the Thoth Tarot known of the coming Sixth Age of the world? Had they foreseen the birth of elves and the other new races of metahumanity?

But these thoughts were taking him off-track. Show me why he comes here, Geraint silently asked the deck. With long, slender fingers he drew another card, which he placed face-up, across the first. He saw the unmistakable image as it turned, and shuddered in spite of himself.

The Nine of Swords. Cruelty. Blood dripped from the fractured blades in the image. The Welshman felt fear, fear for Serrin, fear for what was to come. Then, a third card slid from the deck, without his even touching it, as though his fear had called it forth to obscure the horror of the Nine.

* * *

A stone's throw away, Francesca Young rebuffed an inept pass by her escort as she drew her tanned legs into the waiting limo. She wrinkled her nose just discernibly at the sight of a troll in the chauffeur's seat, but he was polite and Forbes Security had obviously spent money on elocution lessons for their operatives. Mercifully, he restricted himself to a "Very good, m'lady" as he eased the powerful machine along Kensington High Street; Francesca was too out of sorts to put up with a driver who thought clients wanted meaningless chatter about London's weather at two in the morning. As she stared out the window, the first sight that greeted her eyes was that of two young fools in tuxedos squaring off in the road while a pair of debs shrieked with delight from the windows of their limo. She felt tired and jaded, fed up with men who ordered salmon after hearing her mention she'd grown up on the Pacific seaboard of North America, then expected sexual favors for the price of a fairly routine meal.

Her mind returned to her work. All afternoon she'd been buzzing over her cyberdeck, a Fuchi 6, installing the smartframe that would operate as a semi-independent intelligence to execute programs that would protect her while she traveled about in the cyberspace of the Matrix. With the new Korean sleaze program, she'd be able to slip past intrusion countermeasures that until now she'd been too wary to confront. She forgot all about her annoying date and stretched out in the back seat. Men were far less sensuous than a hot program.

She was almost asleep when the limo delivered her to her doorstep; six minutes more and her head hit the pillow in her bedroom. In vain did the tortoiseshell cat grumble for his food. Daddy's little rich girl slept, but that didn't mean the cat would have long to wait. Not much time passed before Francesca was awake again, screaming in terror. It was the same nightmare and it always woke her at the same place, just as the last scalpel had been cleaned and was being put back in the case.

* * *

The Empress. Sitting demurely in her bower, holding flowers, and dressed in blue-green, the serene figure gazes out contentedly over the bounty of the earth. Her curves are sensuous and strong, and she is crowned by the sky above her throne.

Geraint almost slumped with relief. Francesca. Well, we certainly know each other, we three. The hint of a feeling slipped past his control, a momentary sadness, the recollection of a precious opportunity now lost, but the impression faded quickly.

His eyes were drawn against his will to a detail in the bottom left-hand corner of the card: seated below the throne of the woman, beyond her sight, was a pelican feeding her young. It was said that the bird nourished her offspring with her own blood, and, in truth, these fledglings were pecking at their mother's breast. Geraint saw blood, blood in his mind's eye and not on the card, and his body almost convulsed. The triangle of tufted hair at the nape of his neck rose and a cold chill ran down his spine. The champagne lay flat in the glass now, having become merely poor, thin wine. Show me help, he begged the cards, show me what I can reach to. Is there anyone there?

* * *

Rani was breathing a little heavily as she gave the five-rap signal on the reinforced door. Her brother Imran drew back the bolts, saw her face in what remained of the streetlights, and hurriedly pulled the chains from their pins. He drew her into his arms and half-dragged her inside, fumbling the bolts and heavy steel chains back into place to seal out the harsh night. He brushed back the hair from her forehead, examining her face carefully. Reassured that she was unharmed, he still wanted to know what had happened.

"It was nothing. Just a pair of dweebs in an alley in Shoreditch, up by Den's chippie, the one who sells that crap cod, you know?" She was talking too fast, unsettled. "One came up behind me and I swivel-kicked him. I don't think he'll be having any kids in future. The other one didn't back off right away, though. Bastard had a meathook with a honed edge. I think he wanted to get some practice barbering." She laughed a little too loudly and tears welled in her large brown eyes. "Doesn't matter. Happens all the time."

Imran hugged her tight again and shushed her, stroking the back of her head. Then he ushered her into the living room with its barred windows, peeling gilt wallpaper, and frayed carpets. She could see Sanjay with his thermometer and glass retorts in the kitchen beyond, the acrid smell of acetone and isopropyl biting through the air. She looked despondently at Imran, then flicked her eyes back toward kitchen, her face almost despairing.

"It's for a bunch of rakkies in from Essex who think

they're going to have fun slumming in the Smoke,'' her brother sighed, trying to prevent a scene. ''Who cares about white human trash? Sanjay won't put any rat poison in it. Promise.'' His lopsided grin asked for comprehension, but her head was in her hands now, her broad shoulders heaving a little as she fought back the sobs. Her brother knew better than to touch or approach her, giving Rani time to master these powerful emotions with her own strength. This wasn't the moment for the usual reproaches about her being away from home; for once, the words died on his lips.

She inhaled deeply and brushed away the traces of tears from her face. ''Maybe they wanted to kill me because I'm not white. Maybe they wanted to kill me because I'm an ork. I only did what I did because they came at me with blades and hammers. But I killed someone not twenty minutes ago, and I don't feel good about that. And when I get home I find my brothers cooking up drugs to feed the habits of a bunch of trancers.'' She sighed deeply and sank back into the chair, resigned and weary. ''Sod it. I'm seventeen years old, and just now I think I've had enough of the world. Or at least the East End of bloody London.''

Feeling too hopeless to talk, Rani climbed the stairs to her room. She kicked off her heavy combat boots, pulled off her woolen socks, and looked at the upturned palms of her hands with their flexible immunoneutral pads below the skin. Not many of her kind could afford such a fusion of biology and tech. The twenty-first century had made it possible, but it couldn't make it cheap. Imran had paid a lot to protect her.

That's one advantage of being an Indian, she reminded herself; a smartgun link is harder to see on me than on a whiteskin. Makes me a lot harder to kill than most of my cousins. The ones still alive know that. The others found out too late. She pulled the padded jacket over her head and shoulders, making a mental note to repair the tear along the right shoulder in the morning. The edge of the meat hook had made a very precise cut, but a few minutes with the monofilament staplegun and the jacket would be as good as new. She tugged off her baggy ribbed pants and clambered into bed, and within minutes was asleep. Rani was too exhausted to be disturbed by the frequent sounds of shouts and gunfire that came up from the streets through her cracked window to her. Besides, she was used to it.

* * *

Strength.

The calm gaze of the woman holding the lion's mouth open stared back at Geraint from the card. He didn't know who she was, but he felt a mixture of calm and excitement after the horror and fear of the earlier images, a sense of reassurance and uncertainty at the same time. Well, powerful lady, I hope we meet sooner rather than later. After the soft-bodied creatures of the last few weeks, you should be interesting.

Geraint grinned, put the pack in its silk and in its box, and then poured a fresh glass of champagne. News was coming through fast from Tokyo and the Hang Seng in Hong Kong; something was popping in the pharmaceuticals markets, or so it looked. He reached for the plug and snapped it into the datajack behind his left ear, bringing the electronic chatter of the cyberdeck closer to his consciousness.

Geraint was in the Matrix now, and he felt predatory. At the same moment, his persona icon showed the place where his attention was directed in the Matrix. The icon had no objective reality among the optical chips, datalines, and computer architecture they called the Matrix, but another operator in the same part of the system would perceive Geraint's "persona" as a Celtic knight grasping a longsword, which represented a powerful attack program in cyberspace. Beside him, his sensor utilities took the image of a pack of Irish wolfhounds, eager and snuffling as they loped along beside him.

Let's go check on the nightlife in Teesprawl, he thought with a smile. Something tells me Zeta-ImpChem might have some interesting data on this. Come on, boys. Time to make money.

* * *

It's the middle of the twenty-first century, but the November fog is not so different from what it was in *fin de siècle* nineteenth-century London. The soup may not be quite as thick, but it boasts a more powerful cocktail of pathogens and chemical pollutants. The famous fog also still provides cover for those who want to slip unseen into the shadows, especially closer to the River Thames, where most of the street lights have been shot out.

At three-ten in the morning, the thermometer is still hovering around zero. Blood is beginning to seep through the floorboards of a room in Whitechapel and soon it will begin to show on the ceiling of the chamber below. That won't worry the girl asleep downstairs; she's a trancer. The drugs won't wash out of her system until a police doctor arrives after the constables smash down her door later on. A young constable, the one who is first on the scene upstairs, will be vomiting uncontrollably in the street outside. The police photographer will be very, very glad he never takes more than coffee for breakfast.

So it begins.

2

Serrin woke with a start.

Seven-thirty. The familiar and unchanging BBC voice, anonymous for generations, was reading off the mundane litany of disaster that comprised world news. The only good thing, the elf thought groggily, was that the BBC was less parochial than the American broadcasts he was used to. You actually did get world news and not just what happened in your city, tribe, or state in the previous twenty-four hours.

He yawned and stretched his whole body until his hamstring gave him a twinge, reminding him not to push it too far. That thought had distracted him from the first part of what the BBC voice was saying about some five murders in London last night, somewhat above the average. The part he caught was about a particularly messy

murder of a prostitute in the East End, hardened police-
man turning white or green or similar implausible shades,
blah blah, blah. Serrin reached for the remote and ran
his fingers over the buttons to switch to trideo. The picture shimmered into focus instantly—not bad for an average hotel box—only to show some airhead prancing
around a weather display that suggested Britain was
doomed both to rain and garbage breakfast entertainment
for some months to come. He eased his long legs over
the edge of the bed and creaked to his feet.

"Message for you, Mr. Shamandar," the telecom
crackled with a cheerfulness utterly unsuited to such an
hour of a British morning.

"Thanks, go ahead," Serrin wheezed, spluttering back
his thick, early-morning cough.

"Mr. Smith and Mr. Jones cordially invite you to a
business breakfast in the Chippendale Suite at nine
o'clock. They politely request that you be prompt. Thank
you for taking this message." The voice squeaked into
silence.

Serrin headed for the bathroom opposite the bed, and
wrenched the tub's brass hot-water tap into life. One of
the few things he appreciated about Brits was the ambiva-
lent quality of hotel baths: lots of towels, excellent, sub-
tly perfumed soaps, and appalling plumbing and cold
bathrooms. The chill guaranteed that you'd want to stay
in the hot water of the bath purely to survive. The plumbing, however, guaranteed that every bathtime was something of an adventure; would you get enough hot water
to fill the respectably large tubs before it ran lukewarm?

Francesca had told him that it was solely the principle
of the thing that made Brits refuse to use decent chiptech
in their hot-water systems. Baths, they seemed to think,
shouldn't be enjoyed too much. It offended their puritanical asceticism. At the time he'd assumed that it had more
to do with plain, old-fashioned British inefficiency.
Strange that thoughts of Francesca should cross his mind
now. It had been five years since they had last met.

With a tug at his heart that he hadn't felt for a long
time, the elf remembered holding a terrified young
woman outside a restaurant full of corpses in San Francisco. Closing his eyes, he sank into the welcoming

warmth of the water as a wave of memory brought back the sweet smell of her fresh-washed hair against his face. Serrin rarely thought about women, nor did he linger on the topic now. He leaned back against the deep tub, turning his thoughts to business and to the fact that the accommodations the suits had chosen for him did not reveal much about them. The Crescent Hotel was neither real class nor the fake kind for Americans and Japanese with more money than true discernment; it was simply a reasonably good place to stay. He guessed that the pair would not give much away in the breakfast meeting, either, that there might be some cat-and-mouse about this job. I'll worry about that later, he thought. Right now, it's time to soak these bones and get out some of the jet lag.

* * *

"Thank you for being so prompt, Mr. Shamandar." The pudgy hand gripped his with routine corporate strength; not weak, not strong, just an in-between reassurance.

The Chippendale Suite could have seated twenty in ample comfort, so whoever was behind Messrs. Smith and Jones wasn't worried about their expense credsticks. The serving table groaned under the weight of a very traditional British breakfast: bacon, kidneys, smoked herring in butter, scrambled eggs in a great silver bowl, poached eggs in salvers, acres of toast that would be as cold as the chill gray morning, yellow butter in white dishes, thick and distressingly dark marmalade, preserves, urns of tea the color of boot polish, and silver pots of Colombian coffee, enough to feed an army of the urchins roaming the streets of the South London Squeeze zone. They'd have died young from gamma-cholesterol furring up their arteries, but then those urchins had a very low life-expectancy anyway.

Serrin turned his mind back to the matter at hand and heaped a Wedgwood plate with bacon and eggs, hoping that the steam rising from the yellowed eggs would live up to the promise of some residual heat in them. The suits settled for coffee, toast, and what the jar label claimed to be Scottish raspberry jam. The mage vaguely recalled some blight having wiped out Scottish fruit-farming several years ago, but maybe the druids of the Wild Lands in the Grampians had restored the land of late.

The leaner suit, Jones, saturnine and with an almost polished skin, interrupted Serrin's meandering thoughts. "We require a skilled operative to conduct some low-risk surveillance, sir."

The opening gambit was not unexpected: nice and vague. Serrin nodded without speaking. Let them come to the point.

"Our client has an interest in a certain key area of research," Jones went on. "And such research is being conducted in facilities in a city not far from London. Naturally, our client observes the proprieties, while aiming to conduct multimodality surveillance."

Serrin winced mentally, hoping it hadn't shown on his face. Where did these people learn to speak like this? He nodded once again, gratified to find that the eggs had retained just enough heat to warm the toast.

"It would not be frank to fail to apprise you that our client has initiated observations in the cybersphere."

Cybersphere? Come on, chummers, cut the gibberish. I know what computerized snooping is and I'm sure you've hired a good decker. But what do you want from me?

The other man, Smith, took up the patter. As he began to speak, Serrin was intrigued by the small ruby embedded into one of the man's teeth. Not exactly standard-issue for a faceless British corporate mouthpiece.

"Our client is anxious that these observations be enhanced by magical surveillance," Smith was saying. "Our client is aware of your reputation in such matters. He has heard among the knowledgeable that you are one who can deal with watchers. If I may put it so, those spirits who exist in the etheric plane in astral space. At least, this is what I gather that philosophers on such matters say."

Smith and Jones exchanged token smiles and then turned back to face Serrin. They've got their act down pat, the mage thought. They should be exchanging banter with Barry Dando on whatever the lame Brit equivalent is of the late-night talk show, not pushing this crap. Who do they think they're kidding with watchers? Anyone into serious research will have hermetics, mages on the company payroll, who'll make damn sure nothing so simple can crack anything that matters.

"Of course," Jones continued slickly, as Smith smoothed an errant strand of hair over his balding head, "those corporate interests that are developing research along the lines in which our client has a primary interest will be vigilant regarding the possibility of watchers being used as observers. Our client would regard such vigilance as a positive sign that those very corporations are developing research along lines in which our client is interested. In short, we want you to use watchers as a lure to test the defenses of certain corporations."

Jones sat back, then lunged forward to grab the coffee pot. There was a twitchiness about the gesture that told Serrin coffee wasn't the only Colombian export Jones had ingested that morning. It had been so long since his last visit to this country that he'd almost forgotten people here still got high on drugs rather than dreamchips. It amazed him that people were so willing to destroy their bodies and minds.

Smith took up the conversation again in an oily, ingratiating tone. "This is not a demanding task, Mr. Shamandar. However, you must be aware that the unfortunate official restrictions under which we live in Britain require that we look beyond our own shores for able operatives to carry out the tasks requested by clients such as ours."

Serrin was growing more annoyed by the minute. Why had they brought him all this way just to beat around the bush? Looking down, he saw that he'd dolloped marmalade onto what remained of his eggs. He decided to brazen it out. It didn't taste good.

"Our client offers one thousand nuyen per day, plus expenses." The fat man sat back, looking smug. The tiny gem glittered in his mouth, adding fake glamour to his crocodile smile.

"Fifteen hundred," Serrin said curtly. "The work may seem easy, but experts don't come cheap." Serrin thought he might be pushing his luck, but he wanted to test the responses of these unflappable suits. To his surprise, Smith agreed at once.

"Very well. You drive a hard bargain, sir. Fifteen hundred was the limit allowed by our client. You will begin work tomorrow. At five o'clock this afternoon, we will have delivered to you a list of the sites we wish you to survey. You will spend an initial period of one week conducting surveillance and then report to us, both orally and in writing, in nine days' time. We are authorized to give you this." Smith handed Serrin a roseate hard plastic rod that he'd retrieved from the recesses of his immaculate Saville Row suit. "This is good for twelve thousand nuyen, plus three thousand for travel and other incidental expenses. You will not need to provide receipts unless you exceed that sum and wish to claim the balance from our client. Your hotel bill will be covered by our client, who wishes you to stay here each night rather than in Cambridge, where your research will be conducted. That will help prevent detection of your work. You can confirm the sum the credstick authorizes in the credit analyzer in the hotel lobby if you wish."

The suits were rising to their feet now, Smith sweeping away some toast crumbs from the expanse of waistcoat stretched over his ample belly. Jones shook Serrin's hand with exactly the same pressure Smith had applied. "Please enjoy your day. We look forward to seeing you again." With that, the men swept out of the suite.

Serrin drained the coffee pot, adding just a little of the slightly yellowed cream from the jug, which spilled some of its contents over the starched linen tablecloth each time it was used.

This was too easy. The fixer had agreed too readily to a fifty percent increase; the credstick had already been cut on that basis. They knew him, they knew watchers were his specialty. Serrin had the feeling that somehow he was being used. But for fifteen hundred nuyen and for a job that couldn't possibly present any danger, he couldn't imagine that it was a sucker deal.

Could he?

* * *

Jones rubbed his chin as he leaned back in the passenger seat of the Toyota Elite. He looked over at the fat man hurriedly tapping the scrambling code into the portacom link, holding his thumb tightly over the scanner as it checked his thumbprint ID. Smith jacked in the electrodes from the link so the portacom could make the backup brainwave-scan ID check, then fumbled the telecom code into the pad. The screen flickered and registered entry of the code.

With a grunt, Smith checked off the portacom and reached for the ignition. As the car began to purr gently, Jones reached into an inside pocket and drew out a small plastic case.

"They got the confirming code, so we're done with work for the day. A little boost?"

"Don't mind if I do," Smith smirked as a bead of sweat ran down from his pallid forehead. His bulbous nose twitched slightly in anticipation, emphasizing the tiny broken red veins. He took the tiny chip greedily, turning it over and over in his hand. "Morpheus hallmark. That's what I like, a little class."

Back in the hotel, Serrin wrapped a muffler around his throat and buttoned up the baggy woolen coat he always brought with him to London, even in what the Brits laughably termed summer. Striding through the hotel lobby, he hailed one of the voluminous black trollcabs, London's finest, yanking open the passenger door as the grinning driver screeched the vehicle to a halt.

"Serena's, and be sharp about it," Serrin snapped as the cab jerked into motion. Inside his coat he clutched his credstick for comfort. As long as he was in London he was going to get some decent talismongering out of this deal. Liverpool Street station and tickets for Cambridge could wait.

3

"The Greens need all the votes they can get for the Regeneration Bill in the House of Nobles?" Geraint's voice was rough with surprise and too many cigarettes smoked into the wee morning hours.

"We're going to need you, Llanfrechfa." When the Earl of Manchester addressed him by his formal title, it meant the matter was serious. "It's the elven faction, I'm afraid. They're out to cause trouble because they think Wales isn't getting a big enough slice of government money, the greedy bastards. Damn it, they've got less pollution and toxic waste down there than anywhere else in the country. What are they whining about? Probably Glendower's doing, damn woman." The Earl of Manchester's antipathy toward women, in general, and the Countess of Harlech, in particular, was legendary. "We have to vote down their amendments."

"How close is it?"

"We could go down on this one. Winstanley will be sure to take note of who supported us at a difficult time." If the earl was implying the Prime Minister's interest, Geraint knew it meant the promise of a favor sometime in the future. Opportunities for stashing favors were Geraint's specialty. "I know you're a Welshman yourself, Geraint, old man, but you can be sure no one will forget your support."

"Of course," Geraint said. "I'll be at the House at two o'clock sharp. Perhaps we can meet in the smoking rooms for a brandy after lunch, sir." Geraint tried for just the right amount of willingness, with a terminal grovel in the "sir." He grinned inwardly.

"Good man. Show the woman who's boss!" The earl's heavily lined face turned to a wash of static as Geraint cut the telecom.

Geraint wasn't much given to the political intrigues so favored by Britain's nobility. Supporting one faction inevitably meant that some other little clique would invariably harbor a grudge, and so he tried to avoid taking sides. When his hand was forced, he went along with the majority and never opposed the truly powerful. All he could do was hope that Rhiannon Glendower wouldn't single him out from among the parliamentary lobby the government would need to muster for this vote. She was the last person he'd want for an enemy.

Almost dreamily he turned and twisted the tiny Chinese dragon spheres. The spheres tinkled and jingled in his fingers, and soon he had them synchronized in their gentle chiming. It was only when his senses suddenly snapped him back into the real world a few minutes later that he realized how far away he'd been, off in one of the fugue states he'd inherited from his mother, who possessed the Sight far more strongly than did Geraint. He couldn't recall anything from his moments out of this world, just a vague premonition and uncertainty. Almost reluctantly, he reached for the Tarot and drew a single card.

The Five of Wands. *Strife*.

He felt unsure about the card, and despite his intimate familiarity with the images, he pulled a well-thumbed old book from an untidy pile on the small bookcase beside his desk. "A tricky and difficult time," read the entry for the card. "The Five of Wands suggests that one will meet opposition that can only be overcome through cunning and resourcefulness. This opposition takes the form of some competing interest, a talented person or powerful group of people who do not share one's plans, goals, and attitudes, and may even scheme against one. . . ."

It fitted the machinations of the nobles, but Geraint felt that the card was pointing to something else, something more shadowy than a vote on a government bill. As the sense of unease grew within him, he tried to put it aside as he prepared for his appointment with Manchester. He ran a bath while brushing the charcoal-gray Italian suit cut with just the right conservatism and inconspicuousness for the House of Nobles. The scents of ylang ylang, orange blossom, and sandalwood rose with the steam. Geraint rubbed the fatigue from his eyes and began the work of massaging his facial muscles. He felt his thirtieth birthday looming ominously close this morning. Maybe it was the time of life when a man's thoughts turned to collagen implants.

*   *   *

"Good. That's settled." Manchester was in an affable mood, partly because of his assurance that the government forces he'd marshaled would win the vote, but mostly thanks to a third fine Armagnac having made its way to his grossly spreading gut. "Oh, by the way, old boy, did you get an invitation to the Cambridge bash this weekend?"

Geraint's ears pricked up. If the earl was referring to some function hosted by the Duchess of Cambridge, he definitely wanted an invitation. Francesca Hamilton was a most attractive woman, still only recently widowed and, most important of all, she was the richest woman in Britain.

"You mean Francesca's do?" He brazened it out as if he'd known about it all along. A mistake; Manchester frowned slightly, but he was too dull-witted with drink to note Geraint's over-familiarity. "Don't know about that. Bloody woman doesn't have many parties I get to hear about. Never enough drink at them anyway.

"No, my boy, there's a high-powered meeting of Nobles in Business at the University Arms over the weekend. Starts Friday morning. Seminars and all that sod. Bunch of corporate wallahs behind it all, as usual. Can't be bothered myself. If you like, take my invitation and I'll tell the stuffed suits I've recommended you instead. I'm off grouse shooting with old Hamish."

"That's extraordinarily generous of you, sir. I'd be most appreciative." Geraint was curious about the meeting, and amused at the thought of his portly lunch companion blasting away at a bunch of hapless game birds with antique firearms, accompanied by the broomstick-thin and notoriously bad-tempered Earl of Dundee. The Cambridge meeting was of interest because it might yield Geraint some useful contacts. His investigations of the Zeta-ImpChem corporate system hadn't come to much; their defenses were so fierce and so stacked against deckers sniffing at their forbidding Matrix systems that he didn't dare risk it. There might be easier ways of finding out what was going on in the pharmaceuticals market. Getting a corporate suit to wax loquacious by plying him with alcohol was still easier than trying to hack one's way past deadly intrusion countermeasures. Human weaknesses were still more predictable than any technology. Cambridge could be a good opportunity.

Geraint set his glass down on the polished mahogany

table just as the first bell sounded calling the nobles into the debating chamber.

The earl rose to his feet with a grunt, the effort accompanied by a thunderous fart, which Geraint pointedly ignored. ''Come on my boy, let's teach those blasted pixies a lesson about the power of the vote. That's what democracy is all about.''

* * *

Francesca hunched over the Fuchi Cyber-6. Decking played such havoc with her shoulder muscles that she'd need a massage afterward, but looking forward to that was part of the buzz. She was traveling light in the Matrix, having loaded a cloak program to mask her operations, analyze and browse programs for quick checks through datastores and structures, and a powerful sleaze program to get past any ID checks en route. As usual, she also had a restore program ready to repair any damage done to her deck's MPCP, the master persona control program that was the heart of her deck's operations. She'd paid a third of a million nuyen for the cyberdeck, and wasn't about to risk its destruction. As a further guarantee, an alarm seed program left monitors behind that would alert her to any pursuit as she sped down the datastream.

She made a quick check on her bearings, the data bits glowing and swirling around the nondescript child that was her persona in the Matrix. This was no more than a routine job, really; checking the datastores of a very minor research group stuck away in Kent would take no more than half an hour, after which she could copy and decrypt anything interesting at her leisure. The job didn't really justify the fee, but they were paying for her reputation. Besides, she needed extra for Rutger, the barman at the Lounging Lizard, where she often had her meets. Keeping him on a hefty retainer greased the wheels of her style, making her negotiations generally swifter and more professional. That also helped guarantee more work to follow. This was just a preliminary snoop, after all.

As she entered the system access node of Howarth Associates' system, a feeble access program tried to check her ID. The sleaze program got her past the barrier so effortlessly that she was actually looking forward to something more challenging further into the heart of the system. Meanwhile she used the analyze program to check the sub-processing unit ahead, identifying it as the SPU controlling the flow of data to other SPUs within the system. Super! No need to get to the central processor, where she'd surely encounter more severe countermeasures and checks. She could work from this basic point.

The SPU had one nice touch in defense: a tar baby trap that would have crashed and dumped her sleaze program without ceremony had her sleaze not been able to fool it. It looked like that sleaze had been worth every nuyen she'd paid for it because the tar baby let her pass easily. Speeding further along the cluster of SPUs and into the datastores, she ran her analysis and data-checking programs while also keeping tabs on the alarm seed monitors. No reaction from the system, no alerts. It was like stealing candy from a sleeping baby.

As she was preparing to exit the system a microsecond's jarring of her awareness kicked her pulse rate over a hundred. The analyze program gave her only garbage about what had happened, but she knew the disturbance came from some other presence in the system snooping on her and the data she'd just finished downloading into her deck. Her alarm seed monitors had not spotted the intruder, so he was probably well cloaked. She leaped from the SAN and into the grid beyond.

Her child persona spun around to see a black figure with a leather bag fleeing into the distance. She gave chase, keeping pace with the figure, wanting only to get a better look. Racing past a bewildered pair of streetwalkers, she followed the figure to a SAN that screamed black IC, the deadly countermeasures programs, at her.

The figure stepped into the SAN, then turned to face her. It was utterly faceless. Where its face should have been, there gaped a bleak nothingness, a vortex of swirling emptiness.

Numbed, half-paralyzed with fright, Francesca suddenly flew back out of her chair, the trodes snapping out of her datajacks and their leads dangling over the work-table.

She was astonished. Checking her deck quietly, she found no damage. The data was downloaded and ready for the frame to decrypt and analyze it. But this was the first time she'd ever been dumped from the Matrix by a simple glance from another decker persona. For all the power of that faceless thing, however, neither she nor her deck were damaged. She'd have expected it to deploy some vicious black IC, but it hadn't. What the hell was going on?

"Right, you ugly bastard, whoever you are," she said to her empty apartment. "I'm coming back with some armor and defenses that'll make even you think twice." But when she gingerly reentered the Matrix and tracked the SAN into which the figure had vanished, her child persona drew back suddenly. It was the entrance to the Transys Neuronet system. No way! Her resolve evaporated as fast as it had formed. She didn't intend to go headlong into the system of the most paranoid and dangerous cyber-research corporation in Britain.

Francesca didn't like letting go of an unsolved mystery, but she knew when she needed a little help. Armor and shield programs executed from an independent frame would be just a start, but first she needed to touch base with some contacts outside the Matrix. She ignored her aching shoulders and back and keyed in the telecom code. He wasn't home, but that was expected. She left a message instead.

"Geraint, you slippery cobber, I've got something a little wild on my hands. Dinner at the Savoy Grill at eight? Don't drink too much—I need your mind intact. RSVP, Welsh boy."

* * *

The government won by a majority of twenty-one votes, the Cambridge meeting looked worthwhile, and Geraint arrived home to find that the Empress had called. He'd been half-expecting to hear from her, yet when he wrote a card to be sent by courier, he put the date for dinner at the Savoy Hotel at two days from now. He wasn't sure what made him want to delay. Some stubborn uncertainty in him just wasn't ready for things to begin happening so swiftly.

* * *

The killer is satiated right now, but he's still learning what needs to be done. With no one to mourn her, what's left of Polly Nichols lies in the morgue. It has begun, but no one has noticed. Yet.

4

"I like the way you do that." Francesca grinned as she sat down at the table glittering with silver and crystal. "Thank you, sir!"

"Hmm?" Geraint blinked at her, unfurling an immaculate linen napkin from its gleaming ring. Her smile broadened at his quizzical, absent-minded expression.

"Oh, nothing. Just that men back in L.A. wouldn't draw back my chair as I sat down. You Brits may be broke, but you sure have manners."

"Not so broke, Francesca. HKB's last set of global estimations show that we own seventeen percent of your gross domestic product. Almost as much as the Japanese, in fact.

"But you aren't here to talk about Hildebrandt-Kleinfort-Bernal," he said, leaning across to light her cigarette. "The lemon sole's good, but I expect you'll want your usual lump of dead mammal with added steroids and antibiotics?"

"Yes please," she said. "Good and rare. And don't forget the growth hormone additives!" Francesca blew out smoke from her cigarette as she dug around deep in her handbag. Just how did women get so much into the space of a purse? Geraint wondered. Legions of credsticks, powder compacts, and chipbooks for addresses bore testimony to the enduring violation of the laws of physics in women's handbags. Staring down into the depths of the bag, she finally found what she was looking for and drew out the slim palm-sized screen. "Take a look at this."

She tapped in a code and passed him the screen. Immediately fascinated by the holographic images that unfolded before his eyes, Geraint drew in his breath at the sight of the faceless persona. With a kind of shudder he set the screen down on the table. He said nothing for a few moments, fingertips wandering distractedly over his chin and lips, then asked simply, "When was this?"

"Just last night. Ever seen anything like it?"

He shook his head. "I doubt I'd even have believed it if you hadn't shown it to me. But I'm no decker, Fran. Why bring this to me?"

She leaned forward, elbows on the table, her fragrance blotting out the scents of food and cigar smoke. "I'm not sure. Maybe because you know all kinds of stuff, all kinds of people. There might be something in that magpie mind of yours. . . . And, well, I suppose it's also that I wanted to see you again. It's been a while." There was the slightest hint of reproach in her voice. She stared at him intently, only a breath away from knocking over her sherry glass. He smiled slightly and moved the glass a little distance from her elbow.

"I know, and I'm sorry. It's been busy." He was glad that the waiter chose just that moment to come pour their wine, providing a welcome diversion while he ordered his thoughts. When he looked back at Francesca, her face was slightly drawn, the embryonic crow's feet around her eyes showing, but her blue eyes shining as always. He closed his hand around hers and took a chance on his intuition.

"You've been dreaming." His eyes met hers across the table, and she sighed as her whole body slumped a little. She looked away briefly, then met his gaze straight and strong.

"Only once. It may be nothing. . . . when it's only once." But her tone of voice said she knew better.

Geraint tried to hide his shudder as he thought of the last time they'd been together and she'd awakened with the old nightmare. He'd never heard anyone scream like that before. They'd been lovers then, lying beside one another. Though her terror had set his own heart to pounding violently, he'd shushed and tried to calm and comfort her. Now he smiled as reassuringly as he could. She wanted that, and she fumbled the hologram pad back into her bag.

"There's another reason." She looked mischievous. "What do you know about Sir Jonathan Ambrose?"

Geraint puckered his lips as a sensation of relief passed through his body, relaxing the tension he'd begun to feel. This was familiar territory. "He's an absolute dweeb, my dear. Ancient noble heritage, pots of money, degree from Oxford, and absolutely no chin at all. He'd be as much use in bed as a Fuchi Sensation without the batteries. Why do you have such appalling taste in men?"

Francesca pretended to look shocked as he directed the arriving steak and fish to their respective quarters with a polite smile. When the waiter had finished scooping the shrimps and cream over his sole, Geraint raised an eyebrow to her and lifted his fork to the feast. She was giving him that old, familiar look. The shadow had passed.

"Look, leave the holopad with me and I'll make a copy, give it some thought. But you'd best keep it quiet for now. Don't tell anyone else until we know a little more. You have work?"

"*May*-be, maybe," she said slowly, tantalizingly. "It's not just for lunch with Jonathan to the Lounging Lizard that I'm going tomorrow. We'll see what Lady Luck turns up with the day's Mr. Johnson.

"And hey, speaking of Lady Luck, what do your cards have to say these days?"

It was a query Geraint did not wish to answer. He paused just long enough to let her know he didn't want to talk about the cards, but she knew him well enough to permit him his cautions and silences. Whatever noncommittal remark he gave faded into a stream of small talk and enjoyment of the gracious surroundings.

*   *   *

Clutching his carryall tightly Serrin strolled down Regent Street, passing the Stuffer Shack on his way from Cam-

bridge station to the University Arms. Three days of
pointless time-wasting had ended in a meeting where
Smith and Jones had been a no-show. All that greeted
him at dinner was a card expressing their profuse apol-
ogies, along with a credstick to persuade him to accept
an additional assignment. A couple of minor nobles who
were major stockholders in Optical Neotech PLC, one of
his surveillance targets, would be attending a seminar at
Cambridge's finest hotel that weekend. Could he please
tag a watcher or two to their rooms after an initial snoop?

God knows what I'm doing here, the mage thought
with a sigh. It's fifteen minutes before midnight and this
could have waited until tomorrow. All the corps I've been
checking out have hermetic circles and goons around their
laboratories, and none of my little spies have been able
to entice one out far enough to fry them. It's all been
standard security, ordinary precautions, the usual drill.
Whoever's behind Smith and Jones could have easily
learned the same without paying me thousands of nuyen.

While passing through the strange juxtaposition of
Cambridge colleges and the cheap burger joints run sur-
reptitiously by the university to supplement its engorged
bequests and landholding revenues, Serrin suddenly had
a flash of spine-chilling awareness. This was rarer now
than when he was younger, this depersonalization, this
sense of being out of his body as he walked and moved
through the world. Of course, the mage was used to astrally perceiving and traveling, of seeing the world as
emotions and impulses and the shadows of souls, but
what he was experiencing for this eternal second was
quite different. At such moments he felt as though he was
splintered across all the metaplanes and beyond, at once
unreal and perfectly lucid. Time froze into stillness as
his legs pounded along the sidewalk. He didn't even notice the police car with its hawk-eyed trolls sliding slowly
along the road past him. Nor did his wayward senses
notice the fine drizzle slowly dampening his overcoat.

I've been looking at what is, he mused. *But what about
what isn't?*

Minutes later, he was sitting on the lumpy bed in his
hotel room, the trid turned on out of pure habit, but the
inspiration was gone. Like a vivid dream recalled only

in fragments and whose message confounds the waking mind, the negative stubbornly refused to turn into a positive. He chewed at the shriveled sandwich that was all room service could scrounge up at this time of night.

All right, he thought, mentally conjuring an image of the suits at breakfast those few days past, I'll play your game. I'll give you a report so complete it'll bore you stiff with detail and show you I've been a very conscientious dupe. I'll take all the nuyen you care to deal out. And I'll take my time finding out what's really going on here. Just maybe you'll discover that I'm a stubborn fragger who likes to know the truth.

*   *   *

Francesca drained the bulbed glass and licked at her lips as she set it down, the simple gesture symbolically marking the end of the meal. "Good wine. I enjoyed that."

"Well, with the Tairngire vintages, at least you know it's grown on soil that isn't completely corrupted by pollution. Not bad. Could have done with a little extra Cabernet Franc, though." The waiter was placing the silver coffee service on the table and Geraint said, "Large Calvados for me, and—Cointreau?"

Francesca smiled. "You remember little details, don't you?"

A trace of a grin played around the corners of his mouth as piano music drifted across the emptying room. He was barely aware what he was doing as he glanced idly at a northern Lord making a fool of himself with a heavily made-up Asian girl at a table opposite. Francesca noticed, though, and her hand gripped the wrist of his left hand, stopping him rubbing at his temple.

"Geraint." Her voice had just an edge of urgency in it. "I've seen that before."

He drew back from her, suddenly conscious of his action, nervous now and not wanting to hear what she was going to say.

"What's happening? What is it?" She knew about his rare moments of Sight. He'd told her about his ancestry and relatives, the cousins with temporal lobe epilepsy, the family curse. So she knew what that dull throb in the left side of his brain might mean, and she had her own nightmares. He hadn't wanted the evening to come to this, and he shook away her query.

"Oh, it's nothing. Too many nights up late among the smoke-filled rooms of the House of Nobles." He distracted her attention with anecdotes of their lordships' scandals and misbehaviors. The fool with the bored girl across the room provided a good starting point. Between them, they unconsciously agreed to a false meeting ground of laughter over inconsequentialities.

Geraint had his chauffeur drop Francesca off at her place, declining her offer of a nightcap. His head was beginning to ache quite horribly, and for once it wasn't due to either alcohol or smoke. He looked forward to simply being safe and secure in his own home, where he might take some drug to smooth the rough edges. The feeling of queasiness in his guts was still only a forewarning. It was not a vital sign; that was yet to come.

Once inside, he threw his cashmere overcoat, slick with the filthy rain of London's night, over an armchair, then stooped to pick up the wax-sealed packet lying on the floor. The seal was the Earl of Manchester's. Inside was a very glossy brochure—"Nobles in Business: Strategies for Success"—listing more corporate sponsors than London had honest policemen. Accompanying it was a personal invitation to the Earl of Llanfrechfa from Charles Nakatomi of Fuchi Industrial Electronics, no less. Dumping it unceremoniously on the hall table, Geraint rubbed his forehead and pinched the sinuses throbbing over the bridge of his nose to stave off the dull ache in his head. He undressed in the palatial bathroom, put on his silk dragon kimono, and made for the enkephalins in the top desk drawer. Just for good measure, he also took a hit of flocculated ibuprofen complex to turn every voluntary muscle in his body to jelly as he collapsed into bed. Better living through chemistry, boyo. We'll worry about the weekend and the after-effects tomorrow. Cambridge, here I come.

5

Imran was late back from Shoreditch, and Rani was fretting over the chicken jalfrezi, splashing ghee all over the kitchen floor and the hem of her sari. Her nerves were still frayed from the attack, not least because she was sure she hadn't heard the last of it. All day the front room, kept only for honored visitors, had seen a procession of cousins and friends who all suddenly developed an inventive range of pretexts for calling, usually soon after Imran had been using the telecom. She knew he was probably putting the word out. Today at least he'd been out of her hair, out hawking some Italian BTL chips and shady cyberware. Usually he traded in kind, haggling and bartering for goods he could then pass on in turn, balancing every deal with the finesse of a watchmaker. He enjoyed the game, reveled in bargaining with his fellow traders and customers, and salted away the favors any ork needed to get by in the world. It upped your survival chances like nobody's business when the racists knew you had heat on call.

Sanjay was happy, too. Most of the nuyen he'd gotten in exchange for his home-cooked drugs had come up good, and one he'd even been able to "tune up," as he put it. He was dulled with poppy now, but he'd be heading for Mohsin's soon, checking out the skillwires and street cyberware. She smiled remembering the day Sanjay had come home, stiff and sore, with the muscle replacements. Though grimacing with pain, he'd lifted her clean off the floor in his arms, not something he'd been able to do since that horrific day and night of agony when she had transformed. The new biceps gleamed under his oiled skin and she could see the enlarged pectorals straining under his sweat-soaked shirt. Mohsin was distant family; street gear was a far sight safer when the scalpel was wielded by one's own blood.

Her reverie was broken by the sound of Imran giving

his signal at the front door. She ran to unbolt the chains and locks, eager to see him. He bundled roughly past her, carrying a heavy aluminized case.

"It's been a good day, sister!" He grinned, but barely gave her a glance, intent on fumbling with the heavy catches and maglock of the case.

"What you got there, Imran? A body?" She was nervous, her attention skipping between the suitcase and the faintest smell of jalfrezi beginning to burn in the kitchen.

"Much better. I have work with the family for this weekend, and this little beauty will be just the ticket."

Rani's face fell, knowing exactly what work with the family meant.

"The real thing, you know?" He caressed the sleek steel barrel of the heavy pistol, handling it with as much love as if it were a newborn baby. "The Ares Predator II, perfect smartgun link," he beamed, holding out the handle to show her the interface. "And a fifteen-clip of armor-piercing! Real UCAS stock, none of that spamming East European imitation." He flourished the vicious APDS bullets with an air of triumph. "You could knock a rhino over with this." He laughed humorlessly. "Yeah, if you could find a zoo that had a rhino left, you know? I'll be busy this weekend, so you're going to have to stay behind the bolts and chains and wait for your brother to bring back serious money!"

Rani did not reply. The moment he glanced up at her from his precious hardware, he saw by her crossed arms and the firm set of her jaw that she was prepared for a showdown. He decided to be reasonable first, insistent later.

"Let's talk about it over dinner. You should honor your brother for doing his work. Where's my dinner, woman?" He was trying to be jocular, and Rani acquiesced with the appearance of a real smile, but only for a fleeting moment. Imran knew that Sanjay wouldn't be any help in his present state, so he scurried to the telecom while she went to the kitchen to dish out his food. He had just finished tapping in Aqib's telecom code when Rani pressed the cancel button.

"No, brother. This one we will talk about alone."

* * *

He had tried the standard appeals and tactics, praising
her cooking beyond remotely plausible limits, telling her
that handsome Ravi wanted to call on her this weekend,
and then finally serving up his usual trump card of tradition. "We survive as family," he had pleaded. "Our
customs and traditions keep us together. You bring me
honor when you care for me in our home, which is your
workplace. But the world is my domain. I am a man and
that is my place. We survive because we hold to what is
established, safe—real. Our father would not wish it otherwise."

That had been unwise, and Imran regretted it immediately. Appealing to the authority of their dead father
was a low blow. Tears formed in Rani's eyes at the mere
mention, but she would not budge.

"Imran, brother, if I were only a nice little sari-
wearing gopi in the kitchen I would have been dead two
days ago. I would have walked up the street to buy
chicken and fish and they would have ripped me apart.
I'm alive because I am not like that."

"If you had stayed at home where you belong, you
would not have been walking the streets at night at all!
Perhaps they were the sort of men who attack the kind
of filthy women who do that. One of them was killed that
very same night, did you know that?" His disapproval
was strong, but she had a crushing rejoinder.

"Me? Take me as a streetwalker? Who'd have *me*?
I'm an ork. Who'd pay to have my body?" As she
shook with anger and hurt, his arguments evaporated instantly. They had transformed together, brother and sister, and that bond was too close for him not to register
her pain. He rose and took her gently into his arms, hug-
ging her gingerly, but he sensed the strength in Rani that
allowed her to express hurts he'd never been able to face
within himself.

"I want to go with you," she said softly. "I want to
help."

"Rani. Sister. I fear for you, you know that. If you
come with us. I will be so worried about you that I won't

be able to do my own job. Please, stay with Sanjay. You'll be safe here.'' It wasn't going to work, and he knew it.

"No. I'm coming. I can use a gun as well as you can. I'll stay out of trouble, but I want to be there. Who could you trust more?''

He accepted defeat gracefully. "It will be family; Aqib, Wasim, and Sachin, maybe Rajiv if he can get away from that wife of his.'' That broke the tension, leaving them laughing together at the thought of poor Rajiv and his huge, domineering wife who ruled the home as tyrannically as any corporate CEO.

"All right, then," Imran said finally. "The job is set for tomorrow. We'll be using a friend of Mohsin's for wheels, because the place is somewhere sixty miles north of here. All we have to do is take potshots at a suit visiting a laboratory. We don't even have to hit him to make our money. I suppose they just want to put a good scare in him.''

Rani was curious to know more. "Why you? Why not hire some slints from the Squeeze? That would be the obvious thing to do.''

"I guess it's because the people racking up the nuyen know better than to do the obvious. They're smart. I think I like working for smart people, judging by the size of the credstick. And we got a slice upfront plus the hardware. Rani, go see Old Chenka tomorrow. Ask for her blessing and a little something, huh?''

His sister smiled ruefully in reply. Chenka, ancient and toothless, always knew whenever the family was involved in a run because they always came to her for a blessing and one of her paper-wrapped herbal mixtures. As always, they would sit in silence, drinking steaming green tea, the old woman rocking slightly in her chair and gazing fixedly at them with squinting, half-closed eyes. Seeing everything, most likely.

Imran had not told Rani the exact target of the run. He figured she didn't need to know until they were well beyond the Smoke, safer because they'd be traveling by night. Otherwise, she might ask too many questions, and he wasn't sure he'd have enough of the answers.

6

Geraint pushed his way through the bead curtain, past the main shop area, and sat down opposite the tiny elf. Skita, the long-haired black and white cat, strolled over, his splendid tail held proudly aloft, and parked himself on Geraint's lap. The Welshman smiled, curling his fingertips around the cat's ears and under his chin, the animal responding by closing his eyes and purring in pleasure. Serena returned his smile, sitting with her hands folded in her lap, the spell focus on the table between them.

As always, she had crafted it so lovingly that it was a thing of real beauty. She had chosen crystal, roseate quartz, and set it within a silver dragon's claw. It also had a small clasp that would let him wear it on a silver chain or as a brooch. Serena always attended to such fine points whether in her work or in her appearance. Today she wore a flowing silk blouse and cotton skirt in tones of dark blue and ivory, the lines classically elegant. She also wore her azure spinel earrings. The deep blue of the stones matched her beautiful eyes, and flashed with tiny points of magical golden light. Serena's head was tilted slightly to the left as she looked at him, and he wondered if she was using her magical skills to probe his mind.

"You're looking tired, my lord." She used the formal term, without any mockery, when reproaching him. "There's gray under your eyes. You've been spending all your time in the world of false power. You will have to let go of that or you will suffer."

She handed him a glass of sparkling iced liquid, cloudy apple juice settling in pure spring water, wonderfully cold and refreshing. He took a deep draught and relaxed back against the pile of cushions. Skita moved slightly, too, stretching out his front legs, licking the side of one paw to wash his ears. The animal seemed to especially enjoy cleaning himself when Geraint was wearing a dark suit, all the better a carpet to deposit white belly hairs. The cat purred with a deeper tone, but then seemed to think better of rolling over to have his belly rubbed. Skita preferred to hold on to his dignity until he was fully relaxed.

"It's just that time of year, Serena. Lots of corps are finalizing the third-quarter turnovers and announcements, and it's been busy in the House. But then you'd know that." More than a few elven nobles counted Serena as a good friend, and it was probably their influence that allowed her to operate beyond the rigid legal constraints of the Lord Protector's Office. She didn't always need to fill out the quadruplicate paperwork or obtain the full array of permits most registered talismongers needed in Britain's highly regulated society.

Serena waved away his words with a tiny, bird-like shake of her head. "You can always find a rationalization, Geraint. There is always the pressure of work, if you choose that. But I see you are not at ease. There is a blockage in your aura. Your left side"—she touched her left temple with her index finger—"has been flaring. You won't accept it, or you don't want to face it, and you tell yourself that you are too busy, perhaps. You have a block there, and your energies do not flow properly. You're creating tension within yourself, and you have been trying to calm it with poisons."

Her expression was almost stern, almost like one his mother had mastered to perfection. If he'd been allowed, he would have lit a cigarette to calm his irritation and to give his restless fingers something to do now that Skita was clearly not to be disturbed in the acme of his relaxation. Serena would not allow tobacco to even enter her premises, let alone be smoked here.

"Serena, I came for business. It's fortunate that I asked for the mask when I did, for there's an important business meeting this weekend and I'm sure there'll be the usual gaggle of corporate mages and opportunistic freelancers trying to probe a mind or two here and there."

The comment doubled as a warning to her not to probe his any further. Geraint reached into his jacket pocket and withdrew the credstick with the monogrammed silver top. It was a little joke between them, an ostentation that went beyond the bounds of his normal vanity, but one that pleased and amused her. He held it out to her, opening the palm of his free hand to receive the quartz focus in exchange. She took the stick and pushed the focus toward him, but would not relinquish the line of query.

"And they will know, as I do, that you are an adept. You would be a better one if you had not defiled your spirit." Serena disapproved strongly of the little cyberware Geraint had implanted: his datajack, the headware memory, the cannula implant just above the first vertebra for swift administration of psychoactives. Poisons, she called them, and she would not budge on that interpretation. "It is not a common gift, yours, to see the future."

This, at least, gave him the opportunity to attempt to divert the direction the conversation was going. "It's not true precognition, my mother would say. Predicting the future is only extrapolating the present. It is merely clairvoyance and some intuitive guesswork that works out from time to time." He took an almost perverse pleasure in denigrating his talent, a carefully imposed "merely" making it seem more domesticated, less an intrusion into a well-ordered life.

"Call it what you will, Geraint. It isn't something you can stop, or control, or subdue. If you will not accept it, then it will break through in ways that will haunt and disturb you." She was silent for a moment, then turned to put the credstick away. "Well, that's done," she said. "Will you have your cards read?"

"No. Thank you." The first word was too swift, the second following a pause just too long. His response had been almost panicky, and they both knew it. Geraint hid his embarrassment by lifting up a complaining Skita and depositing the cat on the warm cushion he was vacating, then brushing the cat's fur off his lap with exaggerated motions. As he was leaving, Serena had a final word for him, as always.

"Then, they have been speaking to you themselves. Listen, Geraint. Listen! If you do not, they will force you to hear. Take care."

For some inexplicable reason, Geraint managed to knock a small trinket off the counter on the way out of the shop, diluting the impact of her words somehow. He hurriedly picked up the bracelet and replaced it in its wicker container on the polished glass counter. Serena stood with arms crossed, watching him half-seriously, half-amused.

"Acquaintance of yours was in the other day," she said.

"Hmm? One of the elven nobles? Haven't been seeing—"

"No, an elf from across the waters. Serrin Shamandar. I would not tell you what he was seeking, of course, but it was an interesting little coincidence." They both knew that neither of them believed in coincidence. Geraint shrugged, smiled away her raised eyebrows, and then headed into the flow of the faceless on Frith Street.

His bags were already packed as he held the focus within his hands. It would take a couple of hours for the bonding, to draw the magic of the thing into himself. He had handled and meditated upon the crystal and metal during its making, of course, and now he needed just a little time with the finished item. It was three-thirty in the afternoon, and within four hours he would be back in Cambridge, five or ten minutes from his old college, shaking hands with the rich, the fat, and the titled. He laughed, his good spirits returning, and sat down with the focus.

Within minutes, he was oblivious to the world, and he did not even register Francesca's call on the telecom. Besides, she was only calling to wish him a prosperous weekend.

* * *

Serrin frowned as he parked the hired bike in the hotel's underground garage. It didn't help his mood to have baleful sodium-molybdenum lighting winking at him from the walls, with their flaking white-painted arrows pointing toward the elevator.

The morning had been tedious, as usual. Down in Grantchester, a couple of miles to the south, his watchers at the Renraku labs had chattered their reports to him. The barrier created by the hermetic mages inside was as thick as a troll samurai's skin, but that was to be expected. The corp's watchers were observing his without undue concern. The little buggers probably leg it as soon as I've gone, doing whatever they do to amuse themselves, he thought.

It had been the usual routine: concentrating on his magical masking and camouflage, perceiving astrally from a safe distance, prowling around the seamless magical barriers, testing gently for any unusual responses or activities. But nothing unusual ever turned up. No combat mages returning the astral surveillance, no body-armored goons roaring forth in APVs. But then, this was England, nothing like what Serrin was used to back home.

Just for the hell of it, he decided to break the speed limit on the flat, straight road back to the heart of the sprawl. Roaring along the riverbank, he seriously startled some students poling flat-bottomed punts along the River Cam, but none actually fell into the stinking water. Serrin had read in his guidebook that ingesting a mouthful of the river water gave you a flat 10 percent chance of death by chemistry, while sometimes a puntful of students got swallowed by one of the paranimals that wandered downstream from the Stinkfens to the east. But the students still went on punting, as if the simple tradition of it all could defy the realities of a ravaged earth. People just went on: punting on rivers of filth, buying demitech that'd kill them more times than it'd work, going to butchers to get questionable cyberware implanted in street clinics, believing in another green guru with a smile on his face and a corporate credstick stuck up his ass.

Serrin had not been feeling his best that afternoon, but getting away with speeding had lifted his spirits some. Wandering into the hotel foyer, distinctly more grimy and unappealing than most of the clientele, he grinned in spite of himself. Maybe it was time for some late lunch and a decent bit of protein.

Striding toward the maitre d' in the restaurant overlooking Parker's Piece, the one patch of parkland left in Cambridge's central zone, Serrin saw the first of the suits and goons arriving for the weekend seminar. Credsticks were flashing at the reception desk, and the troll chauffeurs looked stereotyped to perfection in their light gray uniforms and visors. Every bulge was in the right place, from the biceps to the licensed pistols secreted at hip and armpit.

Heading up the stairs toward the Churchill Suite were a pair of elves, their spell fetishes in plain view. Security was going to be obvious and strict. Serrin could understand why his employers had asked him to do a little tailing out of town if he was supposed to be checking out a couple of the participants here. From a purely logical point of view, he'd never doubt that this was the real purpose of his expensive jaunt at his anonymous employer's expense. But that unknown something that hovered beyond logic wouldn't let him rest with that.

He picked at his food, gripped by restlessness. He hated having a definite job to do and then having to wait around to do it. He amused himself with crazy ideas of bluffing his way into one of the laboratories by claiming to be a corporate exec or some university science whiz, or of rustling up a fake ID and doing something outrageous purely for the hell of it. Not that he ever did such things, but fantasizing about it passed the time.

He was staring gloomily down the hallway, dawdling over the remains of a crème brulée that had resolutely failed to ignite his appetite, when he saw the hint of a face vanish into the elevator. His heart missed a beat, damn nearly missed a second, and he had to swallow hard to keep from throwing up right there in the middle of the restaurant.

Mustering as much nonchalance as he could in his shaken state, Serrin strolled to the reception desk. Having dressed for lunch, and looking more respectable than usual, he thought he just might get away with it. Besides, he was booked for the whole weekend, so he really was the part, whether he looked it or not.

"Excuse me. The gentleman who just arrived," he breezed to the receptionist, "he's an old friend of mine. Which is his suite?" He took a chance that Kuranita wouldn't have taken an ordinary room. The receptionist might be fooled by that little touch, and thus give it away. She was cooler than that, and she didn't. "I'm sorry, sir. We cannot provide room numbers of guests without their express permission.''

"Of course, I understand. I'll catch up with him later.'' He smiled politely, but he'd seen all he needed to. The ID was still flickering on the vidscreen. James Kuruyama, Communication Management Associates, Chiltern Suite. So it was a false ID, although the company seemed to be plausible enough. Serrin dimly recalled CMA as a subsidiary of the great megacorporation that actually employed Kuranita these days.

But what the hell was Paul Kuranita, Deputy Head of Active Security for Fuchi Switzerland, doing here under this alias?

Back in his room, Serrin had a lot to think about as he took his fetishes and focuses from their silk wraps. Next he unfolded the outer casing of his attaché case, drew out the components of the Ingram, and began to assemble them, screwing and clipping the gun together. When he had finished, he hefted its weight in his left hand for a few moments before slamming a clip of ammunition home with a pleasing click.

In all the years since his parents had been murdered, the missile striking down the Renraku chopper with unerring accuracy, Serrin had never been able to get more than a lead on a single name.

Paul Kuranita.

The man had been untouchable, a brilliant freelance samurai whose movements were untraceable, until the troll in Jo'burg had left him so badly burned that all the reconstructive surgery and spare parts his millions could buy had not been able to put him back together. For six years, Kuranita had worked his way up the ladder of the Fuchi organization. Deputy Head of Active Security for Switzerland sounded like a joke, unless one knew that the Head was hopelessly senile and no more than a figurehead. The joke was even less amusing because of how powerful the Swiss division was in coordinating all of Fuchi's European activities.

Serrin had never been a hundred percent sure of Kuranita's complicity in his parents' deaths. The evidence was only circumstantial, but then it could never be more than that with someone like Kuranita. Now, however,

fortune had brought the assassin to Serrin, and he wasn't
going to pass up his chance.

He began to plan carefully. Immediate magical surveillance would be a mistake, of course, but perhaps
some nuyen thrown to the garage attendant for information on Kuranita's limo would be good for starters.

By the time the mage had made his plans, the world
beyond his room had fallen dark. Passing through the
lobby and down the emergency stairs to the garage, he
did not see the nobleman gawking almost stupidly at him
from the reception desk.

Geraint had no time to chase after the elf, as he was
immediately stopped in his tracks by a relieved Earl of
Smethwick. The earl was delighted to see him again and
would really love to introduce Geraint to some distinctly
tipsy young woman from OzNet who was digging up bits
for a trid feature on the seminar. The pressure of Smethwick's hand gripping his forearm unerringly conveyed the
message, "Get this gopping bimbo off my tail and I'll
owe you a massive favor, friend," with pressing urgency.

With just the hint of a sigh, Geraint decided to do
Smethwick a good turn and turned to the woman, a
blowsy type who clearly favored applying her make-up
with a trowel. Geraint's first few applications of insincere
Celtic charm seemed to be received with an almost de-
votional eagerness by the tridjock. She'd probably been
given the cold shoulder by almost everyone else here that
evening, and there was something almost touching about
her relief at finding someone willing to talk to her. Hell,
maybe her job was on the line; she was obviously only a
junior. At least I can buy her dinner, Geraint thought,
and make sure I don't let anything slip.

He took her arm in his and headed for the flambée.

* * *

"It is not really predictable. I don't think this is such a
well-planned step."

"Look, he can't get close to the man. There's no
chance of anything serious happening here. The important thing is to put that name into his head. He's spent
days doing sweet FA, and now he's got something to sink

his teeth into. He won't get to Kuranita, but he'll start investigating. He'll meet the Welshman and the two of them will begin asking some questions. It will be some time before they can find out what was going down all those years ago, but when they get to the answer the timing will be more or less right. After all, that's a step we can control.

"Sure, there's a whiff of the wild card about it, but you know Calcraft's Cumulated Inexactness Theorem. A sufficient number of wild cards come down to a highly probable hand of cards at the end of the day."

The thin man scratched at his yellowed teeth, picking the last remains of shrimp from between his incisors. He looked, for several moments, as if he were weighing the delicate balance of the matter with every gram of intellect he could bring to bear. Finally, he sat back and tapped a cigarette on the mahogany arm of his chair.

"Charles, that's utter bollocks!" They both burst out laughing, then broke into contented grins. "Okay, let's check the conditioning. I think he's pretty much done by now. Let's arrange the logistics."

* * *

Wheels turn.

Annie Chapman has less than three days to live.

So it continues.

7

Serrin sneaked up quietly behind a peaceful Geraint, who sat reading his *Financial Times* in the breakfast room at the unspeakably early hour of seven-thirty in the morning. The seminars were to start at nine, but still no sign of most of the hotel's honorable sirs and ladies so early in the day.

The Welshman was too engrossed in the headlines to notice Serrin's soft footfall.

"One day, Geraint, you're going to catch some rather unpleasant social disease. Mind if I sit with you?" Serrin didn't await the reply, but instead took the chair opposite and began to help himself to grapefruit slices from the silver bowl.

"I didn't think you'd noticed me, old man," Geraint said, looking up from another fiercely worded editorial railing against the state of the British economy. "You seemed in rather a hurry as I was arriving. Welcome to the dreaming spires of Cambridge." He proffered a lordly hand in greeting.

Serrin waved away the formality. "I had people to bribe. I saw you when I got back from out of town. Just before midnight in the coffee shop with a most disreputable-looking young woman. Like I said, chummer, mind you don't catch something."

"I've been inoculated against most of what's out there, and anyway she was very drunk. It wouldn't have been right, don't you know; true gentlemen don't behave like that. Anyway, you old reprobate, what have you been doing these last seven years—and what brings you to England?"

They settled down to reminiscences of time apart as the room began to fill around them. Serrin spoke of years in hotel rooms, orbitals, and shuttles, the skeletal details of one or two of his many runs. Geraint noted the lack of any personal revelations. The elf always did hide behind lists: numbers, cities, dates, and places. Serrin didn't speak of L.A. or the Bay area. But that had been so long ago, and they had been so young and a lot less knowing of the ways of the world.

Serrin had grown thinner, Geraint observed as he studied the other's face. He noticed, too, that the elf's hands shook just a little now. Though Serrin had been shot up seriously not long before he and Geraint first met, the elf had possessed an energy in those days that now seemed to have turned in on him. Behind the effort to appear glad and pleased to see his friend again, Geraint felt a little saddened.

"So that's about it. Amsterdam, Paris, Seattle, and now the delights of the bally old Smoke for this year. But hey! What about you? I read a profile of you in one of the UCAS business datanets sometime last spring. They tipped you as one of the fifty brightest comers in European speculative finances. If you'd been a racehorse, I'd have backed you to win the Derby!''

Geraint broke into a bright smile as he opened a new pack for the first cigarette of the day. Serrin reached across and helped himself, dismissing the silver lighter as he struck an old-fashioned match and lit both their cigarettes. Feigning a voice from an ancient American detective movie and pulling an imaginary raincoat closer to his neck to keep out non-existent rain, he whispered, ''I wuz pleased to see my humble match lit as brightly as the dude's flashy Zippo.''

Geraint leaned back and locked Serrin in a close gaze. ''You always could raise a smile, old friend. I looked for you after it was all over, you know. I hoped that someone in Tir Tairngire might have been able to give me a lead, but you'd gone to ground and your people were very silent. Very polite, but very silent. I didn't forget you.'' Their fingers reached out, and they held their hands clasped strongly for a few seconds across the table.

''I know.'' The elf's voice was soft and his expression downcast. ''Geraint, it was all too much for me. I was older than you, but I guess I felt I could never hold on to anyone I cared for. Not after the killings there. I don't think I've ever been able to, not since my parents died. I guess I just keep running. If I keep moving, and I keep doing things, then I'm always going to be alive. If I stop, I see that my hands are shaking and my leg pains me. That's what I get if . . .''

His voice trailed away, and he took a deep drag on the cigarette, coughing slightly as he began to stub out half its length in the cut-glass ashtray. Then his expression changed, and he leaned forward across the table.

''Geraint, there's something going on here that I don't understand. Paul Kuranita's here under a false name. Registered as James Kuruyama.'' Geraint looked startled, uncertain what to say. ''You know what that means to me.''

''For God's sake, are you sure?'' the Welshman hissed.

''Positive. I spent two years building up his profile from the records of all his operations. Cost me half a million to trace everything, but there isn't any doubt. What the hell is he doing here?''

"Look, don't be too hasty. The seminars and lectures go on until seven o'clock tomorrow night. Don't do anything foolish; let's both try to find out something about it. Know where he's staying?''

"Hotel ID had him in the Chiltern Suite." Serrin looked grim.

"Give me a couple of hours. I'm down for a real stinker at ten, a three-hour marathon on drug markets and viral degeneration syndromes. Basically it comes down to how many billions of nuyen the drug companies can make out of the crumblies before they hit their ninetieth birthdays. I have people to see there, and I need to be seen nodding enthusiastically during their speeches, if I can force down enough coffee to stay awake, that is. I'll inquire very discreetly about—Kuruyama?''

Geraint began leafing through his massive collection of brochures. "I have a feeling he's down as a teleconferencer: not attending seminars, just watching from his hotel room. It's what the paranoids do if they don't want a legion of trolls with automatic weapons around them every second of the day. But think it's just possible that at some stage he might want a face-to-face with someone over a few drinks. Let me check this out and get back to you. Give me—no, not a couple of hours. Meet me here for lunch.''

Geraint leaned forward and fixed the American with his steely gaze. "Don't do anything crazy in the interim. If it is Kuranita, you won't be able to get to him unless you've got a grenade launcher with you. And even that might not be enough. He may be booked into the Chiltern, but he's probably staked out on the other side of the building.''

Serrin nodded his acquiescence. "Yeah, I guessed that. Every other room in the place has a barrier up, too. I tried just a tad of snooping last night, and had a pair of security mages show up within five minutes to gently warn me against further attempts. I think I'll just get my pants pressed by valet service or something.''

"Trousers, boy, trousers! You're not back home now. Speak bloody English." They laughed as Geraint got up from the bony remains of his kippers, then pulled down the jacket sleeves to regulation half-past his shirt cuffs. Serrin smiled at the gesture, unself-conscious as it was. The nobleman always was that cool and elegant, except just that one time all those years ago.

"Hear from Francesca at all?" Serrin asked, trying to make the question sound like a throwaway. Geraint had been waiting for it all along.

"She moved to London eighteen months ago. Flies out to Jersey a lot, likes the beaches there. One of the few places left where you can walk along without tripping over other people every step of the way. She's doing fine. I had dinner with her a few days ago. Look her up, she'd like that."

Whipping out a gleaming pen from an inside pocket, Geraint scribbled her telecom code onto a paper napkin. He preferred to defer the query that way, not wanting to suggest that the three of them meet back in London. That might be just a little too awkward.

Serrin returned to his room and started filing his report on the laptop. He checked through his diary and noted every time and place he'd been, letting his employers know they'd got overtime and value for money. He knew he still needed to run checks on the Optical Neotech guys at some point, but that could wait. For now.

* * *

If Rutger had spiked the Johnson's drink, the man was showing no appreciable effect of it. He was a New Yorker, a hard guy from the Rotten Apple, and he had briefed her quickly and concisely, with an answer prepared for every query Francesca could muster. But there was just one possible slip in the fifty-minute workout that had intrigued her.

"I must emphasize that my client's interest in this matter is confined to the seeding of the target's system with the corrosive. It is entirely possible that you may encounter an unfriendly operative once in the system. Under such circumstances your contract permits you to withdraw from hostilities if you are endangered, and we add the proviso that under no circumstances are you to enter any other system.''

She pondered that one over breakfast the next morning, which was Saturday. The job would pay well, as befitted the task. Being a freelance security consultant was a discreet cover for her. To those in the know, it said, I bust systems open as well as test them.

This one was a bust. Someone wanted a nasty corrosive virus dumped into the computer system of a Fuchi subsidiary. The virus came in its own autodegrading chip; any attempt to do anything other than download it into its predestined target would melt the cyberdeck into which the chip was loaded. She hadn't paid all that money for a Cyber-6 to have a melting chip rakk it up, and she wasn't going to take too close a look at the thing. Thirty-five thousand nuyen were also a slamming good reason not to fool around.

Get this one right, Francesca, and the employer could become a gravy train. This could be holidays in Sri Lanka until the gray hairs started sprouting.

''I wonder why he said that, though, Annie.'' As usual Francesca had asked her friend to be nearby in case the IC got nasty and she needed someone to take care of her after getting dumped, or worse. It had happened before, just once, when she'd foolishly strayed into the black IC of that Edinburgh system. On that occasion Annie had been able to give her the kiss of life in time.

''Who knows? Just do the job, honey.'' Annie sprawled her six-foot length over the leather sofa, stretching her legs—and she did have fabulous legs, long and lean and muscular. If all went well now they might celebrate by going out on the town tonight, Francesca the blonde in black, Annie the brunette encasing herself in something white, tight, and very, very inadequate to the purpose. They didn't ask too much about each other's lives, speaking of their relationships with the flippancy more common to men talking about women, but it worked at that level. They didn't talk much about their work, either. Francesca needed to keep quiet about what she did, while Annie proclaimed herself a model. Francesca knew what that meant, though. If Annie's hard edge didn't give her away, the high rents she had to pay on her flat around the corner did. But they shared a certain wary mutual respect and unspoken trust. Each knew the other was someone she wouldn't regret having as a companion while getting far too drunk. That counted for a lot.

Francesca's thoughts turned back to the run. The priorities for this job were different from her last. No subtleties needed here; it was bod mode all the way and the most vicious attack program she could muster. She wasn't as happy with the attack stuff as she could have been. She'd gotten it with area-effect rather than high-penetration, thinking the shotgun approach was best when she couldn't be sure what the Fuchi boys would have built in. Still, the Filipino armor program she'd hawked from Paris looked as if it was good enough to buy her the extra time and defense she'd need when up against the heavy IC. She also had a reliable medic program to keep the MPCP rolling when the guano hit the fan; that venerable utility had done yeoman work for at least the last couple of years.

The key to it all was programming the smartframe. She was going to use it as a decoy, she decided, rather than to cover her butt as a defense back-up. That meant she'd have to program it with instructions to confuse, detour, delay, and generally frag with anything she might encounter while dumping the virus into the Fuchi system. She'd contemplated exploring the system in sensor mode, trying to learn what she could in order to better instruct the frame, but then thought better of it. One mistake could place the system on alert, and she wasn't about to hand out any advance warnings.

Chewing her lip, Francesca keyed in the instruction codes. When in doubt, she figured, nuke the bastards and shoot 'em when they glow in the dark. Let's bust through to the CPU and frag anything else.

The adrenaline was pouring through her veins now. Second-guessing Fuchi's strategies, she used her experience and skills to anticipate what she might find, allowing for just a bit of the smartframe's capacity for contingency programming. She flew as high as a kite, and by three in the afternoon the cyberdeck was humming. Francesca jacked in to her deck and entered the Matrix.

Optical Neotech, here I come. You are about to get squared.

* * *

The resistance was just what she'd expected. She'd battered through the IC, the frame smoking her from one crucial attack, and then she'd downloaded the virus into the CPU. She was thinking that was the safest bet when the thing suddenly appeared in the glowing world of cyberspace as a reptilian worm with the head of a moray eel, a really evil-looking beast. It snarled at her, spat hatred, and began gorging itself on subsystems. The IC began to weaken around her, its force diminishing as it faded and dislocated, fragmenting in a burst of nothingness.

The corporate decker had been there, of course, a multi-armed Kali whirling shortswords and dripping venom from his blades. Flashy, but strictly the mark of a wage slave aiming to intimidate rather than wielding true threat. Admittedly, she'd also chosen flashiness, her laser-firing chainsaw ripping arcs of blue light across the distance, blinding and driving away the assault.

Francesca was headed out of the system when she saw the ghostly figure from her last run floating off toward the SAN. The cloaked figure carried a bag, and her pulse and endocrines went through the roof when she saw him. Whatcha got in the bag, Faceless? You wanna fight for it?

She hammered toward him through a blur of abstract space, exiting the system and downlining past another SAN, not caring which system she'd entered. She switched to attack mode, too full of herself to register the menace he presented.

The cloaked figure turned to face her oncoming rush, and as he did so he opened his bag. Inside were surgical instruments: vicious pincers, blades, saws, and a long, dreadful, ivory-handled scalpel. Taking this last instrument in his taloned hand, he swiped at her.

Francesca panicked, desperately trying to dive into the SAN and escape the maniac. She was paralyzed and he knew it. This time he had a face; a terrible, fleshy, con-

torted grimace suffused with madness and hatred. His
visage expanded into a ghastly rictus as he pocketed the
scalpel for later use and reached out with his hands,
grasping for her throat.

Whore!

She felt the word expand out of the persona, an insult
spat like venom from the deepest reaches of whatever
elemental madness seemed to possess the thing. She felt
warm hands close around her throat, felt her limbs jerk-
ing spasmodically as he strangled the life out of her, felt
his hot animal breath on her face as his eyes bore into
her soul. She choked as her heart pumped frantically, her
hands scrabbling ineffectually at his hideous face, her
screams silent as her windpipe ruptured and the world
was shredded black.

It was an hour before Annie could bring her around,
and then her terrified screams roused the building security. She was shaking uncontrollably when Annie hit her
with a tranq patch, then put her to bed.

There wasn't going to be any partying for Francesca
that night, nor for many nights to come.

8

"What did you get?" Serrin was eager to hear, stubbing
out the last of a string of cigarettes that bore witness to
his impatience.

Geraint frowned slightly, dumped a pile of papers on
the table and smoothed back his dark hair. He fussed
over the gold fountain pen in his pocket, sighing in frustration. It hadn't been a good morning, and to top it all
he'd returned to find a missive waiting for him that was
definitely unwelcome. The Earl of Manchester's personal
secretary regretted that Lord Powys was unable to sit in
on the committee stage of the Gwynedd Demarcation Bill
next week, and since a trustworthy and reliable Welshman would be needed . . .

Wonderful. Now he could look forward to being bored

silly in a debate with aggressive Gwynedd elves over small print, while trying to politely kick some government lord under the table to keep him awake. At least he'd gotten something for Serrin, though he wasn't so sure how the elf would take it. Geraint decided to play it down for starters.

"Next to nothing, my friend. The Communication Management people are apparently here for the specific purpose of observing this afternoon's seminar on biomolecular technology in comm systems. They aren't talking to anyone, and the brief they submitted has been printed in the program. It doesn't say much, so far as I can see. But a little bird did whisper something in my ear."

Serrin edged forward. "What kind of bird? As long as it wasn't a blood kite, I want to hear what it said."

"It was one of Nakatomi's boys from Fuchi Industrial UK. Drunk as a skunk at ten in the morning." Geraint's face crinkled slightly with disapproval. "Chap reeked of brandy and bimbo at a frankly disgraceful hour of the day."

"Spare me the jazz," Serrin said with a shrug. "I know places back in Seattle where no one will believe you can cut it at all if you *don't* smell like that, know what I mean? What did you get?"

"Just this: Kuranita is supposed to pay a call on Fuchi's labs out at Longstanton this evening. CMS is a Fuchi subsidiary, after all, so it wouldn't look odd. If I read my contact right, that's Kuranita's real motive for being here. The seminar's just a convenient cover."

Serrin was satisfied. It was impossible to get anywhere near Kuranita in the hotel, and if he tried any more magic around the place it wouldn't just be hotel security knocking politely at his door. Next time, they'd have an official from the Administrative Bureau of the Lord Protector's Office along with them. If Serrin was carrying any permit not perfectly in order, they'd deport him instantly and confiscate his precious magical gear. And even if all his permits were up to snuff, they'd probably still find something in the small print anyway. And that was before they found the Ingram. . . .

So he would wait. He'd been out to Longstanton, north

of the city's sprawl, and it was easy to hide out there. The labs weren't far from the Stinkfens, the polluted miasma of marshland and waters that befouled most of old East Anglia, so there wasn't exactly a high density of population and homes to worry about.

Serrin looked around the room, taking in the scattering of foreign faces, many Asians among them. "I thought this was Nobles in Business, Geraint. You can't tell me that these chummers are all scions of Britain's blue-blooded aristocracy."

"My dear fellow, you misunderstand. An event like this brings together two groups of people who need each other. On the one hand, a selection of British upper-crust, a bit short on cash, but who badly want to believe they can succeed in business. Most of them haven't a prayer, of course, since they're swimming with sharks. On the other hand, you have greedy foreign fat cats who have money and power, but who can't buy that elusive quality, style. So they buy the presence of the nobles, hoping some of it will rub off on them.

"Both sides are doomed to disappointment, obviously. The nobles usually have as much business acumen as a lobotomized troll, and the greed merchants wouldn't know style if it sandbagged them. Still, at least the chaps who pay the tab get traditional British room service, with butlers and valets on tap, and a carefully planned percentage of forelock-tugging and 'by gad, you are a card, sir.' Nobody in Britain actually speaks like that anymore, of course, but you seps seem to think we do, so we maintain the pretense to keep the rich tourists happy. Bentinck, the Tourism Minister, is an absolute past master at it. He's probably got the entire works of Dickens in headware memory and a skillwire in advanced groveling. Still, it's all good for the economy. End of lecture."

Geraint waved away the oncoming threat of the hors d'oeuvres trolley. "I think I'd better stick to something green and safe. Too much gamma-cholesterol in the bacon strips this morning. Must have fed the factory pig the wrong goo."

"But, Geraint, what about your Conservationists?" Serrin said. "They seem pretty much the traditional old Brit to me. And what you're saying about class and style,

that's very British too. I think the folks back home know
they can't buy class, no matter how much we pay for
implants or the loveliest cybereyes or clonal facelifts or
any other cosmetic trick of the modern age. But we recognize it in you guys. That's real.''

"Granted. But you're missing something,'' Geraint
gestured with his fork.

"What's that?''

"Humor. We don't take this terribly seriously. Deep
down, British people know that life's tawdry tapestry is
something you have to get through with a certain decent
detachment. Look, I spent hours this morning listening
to some Swiss corporate mercenary drone on about the
role of speculative finance in the development of viral
agents to counter the diseases of old age. Medicine? No,
it was all about money.

"What his arguments came down to was this. Stuff the
poor countries, because their per capita income is too
low to pay for the drugs, and no one lives long enough
to need them anyway. Ignore the richest countries, because the smart money there is on clone-tech and tissue
replacement banks. In the future the very rich will never
grow old anyway. His position—and this is where he got
really excited for just a few minutes—is that smart inves-
tors will focus on the middle group. That group can't
afford the real cutting-edge work, but who has enough
money and enough crumblies to become a sound market
for the cheaper viral repair agents.

"My friend, what medicine comes down to is, where
is the best market? And not even the best market now.
That's not enough. We need venture capitalists with the
foresight to know who will be able to afford to delay
death in the right way in years to come.

"Oh, and there was a nice little rider in the next pre-
sentation. Some people might think that developing
clonal technology—the thing that really works—for the
very rich and then letting it trickle down to the rest would
benefit everyone. Producers get economies of scale, con-
sumers get what they need. However, it turns out that
you can't dispense the new products to the mass market
because then the corps wouldn't have big enough pro-

duction runs for their simpler, cheaper products. Long-term profits would drop, discouraging further research.

"It's political, of course, as well as economic: we can't allow those with less money to enjoy the same advantages of those with more. Dear me, no. Can't have billions of little Indians and Chinese running around with extra-long life spans. Think of the pollution from over-population. And all this from men living in the most destroyed and polluted countries in the world."

Geraint gestured with his hands, palms out before him, fingers extended across the table toward the elf. "That's why the nobles and the moneymen are in there. They're protecting each other's inalienable right to scrag the rest of the world. I mean, what else would be freedom, democracy, and the Anglo-American way? Not to forget the Swiss and Japanese, of course. Actually, they're rather better at it than we are these days."

There was a long silence after that tirade. Serrin had never heard anything like this from Geraint when he'd been a fresh-faced young student in California.

"Spirits, boy, you sound like one of those goldarned Commies." Serrin made a limp attempt at humor. He wasn't sure what to make of his friend's outburst.

"Serrin, you know the other side of the coin. There's little more decency between these people than they show the rest of the world." Geraint paused, mouth tight. "That's why you want to hunt the person who killed your parents."

The blow struck home. The elf's hands balled into fists and his face contorted with tension. Silence descended heavily between the two men.

"What are you going to do, old friend?" Geraint's voice was almost tender.

"I don't know. I've been out to Longstanton. I'll stake the place out to see what opportunity turns up."

Geraint had known Serrin would try this, and had his reply well-scripted. "You can't know exactly where Kuranita's headed. Longstanton isn't the whole Fuchi complex, but it's three rakking square miles and that's a lot of entrances to cover."

"There are only two main gates, and he's sure to head

for the security complex." The elf twisted his gaze, avoiding Geraint's eyes.

"Serrin, you don't have the weapons to hit the guy. You'd need an expert sniper with an MA 2100 or better and every trick you could build into it. You'd need infrared, APDS to get through the ballistic armor, and you'd need smoke, flare, and heaven knows what else to have a cat in hell's chance of getting out alive. And even if you didn't care about that, and you got lucky and hit the guy in one chance in a hundred, you know as well as I do that a man like Kuranita will have a couple of doubles running around as safeguards. Sure, he'll be going for the security complex—almost certainly by an indirect route, while a doppelganger takes the obvious one. Unless he's going to double-bluff, of course.

"How can you know what someone like that will have planned? You're no street samurai, friend. You couldn't even get close to him with what you do have. You know there'll be corporate mages checking the astral for miles. You wouldn't even get within range before they fried you."

Serrin shook his head. "I took precautions against that. Don't forget, I've been earning my nuyen by snooping around here all week. Got a little something to help on the masking front."

"So that's what you got from Serena," Geraint blurted.

The mage looked astonished. "You been probing my mind, you bastard?" He was angry and threatened by the possibility. Geraint waved away his anger with a smile.

"You should know I don't have any talent in that department. Much simpler: I got pretty much the same thing from her myself, only yesterday. She said you'd been in. And no, she didn't say what you'd bought there. She just said it was an interesting coincidence that you'd stopped by just before I did. Nothing more to it than that."

Serrin relaxed, slowly, but remained slightly on guard. Geraint pounced on his uncertainty with a final warning.

"Fine, so you're masked and you manage not to get noticed by any of the—five or six?—mages who'll be there. The lab will have a couple in the security department, I guess, say two more covering the perimeters, and Kuranita's retinue will include another pair. Call it four.

Do you really think they won't be protecting him with enough sustained spells and spell locks to guard a Swiss banking satellite? Come on, don't be foolish. Take any kind of shot and we won't be chewing the fat over breakfast tomorrow. Let it go. You can't touch this man. Not here, not now.''

It was the truth, and Serrin knew it. "But I have to go.''

Geraint nodded sadly. He'd known this was something beyond reason, but he had to try. There was only one thing left to do.

"Of course you do, you dumb sod. But you can't go alone, and I don't want you getting us both killed by doing anything silly.''

The elf's eyes shone brightly as he looked at his friend. When he spoke it was with an almost childlike naivete. "You'll help me?''

"What are friends for? I have a little more skill these days.'' With the fingers of his left hand Geraint drew the skin on his right palm tight. The implant beneath was well-disguised, scarcely visible even now. It was a beautiful job, and Serrin admired the near-perfect concealment of the smartgun link.

"I felt I needed it after what happened. If I'd been a better shot all those years ago we'd both have someone still alive today.''

"It wasn't your fault. It was dark, raining. She should never have run down that—''

"I don't blame myself. Not now, anyway. But I thought some personal enhancement in that direction wouldn't be amiss. I got myself a skillwire too. I'm not bad, either. I've yet to fire a sniper rifle in real action, but I can bring off a head shot nine times out of ten at eighty yards. I don't think we'll get that close, but I'm bound to be a better shot so you should stick to covering my backside. And I hope that bike of yours is bloody quick.''

Geraint drummed his fingers on the table, planning his moves. "Look, I've got to get back to the Smoke. We'll need rather better resources than we've got here, and I don't really fancy getting a two-thousand nuyen Gieves suit covered with fenland muck. I can't leave until four, but there's the non-stop express shuttle at four-twelve and

I can be back here by, oh, seven. I'll bring whatever I can lay my hands on. Ideally, we could use a rocket launcher, but it's probably too short notice.''

The mage was open-mouthed. Geraint's eyes twinkled back at him. "Only joking. We'd have to raid an Integrated Weapons Systems armory to get one of those, or maybe the Ministry of Defense. Not enough time." He chuckled, his mind shuffling through the contacts he could chase down, hoping that Haughtree, at least, would be at home. Haughtree was the one man he could be sure of in this kind of situation. Thirty thousand nuyen for the cancer op in Zurich made Haughtree a very trustworthy friend.

"Meanwhile, Serrin, you can go check out those Optical Neotech guys. Got something for you on that one; the senior, Peter McCumber, has an extremely shaky cred balance. File a report stating that your sources inform you that he's taking bribes from a subsidiary of British Industrial. Tell your employer to check transactions at the Chartered Imperial Bank. That should earn you a nice bonus. Buy me dinner at the Carlton sometime."

Geraint made to leave, but Serrin grabbed his arm and looked hard into his eyes. "Why are you doing all this?" It wasn't mistrust in his voice, only a little wonderment.

Geraint opted for fatuity. "Because I'm a bored, decadent, minor noble looking for a little excitement in a humdrum life, old friend."

Serrin still looked baffled. Geraint laughed softly and clapped the elf on the shoulder. "Catch you later," he said.

9

Wasim pored over the map as the ancient British Industrial Midlander rattled along the highway. He was hunched up in the back seat, packed between Sachin with the guns and Aqib with a cylindrical steel tube and a box of grenades. "Ten miles, then to the northern zone and past the Bar Hill squatzone. It's on the right."

The car leaped over one of the ubiquitous bumpy testimonies to the woeful quality of British roads. There was a thump as someone's head struck the roof. "What a pile of plazz!" Sachin complained, rubbing his head ruefully. "I thought they'd stopped making these buckets ten years ago when they closed down the Birmingham factory. Didn't close it down soon enough, if you ask me."

"Best Mohsin could do, Sach." Imran's smile flashed in the green light from the dashboard. "Hey Rani, you got Chenka's little helper there?" Next to him, his sister retrieved a plastic ziplock filled with little packets. She broke the seal and handed around the crinkled paper sachets of brown dust.

"What do we do? Swallow it or snort the stuff?" Sachin asked.

"Probably supposed to make tea with it," Aqib muttered and they all laughed, remembering the old woman and her notorious teas. Rani had suffered from a bellyache all day after leaving Chenka's filthy flat in the tenement high above the Stepney squats and rat warrens. The stench of urine and ammonia had been worse than ever.

"Swallow it," Rani advised. "And I've got some instant energy to go with it." She passed around the ricepaper wrapped sugar and coconut balls, lurid with yellow coloring. But they were syrupy and moist, and they helped get the chokingly dry dust down their throats.

They were into Cambridge when the herbal high began to hit them. Even Aqib's brown cybereyes, a real status symbol among them, seemed to shine a little brighter now.

"I've got cotton mouth," Imran complained as he ground his teeth. "We got anything? I'd even take green tea."

It was a problem Rani had anticipated. She opened the seal on a guava drink, an expensive luxury which had set her back plenty because it boasted real fruit and not the usual array of artificial flavorings. Perhaps it did, too, she thought with surprise as she gulped down some of the warm but welcome fluid. The men were complaining for their turns, so she passed the bottle over her shoulder to Sachin. Then she resumed her tight grip on what claimed to be a Bond and Carrington pistol in her lap. It was probably as genuine as a tridjock's smile, but the barrel was clean and smooth and the trigger mechanism had seemed fluent when she'd practiced with it. Now, though, it was armed with live ammunition and with that she had not practiced.

This sure better work out, she thought grimly. It seemed a lot of dosh just to throw a scare into somebody by taking a few potshots at him, then legging it back home in a hurry.

She was starting to have a very bad feeling about all this.

*   *   *

Geraint had called Serrin from the rail station, arranging to meet at a pub on the north side of town. Serrin arrived just at half past seven but didn't immediately spot Geraint. The nobleman looked very different dressed in nonde-script baggy clothing instead of a designer suit, but he wasn't conspicuous, especially the way he sat quaffing a pint of ale like any local.

"How do you know about a place like this?" the mage asked.

Geraint looked mildly offended. "I spent three years as a student in Cambridge, old friend, and I did manage to mis-spend some of my youth in moderately disrepu-table places. It's a pity the old laserball machine's gone, though. I fancied dumping a few quid into it for old times' sake."

Geraint laughed softly and his expression changed to one Serrin could not quite identify. "I had my one and only experience as a boytoy here," the nobleman said. "I was twenty, she was thirty-one, and I used to take her home from the fish and chip shop over the road. That's gone, too, of course. Take a guess—it's a burger joint now. I suppose that's because the few fish left in the North Sea are so polluted with chemicals and sewage sludge that the price of decent cod is something wicked these days."

Serrin looked quizzically at Geraint. "I can't imagine you with someone from a fish and chip shop."

"She used to call in here after work on the weekends. There was a serial rapist around at the time and most of us were on escort duty. One time she decided to stay in my rooms, which were just down the road. She was engaged to some fellow in the air force, but really just for the sake of the kids from her first marriage. Security for her declining years, I suppose. He was posted out all over the place, but one day he flew in and they got married there and then. I sometimes wonder what became of her. You know how it goes."

Geraint sat remembering, hands clasped together under his chin. Serrin allowed him a few moments, then turned the talk back to more pressing matters. "What did you get?" He'd seen the battered cloth carryall, which did the job of keeping its contents shapeless most effectively.

"Let's go for a ride. I don't imagine the walls have ears, but best not to take any chances."

They drained their glasses and signaled to pay the ork barmaid, who didn't look at Serrin any too kindly. The mage guessed that elves of more exalted lineage than his might be none too popular, with their airs and graces, in a pub like this. In her eyes he would probably be tarred with the same brush. Revealing himself as an American could easily make matters worse, so he only nodded when Geraint said, "Thank you." Reaching the door, Serrin and Geraint carefully gave way to a bunch of local fenland orks shouldering their way into the bar.

* * *

They skirted away from the side road well before coming to the old farms area, careful to give it a wide berth. The land here was too polluted from the outflow of the Stinkfens to be officially considered habitable, but squatters would surely be about. Serrin detoured south and east before circling back to the highway; the sound of a bike engine might well draw some of the squatters out for a look. A road bike was worth a lot of barter to people that poor. It wasn't likely they had much in the way of weapons, perhaps only knives and stones, but an old shotgun was also a possibility. Serrin switched the headlight off, and let the bike coast over the sodden, barren fields. He got as close to the edge of the fens as he dared, then began to loop back westward. After crossing the road, he parked the bike beside a dead tree stump, laying it flat to the ground.

"We'll head for that rise," the mage said, pointing to a gentle curve in the distance.

"Get the armor vest on. You got your Ingram? I managed to pick up some armor-piercing for it." Geraint handed Serrin the clip and a small vial.

"Here's something useful from the chemistry set. Crush the vial if you have to start firing. Inhale the stuff. But don't do it if you've got a troll less than ten feet away because it'll blow your brain out your ears and you won't be able to see a thing for a few seconds. Do it while he's two hundred yards away. With this stuff your hands won't tremble if you do have to start shooting. And if you have to run, it'll get you moving faster than a cheetah with a red chili enema. Even with that leg of yours. And when I tell you to run, you damn well better. Don't shoot unless we're getting out. Use whatever magic you've got to defend us just before I start shooting. I'll tell you when.

"Got all that?"

Serrin was impressed by the authority in Geraint's voice. This was a very different man from the boy who'd panicked on the streets of San Francisco. The elf slipped the vial into his pocket, deciding this wasn't the moment to challenge Geraint on his use of drugs.

"Good." The Welshman wasn't waiting for a reply. "Next item. Take this." He handed Serrin a lacquered canister topped with a ring-pull. "Use this when we move out. Three seconds after you pull the ring, you'll get smoke cover, which will scrag IR into the bargain. Just dump the thing on the ground behind us." Geraint was adding the folding stock to a customized sniper rifle as he spoke. Serrin thought it looked like the MA 2100, but the thing was glinting with add-ons. He'd been on runs with a lot more firepower than this, but this Welshman was beginning to look like the real thing.

Geraint glanced up at him in the moonlight as he completed his work. "You do realize this is bloody madness, don't you? Two people out here against scores of them in there. I must be insane doing this. You'll have to cover us damn well with your magic. Hope you've got something that'll keep the corp mages from spotting us too quickly or else we're sitting ducks. If it's a two-minute walk to that hill, it's fifteen seconds running with the drug, twenty if we don't move fast enough. That's too long if we're out in the open. What's your plan?"

Serrin was busy himself, locking together a series of bizarre stone plaques around a leather strap, jiggling them into place, and finally tightening it around his shoulder and hip. "I thought I'd better put a priority on protection and disguise. I've got to make it as hard for them to see us as possible, and that means everything—magical detection, IR scans, ultrasonics—though I don't think chiphounds will be a problem. We should be well away before they can get them out of the compound. This little bunch," he added, gripping the belt around his body, "adds some power along the line. I won't bore you with the details. Key thing is a chaotic shift. How much do you know about spellcraft?"

"I thought a chaotic world spell messed up the sensing of the magician who got hit by it."

"Same principle, different way of going about it. I spent a year researching a version that centers the effect on the casting magician. Screws up most forms of detection in a constantly shifting area centered on me instead of a target. I don't think they're going to have time to run a computing of average transients to figure out the algorithm for the shifting. Besides, it's keyed to magnetic field fluctuations. I always knew that funny little deposit of magnetically sensitive ferric bone above my sinuses was good for something. They won't work that one out. Nice big area, too. The barriers I'm erecting are a bit more limited in scale, but we shouldn't have to worry about anything less than a cascade of automatics or a firework display of multiple grenade launchers."

Geraint slapped him on the shoulder. "Don't know much about these things, but it sounds good to me."

"When you're alone out there, it's a good idea to design something that doesn't force you to depend on anyone else. But it works just as well when you're working with another person, too. Only problem is, the drain is pretty heavy. I'll be a bit groggy for a little while. Make sure you shoot straight.''

They set off for the hill, their boots sloshing in the fouled waters of the field until they reached the incline. They crawled to the top on their bellies, and looked down over the Fuchi site three hundred yards to the west. The headlights of the first convoy began to crawl along the road toward the front gates after a frozen half-hour.

Geraint slipped off the woolen gloves, breathing on his hands to keep them warm. He edged the rifle forward and squinted with his left eye as he lined up the IR sight, ignoring the cars and aiming just inside the gate. As the cars got closer, he drew back and looked away from the glare of their lights.

Serrin was scanning the scene with binox, shifting to IR and low-light. Casting his spell as silently as he could, he made the briefest of checks as the cars spilled their human contents out onto the tarmac inside the gates.

''Geraint, I don't think it's him.'' Despite the elf's low whisper, his voice was urgent, stressed. ''Hold your fire.''

''Checked the plates?''

''Yes, it's the right limo, but that's not him. It's a damn good double, but not good enough. Something feels weird here. I'm sensing that they're not paying much attention to this side of the place. They're looking south.''

Geraint was still peering down the sight, but with the slightest of movements he could see that the security guards were all looking that way. ''Of course they are. It's where the gates open.''

''No, it's more than that. I don't dare probe, it'll give us away. But I—wait a minute. North, look!'' he hissed.

Geraint lifted his eyes away from the rifle sight and gazed out toward the far gate. Two shadowy vehicles were headed that way, gliding silently across the fields. They were going straight for the smaller northern gate, on the far side of the complex from the security compound. ''We were right. The dummy's coming in from the south. Here's the real thing.'' He shifted position, drawing the gun around gently to face the far gate, settling to his aim again. "Two cars, say ten men. I can down four of them before they know what hit them. Let's pray one of them is who we're looking for."

Geraint never made that shot.

Whatever the noise was, it made them both suddenly duck their heads, utterly bewildered. Then they heard the drone of a helicopter, coming in low from the west. It had to be one of the IWS-licensed super-stealths; the thing was almost over the far wall before they heard it. Serrin began his spellcasting as Geraint desperately tried to revise his plan of action, waiting for the chopper to land, certain that *this* must be their man. The sudden flare took him completely by surprise, ruining his aim.

Then the gunfire began.

* * *

Aqib's improvised launcher worked pretty well the first time. The flareshot landed whack in the middle of the compound, illuminating a large group of black-visored orks and trolls waving down the chopper. The gates were already opening when Sachin's Ceska started chattering. He and Wasim were almost whooping as their guns spat, and Imran had his beloved Predator readied for some carefully aimed fire.

Rani was the first to realize something was very, very wrong. "Look out! They know!"

The security men were already storming out of the gates, and a couple of real grenade launchers were coughing missiles at them from the security tower. Damn Chenka's powders, Rani screamed to herself. The men's blood is too hot, they don't see.

It was swift and bloody. Aqib's launcher disintegrated as he let fly a second time, the young Sind samurai thrown backward, arms bathed in flame. To her left, another blast exploded Wasim's body into bloody shreds of gore. The others had no time to take in the horror of it as a great pillar of flame roared to life behind them, then began to streak across the brilliantly lit terrain at staggering speed.

In the distance, Serrin gasped, appalled. "Christ, a fragging fire elemental. Those guys are dead meat."

Geraint wasn't stopping. He'd already torn the top off his vial and was screaming at Serrin to do the same. As he turned, he dropped the rifle and dragged a Bond and Carrington pistol from his padded jacket, loping away across the mud and muck toward the stashed bike.

Serrin wasn't hanging around to argue. Whatever it was they'd strayed into, there wasn't a hope in hell of finding Kuranita in this madness. He could only hope his spell would cover their exit, given that security was looking elsewhere.

His leg betrayed him. A deep rumble from the area of the compound set the ground to shaking underfoot, and the elf stumbled and fell. Mouth choked with mud and the sour taste of saline and acid, Serrin dragged himself to his feet, his pulse racing crazily. To his right, two figures were racing desperately across the road with the retina-searing elemental close behind. A detachment of security also was hot in pursuit, SMGs chattering.

Serrin didn't know why he did it; it was crazy and stupid. Dropping his sustained protections was absurd under the circumstances, but something told him that no one was after him, no one had seen him. He began to chant slowly. He got lucky. The elemental wasn't a tough one, its force fairly weak, and it took the elf mage no more than fifteen seconds to banish the spirit. The spell sapped the creature's power, and its flames flickered and died. All those other people had to do now was evade a posse of heavily armored and cyberware-toting hulks with automatic weapons.

Well, at least I've bought them a chance, Serrin thought grimly as he turned and ran. In his haste he didn't hear the car engine revving in the distance. He never knew that she'd seen his face in a chance flash of light. He was unaware of what she would remember all her life.

Now some of the troopers were searching around, well-trained enough to hunt the source of something that could dissipate an elemental. Serrin's leg throbbed viciously as he lurched toward where he thought they'd left the bike. The leg felt as if he'd been hamstrung with a meathook. Distantly he heard Geraint's desperate cry to him, but the drain was beginning to take its toll and he could do no more than half-run, half-limp onto a riverbank that shouldn't have been there. He just managed to crawl over it, hoping to find some cover where he could hide. A foul liquid bubbled up from his lungs, and his breath came in ragged gasps. He stumbled again and landed up to his neck in water and reeds.

The last thing Serrin saw before passing out was the river serpent. The thing was probably ten yards long. Rearing over him, the beast opened its powerfully muscular jaws to reveal its dagger-sharp teeth set in a huge, gaping maw as black as the entrance to hell.

10

Geraint retained enough self-control not to exceed the speed limit as he headed through Bar Hill's dreary low-rise houses on the way back to Cambridge. His thoughts, however, raced furiously.

Serrin had vanished into the night. Geraint, meanwhile, had hordes of heavily armed Fuchi security guards rushing toward him, forcing him to take off on the elf's bike, praying no copters were after him, too. It was bad enough that Serrin had disappeared. Now he also had the unexpected arrival of another group of raiders at the lab to disturb and confuse him.

Geraint turned everything over and over in his mind, trying to recall what he and Serrin had said and where they'd said it, wondering if their conversations had been bugged. No matter how many times he mentally replayed scenes, however, he couldn't make any sense of it.

Entering the main sprawl zone north of Cambridge, Geraint realized that he couldn't return to the hotel. He could hardly stroll through the front lobby with his clothes torn to ribbons and caked with mud. Even his famous sang froid wouldn't let him get away with blithely leaving a muddy trail of wet clods on the carpet behind him. Hotel security was bound to make a discreet notification to the police, some of whom must certainly be special friends of Fuchi. Things could get supremely nasty. For the same reason, dumping the bike in the selfpark garage and heading straight for the elevator was a no-go. The attendant might see him, and there would be videoscans even there.

Rakk it all, he'd have to go back to London, which meant no motorway travel, not on a motorbike. Forty miles of back roads all the way to the outer orbital. Wonderful, he thought. I hope it hasn't changed much since my student days. I haven't driven along here in ten years.

Hitting the roads, Geraint had the impression they hadn't been repaired in a decade, either. South of Royston he had the sense to turn off the main road and take a detour around the decaying sprawl suburbs. He saw the barricade and the lurking wrecker gang just in time. Had he continued straight on, he'd have already been dead meat.

Cursing his bad luck, Geraint now found himself in a warren of back streets. He slowed the bike while he tried to figure out where he was and where he was going. The street lights had been shot out long ago, and all he had was the weak light of the moon and his own dipped headlight. Realizing that he'd completely lost track of his direction, and had no idea how to get out of here, the hair began to rise at the back of his neck. One thing was certain, though; he had to keep moving. At one point he decided to turn around again, and was making a slow U-turn, when suddenly he saw before him a ragged group edging out of the shadows and blocking his path.

"Nice bike, term," a rough voice called. "Make you an offer!"

There were sniggers audible above the bike's revving engine. The punk at the front of the pack was hefting a hunk of wood that looked like a railway tie. Some of those hanging further back were carrying rocks, more likely chunks of plascrete.

Geraint began to sweat. How am I going to get out of this one? he wondered desperately. A single hit would wing me. Then I'm off the bike. Then I'm down. Then I'm dead. Got no choice, I guess.

As the punks fanned out around and in front of him, he drew his pistol, hoping it was visible in the glare of his headlight. Their reactions said they saw it, but they were poor enough to have nothing to lose. They no doubt lost a member or two every week in a gang fight, so the prospect of losing a few more now probably didn't terrify them much. Not if they saw a motorcycle and a gun as the prize to be won.

"Spare me that glop, you wankers!" Geraint made his voice tougher than he could possibly feel right there and then. "Bond and Carrington MC-40, armor-piercing rounds with high-reaction reload. Six of you die, maybe eight. I got a smartgun link, so you could even count to ten if you get unlucky."

The rabble was shifting uneasily now, but they held their ground. Impasse. Then Geraint had a flash of inspiration.

"In about eight minutes the slint on my tail will come edging round the shadows here. Nice Toyota bike. A real banger. Why not wait for him instead? Set up a sweet little ambush. That way half of you don't get splashed.

"And since you'll be doing me a favor," he added, revving the bike's engine to make a dash for it, "I think a little remuneration would be in order."

He drew a wad of bills from his jacket. Thank the Bank of England for stubbornly refusing to accept that credsticks were the only way to do business these days. He flung the paper into the air, then watched as it fluttered down like a ticker tape parade of fifties and hundreds. The next instant he was scorching away from a dead stop as the snakeboys ran to grab what they could, some even dropping their improvised weapons in their urgency to stuff bank notes into their pockets.

Geraint crouched low over the handlebars and prayed to an obscure Welsh saint that nobody would throw a rock just for the hell of it.

He got lucky. Before the hour was out, he was standing in the service elevator of his apartment house, hoping that no one would see him coming out at penthouse level. Stripping off the jacket and trousers, he bundled them into his carryall and emerged from the elevator feigning a drunken stagger. Muddied nobles in armor jackets might worry security. Half-naked nobles lurching home in a state of terminal intoxication certainly would not.

Breathing heavily, he got the magkey into the lock and half-fell into the hallway, slamming the door behind him.

Time for a bath, coffee, and a good shot of GABA-interactive neuromodulator complex, Geraint promised himself, and it didn't matter much in what order.

* * *

Imran was still in a state of shock, sitting on the tattered sofa staring emptily into space. When he and Rani returned home, they'd had to rouse a severely doped-up Sanjay to open the door. The place was a pigsty from Sanjay's rolling with a wretched street girl he'd probably lured back to the house with the promise of opiate oblivion. Rani chased the girl out, barely giving her time to cover her scrawny, eczema-riddled body. Sanjay met Rani's complaints of disgust with a mere shrug and a blank gaze from his heavily dilated pupils. But the mess gave her something on which to vent her anguish and frustration, and she felt a little calmer after making some tea and allowing herself a shot of the fierce, peppery spirit they kept for emergencies.

Imran was half-catatonic, and there was no one to talk to worth the effort, but still she tried.

"It was a set-up, Imran. They knew we were coming. They knew our exact location. Now you . . . you . . . you rakking sod . . . you're going to tell me everything you know about who hired you for this job. Where you met them, what they looked like, who gave you the contact. Everything!"

A bead of sweat trickled down Imran's forehead. He wasn't listening. Instead he babbled a little about the families they'd have to phone, in whose sitting rooms the women would have to mourn and bewail the dead, who else would have to know. He recited a litany of cousins as uselessly as a nervous Catholic fumbling a string of rosary beads.

Rani slapped him hard, hoping to jolt him back to reality. He looked up at her with total incomprehension, then his face puckered with rage. Leaping angrily to his feet, Imran smashed her across the face with all his strength—not just a slap but a hard punch—sending her flying across the room. Then his anger evaporated just as instantly. He fell to his knees and began to cry.

Rani was horrified, but hurt also, her ears singing from the blow. Something broke between them there and then. She looked at Imran, and though it was only later that she realized it, Rani lost respect for her brother at that moment. She hugged and consoled him, but she was already thinking about what to do next. It wouldn't be her brother asking the questions on the streets now.

* * *

Geraint decided that it would be safe to cut and run at about five o'clock. He'd ended up falling asleep right after his bath, and the alarm almost didn't rouse him for an early train back to the hotel. It wouldn't seem unusual for a noble to have spent the night away from the place, he figured. Some of them would have used personal helicopters to get back overnight, so he wouldn't be specifically missed.

"Going to the ATT time-series seminar this morning?"

Geraint looked up from his coffee, all he could face this morning, at the puffed red face of the Marquis of Scunthorpe. He tried to hide his dismay.

"Um, looks interesting, yes, yes, I thought I'd go. How's the lovely Tamsin?" It always pleased the rubicund, bloated Yorkshireman to have noble acquaintances praise his fiery and beautiful wife. You poor bastard, Geraint thought, as he always did. She only married you for the money and the title and you don't even notice that half your male domestic servants walk around with permanent smirks on their faces.

"Jolly chipper, old feller, jolly chipper!" The Marquis parked his spreading pin-striped posterior on the armchair with a grunt, and preened his handlebar mustache. "Well, I thought I'd take a doze in the British Industrial thing. All that mathematical stuff is a bit heavy on the old gray cells. Have a natter with old Walter over lunch instead. D'you care to join us?"

Geraint couldn't contemplate a more awful lunch prospect than being closeted with the two Yorkshiremen.

Walter Crowther, head of British Industrial's infamous Foods Division, was renowned for his enthusiasms. All the while totally losing his appetite, Geraint would have to listen to endless details of how factory animals could be stuffed full of synthetic hormones and growth enforcers. Crowther had a ghastly ambition, and talk of it was always prefaced by "Did I ever tell you . . . ?" This was the signal for a set speech about how he was hoping to breed a rabbit the length of a telephone pole so it could be neatly chopped into Rabburger Bunny Chunks in an endless series of slices. "Length of a cricket pitch I'd settle for," he'd then say, the cue for him to begin reviewing England's cricket team for the last sixty years. Geraint just couldn't face it, but catching sight of a chambermaid hefting a trolleyful of fresh linen into an elevator gave him an idea.

"Tied up, old chap. But I'll tell you what, I'll stand you a brandy in the Marlborough Bar after lunch. Like to hear you and old Crowther's opinion on Sutcliffe batting at number six." The fat face opposite beamed with pleasure.

Got out of that one nicely, Geraint reflected as he reached the fifth floor. Now let's find that chambermaid. He checked his jacket's innermost pocket, the one with the fiberseal just below the Gieves tag. The notes rustled reassuringly within it. Don't know why anyone ever uses credsticks, he mused. Cash certainly seems more useful with the lower classes. Grinning to himself, he turned the corner and strode along the plush pile toward the "Rooms 510–518" sign, all fake gilt on fake hardwood.

The girl was only too happy to do as he asked. She didn't earn that much in a month.

* * *

Geraint was back in his own flat in London by six-thirty, with the entire contents of Serrin's hotel room spread out before him. He hadn't dared risk going out to Longstanton to look for the elf, consoling himself with the fact that the local news had included no reports of trouble at the Fuchi site.

You travel light in the world, old friend, Geraint thought,

as he rifled through Serrin's meager belongings. He didn't open the sealed electronic book; that would have been a violation somehow, even though he feared in his heart that the elf was dead. Serrin had left behind some of his permits and licenses, though Geraint guessed they were probably duplicates for backup. The mage wouldn't go out into the bureaucratic British world without every bit of official paper he needed. There were clothes in the suitcase, but they lacked any individuality and identity. Well, whatever the elf's indifference to style, at least Geraint had retrieved his belongings for him. The chambermaid had his number and instructions to tell Serrin where to pick up money in Cambridge if he came back to the hotel. She was Welsh, so Geraint had figured he could trust her. Hell, he thought, I own the land her family lives on. Guess I'd better be able to trust her.

The beep of the telecom startled him. It was the autocheck, the soft chipvoice asking if he wanted messages from the preceding forty-eight hours retained or erased. He instructed it to play.

There was another summons from Manchester's secretary, so he paused the playback and made the call, confirming his willingness to serve King and Country by sitting through the tedium of the House of Nobles committee rooms. After that he poured a Chartreuse and let the machine complete its messages. A face he hadn't seen before appeared on the screen. She was very attractive, and he attended carefully.

"Hello, Lord Llanfrechfa. You don't know me, but I'm Annie, a friend of Francesca's. She needs help at the moment and I thought maybe you could. I found your name in her date book, and I think she's told me you're friends. Could you stop by here? Francesca's in a little trouble. I'm not sure what to do this time. Thank you."

There was a clear edge of distress and uncertainty in the girl's voice—not really what Geraint needed right now. "Oh God," he sighed, sitting back and rubbing at his face. "Serrin's vanished, maybe dead, and now this. What the hell has Francesca gotten into now?"

He checked the time-date stamp of the call and realized that it had come in more than twenty-four hours before. When he tapped in Francesca's telecom code, all

he got was the ansafone, so perhaps she was still unable to take calls. Annie hadn't left her number, so he'd have to make the short haul to Knightsbridge in person.

* * *

Francesca was dazed and still sedated, but he got the gist of it out of her. It was hard to tell, though, whether her incoherence was the effect of the IC having ripped through her brain or whether it was the drugs talking. She was shaken, but the damage was not as bad as he'd feared. It certainly didn't seem irreparable.

Geraint held her hand and sat on the patchwork quilt spread over the huge bed, downplaying the conference, not wanting to mention Serrin. Mercifully, Francesca didn't know that the mage was in town, so she didn't ask after him. They talked gently into the late evening hours.

"It was Annie who saved me," she mumbled for the fifth or sixth time. "She pulled the jacks when she saw my face. That's twice she's done that now. Good girl, Annie. Well, not what you'd call a good girl, but she is really." She was rambling a little. He thought it was time to tuck her in and leave. The Careline doc would be back in the morning to make another check, and it was the best coverage money could buy.

"Maybe I'll drop in on the lady and thank her," he said, rising from the bed. "It's good to know you've got such a friend."

She made to get out of bed. "She's just around the corner. Hanbury Court. You know, jus' round the corner. Call it a court even though it's just the next floor down. Round the corner, down the stairs and number fifty-five on the circular balcony. I ought to go see her myself. Say thanks properly. Good girl." She was struggling into her robe.

"Come on, you're in no fit state," Geraint said calmly, but she pushed her feet into some slippers and took his arm. "Fresh air will do me good, Geraint." She grinned up at him, suddenly coherent again. Her face was flushed from the tranquilizers, but she walked fairly steadily. What the hell, he thought.

Geraint checked to see that she had her magkey as they

closed the door behind them, then circled around to the mezzanine stairs and toward number fifty-five. When Geraint knocked, he was startled to find the door just slightly ajar. It swung silently open even as his hand rapped at it.

The living room was quiet, the trid on very low. Behind the settee a black lacquered lamp lay on the carpet, the shade tumbled askew. Geraint's nerves began to jangle. People who lived in a place like this didn't leave their doors open. Most of them rarely even spoke to the person who lived in the next apartment, and they paid big money for security. Doors did not get left open.

Francesca looked puzzled, dumb, as if trying to focus on the scene. "Where's Annie?" she murmured.

"Don't know. This seems a bit odd, but I'm sure there's nothing to . . ." Geraint's voice trailed away as he saw the hint of a stain in front of the door to his left. He couldn't be sure, it might be no more than spilled wine, but his guts were beginning to churn and he was afraid.

"Fran, why don't you just, uh, sit down there and I'll call down to security." He steered her to a plush chair facing away from the far door, and reached for the telecom pad on the table beside it. That way he could open the bedroom door and peek in unobtrusively while pretending to make a call. She'd never see him.

Francesca turned around in the chair and saw his face just as the blood drained out of it. She staggered to her feet and got to him before he was able to react, stunned as he was. Feebly, he clutched at her face, trying to turn her head away from seeing what lay in the bedroom beyond. "Just don't look, just don't look," he managed to gasp, but it was too late.

Geraint would never have believed a body had so much blood in it. Great pools of it were congealing on the carpet and the covers, and the far wall looked as if someone had flung a bucketful of blood from one end of the room to the other. The curtains were dappled with it, drops still leaking onto the parquet tiles by the window. The great gash across Annie Chapman's throat found its hideous, enlarged echo in a ragged, bloody gash across the breadth of her stomach. A ribbon of internal organs had been flung in a ghastly pile around one shoulder of the woman's body in a horrific parody of modern fashions.

Geraint reeled back across Francesca's unconscious form, fell before he could get to the bathroom door, and vomited until he thought his heart would burst right through his chest. Scrabbling at the telecom pad he had dropped to the floor, he frantically tapped in the code for emergency. He had just barely managed to regain his self-control when the uniformed troll arrived, hefting his IWS taser and netgun in alarm.

"You won't be needing those," Geraint said. "Just call the police." He gagged again. "I really wouldn't look in there if I were you," he managed to add, but the security guard had sniffed the carnage and couldn't resist taking a look for himself.

Geraint was calling up Careline to take care of Francesca when he heard an unmistakable noise. It was the troll, half-retching, half-sobbing, in the room behind him.

11

Rani knew it was useless questioning any of the neighbors in the faded five-story Victorian apartment house. Imran, like any decent snakeboy with any vestige of self-respect, only hung with those who considered themselves tough, mean types. No way did that include the trancers squatting in the rat-infested ground floors, or the meek and fearful old folk upstairs. Her brother was still sleeping, but Rani would find out whatever she could from his friends.

Being an ork and—worse—a girl, Rani knew the reaction she was likely to get. But with three family members dead, nothing was going to stop her trying to dig up any possible scrap of information. She really didn't expect trouble, but she decided to pack the long knife anyway. After thinking long and hard about it, she went to get Imran's Predator too. Partly for extra security, but mostly because she felt tougher with the gun bulging inside her jacket. Today she'd need all the fierceness she could muster.

Passing some kids playing with the remains of a dog in the street, she crossed over along Whitechapel Road. It wasn't far east to the wooded, gentrified corporate enclave of Limehouse, with its media elves and chardonnay-sipping kens and kylies, but it could easily have been half a continent and half a lifetime away.

Along the main road, Rani smiled wryly at a double-decker tourist bus parked to allow the mostly American and Japanese tourists aboard the opportunity to buy baked potatoes and hot chestnuts from a street vendor. Hot smoke from his barrow poured into the freezing air of the November morning.

"Cor blimey, mister, that'll be two quid. Cheap at half the price and no mistake," the cloth-capped urchin pattered cheerfully to an admiring American snapping away with an accessory-bedecked portacam. Chestnuts, huh! Extruded fungal residues, matey, and that's if you're lucky. As for the jacket potatoes served with a plastic beaker of real Lancashire hot pot, she didn't think the rat meat in it came from Lancashire. With the slightest shake of her head, Rani crossed over and cut through Old Montague Street, heading for Brick Lane.

She found who she was looking for in their usual spot, hawking stolen cameras and other goods near the back of the fruit'n'veg stall. The men looked momentarily surprised to see her dressed so differently, but Kapil barely missed a beat before resuming his pitch. Business was slow this morning, though the regulars would surely stop by later to see what had fallen off the back of sundry lorries over the weekend. By the look of the cartons discreetly stashed next to the pulpy tomatoes, quite a few lorries had coincidentally lost some of their cargo of late.

The boys might be in a better mood later after they'd pocketed some more doshi, but Rani had no time to waste. Kapil seemed deep in conversation with a rodent-faced white kid, so Rani grabbed Bishen, his partner.

"There's been trouble, Bishen," she said. "Trouble that left family dead."

"So I heard. Where's Imran?" Bishen asked, sounding like he didn't want to know.

"He took a little flak. Nothing serious but he's out for a while." She'd prepared the lie in advance. "I'm trying to find out what I can about who fixed him for this run. There's a score to settle."

"That's men's work, Rani. Tell Imran to see us, and we'll see what we can do." The man started to turn away, but Rani grabbed his arm.

"No time for that! The trail will be cold. I got to find out as much as possible right now, so my brother can follow up the right way when he's better." It was a clever pitch, acknowledging her brother's primacy, but Bishen wasn't having any of it. He folded his arms adamantly.

"Look, Rani, go back home, huh? Tell Imran to come talk when he's ready. Nothing much we could tell him anyway."

He turned away, head down, kicking at the remains of some produce rotting in the gutter. She'd gotten her first brush-off of the day, but Rani was sure it wasn't going to be the last.

* * *

Rani had almost worked her way up to Bethnal Green by the time she succumbed to the smell of hot bagels wafting up the street. Rubbing her hands together to warm them a bit, she decided to try raising her spirits with a hot soystrami and soykaf. All she'd gotten for her trouble this morning was a string of no one's heard anything, no one knows anything, no one's saying anything, and we'll talk to Imran, girl. Raising the best smile she could in response to the wrinkled vendor's chitchat, she took her tray and retreated to a distant corner of the cafe. The place was filling up mostly with street sharks taking their morning break and flyboys and night girls just waking up to another pointless day or maybe heading home after a long night of oblivion. There was also a sprinkling of down-and-outs with hands cupped around the cheap soykaf they would nurse in sips long after it had gone cold.

She was lucky to spot the retractables, though the cybereyes would have been a dead giveaway. As Mohinder came through the door, the people seated at the counter quickly made a space for his powerful frame. Hand razors made anyone nervous. He strode slowly and deliberately; dermal plating, she guessed. The man had gotten lucky once with a big rollover in east Whitechapel: a bunch of foolhardy pixies had strayed in from Limehouse and some big credsticks had changed hands. That was a long time before Imran knew Mohinder, of course.

Careful not to let him spot her right away, Rani waited till he left the restaurant, then followed the big man to Sheba Street, where he ducked his frame through the small doorway of a demitech store, its frontage reinforced with steel-barred windows. She had a pretext in her pocket, so she took a chance on it.

Mohinder was just mooching around, waiting to see whether it was safe to ask the owner about what was under the counter. At first he ignored Rani, then shrugged when she discreetly showed the bulge of the pistol. One hard-eyed glance at the nervous man behind the counter got them behind the curtain and into the cramped little storeroom.

"You know about these," Rani said, producing the Ares Predator. "Does it look sound?" She tried to sound like she'd been sleeping in gutters for a month.

Mohinder took the gun in his huge hands, tested its weight and balance, checked the mechanism and the barrel. "Uh-huh. Give you thirteen hundred." He detached the ammo clip and nodded with newfound respect. "Twelve armor-piercing in the clip," he said, checking. "Give you a premium on that. Call it fourteen fifty."

So he hadn't been in on the deal. Of course not; he'd have wanted it for himself, surely, if he'd known. But he might know someone who'd seen something. She spun the conversation out a while longer.

"Fifteen."

He looked coldly at her. "Don't push your luck, woman. If I say fourteen-fifty, that's what I pay. Not a nuyen more. You don't want it, go away."

"Okay, I'll take it," she blurted, quickly backing off from his annoyance. "I need something as a replacement, of course."

"Huh," Mohinder grunted. "Imran know about all this?"

Ace it, he knew all about her. She was beginning to loathe the sound of her brother's name. "You're buying it from me, not him. I just need a little something for the house. To keep behind the door when he's away."

That worked. "Nice little Ceska be just right for you. That's eleven hundred, and you can have a spare clip of ammo. Yes?"

She waved the Predator goodbye, hoping the sacrifice wouldn't be entirely in vain. Taking a deep breath, she began her pitch.

"Something important to my family, big man. Someone paid Imran for a run. It was a set-up, and now three're dead."

To her surprise, he didn't seem to have heard about it. "Imran didn't say anything to me." His arrogant annoyance gave her an opportunity to push further.

"He made a mistake there. Other people died for it. I need to find out who was the fixer."

"Imran's hiding behind skirts?" Mohinder was contemptuous now, turning to leave. In desperation, she stood in his way, arms open beseechingly.

"Mohinder, he blew it! I need to find out what I can, then go back to Imran and the family and see what they can do. It's for the family." The implicit promise to remain in her proper place if she could just get some information seemed to count for something. He nodded as he waved her out of the way.

"Tell Imran to come see me at the Toadslab. I'll have the pistol by Wednesday. I'll bring the money, too. I don't carry that much around if I don't have to."

Rani was dismayed at the thought of such a delay, but it was the only hope she'd gotten all day. She smiled and bowed her head respectfully as Mohinder headed out past the shop counter.

"Eight o'clock. Place'll be lively by then." His hand razors snapped out of their sheaths as he opened the door. "Now I got to see a man about some money he owes me. Huh. Bye for now."

* * *

Seated on ancient leather in the House of Nobles, Geraint's thoughts wandered as an irate elf filibustered about road barriers and police patrols in northern Wales. He was only stuck here in the Westminster chambers to make up the numbers for the votes and he knew it. Damn Manchester, he thought, why's he wasting my time like this?

Geraint hadn't been able to do much more about Serrin. Returning to Longstanton would be far too dangerous. Inquiries among his contacts in the Home Office revealed no dead elves washed up downriver or found floating in a lock. Then again, the body wasn't likely to turn up as a statistic in official body counts if it had been Fuchi security that got Serrin. On that score, he could only hope against hope.

Francesca was coming home from Maudsley Hospital tomorrow night. He'd ordered some flowers delivered, and he intended to make a second trip to the ward this evening if he ever managed to escape the interminable wranglings of the House. Doctor van der Merwe, the smooth and unctuous South African doctor, had reassured him of Francesca's progress in a tone of voice that strongly suggested he believed that most people had IQs smaller than their boot sizes, and that they needed medical matters explained in words of two syllables at most. Geraint's testy reference to his own degree in neuropsychology hadn't made a dent.

He got away from the House just after six, the guillotine on the bill promising a merciful release after tomorrow's business. Knowing Francesca would ask what the police had to say, he decided to check with them again.

It was purely by virtue of his title that he caught a couple of minutes with Chief Inspector Swanson. Tweed-suited and smoking an especially malodorous pipe, the pudgy man sat behind his spacious desk, obviously irritated at having to deal with the nobleman.

"We'll make all possible inquiries, of course," Swanson said, "but forensics didn't come up with much. Besides, we're stretched on manpower right now. A gentleman like yourself would know about that, of course."

Geraint didn't take the edge of reproach well. He wasn't responsible for the Home Office's funding of the force, and it had already been a long and tedious day. He snapped back a rejoinder suggesting that the police weren't doing all they could, and Swanson's expression changed to one of cold formality.

"Sir," the man said archly, "my men have had to deal with eleven murders over this past weekend alone. We've got a racist troll butchering in the East End, and our men are out in cars trying to stop a riot developing. If half of what I'm told about the Squeeze is correct, we'll be getting a regular wagonload of bodies across the river any day now. And, sir, in the case of Miss Chapman there is a slight complication owing to gentlemen such as yourself. Because of her line of work, certain individuals have let it be known that overly enthusiastic inquiries might reveal rather embarrassing associations. That, of course, makes matters increasingly difficult for us. The disabling of the security monitors in her flat suggests that such an individual might have been involved in her demise, too. Now, sir, we'll do what we can and I will notify you if we come up with anything. In the meantime, thank you for your statement, which has been most helpful."

Swanson stood up and offered his hand in dismissal. Geraint should have realized the man's predicament. Annie Chapman was a high-class prostitute whose clientele would have included nobles, members of parliament, and corporate high-fliers. Strings were being pulled to prevent any publicity involving them. No wonder the murder hadn't made the news.

Feeling defeated and depressed, Geraint drove across the city to the hospital, where Doctor van der Merwe informed him that Ms. Young was in preliminary sedation before her final neuroconditioning session. Looking into the room, Geraint was pleased to see the fine bouquet of orchids and tiger lilies Simpson's had sent over for him. They were her favorites.

*   *   *

Back home, Geraint restlessly took up the Tarot cards. He'd been avoiding them for days, afraid to ask. But as time passed and no sign of the mage was forthcoming, the cards were the only source of information he had.

Closing his eyes, shuffling smoothly and silently, he felt himself drift a little, almost as if he could hear the soothing wash of the Thames far below his sealed windows. He stopped, cut the deck and half-fearfully turned over the top card. Feeling a wave of blessed relief to see that was not one of ill omen, Geraint realized just how much he'd been dreading what the cards would tell him.

The Wheel.

So, you will not answer me except as a riddle. Serrin is in the hands of Fortune, and I cannot read that fortune now. At least you leave me with room for hope.

He shuffled again, thinking about Annie, remembering her face on the telecom rather than the horror of the bedroom. He cut again and the great bony figure was no surprise to him.

Death.

Well, of course. He continued to shuffle, this time hardly aware of what he wanted to ask or know, his thoughts divided between concern for Francesca and his frustration at trying to get something, anything, out of the police. He cut to reveal another card and the dead girl's face returned to his mind.

Death.

This time the card surprised him. It was very rare for the cards to repeat such an image. Another death? Fran? But when he registered no fear at the thought, he felt the card was not warning him of that. He was confused, for a moment afraid that it might mean Serrin, but the Wheel had already told him that was not the meaning either.

I'm just clutching at straws, he thought wearily. I can't get this clear now. He tried to focus his mind by asking the deck for a card representing himself. That often helped to clarify matters.

The Fool.

It was the standard signal from the deck that Geraint should probe no further. But this time, just for once, he felt that the horned, green-clad man grinned at him for a reason. The Fool is all things, he mused. Right now, I can't get anywhere with anything. I don't know where Serrin is, my days are filled with meaningless routine, there's nothing I can do for Fran, I get nowhere with the police. Looking at the card, he thought how it was a complete contradiction. But then, that was the way with card zero.

"Oh, rakk it!" he cursed aloud, thinking he should just get himself completely steamed. Drink a gutful of Aussie Shiraz and watch the second innings from Adelaide over the satellite.

The drink, yes, but Adelaide, no. That night Geraint was asleep before the fall of the first wicket.

12

His vision swam slowly in and out of focus as he coughed and spluttered, dimly aware that someone was trying to force a liquid down his throat. The stuff smelled like horse manure and tasted even worse. Feebly attempting to push the administering hand away, Serrin managed to prop himself up on an elbow and tried to take in his surroundings.

He was inside a decrepit wooden hut, unlit except for the last of the daylight filtering in from the mist. It was close to dawn or dusk, he guessed, but he couldn't see much through the open doorway. The place looked as if it were built on wooden supports, and he was sure there was water right outside.

The woman sat back on her haunches, watching him attentively. She was dirty, unkempt, and wearing a simple garment tied around the waist with a length of thin twine. It looked like a piece of old sackcloth.

"How are you feeling?" Her voice was surprisingly deep for a woman's, slow and languid.

"Oh, I think I'll survive," he croaked, but he felt dreadful. "How did I get here? Last I remember, something that looked like the bastard offspring of the Loch Ness monster and Bigfoot was about to snack on me. It was a toss-up between drowning and being eaten alive."

She smiled as if at a child. "Ramalan brought you here. He would not have harmed you. He is old now, and had already fed that day. Eels are plentiful this year. He was only just roused from sleep. He wanders a little in his dotage." A wave of water lapped up to the doorway, almost washing into the hut. She smiled peacefully. "He is outside now. I think he will sleep again in two, three days. I must keep him closer in future. I never know what he may bring back, elf."

As she talked, he looked around the room. Serrin realized he was lying on a bed of what appeared to be dried reeds, but nothing else in the room indicated where he might be. He dimly registered a couple of simple pots and urns, some wickerware and a rag or two, but that was all. He rubbed his eyes and turned back to the woman.

"Who are you, lady? Where am I?"

Her face remained impassive. "You are in the marshlands, elf. you are safe, but you must rest."

He groaned. "The Stinkfens? Spirits, lady, my lungs are in a bad enough state already. I don't mean to sound ungrateful, but the night air here'll be the death of me."

"If you had not been brought here, the walking dead would have killed you. Anyway, the air is not so unhealthy here."

"The walking dead?" He wondered if she were mad.

"The men from the laboratories," she said with a frown. "Those who carry guns and wear armor. They are dead men; their bodies and hearts are destroyed by the wires and machines within them. You know this. You use Power too."

"You're a shaman?" Serrin asked. "But you don't carry any—"

"I am a druid. I am of Wyrm."

"But I thought you people, I mean druids, I thought that was all about stone circles and white robes and mystical Albion, all that stuff." At once he regretted these shallow words. "I'm sorry, I can't clear my head. Truly. I'm not from your country, I don't know much about you. Please forgive my ignorance and bad manners."

The woman waved her hand to indicate that she took no offense. "Those who walk the Circles have their own places and their own hearts and minds. I endure here. I heal and purify as I can. I am not alone; there are others here, in what remains of the village, and there are many who make their living here, beyond the man-sprawl. They travel the fenlands in their punts and coracles. We are beginning to live again as we all will, if this Earth can be healed. We do what we can.

"Now drink, and sleep. I still have work to do on you."

She reached across him and picked up the crude pottery mug she had placed on the table. Shushing away his feeble protests, she made Serrin drink some disgusting green liquid, while she smoothed the hair back from his forehead. Then she pushed him gently down, and began to massage his head and neck.

He felt Power flowing through her strong hands, into his head and nerves, and a wonderfully cool calm began to radiate through his body. With his eyes closed, Serrin saw his own body in his mind's eye, a network of cool blue nerves shining over his chest and arms, stretching out over his pelvis and solar plexus, down the length of his legs. He gave a little gasp when the encroaching net met the most ravaged part of his long-damaged leg, and then relaxed after a momentary resistance.

With a long, deep sigh, the mage let himself float gently back down into sleep.

* * *

As the woman showed him around the village, Serrin became uneasy. Much of the place had sunk half-underwater because of the rise in the fen waters created by decades of polar thaw. Some families lived on the top floors of three-story buildings whose lower levels had been lost to the waters, and the whole of which were threatening to sink into the marsh. This barren land offered little in the way of building materials, but a few wooden houses looked relatively recent. He was utterly baffled when they came upon a grove of young willows on one isolated shallow hillock.

"A few trees grow now," the woman said. "Power is not only for healing people—or elves. Much of this water is almost pure now, but at any time the dead men with their factories may bring more poisons. I must be ever vigilant. The battle is never-ending. But in this place we have a small victory. Look, isn't she beautiful?''

The druid picked up a small child who had ventured out to peer through the open window of a house they were passing in their boat. The little one had all the mischief mixed with shyness typical of most three-year-olds, and she was lovely, with silky brown hair and big, deep brown eyes. She stretched her small hand away from her mouth and waved at them and then, almost overcome by her own temerity, she ducked out of sight, only to reappear again and stare at the tall, gangling elf.

"She's a pretty little girl."

"Her parents' last child was stillborn. Before that, her mother had two miscarriages. Before that, the mother bore a monster, a wailing thing with two heads and skin peeling red raw from its body. It lived for three days. The land and water drip with poisons. Now you must understand why I am here, elf, and why I would die for this place. I have the animals and plants to care for, too, but I do not think you would really understand that." Only the whiteness of her knuckles gripping the oar gave away the force of her emotions.

"I don't know what to say." Serrin was ashamed, as if somehow he was part of those who had done harm to these people. Then he realized that every time he bought something advertised by a sanitized, smiling corporate bimbo, he really did become part of it.

Something fractured within him. Why am I affected by this? he pondered. I've seen enough streets paved with starving children and beggars with limbs ripped off by street samurai or gang kids who did it for the sheer sadistic pleasure. I've been places so polluted it takes round-the-clock work just to keep 'em from spontaneously exploding into flame. I've worked for people who I know damn well dump filth and effluent by the gigaliter. She must have done something to me with that healing. How does her Power flow? What has it done to me?

Still, he recoiled from what he felt and saw. It was simply too painful to embrace. And he knew this place was hardly paradise; the people who lived here would argue and steal just as anywhere else in the world. The thought did not bring consolation.

They were stopped on the way back to her hut by a small punt laden with bales of swamp hay, pushed along by a young man. Serrin's first thought was that it was rather late in the year for that. Then he wondered, how the hell do I know that?

The man looked up at them as the punts drifted past each other. He had one eye missing and an ugly mass of scar tissue where one of his ears should have been. His face opened in an almost toothless smile as he saw the druid, then he looked away uncertainly from the stranger. Shyly, he looked back again, and nodded in greeting to Serrin.

Serrin didn't know why, but as he turned away he was aware that his hands were shaking slightly. Then he realized that they hadn't been shaking all day, something that hadn't happened for nearly thirteen years.

He hoped the shaman did not see the tears welling in the corners of his eyes.

* * *

"I don't even know your name," Serrin said as he hungrily spooned up the stewed grain; it had an edge of spiciness that wasn't obvious until it hit the throat. It was very welcome to him.

"You don't need to know my name. Have I asked yours? To some, knowing the name of one with Power is power in itself."

He nodded, feeling foolish. "Of course. I'm sorry." He shifted tack. "I must find my way home."

"Of course. But first you will tell me some things. What were you doing among the dead men? Do they pay you with their worthless money?"

He ducked that query. "I sought a man—one of the dead men, you would say. Definitely, very much a dead man. More machine than man, if he ever had a man's heart. He murdered my father and mother." She nodded in a matter-of-fact way, as if such things happened regularly and routinely. "Over at the Fuchi laboratories, at Longstanton . . . I was separated from a friend there, a man I haven't seen in many years. He was helping me out of friendship. I hope he got away. He will be worried about me. I need to get back to let him know I'm still alive, for a start.''

"Do you work for those who blaspheme creation?"

The words stunned him. He had no idea what she meant, and said so. His reaction seemed to satisfy her.

"There is a place to the north of where you were found. I do not go close, but I sense the energies there. There is pain inside it, and they keep animals there, and so they will torture them as they always do. But there is an evil there that is different even than that, and a confusion also. I fear that place. I feel the confusion serves to make it easier for the evil and pain to triumph.'' She was struggling for words, not certain how to express herself. "I have not been close, as I say. There are many dead men there. I did not think you came from that place.'' The shaman allowed herself a small smile of pleasure that her intuition had been correct. "You are not evil any more than you are a dead one.

"But how alive are you, elf?''

Again, he did not want to face her probe. Instead, he was untying the belt of his most precious possessions. Unlocking the sequence of plaques, he handed her one of the stones. It was beautifully crafted, from Tir Tairngire, and it made his heart heavy to part with it. "It brings help in healing. It does not heal in and of itself, but when healing power is used, it makes such work more effective, more assured of success. You heal much in this place. You will use it so much better than I.''

She pushed the stone away. "Elf, you are not healed. Your body is well again, but you have a long way to go before you are healed.''

The stone would be a real loss to him, but he ached for her to accept it. "Please. For the child we saw. For the man on the punt. For everything this fragging rotten world dumps on you. It was made by one of my people, and it is a true part of me. I don't have much of me in the world and, uh, sometimes I try to hang on to little things, scraps and papers and possessions, until I get mixed up and leave myself behind with them. But this is Power and I want you to have it. Perhaps it will mean I am remembered here.'' Serrin felt embarrassed by the strength of his need. "I don't usually think about such things."

She took the stone then, quietly turning it over and over in her hands, beginning to fill with the wonder of it. She gestured him to silence as he began to apologize that she would have to bond it, that it would take time, and so he sat quietly looking out into the gathering evening mists. He knew too much and had seen too much of the world ever to be at peace with something as simple as this beautiful, blighted place, and he didn't know how to deal with that.

As if searching for respite, his thoughts turned again to Cambridge and what the hell he would do when he got back there.

13

Rani had attended too many weeping family scenes in the last three days to have much enthusiasm for any more of them, but at Sachin's wake one of his cousins made himself useful. She had overheard him in the kitchen, berating Imran for having taken the young man on such a dangerous run. Imran had whined that he hadn't known it would be dangerous. The mission had seemed so simple and straightforward. His angry interrogator had then asked why Imran was not out on the streets seeking vengeance. Rani could not make out her brother's reply because just then a whole gaggle of cousins had come teeming into the hallway, jostling Rani away from her listening post just beyond the kitchen door.

Imran had evaded her attempts to question him, spending most of his time away from the house, rising early and not returning until late at night. What she had just overheard suggested that he wasn't making any moves on the street.

He hadn't even missed his Predator, though perhaps that was not so surprising. It was Rani who had picked it up as they fled to the car. Imran might have assumed he'd lost it. Afterward, they were all in such a state of shock that she'd forgotten about it, too, until its weight jammed into her ribs when she finally collapsed on the bed. What was surprising was that Imran had never asked about it. Perhaps it was because he felt ashamed and powerless. Whatever he was doing with his days, he was lying low, avoiding his usual chums and fellow gang-boys.

When he still wasn't back by seven o'clock Wednesday evening, Rani changed into her jacket and thick cotton trousers and geared up for a trip to Bethnal Green Road. She took the knife, as usual, and she raided a small can of ammonia complex from the kitchen cupboards. A faceful of that stuff would stop even a troll, unless he had the kind of cyberware that would make him an instant killer anyway.

Shutting the door behind her and then checking the three locks, Rani paused as the November night mist closed around her. This mist would turn to heavy fog before many more hours had gone by. She pocketed her keys, hoping this wouldn't take long. Knowing Mohinder, he'd probably turn up three hours late on purpose and she'd have to walk home in ten-foot visibility carrying more than a thousand nuyen on her. Maybe no one in the restaurant would notice a package changing hands. Whatever happened, she'd have the gun, knife, and the gas on the way back, none of which would make her an easy mark for anyone.

Rani set off down the street, smiling despite her fears.

* * *

The Toadslab, the East End's most singular restaurant, was doing a roaring trade by the time Rani arrived and pushed her way inside. A large group of orks and dwarfs sat along the far wall, the trestle tables groaning under the weight of food and tankards of foaming beer. Rani was glad to see as many females as males among them. It made her feel less conspicuous as a female Indian ork out on her own.

The large group wasn't any local gang she knew of, but a glance around the room showed her the emblems

and tattoos of various other gangs of whom she'd heard
Imran speak. She saw nose-rings, stapled jeans, rat-tail
bracelets, rusted skull badges, the full litany of signs and
symbols. Each little group sat in its own area, respecting
the territory of the others but making their own presence
known. A handful of solitaires strong enough to command respect passed through the crowd. The outsiders
didn't seem to arouse either contempt or dismay among
the locals, and she wondered how they had earned such
acceptance. Probably because there are forty or fifty of
them, she thought; that might do it.

It was a double birthday celebration, she realized. An
ork and a dwarf stood up to cheers from their family and
friends, and behind the service counter three of the ork
waiters were grinning, their huge flat scoops laden with
steaming food. As soon as the standing ork at the table
seemed ready to speak, food began to fly through the air
toward him.

A great cheer and an outbreak of foot-stomping broke
out as the waiters pulled out all the stops for this one.
With superb coordination, they flung the first volley of
foot-square slabs of toad-in-the-hole fully thirty feet to
the gathered throng, who grabbed the batter-fried sausage slices and slammed them down on their plates. One
of the dwarfs managed the rare feat of impaling a de-
scending slab on his fork, while the standing ork mis-
timed his grab and got hit full in the face by a greasy
serving. The cheers grew louder.

Food continued to fly through the air as a young ork
girl came rushing out of the kitchen with another massive
flat pan of the sausages in batter. She dropped it onto the
serving counter, shaking her cloth-swathed hands to show
how hot it was. As one, the waiters spun around, made
deft cuts with the honed edges of their scoops, then turned
around again and unleashed another volley of foot-square
slices.

Rani remembered having once seen synchronized
swimming on the trid, but it had absolutely nothing on
this. The waiters were poetry in motion, moving as one,
their aim perfect, body movements in total harmony with
the rhythm of the bhangratech pumping out over the ancient speaker units. It took them less than two minutes

to deliver forty portions to their hungry and expectant customers. They completed their act by delivering a steaming pan of glutinous, rich gravy by the simpler method of carrying it across the room. The party managed to spray most of it over the table and themselves as they slam-dunked their slabs of meat into the viscous gunge.

Rani was tapping her feet to the insistent beat of the music by the time her own slab and beer arrived. Perhaps it was her obvious pleasure that made Mohinder frown as he sauntered over, dressed in the heavy synthleather go-gang jacket he favored for evening. It was voluminous enough to conceal a grenade launcher; sometimes it did. She saw his disapproval and stopped enjoying herself so visibly. A good little Indian girl shouldn't be seen having fun alone in public.

"Imran not showing his face, huh?" Mohinder sat down and helped himself to a chunk of spicy sausage from her slab, swallowing it whole and licking his fingers. She wondered if people with retractable hand razors ever made mistakes when they did that, rather hoping they did.

"He wanted to come, but he's been out all day and night."

"I don't usually do business with women, Rani. Well, not unless they're selling something besides guns." He leered unpleasantly. From most people, the remark would have had sexual connotations, but from Mohinder it probably referred to street prices for transplantable organs. In most cases, at least.

"But they say you do business when the goods are worth it." She pandered to his ego, unfailingly the largest part of any chauvinist.

"No complaints, Rani. Nice heat. I might even keep it for personal use." His expression changed to a crafty smirk. "Show me some affection, lady." He leaned very close across the small table, and she shuddered in repulsion for a moment until she realized what his gesture meant.

The package was pumped down his arm by the force of contracting muscle, then deposited inside her jacket as he caressed her right breast. He disgusted her, but she had some of what she'd come for. At least the slint hadn't tried to kiss her; that would have been too much.

He ripped off a great strip of batter and crammed it into his mouth. He was clearly about to leave, looking around at the door, lifting his huge hands off the table and straightening his jacket.

"Mohinder, I'm still trying to find out what happened that night. Who set us up."

"But now that Imran's spending all his days and nights on the streets he'll be able to find out, huh? He tell you who hired him?" Mohinder's brows frowned at her.

"Of course, but he won't tell me where, nor any of the details." She had to lie. If Mohinder knew that her own brother hadn't told her a thing, he'd never trust her with any information he might have.

"I don't think you're leveling with me, gopi. You've still got the smell of the kitchen about you." He stood up, stretched his arms out behind his back, then folded them across his chest. "But you're lucky. This afternoon I cut a fine deal. I'm a happy man tonight, Rani, so perhaps I will tell you a little something."

She stretched across the table eagerly.

"But first you promise to put a word in with your man Mohsin, huh? Not that he wouldn't do a good job for me anyway. He knows not to cross me. But family gets best treatment, and I'm not family, so you put in a word, right?"

Rani gave him her most winning smile. "I'll threaten to dose him with one of old Chenka's powders if he doesn't give you the best!" Chenka could make up anything, including poisons and toxins that would send a troll's guts into spasms for a month.

He laughed contentedly. "Deal." He placed his huge paws on the table, staring straight into her face. Rani did not flinch from the inhuman stare of his cybereyes. "Well, Imran got a job I should have had. If your family had been working with me, little one, they'd be still alive and safe. Your brother is a greedy fool. Pershinkin hired him. The little rat would be an intermediary for some heavy rollers, yeah? Can't tell you where to find him, though. He's vanished. Wouldn't mind a word with him myself. Not that you'll see him—but if you do, tell him to look me up sometime.''

Finally he turned to leave. ''Don't you forget to have that word with Mohsin, girl. Now I got to sort out Typhoid Mary. Later.''

Without another word, Mohinder stood up with a howling scrape of chair legs, then shouldered his way through the crowd toward a gaunt young woman. She was dressed in black and wore her hair in a mass of tangles. A datajack showed on one temple, but she sat nervously avoiding everyone's eyes and playing with a near-empty glass. Mohinder made only the slightest beckoning motion with one finger and she stood and followed him out of the noisy restaurant.

Rani pulled on her jacket and headed out into the thickening fog as the birthday party guests began emptying their pockets to pay the bill. She'd gotten what she'd come for.

* * *

Pershinkin.

A real freak. Part-Ukrainian, part-Indian, part-Italian. Spoke eleven languages, lied fluently in all of them. He drifted in and out of Spitalfields, Whitechapel, Bethnal, even the Squeeze. Chipped to the cybereyeballs and as fast and elusive as a greased piglet on crack.

Pershinkin was a big-time fixer, a conduit for corporate money stretching out to hire poor street muscle from across the river while his employers sat safe and cozy in their Estates penthouses and boardrooms or some other safe patch. Nobody ever knew how to find Pershinkin. He only appeared when he had to fill the bill for some work.

Rani had heard Imran mention the little man a few times when in a boastful mood. She'd never seen him, but she had a name and that was a start. At least she could confront Imran and force something out of him now, though she'd need Sanjay's help if the wretch ever came out of his stupor.

She was most of the way down a deserted Brick Lane before she realized just how thick the fog was. She coughed into her hands, the sound quickly sucked up by the wet night. The street lights along here were intermittent, and the little light they emanated diffused into a purulent yellow haze at unpredictable intervals along the street. As an ork, her low-light eyes gave her an advantage most nights, but in a fog this thick even she struggled to see more than a few yards ahead of her as she padded along the wet sidewalk.

Near the junction with Mile End Road the fog began to thin out, a gap in the pea-souper suddenly revealing a circle of figures standing there. Their features were dim, but their intentions were obvious. The curved blades and chains made sure of that.

"What have we here, boys?" said one.

There was an answering voice from behind her. "Dear me, a little Indian girl out on her own at night. Bad gopi girlie." There was a nasal snigger.

The acne-scarred face of the snakeboy advancing slowly toward Rani broke into a grimace of pure hatred. "Well, well, that's none too smart, huh? Oh and look, it's an ork, too. The kind of filth we don't need on the streets of our country. Wouldn't you say, boys?"

Rani was dead and she knew it. Her terrified eyes took in the white flash marks on their jackets and on the forehead of their yellow-toothed, crazy leader. His twitching hands said he was high as hell on something, and the motif told her: White Lightning. Anti-metahuman, pure racist, neo-Nazi street scum.

All that was left to hope was that she could kill or maim as many as possible before they ripped her apart. She drew both knife and pistol, clenching them with trembling hands.

The leader's face broke into an insane cackle, staring at her, pupils dilated to the max. "She's going to make a fight of it, boys! Oh look, a little Ceska pistol! Frag me, it's going to rip my ballistic so bad I'm never gonna scrag another rakkin' subhuman again!" He clutched at his chest in mock agony. Head shot for you, you wanker, she promised him silently. One or two of the shadows behind him seemed just a little less eager at the sight of the twin weapons. Take him out and you might just reduce the odds, girl. Maybe only half a million to one.

DaG '92

Don't think it.

Do it.

She armed the Ceska, drilling him right between the eyes. He dropped like a stone, blood spurting gore over his chest and the pavement. A low growl broke out from the others and they advanced on Rani, moving to flank her on either side. She realized that now they would have to avenge their leader.

Well, that's one fascist scumsucker gone, thought Rani. If I knew who to pray to, I'd beg to take out another dozen before I die. She aimed at the closest gangboy, a drooling one-eyed skinhead with a ribbed scar running from forehead to chin. Before she could squeeze the trigger, something heavy hit her in the back and sent her shot flying wide. Running now, the gangers were still coming at her.

The first creep was four yards away and screaming, his knives ready for action, when his throat suddenly sprayed crimson and his scream turned into a ghastly dying gargle. Something from behind her had hit him, but she hadn't any time to wonder what was happening. The gangboy staggered backward and half-knocked down the one behind him. Without pausing for thought, Rani kicked him sweetly under the chin, feeling the pleasing crack of a breaking jaw as her steel boot cap connected with his face.

Spinning to her right, she slammed two pistol shots straight into the stomach of another skinhead just as his weighted throwing knife whirred past her face. A sear of pain told her that she might suddenly have one less ear than before, but what did that matter when she was fighting for her life? Rani was dimly aware that other figures were struggling elsewhere in the fog, and then she heard some rapid cracks of gunshot, but not many. She was looking for the next skinhead to attack when she heard the footfalls in the distance, heading up from Whitechapel Road. She also heard the marching cry, "Light-ning! Light-ning!"

Sod it all. Reinforcements.

"This way. NOW!" Standing before her was an ork, a grim-faced brute in filthy leathers and with blood on his knife and hands. She stood shocked for a moment, unable to move. He slapped her hard across the face and screamed, "NOW, you acing git!" He grabbed her arm and began to drag her out of the street and into the shadows.

Rani no longer had any clear idea of what was happening, but she dimly registered that this was no cretinous White Lightning attacker. He was an ork like her, so she let herself be carried along in the group that coalesced out of the fog. Shadows and forms seemed to flow along the back streets as they hurried along, the chanting behind them become screams of fury. They've found the bodies, she thought.

Then she was being pushed roughly into an abandoned, tumble-down building. All around came the monotonous sound of water dripping steadily from an unseen ceiling. As she looked up, one heavy drop hit her square in the face, and she blinked to regain her vision. Hands pushed her behind a mass of what looked like collapsed brickwork, a wooden door appearing out of nowhere as though by a conjurer's sleight of hand. A flight of stone steps opened up below it.

"Down." It was an order.

"What the f—"

"Down. Or d'ya want anovver fifteen rounds wiv White Lightning?" A dwarf with a broken nose and a face not even his mother could love gave Rani a push. She stumbled through ork and dwarf bodies, half-falling down the first few steps until the broad back of another ork female stopped her.

Well, she thought, I may not know where I'm going, but it's better than being dead. She drew in her breath and hurried down into the gloom and stench. I hope.

14

The group was assembling into a marching order as the last ork down pulled the trapdoor shut behind him and fastened the array of huge bolts. Looking around her,

Rani saw that they were in an old, low-ceilinged brick tunnel with a pair of parallel rails running down the middle. It was too dark here for low-light eyes of any use, and so some of the group were lighting up simple flash-tubes and pointing them down the curving tunnel. It was a tight squeeze for the orks in the group, who ducked their heads low under the brickwork ceiling. As the last dwarfs scuttled down the steps, an ork male at the front of the group yelled them to attention. Aside from his flash tube the ork carried a pistol that made a Ceska look sophisticated.

"We got an hour to get the stuff back to the Ratskinks. Let's move it."

No one said anything to Rani, seemingly unconcerned by her presence. Ducking her head, she followed the single-file column up the tunnel.

Bang it, she thought, I'm in the Undercity! That realization shouldn't have been so startling, but perhaps her amazement spilled over from the fact she'd just shot two attackers. The adrenaline still pumping through her blood fueled a string of fantastic thoughts. She'd always dreamed about this city under the streets of London, fantasizing about adventures down here. Tough men and strong women, living wild. No shuttered windows and barred doors. No street Nazis. No Lord Protector, Templars, baggies, no one telling her she was only a girl and had to stay at home. No White Lightning telling her she was a piece of worthless ace that had no right to live.

Rani was elated, not even registering the throb of pain from her left ear.

"Where are we?" she said to the figure in front of her. It was the same female ork Rani had plowed into on the stairwell.

"Shut the rakk up and just keep moving," was all she got. Her head bowed even further and her spirits sank. Stuffing her hands into the pockets of her jacket, she trudged silently along.

Just before they reached the old Tube station, Rani realized she was in the company of the birthday group from the Toadslab. That meant they must also know the surface world, and must sometimes walk the streets of

Spitalfields and the rest of the East End. Maybe she could talk with them after all, given half a chance.

As she took her turn stepping through a hole in the wall, Rani joined the others on the platform of a long-abandoned underground station. The rails beyond the crumbling edge of the platform were awash with stinking water, and any identifying station signs had long ago flaked off the walls. Random heaps of bricks and rubble littered the ground. A pair of ragged brown rats dived into the water as the first ork in the group swung a lazy boot at them. It looked like one of those ancient trid scenes of London during the Blitz, whatever that was.

She joined the group splashing along the new tunnel, relieved to find the water only a few inches deep and her boots high enough to keep her feet just about dry. The line of orks and dwarfs were silent, marching along in silent determination. At one point the bodies ahead obscured the light from the flashtubes, causing Rani to slip and turn an ankle on the hidden metal rail. All that kept her from falling were a pair of great arms grabbing the back of her jacket and hauling her back to a standing position.

"Move it, girl. We're already late." For a group that had saved her life, these people didn't seem to have much sympathy for her now. But she held her tongue, which seemed the best policy at the moment.

When they reached the next access point, the front marchers were lined up beside another gaping hole in the brickwork and they ushered the middle of the group to the front to lead on. Rani was now near the front, able to see what was ahead of her before she stumbled over it. She began to smell the entrance to the ancient Victorian sewer long before they reached it, her nose crinkling with disgust. Mercifully, the flow didn't seem very deep. As the group fanned out to double file, the dwarf marching next to her began to speak.

"Watch Smeng," he growled, pointing to the new leader. "There're some deeper pools at the junctions. He knows where to put his feet. Follow him exactly or you'll get a faceful of upper-class drek." He grimaced and held his nose. She looked down at him with a sudden thought: *I've got a real advantage being an ork here. If I were a* dwarf, I'd be two feet closer to kissing the turds. Perversely pleased with possessing that advantage, she followed close behind the hulking ork at the front.

A dwarf behind her had just muttered the words "Nearly there" to no one in particular when a creature looking like it had dragged itself straight from the depths of hell reared up out of the filth in front of them. As it leaped forward, a slow wave of stinking sewage broke over the leading ork, who reeled to one side as he took a full faceful of muck. As the flashtubes behind her illuminated the monster in garish, underlit neon, as Rani grabbed frantically for her gun.

The beast looked vaguely like a troll. It was about the same size and shape, and had arms, head and a torso in roughly the right proportions. Its skin was as thick as a troll's, too. But around its neck suppurating gill fronds heaved and disgorged a foul, reeking acid, and its clawed hands showed fused, knotted fingers tipped with keratinous claws longer than steak knives. A great tooth-ringed sucker slobbered where its mouth should have been, and its eyes were red-raw and pupil-less, pulsing wildly below a forehead whose bony nodules were encrusted with ordure and mucus. Huge muscles stretched across the thing's body, veins as big as telecom cables bulging out as the creature flung aside the retching ork and extruded a serrated, cartilaginous tongue from its sucker-mouth.

Not finding her gun, Rani grabbed at the aerosol can of ammonia complex as the people behind began to panic. "Mutaqua!" someone screamed. "We're goners!"

It was eight feet away. In a blind panic, Rani pulled out the aerosol can and sprayed wildly before her, looking away from the thing. It was a crazy thing to do, but she was as terrified as everyone else.

A scream like someone burning alive exploded through the tunnel, half-deafening her, and then she heard a thunderous splash. Peering over the arm she had flung over her face in a vain attempt at protection, Rani saw the creature clutching at its face in horror as skin and membrane peeled away. Dripping folds of blood-soaked flesh hung limply from the mutant's visage. It opened its mouth and howled in sheer agony. The flesh around its mouth tore like melted cheese, revealing gums and muscle beneath the strings of flesh.

By the time the mutant turned and began to thrash blindly down the tunnel away from them, bare bone was showing through what remained of its disintegrating face. It staggered a few paces before the massive body collapsed face-down into the churning sewage. The thing convulsed once or twice, tried to raise itself up on its fists, then slumped into the muck. It did not move again.

Rani held on to the can as if her life still depended upon it. She didn't move a muscle either.

The leading ork was getting to his feet now, wiping muck off his face and hands. When he looked at her, it was with a very different expression than before.

At first he just stared, and Rani stared back. They remained so for a second, ripples of water from the monster's final spasms lapping against their legs, their breath coming in shallow heaves. Then the ork bowed his head, and bent just a little from the waist.

"Life saves life saves life," he said simply. A gentle hubbub rose from the others. "You are more than you seem. This I do not forget." He spoke slowly, putting his whole being into the emphasis on the *not*. "Come now. We can talk later. We have business first. Nearly home."

Indeed, it was not far. They went a few more yards, past the motionless body of the dead thing that had tried to ambush them, then came to the secret entrance leading to the caverns of the Undercity beyond.

* * *

"Where are we?"

Rani was astonished. After a couple of miles of progressively more disgusting sewer tunnels, and an unwanted soaking in sewer effluent, this cavern was clean, though bare and unmarked. The dusty, dank air was not so good, either, but one could live in such a place. Orks and dwarfs were using buckets of water to clean the filth off their boots.

"Old Civil Defense underground," the leading ork said without looking up. "Hundred years old, maybe more.

Abandoned them when they built deeper and bigger bunkers to save the nobles in case of a nuke attack. Good place. Easy to defend. Our home.'' It was plain that they finally trusted Rani enough to give her some information. ''Sometimes we get trouble with the Gleedens from the deeper tunnels, but they're slim from all the dumpchutes down there, and we do business with the Ratskinks anyway. Keeps our patch safe.'' She had no idea what Gleedens or Ratskinks were, but she didn't like the sound of either one. This certainly was another world.

''The, um, mutaqua? Get many of them down here?'' She tried to sound nonchalant.

The ork handed her a bucket and some rags. ''Not many. They usually don't make it up this far from the deeps. Mutated dzoo-noo-qua—no one knows how they got down here, but they're motherrubbing dangerous. Don't know what you have in that can, gopi, but it was tailor-made for the job.''

Rani merely nodded. She didn't have any idea exactly what it was that had turned the mutaqua's face to bloody jelly, either. In a sewer, it could hardly have been the ammonia. She wondered whether she'd grabbed a can of something else from the kitchen in her haste. At the back of her mind, a little plan was hatching about the fortune to be made selling the stuff to the population of the Undercity. She was just congratulating herself on her canny presence of mind when she realized these orks were not likely to be what you called rich. Oh well. That'd teach her to start thinking like her brothers.

A powerfully built dwarf came over and handed a black plastic package to the ork with whom she'd been talking. Whatever was inside slithered and squirmed a little. She knew better than to inquire about the contents.

''All right, peeps,'' the ork said. ''Kurak's waiting. Let's go. Fun-time's over for the evening.''

She was suddenly aware that it was very late, and after the tension of dealing with Mohinder and the fighting of this night, her muscles were beginning to feel very heavy. Her eyelids drooped and it was a real effort to put one foot in front of the other as she walked along.

''Sorry, gopi, uh, sorry again. Hey, what's your name?'' The big ork grinned at her. She told him, and he said, "I'm Smeng. Yeah, Rani, we're going to have to blindfold you now. Should have done it before, really. Make sure you don't see what you shouldn't. Nothing personal, you know."

Without complaint she let them bind a thick, smelly cloth tightly across her eyes. As they marched her along, she was really too tired to try to figure out how far they'd gone, dimly thinking they might be back-tracking at some stage as guttural yells to sentinels got them past blocks and checks.

By the time they removed the blindfold, Rani was almost dead on her feet. She looked dazedly around at a large chamber with strange faded maps posted on the walls and dim lamps suspended in arrays along the ceiling. She blinked like a rabbit caught in the headlights of a car.

"We take a little juice off the electricity cables. Service ducts aren't too far away. We do a little freelance rewiring from time to time." Smeng grinned at her again. Maybe it was just the lateness and exhaustion, but she was beginning to like him a little.

"Rani, I got business to take care of." He held the black package protectively to his chest. "Got to figure out what to do with you, too. Sleep on it, huh?" He unlocked a side door and ushered her into a little four-bunked cell. She'd have slept in a radioactive bomb crater if he'd put a bed in it. She could hardly take another step.

Maybe it was the excitement of the night, maybe some premonition, maybe just exhaustion that kept her awake an extra few minutes after Smeng had locked her in. She struggled to pull off her befouled clothes, then snuggled under the gray blankets smelling of naphtha. She lay there awhile, her mind racing too fast for sleep. When she heard murmurs and saw the light grow brighter in the crack under the door, she draped the blanket around her and crept through the dark to listen.

There was laughter, a few chinking sounds that could only have been glasses or mugs brought together to seal some bargain, then the stray word caught here and there. She didn't hear her own name mentioned, but she heard Smeng speaking and other higher-pitched voices raised in reply. One word, though, sliced through her confusion and fatigue to jolt her fully awake.

Pershinkin.

That gave her something to think about! Rani managed five seconds' thought before her body told her she'd pass out on the floor if she didn't get back into the bunk. She settled for the latter.

15

Francesca did not surface until nearly noon. Wrapped in one of Geraint's terry bathrobes she stumbled out of the guest bedroom, rubbing her eyes like a child and then bumping into a china cabinet in the hall because she wasn't looking. Smiling indulgently, Geraint took her elbow, steered her into the bathroom and showed her the control panel.

"Red tab for the shower motor. Thirty-second floor so we need a motor, yes? You remember." She gave him a sleepy grin and squinted at him appealingly. "Flexidryer there if you need to do your hair. Shower gel in the sachets next to the shampoo. Girl's stuff is in the pink sachet." Geraint grinned at her pretense of a frown. Nice to have her back here, he thought.

"I brought over some clothes from your flat. I wasn't too particular, but at least there's a selection."

She gave a sleepy "Mmm" and reached out blindly to put her arms around him, half a hug and half just holding herself up.

"You okay?" he asked. She nodded dopily. Geraint decided she was coherent enough to carry out her ablutions in private, so he went out, closing the door behind him. The shower motor immediately hummed into life. She wouldn't want any breakfast, he guessed, so he just dumped some oranges into the juicer and scooped some Kenyan into the coffeemaker.

While waiting he jacked into his deck and downloaded some data from the Korean index. After his stint in the

House of Nobles, he was itching to make some money again.

Francesca emerged from the bath brushing her long, fair hair with the brush from the overnight bag he'd brought for her. Somehow he thought it was best not to give her the usual female guest things. He had intuited that she'd feel better finding her own possessions around her when she finally awoke. But he had been wrong about breakfast.

"Geraint, sorry, but I'm so hungry I could eat a horse. God, I could eat a troll." She sniffed at the brewing coffee, and gulped down the juice. "Smells good. What's in the fridge?"

He remembered her tastes and had shopped accordingly. "Waffles, real thing, of course. Strawberry, ginger, and melon preserves. And you're a real good girl. I might just be able to come up with some ham and eggs."

She gave him a knowing smile. "Uh huh. And what do I have to do to be a real good girl?" It was the same kind of smile she used to give him in the days when they'd breakfasted under more intimate circumstances— a complication Geraint didn't want now. The doctors at Maudsley had probably given her a subcutaneous implant; if so, it would play havoc with her neuroendocrines for a couple of days at least. This was certainly not the right time to get into all that again.

"Just sit down and watch the screens. Let me know if anything comes through from Manila. But don't you dare let me find you with a datajack plugged in when I come back," he said, heading for the kitchen as the lure of coffee drew her to the table.

* * *

"Damn it, Geraint, I'm getting a tummy," she complained, rubbing her lower abdomen. This was after stuffing herself with smoked bacon and eggs and more waffles than he could remember toasting. The ginger and melon had taken a healthy bashing, too. He felt good.

"Well, Fran, we're both closing in on the big three-oh. Just one of life's little indignities, I'm afraid. Past twenty-eight and it's all downhill from there. I can give

you the address of a good shadow clinic if you're really
worried,'' he joked, but kept a perfectly straight face.
They held hands, lost for a moment to the world.

Then the moment was gone, shattered by the buzz of the
doorbell.

"Can't think who that might be. Surely the God-
squadders selling redemption wouldn't get past security.
Oh well.'' Geraint got to his feet and padded off down
the hall to use the intercom. It seemed like a lifetime
since he'd heard the voice on the other end.

"Open the door, you Welsh poseur,'' the elf chirped.
"I got the money and I made it back to the Smoke. Come
on. Who've you got in there?''

Geraint felt awkward when he opened the door, but he
embraced the mage, biting on his lower lip to conceal
his emotion. "Serrin, ace it! I never thought I'd see you
again. Hey, Fran's here. She's got troubles too. . . .''
But the elf had already seen Francesca standing at the
end of the hall, watching in curiosity.

Serrin took in the scene before him and jumped to
hasty conclusions. Francesca was wearing what looked
like Geraint's bathrobe, it was the middle of the day,
what else could he conclude? He felt like an intruder on
their happy little love-nest.

"Hey, look, if it isn't a good time to—''

Geraint hushed him to silence. "Come in, come in,''
he said. "It's been a little eventful all around lately.'' He
breathed out a sigh. "Guess we've got some catching up
to do.'' Geraint looked the elf up and down with a concerned eye. "Hell, you look skinnier than ever. Ham and
eggs in the fridge, waffles ready for the toaster, go get
yourself some brunch. Make some more coffee too. Go
on, make yourself useful.''

The elf looked down at his scuffed shoes, uncertain
how to behave.

"Sack of oranges out there,'' Geraint went on.
"Squeeze a jugful. Go on, move it, move it!'' He laughed
good-naturedly as Serrin shuffled off to the kitchen, not
sure where to look.

Francesca was staring at the pair of them, mystified.

"My life hasn't been so quiet recently, either,'' he said
by way of explanation, sitting down with her again. "Wait

till we get some more coffee and juice and we can talk it all through.''

* * *

Geraint steered Serrin's curiosity away from Francesca's mishaps in the Matrix. He thought she might not want to remember all the gory details right now, so instead he engaged the elf in reminiscences of that fateful night north of Cambridge.

"I don't know who those other poor suckers were out at Longstanton, but I doubt any of 'em got away alive.'' Serrin had recounted the broad details of their misadventure for Francesca's benefit. "I dispelled the elemental that was after them, but the Fuchiguards probably got 'em anyway. Poor bastards.''

"I lost you, couldn't see you in the dark,'' Geraint said. "I stayed as long as I could, but then I had to make a run for it. The troopers were right on my tail. Clazz, that bike of yours is a rough ride.''

"Where is it? The rental company will get nasty if it's not back tomorrow. Only took it for the week.''

"Don't worry. It's extremely disreputable-looking but safe among the BMWs and Rollers in the garage downstairs. Laughton got a nice tip to toss a tarpaulin over it and forget all about it. So, where'd you end up?''

Serrin spoke of the river serpent and the druid, but Geraint could see that the elf was not comfortable telling the story, becoming either over-discursive or vague on detail. He had clearly been affected by the experience. The mage shifted the conversation as soon as possible.

"Anyway, I managed to finish my report on the train down. Filed, sealed, and delivered. I was supposed to meet the delightful Smith and Jones yesterday, but they left an address for delivery with the hotel. And it must have arrived damn fast. I got my last few thou by straight debit over the desk.'' He flourished a credstick happily.

Geraint was surprised. "But Serrin, aren't you at all keen to know who was employing you? I mean, after what happened this weekend. . .''

"Whoever hired me had nothing to do with that.

Strictly solo, my chasing after Kuranita. They didn't ask me to.''

''Mmm.'' Something was nagging at the back of Geraint's mind, but he let it pass. ''Guess you're right.''

Serrin was mumbling some thanks for the meal when Geraint suddenly got up and walked over to his work consoles.

''I think I want to check something out. Won't be a minute. Talk amongst yourselves, ladies and gentlemen.'' He jacked into his cyberdeck, leaving Serrin and Fran to catch up on the many years since last they'd met. For his part, Geraint was making a little run through the Matrix to the Crescent Hotel system. While the Americans were speaking of Paris, Florence, New York, and Nagoya, he was locating an entry in a datafile. Hotels usually only data-dumped at midnight.

The address Smith and Jones had left for Serrin was in Charterhouse Street, among a warren of tiny registered offices in the heart of the city. Most of them consisted of no more than one man with a dozen telecoms and wall-to-wall datastores.

Registration Services PLC was the name assigned to the address. That could mean anything: a fast-license service to deal with the Lord Protector's Administrative Bureau, a business-data investigation franchise, maybe only a drop address. He engaged the browse program, cursing the names Smith and Jones. If they were McAllister and Hendrick, they'd be a damn sight easier to find.

The icon of the little browse clerk had just reached the fat Jones file when a subfile slipped neatly out of the folder and whipped through the datastore's far node. Deleted, headed for limbo. Geraint followed it, the clerk puffing and panting beside the icon of his knight. Hell, I ought to reconfigure that program, he thought idly. Make it a squire or something more appropriate.

Limbo he perceived as a mortuary, a little flourish of his occasionally morbid sense of humor. The clerk checked name tags, flipped back a sheet, and jotted down a swift note. In the distance, the white-coated attendants were immobile. Datafiles would only be permanently erased at the end of the working day, and from the dated tags on the slabs it looked as if Registration Services hadn't made its final deletions as promptly as they should have. He made his way back to the main datastore, where the clerk hummed and hawed as he flicked through the Smiths and Joneses. Geraint made another mental note to upgrade his browse program sometime.

It had taken under a minute. He gave instructions for data compilation and left the laser printer to its work. That took less than a minute too. By the time Francesca and Serrin had journeyed as far as Cairo in their talk, Geraint was back at the table, leafing through the 129 entries.

The entry that got deleted just as he'd entered the datastore was one of the possible candidates. "Jones, Melvin Aloysius." Aloysius? "Opened an account with Registration Services PLC two days before you were approached, Serrin. Only one other Jones from the start of November, and he's got a very plush address in Hampstead. Anyway, Mellie-boy simply used the place as a dead-letter drop. Nothing else received that's been recorded. Oh ho! Surprise, surprise, look at this. Package received at eleven forty-four this morning." It was the other entry below that which was really making his mind spin. "When did you send it off, Serrin?"

"Just before eleven."

"And you got paid—when?"

"Money was there when I checked out. Just before noon." The mage frowned, unsure or unwilling to discover where all this was leading.

"Does that tell you something?" The elf's face betrayed no insight.

"What it means is one of two things. If they weren't expecting anything else and didn't want to check the package you sent from the Crescent, they made the payment by electronic transfer. Or else they collected the package and then paid you. If so, they collected it within, oh, say, ten minutes. No way would Registration Services have been able to deliver it that fast. Someone must have been there waiting."

"Maybe Registration Services checked it for them, then notified them and paid me."

"No way. These people get paid precisely because they *don't* check packages. Strictly monkey see nothing, hear nothing, say nothing. For one thing, checking the package would risk having to deal with the official licensing hassles.'' Geraint stood again and strode back to his console. ''Let's have a look at the record.''

The printout took two seconds, since he knew exactly what he was looking for in the data. ''Well, I never. Package is recorded as delivered by hand and received at eleven forty-four. Same time receipt and dispatch. Someone was there to collect it. Now, don't tell me they were hanging around all day on the off chance you might come up trumps after a no-show at yesterday's meeting. Seems to me like someone knew when you would be delivering.''

There was a long silence, broken by Serrin's next query. ''Is there an address in the file, a forwarding address of any sort?''

''No forwarding address. They have to give a home address, though, for administrative purposes.'' Geraint sounded almost scornful. ''Good old-fashioned British red tape has its uses for deckers sometimes. All that admin needs a lot of data storage. Unfortunately, it's somewhere in Goiania.''

''Where the frag's Goiania?'' Serrin said.

''It's a tiny oasis of, oh, about six million down the road from Brasilia.'' He remembered it because he'd gotten lucky with transactions on some of the last of the minerals down there. ''Did, um, Smith and Jones strike you as, ah, South American in any way?''

''Are you kidding? About as much as your old granny.'' Francesca joined in the smiles at that.

They were stymied for the moment. Geraint suggested that one of them could visit Registration Services with a hefty bribe, but that probably wouldn't work. One whiff of indiscretion and such an agency was dead. On the other hand, their ilk sprang up like weeds every day. If one got a bad name among the corporations, all they had to do was relocate somewhere else in the city under a new one. Maybe there was a chance after all.

The one final worry was that Serrin's employers must, at the very least, have had a spy at the Crescent Hotel. Seeing the elf arrive there, or maybe just bribing a hotel clerk to alert him to that fact, the spy could have gotten over to Registration Services by the time the package arrived.

They were stuck again, and sat looking at each other blankly for a bit. Finally Serrin shrugged and began to ask Francesca what she'd been doing while he and Geraint were getting shot at over the weekend. After a long pause, she described her encounters with the bizarre figure in the Matrix, but she was obviously avoiding the details.

"I've never seen anything like it before. After the first time I thought about hunting him down, but after the second, I think I'd prefer not to see him again." She gave a little shiver. "I haven't analyzed my deck to find out where he went the second time. I was so busy hunting I didn't really register the SAN I'd passed. My deck will have the information, though. The first time the bastard went into the Transys Neuronet subsystem, which is not somewhere I really want to stick my pretty little nose."

Just then Serrin had a moment of complete illumination, almost an epiphany. Slapping one hand to his forehead, he shushed Francesca, then leaned back dramatically in his chair. Spreading his arms wide, he managed to avoid falling backward solely by the expedient of getting his feet stuck under the table. As he struggled to regain his balance and composure, the other two broke into gales of laughter. When they finally stopped, the mage revealed what he'd understood at last.

"Look, this is important. I just realized something. I told you that what I was doing at Cambridge was a waste of time, yes? Astral checks, watchers, detections around all the places—Fuchi, Renraku, ATT, Parawatch, blah di bloody blah. But why was I watching those people? What I should have seen was who I *wasn't* watching.

"Transys Neuronet is out at Over, just north of Longstanton. I wasn't asked to check them."

The druid shaman's words floated back into Serrin's mind: bad energies, a place north of the Fuchi complex. Same place?

It didn't take Geraint long to download maps and files. They spread them out across the table, pushing the swath of greasy plates onto a service trolley and rolling back the linen tablecloth.

Serrin pointed out various locations on the first map. "Look at this other stuff. Strictly small time. And right on the edge of the Stinkfens and who the hell would want to be there? Cost a fortune in detox if you wanted anything serious. Fly-by-night places. Probably making demitech and dodgy cyberware." Serrin's mind was beginning to race now. "Transys is the only important target I wasn't asked to check. Now I'm beginning to wonder."

They each chased their own thoughts for a time, trying to put it all together. After a while, Geraint slapped his hands on the table. "What have we got?" he said. "Francesca chases something wild into the Transys subsystem here in London. But it was something she met purely by accident. So what?"

Francesca disagreed. "Who says I met it by accident? And don't forget, the second time I was specifically asked not to enter any other system apart from the Fuchi subsidiary where I was virus-dumping."

"Fuchi?" Serrin hadn't heard any of the details of Francesca's run. There hadn't been time yet. "But we were out at a Fuchi installation."

"Unbidden. No one asked us to go," Geraint observed dryly. "But let's say, just for the sake of argument, that it was Transys paying you. That's why they didn't want you snooping around their place."

"Yeah, okay, but why? They have mages a darn sight fancier than me. So why bring me all the way from Seattle to snoop somewhere just down the road from one of their own research labs, and in a totally pointless way?"

"I don't know the answer to that," Francesca said, "but just as you were told, implicitly, that Transys was a no-go area, so was I, indirectly." Francesca was beginning to look more alive and alert. "What about that?"

"And we all ended up with something related to Fuchi." Serrin was chasing that theme again. "So, is Transys hiring us to shaft Fuchi? Poisoning a Matrix system and taking pot-shots at a big wheel at Longstanton?"

"Nobody asked us to get Kuranita," Geraint insisted. He just couldn't see a way past that. "And what about those other poor sods who got burned at Longstanton?

Did Transys hire people for a raid that hadn't a hope in hell? Strange thing to do, paying people to make a complete hash of everything. Francesca was hired to make a real hit, which she did. It just doesn't match up." Geraint retreated to the coffee maker.

The argument went on for at least two more hours, but they just kept treading over the same territory and running into the same blocks.

By the time the sky had washed from gray to black over the rain-lashed streets of London, Francesca had begun to stifle a series of yawns. Serrin, meanwhile, had begun to cough heavily, getting almost red in the face.

"You need something for that," Geraint said, heading for the bathroom.

"Yeah, it didn't get any better in the Stinkfens." Serrin turned his chair around to face the departing figure. "If it hadn't been for that lady I'd probably have died of pneumonia."

When Geraint returned he was carrying a big glass bottle filled with viscous brown liquid.

"What the frag is that?" the mage complained as he took the bottle. "Dr. Jerome Browne's Original Victorian Cough Syrup. This some kind of joke?"

"No, dear boy. Most assuredly not. Prescription only. Works like a charm. Uses a tried and true recipe from East Anglia. That land has always been thick with mists and general unhealthiness, and this stuff was all the rage two hundred years ago. The original mix came back on the market a few years back. I swear by the stuff."

"Swear at it more likely. It smells like some monster with killer gut-trouble got this bottle stuck up its—"

"Shut up and take a good mouthful, you coward," Geraint taunted.

The elf complied, spluttering and pulling a disgusted face at the filthy taste. "Oh, that's evil. Are you sure it works?"

"Just wait and see." The noble did not think it prudent to tell Serrin that the original recipe included laudanum and a nice shot of opium to soothe the inflamed membranes of the lung lining. By the time Geraint had put on his overcoat to go check out the contact address, his two friends were both sound asleep in the chairs where they sat.

* * *

The man flicked at a grease spot on his tie with a vestige of irritation as his subordinate passed through the automatic door. The waiting game was almost over.

"What was in the report?"

"Oh, very punctilious. Dates, times, places, expenses. He'd make a wonderful bureaucrat."

The figure lounging in the recliner snorted derisively. "Doubt it. Indeed, we're hoping that's precisely what he wouldn't make. Did they make checks?"

"Uh-huh. Checked the Registration Services system. We triggered the Jones file when the Welshman came browsing. He grabbed it from limbo, thinking he was being real clever."

Sniffing and exhaling, the older man brought his hands together in his lap, a study in concentration now.

"Well, there really shouldn't have been anything in there. I think it would have been too much to leave any trail in that file. They'd have smelled a rat."

"What do you think they'll do?"

"They've got lots of avenues to explore, but I doubt Ms. Young will be doing much Matrix-hopping. We sit tight. It won't be long now anyway."

"We could take the kidney option." They shared an unpleasant laugh.

"No, I think we were right to reject that one. Someone in the Met police might have begun to wonder if we'd dished up that little item to the Chief Superintendent. We can't be sure they'll try the police again anyway. Besides, maybe Swanson wouldn't dispense the information. No, let's wait. The pot's stirred and they're resourceful enough. After all, that's why we chose them."

* * *

Now the wheels begin to turn more swiftly. Elizabeth Stride does not suspect what is going to happen to her, but it will be swift, final, and terribly messy.

16

Rani felt weak and shaky when Smeng unlocked the door
and brought her a bowl of soup and a cracked paper cup
dripping soykaf. Draining the cup, she found that the
powdered soya milk had formed a disagreeable sludge at
the bottom, but at least the stuff had been hot. Following
it up with the thick soup, Rani felt a whole lot better.
She'd have preferred solid food, but her stomach gurgled
with satisfaction anyway. The belch she stifled with a
hand over her mouth.

He grinned, looking down at her. "No need to watch
your manners here, girl."

Rani smiled, but she had some questions. "Why did
you help me last night? What's it to you? And what were
you doing in the Toadslab anyway?"

He shook his head to halt the torrent of questions.
"Hey, not so fast! Don't rush me, girl. Two of our blood
had birthdays so we went out on the town. We also had
a little business up there, something to collect and deliver, remember?" She nodded and he went on. "We
don't get out too often. Six of us hadn't ever been above
ground in their lives. It was an interesting time for them.

"As for you, well, we were just on our way home. We
can smell the fascists a mile away. Sometimes the skins,
White Lightning and their friends, learn about one of our
little jaunts up to the surface and lie in wait for us. We've
lost blood to those slints a few times. It's always good to
have a chance to settle the score. You're an ork, ain't
you? We got the same enemies."

She smiled sadly. Growing up meant learning the ways
of the world, but when those ways included crazed fascist
street thugs, learning the lessons wasn't much fun. She
decided to pursue other queries.

"Who lives down here? I mean, I've always wondered,
ever since I was a kid and my uncle Ravi used to tell me
about the Undercity. He used to sit me on his knee at

Saturday tea-times and we'd have chapatis and bhuna, and he'd go on about India and the dust and heat and the sacred places and buildings, and then he'd talk about the city beneath the city. He'd never seen it, of course, and I used to think he was making it all up to entertain me. But I didn't care. It was swell.''

Smeng looked at her as though weighing something in his mind, as though trying to decide whether he could trust her.

Finally he gave her a smile and held out one hand. "Well, come see a little of it then. I can't show you much, Rani, because it's not safe to let spitsiders know too much about the place. You understand?'' It wasn't really a question. "Some of our people believe that overgrounders who find out too much should never be allowed to leave. But without your help some of us would be dead now, so we owe you. Strictly speaking, I guess we're quits, but I wouldn't hear a word about keeping you here.'' His tone suggested that some of the others might have demanded that precaution.

"Anyway, come on. Work to do.''

Smeng ducked his head under the door and headed back into the first tunnel complex, leading her by the hand. Both of them had their pistols readied. Rani would have thought it was safe here, but maybe having your weapon ready for use at any moment was the trick to staying alive in this new existence she'd discovered. Not that life expectancy was ever ensured.

Eventually they came to a connecting passage, and Smeng pointed out the various routes they could take.

"More Civil Defense that way,'' he growled, pointing sharp left. "Most of the dwarfs hang out down there. They strip stuff out of the tunnels and service ducts. Last year they even got a half-mile or so of copper cable, the lucky buggers. Bought them enough beer to keep them sozzled for a month. You get a power failure overground, and I bet you fifty-fifty it's because of a crack team of dwarf cable-strippers.'' Smeng laughed and it sounded like distant thunder.

"Down that way,'' he said, indicating another direction with a sweep of his right arm, "well, that leads to other territories. We got all sorts down here. There's a great network of mail tunnels below the old sorting office complex, but it's too much of a warren for anyone to live there. We guard some of the exits, and so do the Ratskinks. They've been allies of ours for a few years now. More of us stay alive that way. They're good kids, most of 'em, though there's the odd trancer and crazy. But then you get that kind anywhere."

"Who are the Ratskinks?" Rani asked. Something small and dark scuttled away down one of the tunnels accompanied by a high-pitched squeaking.

"Street kids, mainly. Dumped into the streets and back alleys by East Enders too poor to feed 'em. Mostly, they die of exposure or starvation, or they get picked up by the meat hunters looking for fresh tissue to sell to the body shops. Feed 'em up, whack 'em full of vitamin shots. When the scans say the body's okay, it's time to cash in." He drew a finger across his throat with a grimace.

"Some of 'em get picked up by agencies supplying nobles with young flesh as pleasure slaves. There's a racket like that at the London Hospital, right on your patch. Pediatrics give 'em prefrontal implants to dull awareness and some heavy motor conditioning for the right reflexes. Unofficial, of course, but everyone knows about it."

Rani was aghast. Mohsin worked at the London Hospital; did he know about this? Good God, did he even participate? His headware implants were the best street doctoring available in the area. She shuddered at the possibilities.

"Anyway, those who don't end up that way may get picked up by a Ratskink and brought down here. They look after their own. The older ones, they protect the kids. The clan leaders, King Rat and his bodyguards, they're old men by anyone's standards here. Clazz, some of 'em must be in their early twenties. They're poor, but they're great scavengers. Corner 'em and they'll fight like demons. Got nothing to lose."

She was silent. To someone from her background, the idea that a family could abandon their young to such horrors was intolerable, and her mind rebelled against it.

Now it was time to move on again. They walked a long

way down the central tunnel, until it opened out into a great arched vault with curved and flowing pillars supporting the ceiling. Rani stared in awe. She'd never been in a Christian church, and wondered if that's what this was.

"Not quite. Church crypt—or at least it used to be. Built by the Templars around 2030. Word is they did some heavy magic down here and then never came back. We've blocked off all the routes to the surface. Hi, term!" This was said to a limping dwarf toting an archaic shotgun as he stomped across the chamber toward the far door.

"Yo, plazzman!"

"Ho, stumpy!"

They traded jocular insults for a bit, then the dwarf hefted the gun barrel over his shoulder and continued on his way. "Hilda and Stan comin' for tea. See youse."

Smeng turned her around. "He means—"

"Trolls, yeah, I know. You got them down here too?" It was a rather pointless question, but he was happy to answer it.

"Troll gang down in the old sewer complex west of here. They're not happy folks. The sewers are really jazzed down there and they get flood waters in from the river. There's seepage from the deep dumps, too, so they also get chemical shock epidemics from time to time. I hear say they're hunting new territory, but they're slim guys for trolls and they ain't got much to bargain with. We ain't gonna let them in, but we may decide to join with them to open up some new areas. Never did like the Blindboys much, so we might get something arranged there. Trolls get the living space and we get the booty. Everyone says the Blindboys got some good stuff. They steam on the surface from time to time. Seem to know how to pick the right targets."

It sounded like the Blindboys were muggers, but Rani wasn't up to asking for more details. She was still overawed by the enormity of this incredible unknown world.

"We better go now. You've seen some of it, more than most overgrounders ever will. You'll keep your mouth shut about it, right?"

"Safe." Rani hardly used street slang in her everyday

life, but this wasn't everyday life. Anyway, Smeng's language was odd enough; half the time he talked about complicated matters such as prefrontal lobotomies, the other half he talked like he'd had one. Guess life down here changed a person.

As they trudged back through the tunnels, Smeng asked Rani what she'd been doing out alone so late the night before.

"It wasn't that late. And I had no reason to expect any trouble."

"You kidding? Fog as thick as a troll's skull, well past anyone's bedtime, and you an Indian girl to boot?"

She bristled a little at that, then calmed herself down. By now she should be used to hearing what being an Indian girl meant, but she probably never would.

"I was doing a little business of my own. The gun, for a start." She emboldened herself with the lie. "Got people to meet and things to collect, yeah?"

He laughed quietly as they passed the first check, three dwarfs with pistols and a series of beautifully concealed tripwires. He showed her how to avoid the mantrap with the triggering plate locked into the narrow rails of the mail wagon tunnel.

"Rani, you ain't no runner I've ever met. You're too young and your face gives you away too easily." He patted her on the back to reassure her he meant no insult or offense.

"Well, no, it's not a regular thing. But I went on a run recently and it was a set-up. Three of my cousins were killed. My brother, he organized it, and now he's hiding his face. He's not going to do anything. Me, I want revenge. I could have been killed myself. You going to tell me that if White Lightning killed a bunch of your people, you wouldn't start making moves to pay them back?"

"No." He sighed. "No, we always try to do what we can. Sometimes we set up a lure and draw them to the bait. And yes, when we get revenge, it always tastes sweet." He stuffed a hand into his pocket. "Sorry, Rani, time for the blindfold again."

Once she was sightless, Smeng led her along by the hand again, whispering passwords or other reassurances to unseen others as they went. It was a ways before they stopped and he untied the rag from her eyes.

They were standing at the bottom of a twisting, narrow duct that they had to navigate on all fours, clambering with gasping breaths. It led upward, taking them to a main tunnel. Feeling a current of air flowing through it, Rani knew she was near the surface again.

Her words about her brother had also brought important questions to the surface. She made her play in the deserted Tube station.

"I didn't have much luck trying to locate who hired my brother for a sucker job that left so many of us killed. All I got is a name. Man named Pershinkin or something." She tried to conceal the fact that she was watching Smeng for a reaction.

He stiffened a little and looked away. "Yeah? Well. Wish you luck with it."

He wasn't going to bite, she thought. Instead, the ork began to tell her where he would leave her, saying that she must look straight ahead when she got out, and not look back at her exit point. "It's best if you don't see too much. Just take a right, a right, a left, and you're in Fenchurch Street. I can't take you where we came in at sun-up, too dangerous. Just keep strolling through Aldgate and you're back at Whitechapel High Street, and then safe at home. You know."

"Yeah, I know," Rani said, feeling almost sad at having to return to the other world.

When they got closer to their destination, she saw the reinforced door, and knew this was her last chance. "Pershinkin," she said. "Would the name mean anything to any of your people who go spitside? Three dead, Smeng, three of my family dead. It matters."

He sighed and motioned her up the last few stairs. "Look, girl, I'll do what I can. Maybe I'll find something out, maybe not, but I can't promise you nothing. We're quits, huh? Now, you keep safe. No more going out alone at night. And you know how to keep your mouth shut about us. You just got flipped and woke up in a dump. Right?"

"I hear you." A little surprised at herself, she hugged

him close. After a moment he put his arms around her and kissed her gently on the forehead.

When the ork had closed the door behind her, she forced back tears and squinted into the gray light morosely filtering through the filthy and mostly broken windows of the warehouse. It was only then that she checked her inside pocket and found the wad of nuyen, forgotten in all the excitement. With a broad smile bringing her face alive, she skipped across the dirty stone floor while figuring what to do with it.

Maybe I'll get myself some slap patches with this stuff, she thought, and better ammo. What the hell, and one of Sunil's saris, too. That lovely purple one with the silver threads.

Her delighted thoughts raced like a child's. At the doorway she peered in both directions, then stepped cautiously out on to the street. At that instant, an entirely new idea flashed through her thoughts.

Banging! It's my birthday tomorrow, Rani exulted. Sweet eighteen. I'll go down to that old Polack store and get some of his firewater, the clear stuff with the plum skins in it. I can get drunk!

What's that like? she wondered.

17

Serrin woke in the darkened room to see Geraint still hunched over his desk, his hands moving in the pool of light from the desk lamp. Beside him a vidscreen was flickering silently, but he was shuffling a pack of heavy, large cards.

The mage stretched out his endless legs and ran the fingers of one hand through his hair. Collecting his gangling form, he pulled up and out of the chair and sidled across the room. "Tarot, huh? Didn't know you were interested in that."

Geraint sighed and pushed the pile of cards to one side. "I was only just learning when you knew me before. My mother used the cards, but I resisted it for a long time. She always told me I would have the Sight, too, but I think I was hoping to prove she didn't always know what was right for me. I've always been stubborn. You know that.''

Serrin looked at the paintings on the upturned cards, knowing better than to touch them without Geraint's permission. ''Think I've seen them before somewhere. Twentieth-century, aren't they?''

''You won't have seen these. I designed them myself. Well, no, that's not strictly true, you might have seen something very like them. Based on an old occult deck, the Thoth. Rather idiosyncratic. I liked the cards, but a few of the images seemed wrong to me. These aren't exactly traditional designs.''

Serrin could see that from the glorious explosions of color, the sweeping ebb and flow of the complex images.

''So I hunted down a woman who was the great granddaughter of the one who had painted them originally. She's an artist, too. I scanned the images and let her redesign some using a paintbox. Very elementary. Actually, she didn't get everything quite right so I rescanned and reconfigured some of them myself. Got what I wanted in the end.''

Yes, my friend, and that's what usually happens, Serrin mused. But what do you do when you can't get what you want? ''Mind if I ask a personal question?''

''Fire away, old chap.''

''What are you worth these days?''

Geraint smiled. ''Don't mind telling you that. Forbes and Dunn could do the same for a trivial fee. Well, it varies day to day with interest and speculations, natch, and about sixty percent is usually tied up for a week or so, but in total, call it eighteen million, give or take one percent. And I watch that one percent like a hawk, mind you.''

''Eighteen million pounds? Spirits, how the—''

''Eighteen million nuyen, dear boy. About forty-five million in sterling, not that I ever bother with it myself. Strictly nuyen for business.''

''My God, your family must be rich. You know, I had no idea you Welshies were worth that much.''

"Well, actually, they're not. I made most of it speculating. As for my father, he owns a lot of land but it's meager as far as rents and properties go. I deal with the estates, such as they are. Since I rarely go back to Wales, I don't like to squeeze the tenants. I think it's a pretty rum do when some absentee landlord charges a fortune of people who are struggling over their heads just to survive, then kicks them out when they meet hard times."

Well, what do you know? the elf thought. He actually cares about those people. Enough not to rob them blind anyway. Good for you, chummer.

"Like I say, I rarely go back there. Bloody disgusting country. Hills that pretend to be mountains, valleys on the more depressing side of desolate. Welsh people are friendly, but by God they're nosy, too. There's an old proverb: a Welshman prays on his knees on Sundays, and preys on the rest of humanity the remainder of the week."

"Well, this one doesn't seem to be like that," Serrin smirked.

"Too right. Won't find me in chapel on the sabbath." They laughed genuinely. Geraint put the pack back into its silk wrap, then got up and flexed his aching shoulders. "How about some coffee?"

"I'll make it." Serrin was about to head for the kitchen when something on the trideo caught his eye. "Hey, what was in that cough medicine anyway?" He'd just seen the time display. "I've been asleep nearly four hours."

"Never you mind. It's an ancient Welsh recipe specially made to stop elves from asking difficult questions."

Serrin had come back with the coffee by the time Francesca was stirring. By now it had also occurred to him that a cough medicine invented in the 1850s might not, after all, have been concocted for elves. He put the tray down, smiled at Geraint's back, and thought: this isn't over yet. Goodbyes aren't in order, surely.

* * *

Geraint had found nothing at the drop address. Even the sight of a hefty chunk of high-denomination notes hadn't unbuttoned the clerk's lip. He even insinuated that Geraint might be an agent from the Administrative Bureau come to entrap him into indiscretion.

Well, good for you, Geraint had thought as he left. If I ever need a dead-letter drop, this is where I'll come.

"So that's a dead end," he was saying now. "I don't see how we can track Messers. Smith and Jones further, unless we hire some street detectives. I know a discreet, good firm, but those two are still only middlemen. Hell, Serrin, they didn't even come to Seattle for you, they used a second middleman there. Even if we find them, I doubt we can do much with the information. Maybe they're back in South America."

As stuck as ever, they reluctantly decided to give up the pursuit.

"What are your plans, Francesca?"

"I think I'm going to spend a few days upgrading my system software. Need some better armor programs and I think the medic must have taken a beating. I'm also going to get me some hot poison."

Geraint gave a low whistle as he sucked in his breath. "You'll never get a license for that. Even the corps have to tread carefully with that kind of stuff."

Poison programs, otherwise known as persona-attacking. It was almost the equivalent of an anti-personnel weapon in the Matrix. The officious British licensing regulators didn't like that kind of thing at all.

"No problem," Francesca muttered. "I've got a corporate contact who's sure to have a global license I can hide under. Did some work for them a year back, maybe the best work I've ever done. I know I can get what I need. They'll know I don't intend to use the program unless I absolutely have to."

Geraint was surprised at that. If Francesca had that kind of pull, she must be outstanding at her work. "Would it be impolite to ask which corp?"

"Unfortunately it would. Not Transys or Fuchi, though. Of course, half the time I've got no idea who I'm actually working for. As long as I get paid, that's enough for me." Her hard edge, that one unattractive feature, was showing again.

Serrin jumped up from his chair with a yelp, making them all start. "Hey, I've got to call the Crescent. I should have checked out or back in hours ago. They'll have thrown my stuff away by now.'' He was utterly panicked at the thought.

"No, they won't,'' Geraint reassured him. "All your things are in the guest bedroom. I had most of it here anyway, so I thought I might as well get the rest sent over. You can stay here awhile. How long's the visa for?''

"Until the end of the month, but—''

"Well, that's no problem. Terms and conditions: one, no spellcasting. The building security mage won't like it. He's getting on a bit now, doesn't want any trouble, what with his pension getting closer. Two, you'll have to pay half the coffee bill, the way you go through the stuff.'' Serrin pushed his mug away guiltily. "You can raid the fridge and freezer for anything else, as you wish. Third, don't stay in the shower for an hour in the morning. Uses up all the hot water, and I get nasty if all I get is cold water. If you can handle all that, stay as long as you like. I won't force you to stay the month, but I'm sure you can manage the weekend.''

"I'd love to stay. If you want, I can conjure a water elemental to do the dishes. Only a very feeble little thing, promise.''

"No thank you! Domestic service people do all that kind of thing. All you have to do is dump the dishes down the chute. Rubberized valves and relays make sure they don't break—miracle of modern technology. In this day and age, we don't even have to see our servants.''

Francesca playfully pretended to swipe him across the head as they laughed together. She got up to get dressed, and scant minutes later she was back in her overcoat, ready to go.

"Want me to drive you over?'' Geraint asked, still a little concerned.

"No, I'm fine. Really. I'll pick up a cab outside. See you!'' She ambled down the hall, and Geraint got up to walk her to the door.

"Give us a call. Hey, why don't you come for dinner Saturday night? Tell you what, I'll get Fortnum's to do the catering and we'll have a bottle of Petrus. Real Welsh beef, too. Chateaubriand or Wellington?''

Ten thousand nuyen a bottle for the wine alone. He

certainly knows how to enjoy his money, Francesca thought a little guiltily.

"Sure. That's a wonderful idea. I'll bring you some champagne for aperitif. Dom Ruisse, huh? That funny bottle with the long tapered neck. Yeah, let's celebrate. Seven for seven-thirty?"

"Perfect. Keep well, you." He closed the door behind her, rubbed his chin lazily, and went to park himself in his favorite armchair.

Serrin gave Geraint a look worthy of one of the Lord Protector's puritanical high officials. "You're a self-indulgent pair!"

"Special occasion, old chap. We haven't been together in a long, long time. I think it's worth a celebration. I saw it, you know; the Tarot told me. Must have been right after you landed at Heathrow." But wait. He was forgetting something, trying to figure out what he'd missed. Of course.

"There was someone else, though. A woman. A strong woman. She was part of it, with you and Francesca. No sign of her yet. But there will be." He also remembered the Nine of Swords. Bloodied blades.

That must have been Annie, he reflected, but tried not to remember that. To clear his head, Geraint thought he'd go make some money. He'd been neglecting that for too long.

"Well, old friend, I'm going to be unmovable in front of the cricket in a few hours, and until then I'm going to be sticking my snout into the trough of speculative financing. Got to check out the West Coast markets. They'll be humming by now. So you'll have to excuse me for tonight.

"There're some good shows in town. Check the text service on the Beeb's C-net, that'll tell you everything you want to know. If you're homesick, OzNet on the trid has reruns of ancient American sitcoms and soaps. Or there might be something on the satellite channels. Avoid anything Italian, though; it's either the worst game shows in the world or atrociously dubbed porn. Tomorrow, we can do some touristy things. Y'know: Tower of London, the Palaces, all that glop. Sound good to you?"

Geraint didn't get the reply he expected. Instead, he

heard the query that every British man dreads in the
deepest recesses of his soul whenever it comes from an
American.

"Um, Geraint, could you explain to me the rules of
cricket?"

18

Rani woke to find that a gang of trolls with sledgehammers was breaking up a road inside her skull. She
groaned, looked at the digital, which read eleven-fifteen,
and turned over. She wanted to get back to sleep, but
she was desperately thirsty. It felt like someone had
washed out her mouth with paint-stripper.

She managed to get downstairs without killing herself
and staggered around looking for the orange juice. I am
never, ever, going to drink that Polish stuff again, she
thought. Why couldn't I have been satisfied with just food
and sweets? When was. . . ? I think I started drinking
about ten. I sure as hell can't remember much after ten-
thirty.

Taking the bottle from the ancient electric fridge, she
dropped the plastic beaker she was going to fill, and
thought, Rakk this! I'll just drink from the bottle.

She drained half of it then and there in the kitchen,
then slouched back toward the living room. That was
when she saw the scrap of paper lying on the floor, in
front of the door with its many locks and chains. The old
letterbox had long been nailed shut, so someone must
have actually forced the sheet through the infinitesimally
small gap between door and floor. That was unusual.

What the frag IS this? she thought, casting a bleary
eye over it. It was a leaflet printed in heavy black and
red ink on garish yellow paper, an advertisement for an
appearance by the Blazing Paranormal Ambulance at The
Subway. In the area to be sure, and they did play great
electroslam, but the date on the flyer was August four-
teenth.

"What the hell is this?" she snapped to no one in particular, and was about to throw the plugger away when the crude scrawl running around the border caught her eye:

> May have something to tell you—Exit to Finchley Rd, remember?—Midnight—Can't risk the daytime—You'll be safe

You bet I'll be safe, Smeng. Hell, I'll even get myself a cab, if I can find one willing to do business around here at that hour.

Rani dragged herself back up the stairs and collapsed into bed with a splitting headache. She dozed on and off for an hour or two, then dragged herself out of the sweaty sheets and made for the bathroom. Splashing handfuls of cold water over her face while shivering in her underwear, Rani found no comfort in the fact that she looked only slightly less awful than she felt. And since that was like death warmed over, the mirror wasn't doing her much of a favor. The window had ice flowers on it, but she wasn't sure if she was shaking because of the cold or the hangover.

Get out on the streets and get some fresh air, girl, she chided herself. Get yourself a quart of juice, stuff down as many high-sugar sweets as you can without puking, and get this body into working order. Tonight you're going to get one move closer.

* * *

"So, what have you been up to these past few days?"

They were savoring the first sips of the chilled champagne, mist forming on the side of the glasses, the long flutes raised to waiting lips. They had sighed as one at the first taste of lemony bubbles exploding in the mouth.

"Well," Francesca replied, licking her deliciously glossed lips, "frankly, I spent a good day stripping my Fuchi-6 and checking it out. I got paranoid about whether someone had been horsing around with it. Ridiculous, of course. No one's going to get past the security, but I wasn't entirely rational at the time. I got the new medic program installed and an armor program like you wouldn't believe. Withstand a tactical nuke, this one. I'll have to wait on the poison, though.

"In the interim, I checked some personnel agencies for my own benefit. Downloaded a few megs of various bits and pieces. Left the dumbframe to wander around it all, run some analyses. It's always useful to see who's been having a surge of interest in people who, er, work in related fields." That was enough about her. "What have you boys been up to?"

Geraint replied with a slight shake of the head. "Not a lot. We chewed the fat over a glass or two. Took Serrin to the National Museum, caught *Hamlet* at the Imperial last night, made a little money. There's a new Paraguayan root extract all the rage with the slammers here and I invested in some, sold some distribution rights, and covered myself with HKB's commodity insurance. Allowing for the premium, should be up forty, fifty thou. Today's been quiet."

"He showed me the Changing of the Guard at Buckingham Palace, then took me around the House of Nobles," Serrin piped in. "I actually had a good time." Geraint made a polite gesture of self-deprecation as Serrin enthused, then he leaned forward to refill Francesca's glass.

The evening drifted perfectly. Before long the liveried waiters began to emerge from the kitchen with a series of delights, though the three of them barely noticed, so caught up were they in each other's company.

Geraint must have paid a fortune for this, Serrin thought as he cut himself another slice of the perfect, slightly pink beef and heaped another spoonful of buttered broccoli onto his china plate. Sure, he had the money to pay for it, but Serrin knew plenty of people who wouldn't treat friends this good.

"Comes from farmlands near home, this beef," Geraint was saying. "I can guarantee there's absolutely nothing in it you wouldn't want to have in your tissues this time tomorrow. The land went through detox a decade ago. The cow this came from actually ate healthy grass under blue skies. Not factory stuff. A bloody miracle. Enjoy yourselves."

They hardly needed the invitation. By the time the servants had brought the pavlova and zabaglione and the astonishing coffee tray filled with fresh cream truffles and sculpted mints, they were experiencing a sense of well-being none of them had felt for some time. When the last of Fortnum's people had gone, closing the door carefully and quietly, they barely even noticed.

Geraint drained the last of the Petrus, fabulously rich and luscious, its aftertaste developing in his mouth and at the back of his throat.

"This wine is empirical proof of the existence of God. And if God exists this proves he must be a benevolent old bastard. I'm always tempted to quote poetry when I drink Petrus." He laughed at himself as he stirred thick cream into his coffee cup. "Only joking. I very, very rarely do that."

"Only to women." Francesca smiled seductively at him, almost a challenge across the table as she leaned forward on her elbows. The alcohol had flushed her face slightly, and she tended to be indiscreet at such times.

I wish you hadn't said that, Geraint thought sadly. Serrin's beginning to wonder now. He thinks something may be going on. He didn't ask me about it, and somehow I didn't feel like saying anything to him.

"Well, that's different. A little John Donne or Andrew Marvell. Life needs some bittersweet romance now and then."

"Donne or Marvell, or the Queen's song. That Babylonian song."

"Sumerian. Dumuzi and Inanna's *Ecstasy of Love* ."

"How did it go? 'Last night as I, the queen of heaven, was shining bright . . .'" She was lost in the recollection, forgetting how the verse continued.

But Geraint did not forget. *As I was shining bright, as I was dancing, as I was uttering a song at the brightening of the night, he met me. . . .*

He looked away, embarrassed and a little pained, gazing out over the skyline. In the winter's chill, London's bright city lights shone under a canopy of stars crisscrossed at intervals by shadowy fragments of the weather control domes. Ten million souls. How many of them meeting like that in the brightening of this night?

With a pang of embarrassment, Geraint broke the spell. "Serrin, can you turn on the box, you're nearest? Check the eleven o'clock news." Anything to keep the talk from getting any more personal.

The elf got up from his chair and took the remote, zapped up the BBC News channel. I assume that's what he wants, the elf thought. When in Britain, assume the locals watch the BBC.

The screen flickered instantly to life. It was just ten past the hour, so they only got the tail end of the politics, followed by the face of a bimbo standing uncomfortably in front of a brick wall, her words caught in mid-sentence.

". . . tonight that the murder took place. The victim has been identified by police as a Ms. Elizabeth Stride. A police spokesman said the murder was unusually brutal even for this district." The reporter's frisson of horror invited her audience to the hypocrisy of feeling shocked all the while they were pruriently interested. "Here in Spitalfields, police revealed, the victim was found dismembered by her attacker. Initial pathscan reports leaked to us say that the body was eviscerated. Senior police pathologist Dr. Leslie Phillips is alleged to have told investigating detectives that the mutilation of the corpse was conducted with surgical precision. The motive for the slaying is unknown, but—"

Seeing Francesca holding her hands to her ears, struggling to blot out the horror of the report, Geraint yelled at Serrin to kill it. A few last words came through before the mage flicked the screen into silence.

"—neighbors state that Ms. Stride received visits from many males and suffered from alcoholism. This is Sian Masterson for the—" and then there was no more.

Geraint drew Francesca's hands gently from her face and held them in his own. "Sorry, Fran. I didn't—"

"It's all right, really. It's just that it reminded me of what happened. You know, poor Annie."

A shock went through him that felt like he'd been kicked hard between the legs. His stomach formed into a tight knot and a clawed hand grabbed his heart and squeezed tight. The concerned words of his dinner guests seemed far, far away.

Serrin realized something was wrong, and seemed to be saying, "Geraint? You all right?"

He couldn't seem to get an answer out. Wanting to hide his distress, he went for the water jug on his desk and, as he did, the sleeve of his dinner jacket caught on the pack of cards he'd left out earlier that afternoon. A single card went flying off the surface of the table. Gripping the water jug with shaking hands, he hardly needed to look down to know what it was.

The card landed faceup. Of course.

Death.

* * *

It was a day that improved the longer it went on. Some time around five, Rani began to feel more like an ork again, after plenty of food and the self-indulgence of what claimed to be a bagel with smoked salmon. Whether or not it was, it cost the same as the real thing, and it tasted bloody wonderful. She was feeling good about a lot of things right now, and fairly secure about her destination for later that evening. She'd done some advance checking of the streets and alleys around the Finchley Road exit.

The nuyen had given her confidence, and she'd managed to pick up a new clip for the Ceska. She'd also purchased a couple of trauma patches from Mohsin's nephew. He'd charged an inflated rate, but she knew the sterilized packs wouldn't have any pinpricks because the boy would never cheat family.

And Imran still wasn't showing his face. Sanjay had found himself a white girl, probably some spotty-faced little thing from the streets who he'd fool around with until he got bored. If the girl was white, then it couldn't be anything serious, and besides, Rani was glad not to have him underfoot in the house. Best of all, he wouldn't be doped to the nines all day. Can't rub a slinky snakegirl if you're smacked out of your tree, Sanjay baby, she reflected cynically.

She checked the gun for the umpteenth time. She also rechecked the canister meter, which showed it still ninety per cent full, and cleaned her jacket. Time I got a new one, Rani decided.

But she had met Mohinder on a street off Brick Lane and he'd come up with some body armor for her, delivered to her door for a little extra. It hadn't left her very much of the money he'd paid her for the Predator, but the vest and thigh guards were good and strong.

She fantasized about a stream of gear coming to her door. It was foolishness, of course. She hadn't the money to become a street samurai, and where she was going at midnight she would be among friends anyway. But she did have boosted reflexes, just enough hardware to get excited about on the day after her eighteenth birthday, and tonight was another adventure.

One step closer to the truth.

Rani did not see the evening news. She had no idea just how exciting it was all about to get.

19

Francesca and Serrin had their arms around him, holding him up. Geraint fought hard to keep his breathing regular and maintain his posture. He felt light-headed, spinning, at the same time aroused and excited and faintly sick. He needed to be able to do a dozen things at once. He hadn't any time to explain. He sat down and jacked in.

"I'm all right. Give me a minute. I know what I'm doing," he complained in a voice suggesting that he obviously didn't.

Francesca plugged in the hitcher jack to accompany him, her observer icon appearing as a comely maiden, while his Knight ventured forth a little unsteadily. Wolves and reconfigured squire at his heels, they headed for a public datanet.

First Geraint checked the tourist guide for the basic story, then he browsed the Rumbelow book in the textual library and downloaded what his squire selected from that. Standard reference, giving him the list of names, dates, places, and some of the post-mortem material. It would be enough for now. Then he system-hopped into Births and Deaths, looking for Polly Nichols.

There she was, poor wretch. He didn't need any details, but he noted the date. Two weeks ago. Polly on the eighth, Annie on the fifteenth, Elizabeth on the twenty . . . first?

The name came to him even before he had time to check the data from the books. Eddowes; Catherine Eddowes. He felt as if he was falling down a pit so deep it had no bottom.

He jacked out and reached into the top drawer of the desk. He thought a GABA agent would do the trick and maybe also a dopamine regulator. Synthesis stimulator took too long, ditto neuromodulator. This called for an enzyme inhibitor, and he thought he'd add a shot of amino agents as well. What the hell, let's have a real cocktail.

Geraint applied the coded green and blue vials to the cannula, and within about forty-five seconds began to feel much more sober for now. Francesca and Serrin were both standing a little unsteadily after the evening's indulgences. Giving them a thumbs-up, he jacked back into the Matrix. Unable to confirm the address he knew, he got up from the desk after a few seconds, leaving trailing electrodes behind him.

"Right." He snapped his fingers to get their attention. "Focus as best you can." He emphasized his words with sweeping movements of his hands, the elegant long fingers extended straight before him. "East End of London, Eighteen eighty-eight. Quick history lesson.

"Jack the Ripper. Murdered five prostitutes. Some say seven, but the first two are questionable. Forget them. First true victim, one Polly Nichols."

Francesca took a sharp intake of breath. She saw what he'd been hunting for.

"Second victim, Annie Chapman. Yes, Fran: Annie Chapman." She was gasping with shock, totally disbelieving. "Fran, what did Annie do? I assumed she was just a friend. What've you got?"

Her head was bowed, her body rocking slightly forward and back in the armchair. Her voice was hushed.

"She was a call girl, Geraint. A high-class hooker."

He'd known, of course, from what the police had told

him, but something in him wanted to pull it out of her, make it real for her. He was looking for confirmation, needing them to accept and believe him.

"Right. Third victim, Elizabeth Stride. What did we see on the news tonight?"

Francesca's head was down, but Serrin was alert to what his friend was saying. Now it was the mage's turn to gasp slightly.

"Yes, there are a dozen Ripper-style copycat murders every year in the East End," Geraint went on. "Some joker dumps a mutilated body on the streets for a laugh. There are plenty of sick people out there who do that kind of stuff. But I get a distinct feeling that we're dealing with something entirely different here. And I have a problem with it."

"Like what?" Serrin was all eyes and ears. He could almost see the energies flowing in the man.

"In the original slayings, the fourth murder was committed the same day as the third. Double event. The fourth victim was a woman named Catherine Eddowes." He paused, waiting to deliver the final bombshell.

"So?" Serrin was uncertain, knowing Geraint had more to say, and waiting to hear it.

"I know a Catherine Eddowes. Well, I don't know her, but I know of her. She lives in—get this—the East End. In Whitechapel. Whitechapel. Ripperland, right?"

"How do you—"

"No, my friend," he said, waving a finger reproachfully at the elf, "I did not avail myself of her services. A couple of years back, I was friendly with the son of the Earl of Manchester. Lawrence was a good contact. He knew people I wanted to meet and he was reasonable company. Used to lose a packet at the High Roller, but that's life.

"Anyway, one night, very late, I get a call. I end up collecting him from Catherine Eddowes'. He's drunk as a skunk and there's someone from cheap trid hanging around outside looking for a story. I get in looking scruffy as hell so as not to arouse the interest of the trid reptile, and smuggle Larry out across fire escapes, punching him in the gut to stop the drunken singing he decides to do.

Got him home to Belgravia, and I didn't exactly want to see him again.

"Oh, our Ms. Eddowes is a whore, my friends, no question. Let's just say that she specialized in certain perversions of a peculiarly English nature. Being Welsh myself, I'm not so inclined. I like to be philosophical and detached about the line of work she pursues, but I can't forget certain details. Afterward, as I say, I didn't ever want to see Lawrence again."

When Francesca spoke, she was hesitant at first, but then her voice took on an edge of creeping hysteria.

"Annie saved my life twice. Who murdered her? I want to know. And Geraint, that thing in the Matrix, it had knives and scalpels and—''

He cut in. "Something's going on here. We all know it. Now maybe we can act. Catherine Eddowes isn't dead—yet. No report of it, anyway. And, yes, she is a whore, but that's hardly a license for someone to kill her. It's the sick scum she panders to who deserve that fate."

My God, what did you see that night? Serrin wondered as Geraint got to his feet. This is a bad world, and you know it, but something got to you that night, my friend.

"We're going to the East End. There's someone about to get butchered and we're the only people who can stop it." The words were melodramatic, but they rung true.

Serrin tried to insert a note of caution. "Why don't we just call—''

"Oh, I will. She's almost certainly ex-directory, but I can deck the number. Problem is, she won't be checking her answering machine this time of night, will she? She's a working girl. She'll plan to do that tomorrow morning, checking the bookings from the punters, with their special requests. But by tomorrow morning, she isn't going to be able to check anything."

"Why don't we just call the police?"

"Oh, sure. We tell them some story about the Ripper they've heard a dozen times this year alone, and maybe they'll get round to investigating it sometime next week."

"But surely they'll listen to you. You being a noble and all that. Surely." Serrin was clutching at straws.

"Are you for real? We'll get a duty constable on the telecom if we're lucky. He'll tell me that the Chief Inspector is dining somewhere, and that he will do his level best to reach him. Then he'll ring off, log the call, and promptly forget all about it. Anyone who's anyone tries to use his name and rank with the police all the time, it's all they ever hear and it just goes in one ear and out the other. Sure, there's a priority line for bluebloods like me, but that won't do the job fast enough.

"Serrin, the police in Britain are as stupid, vicious, and corrupt as anywhere in the world. Forget the image of the friendly bobby riding his bike and wearing the silly hat. They're uncaring rakkers just like the ones where you come from. And here we don't have Lone Star or anything like them. No, friend, if we want to deal with this, we'll have to do it ourselves."

"Geraint, why are we getting into this?"

Francesca's question was a good one. He didn't have a rational answer. "Will you trust me this one time?" She nodded, hesitant, then becoming more certain. His head was still afire, something was drawing him on and he couldn't be deflected now. "Serrin, take the book there. Yes, that's the one, the old Tarot book. Check the truth of what I find." He took up the pack, shuffled rapidly, and said to the elf, "I'm asking if there's someone behind this, you got it?"

The elf nodded, though he was unsure exactly what the Welshman was up to.

King of Swords.

Geraint sighed, holding his head in his hands. Serrin read from the book. "Mental prowess . . ."

"It's reversed, Serrin, see?"

The elf looked up from the book and stared at the card, the head of the throned King pointing downward, and nodded. He started again.

"A cold and cruel impersonality bordering on the sadistic. A calculating and shrewd person, who knows what he wants and how to get it. At worst, a quality of elemental evil backed by brutally efficient planning. Arguably, the worst-aspected card in the entire pack."

"Spirits, Geraint," the elf said, "what are we getting into?"

Francesca wiped at her forehead with the back of her hand and slouched down in her chair. "Why are we getting involved with this?'' she asked again. But at the back of her mind was Annie Chapman. She wasn't asking the question because she didn't want to get involved. She was asking because she wanted to hear what kind of ideas Geraint had for dealing with it. He was the only sober one there after all.

Geraint turned up the next card.

Justice.

''Do you need to ask?'' He turned to look at the elf. The slightest shake of Serrin's head told him all he needed to know.

''Look, we need to take some care here. We can't just get into the car and pile across the river. Let's think it through first.'' Serrin's caution was sensible.

Geraint explained his plan of action. ''First of all, I've been trying to call Catherine Eddowes. The deck's on auto-repeat dialing through the telecom interface. It's already got the answering machine, but we'll plug away and hope. She just might answer if she gets an alert from her phone that she's being called every thirty seconds. We can afford ten, fifteen minutes at least.

''Second, I'm running a program looking for every Catherine Eddowes in London. It's not likely to be a common name, so I'm using an analysis frame to search for every one in the public datanets. If we come up with an alternative Catherine Eddowes who's a seventy-five-year-old retired author up in Wood Green or a five-year-old crèche regular, I think we can check them off the list.'' Geraint paused a moment, unsure how to phrase the next part.

''Third, there's the minor problem of the fact that you two are, pardon me for saying so, as tight as judges. You've gone through the equivalent of at least a bottle of wine each and, unlike me, you don't have cannula implants to get you over that hurdle in a minute flat. I've got some enzyme shots, but that'll only handle the peripherals, I'm afraid. Your brains will continue to have a very hefty slug of alcohol swimming round in them for about half an hour; modern technology can't get across the blood-brain barrier much faster than that. That alone is a great reason for spending a quarter of an hour plugging away at the telecom and hoping we don't have to set foot outside this flat tonight.''

Francesca and Serrin exchanged glances. A few minutes ago Geraint had barely been able to stand upright. The change was impressive.

He gave them both a slap patch with the degrading enzyme, then opened a wall safe after its security system had run a retina scan on his eyes. The seamless edge slid soundlessly open, revealing a space the size of a small wardrobe. He rummaged through the safe contents.

''I think we should take body armor for a start, plus IR lenses and Bond and Carringtons. What are you most comfortable with in the pistol department, Fran?''

''I've never carried anything more than a light—a Colt, usually. Never needed anything more. I've hardly ever fired one of those.''

He casually tossed her a Bond and Carrington light with a hefty clip. ''Twenty shots in the clip, and a spare. That should do the job. Serrin's got his Ingram and I'll take my usual. Okay, that's done. Now, I don't exactly have an anti-personnel armory here, but we should be able to come up with a few extras. Slap patches for a start. Take the best trauma I've got.''

''You figure we're going to get seriously hurt?'' The elf looked grave.

''Serrin, we may walk in to find someone very close to death. The best trauma patch in the world may be no more use to her than using a feather duster to beat off a troll samurai, but we can only hope.''

He mused before the shelves of the safe. Serrin could see a startling number of credsticks stacked up in the top row, each taped and labelled. Geraint pocketed a couple and took a hefty wedge of notes into the bargain, but that wasn't what was on his mind. ''Maybe we should reconsider,'' he said. ''Do you have a pistol license, Fran?''

''Yes. I had to file a residency request, which is still in the works, but the Lord Protector, God preserve, decided I was a fit person to carry a Colt. I think my corporate references may have had something to do with that.''

''Well, technically your pistol isn't covered by that, but it is functionally identical and I think your Colt de-

veloped a sad fault in it yesterday, right?'' She grinned.
''If you're caught in possession you'll get fined but you
won't get deported. Serrin's Ingram is a trickier problem.
I assume you have no license for that, my friend?''

''Well, er, no.'' Serrin obviously didn't want to discuss how he'd acquired the weapon.

''Right. If the baggies catch you, it could be serious.
If you fire the thing, you could end up as a guest of Her
Majesty's Prison Service. That is not a prospect you want
to take lightly. So, maybe you should leave it behind. I
can offer you a large net-gun instead. Non-lethal, con-
straining, purely self-defense. They catch you with that
and you get deported, of course, but then that's not really
a pressing worry right now. You'd only get fined a few
thou. What do you say?''

The elf grumbled at first, but he could see the wisdom
behind Geraint's suggestion. He accepted the hefty
weapon and was figuring out how to conceal it under his
voluminous greatcoat when the laser printer began its
smooth flow. Geraint ran over to pore over the printout.

''Five of them. More than I'd expected, given the
name. Well, well, one's just gone on holiday to France,
poor woman. Not something any patriotic Brit would do,
never mind. Her flight left on Friday, so she's out. One's
a civil servant, age forty-six. Think we can forget her.
Number three's a cab driver in Westway. Twenty-seven
years old. She might be a possible, servicing dubious
gentlemen in the back of the cab in Paddington, but right
now she's in the Royal Marsden having a retina-tightening
eye operation. Someone could try to murder her there,
but they've got incredible security. Not very likely, I
think.''

''How the hell are you finding all this out?'' Serrin
muttered.

''Easy. Once I have the names from the public datanet
it's pretty simple to check vehicle licenses, air and rail
and coach departure bookings, hospital lists, and the like.
But I daren't risk what I really want to do, which is check
through Metropolitan Police files on the Met's own network.

''Number four is a troll in the Squeeze. Mind you, the
data is five years out of date. Census data down there is

pretty patchy even in these days of compulsory poll tax. She's registered as having been a local counsellor in Croydon in 2044, which makes her one of the radfems. That was a real hoot, that business. Anyway, even if she's still around I think we can safely eliminate a radical feminist troll from our list of possibles.'' Geraint allowed himself a grim smile, which spread into a broader one as he scanned the last entry.

''Bringing us to number five. Who happens to be, good heavens, a retired travel writer living in Wood Green. Hmm. She's sixty-six and specializes in scripting trid documentaries about vanishing cultures. Oh no, I don't think so.''

Serrin was puzzled. ''But the Catherine Eddowes you know isn't on the list. I don't understand.''

''That tells us one of two things. Either she's moved and isn't registered at her new address, or she's where she used to be and census data is incomplete, which is more than likely down in the East End. Over a million and a half Londoners do not appear on any official lists, and that doesn't even count the Undercity. There are plenty of places where census officials wouldn't go even if toting a vanload of SAS laser packs at their backs. Most places with a Metropolitan Police security rating of C or worse have very incomplete data. And we're heading into a C zone or lower, no question.

''You people sobering up, by the way?''

Francesca ruefully admitted she was getting there, but the evening wasn't turning out to be exactly what they'd expected. A warm haze of alcoholic glow over coffee and truffles had been an inviting prospect, but that was starting to seem all very distant now. Serrin nodded as he fingered the unused patch in his pocket. He'd let his own body deal with it naturally.

Geraint made one final check on the telecom. ''Getting nothing but the answering machine. I'll leave a short message on auto telling her to barricade herself until we arrive. She won't take any notice even if she gets it, I suppose, but we have to try.''

Serrin had a final consideration. ''Hey, what if the media are onto this? We might end up with a posse of tridjocks down on the site. They might even get there first.''

"Well, if we do, that's great. We can just turn the car round and go home. But we know something they don't."

"What's that?"

"We know about Annie Chapman. That barely got reported at all; some of her, um, more discretion-minded, shall we say, clientele wanted it that way. So it would be a fluke if anyone in the media noticed, and as I say, we get a bunch of copycat murders every year. Even if a bright little thing noticed the connection, by this time of night her desk editor will be downing his fifteenth whisky and he'll just tell her to check it out tomorrow. Murders don't get any more than a single soundbite in London unless the victim's a VIP. They're too common these days."

By the time they had struggled into their armor and packed their weaponry, Geraint needed a minute to stuff a black bag full of bits and pieces: tools, scraps from a survival kit, even a small respirator. He carried it down the hall as the others followed him, and then the grim humor of it became apparent.

"Geraint, that bag. It looks just like—" Francesca shuddered.

"Doesn't it just? Let's hope we're not going to be too late to find a killer toting one just like it."

It was just eleven-forty when they left the house. Across the city, a very nervous Indian girl found that her hands were shaking as she bent to put on her boots. Soon she had the door locked behind her, had hailed a cab, and paid the troll the fare upfront. She sat in the back of the cab, gazing through the barred windows, the cracks in the plasglass streaming from a central impact location. That told her the windows were bulletproof. It also told her the cab had been shot at, which was pretty standard. Kids just want to have fun, after all.

20

Midnight was closing in on them by the time they parked the Saab in Aldgate. The club wasn't exactly classy, but the troll bouncer's eyes lit up when he saw the notes Geraint waved under his snout. He got a nice advance, a promised fee per hour for making sure no one ran off with the car, and the further promise of a handsome bonus if the Saab was safe and undamaged when they got back. Geraint made a showy display of activating the car's defense systems.

"Look, if anyone does touch it, some pretty unpleasant gas will start billowing all over the place, not to mention the ultrasonics, so make sure no one even gets close, right?"

The troll took the money and gave Geraint a greedy, confident grin. He opened his Italian-designer jacket and displayed a fine range of heavy throwing knives inside. "Don't worry, boss. Anyone gets too nosy, you got their nose waiting for you when you get back. I'll rip it right orf of their face. Pay me by the nose?"

Geraint smiled and walked away. "You'll be paid well, term. See you soon." I hope, he added to himself.

"We had to park farther away than I would have liked," he told Francesca and Serrin. "Let's hope we don't have to make a run for it. Any closer to Houndsditch, though, and we couldn't have relied on the car being in one piece when we got back. Tires would have been stolen and we'd probably find the doors beaten in just for the hell of it."

"Is all that stuff you told Mr. Ugly true?" Francesca asked.

"Does it really matter? I certainly do have some defenses and alarms but unfortunately nerve gas isn't licensed as one of them. Don't know what this country's coming to."

They edged down the increasingly dark side streets.

Some of the street lights had been shot out, but most had been dismantled and their cables and wires stripped for the copper. To their right, one of the very few remaining church clocks began to chime midnight.

"Hell, Geraint, I don't like this at all." Serrin's stomach was protesting his fear. On top of all the food he had eaten, it didn't feel comfortable at all.

"Okay, stop. Here. It's the third house along on the left—see? Yeah, the one with the figure on top."

Against the glimmering sky with its suffused glow of distant neon, they could dimly see the small statue perched atop the roof. Eros, the child archer.

"Serrin, time to do some checking. Top floor, back of the building."

They'd discussed this move before setting off. Serrin hadn't liked the idea of investigating with his astral body; being in a trance in the unlit mean streets of London's East End was not a particularly comfortable thought. Instead he would simply assense the area first. He was startled by what he found.

"There's a spell effect in the area. Detection spell. Someone's running a detection spell." Reacting swiftly, the elf dropped his astral perception and muttered a few words to activate a spell of his own. Probing for enemies, what he sensed within the building confused him.

"Someone in there doesn't like me much. But I can't tell if it's specific. It feels more like a spellcaster is expecting enemies to arrive, but I can't figure out just how specific it is." He stopped speaking and concentrated once more; the effect was like watching someone listening to instructions being delivered via a hidden ear-piece. "There's some masking here, I think. There's also some kind of—oh, frag it, I can't tell."

Switching his spell, Serrin began to search for the presence of a mage close by. He knew there must be one, surely; it couldn't be just a spell lock, that wouldn't make much sense. Screwing up his eyes in concentration and probing again, he shook his hands in annoyance.

"Check the woman!" Geraint hissed by his shoulder.

Of course; so absorbed in hunting for the source of the spell he'd detected, the mage had forgotten that part of the original plan. His mind probed for Catherine Eddowes.

"Got her! . . . No, she's gone!" He was furious with himself, wishing he'd learned these mundane spells with more force. He concentrated all his magical energies into the detection, adding resources he'd been withholding for defense in case the target of the detection reacted against him with hostility.

"Bingo!" She was at the back of the building. Then the elf reeled backward as if kicked by a mule. The scream reverberated right through him. He wasn't going to try that again.

"Geraint, I think—"

His voice trailed away. They looked at each other and readied their weapons, but Serrin begged time to prepare some magical defense. There was a mage about, somewhere, and he sure as hell didn't want to be caught with his pants down.

Geraint stuffed a handful of notes into the hands of the ork pimps lurking by the doorway. Bored and uninterested, they put down their stunprods and ushered the motley trio up the stairs. They'd seen it all before. The runners' feet hammered up the wooden stairs, and as they reached the top floor, Geraint virtually fell into the tacky wooden door. It bulged in its frame, but it didn't give way. From within, they heard a loud bang. The door began to splinter as they beat against it, but it so resisted their attempts to force it open that they guessed some heavy furniture must be piled up against it.

The orks came running up the stairs behind them just as Geraint and company managed to force open a wedge between door and frame, pushing laboriously at the wardrobe lodged there. The pimps were yelling, menacing, clearly intending to attack them. Geraint screamed to them that someone was being killed, but Serrin decided it was no time for conversation. Throwing a powerball spell into the orks, the elf almost fell to his knees as the orks reeled back down the stairs. One collapsed unconscious and the other could do little more than hold his head, groaning in system shock. Geraint glanced at the elf furiously as he labored to force the door.

By the time he could drag himself through the wedged

door and climb over the wardrobe, the wave of cold night air from the open window told Geraint that Catherine Eddowes' attacker was gone. He half-stumbled over the barrier and slid to his knees in the slick pool of fresh blood. Gore covered his hands and the sleeves of his jacket, and soaked the legs of his trousers. To get to the window and look out for any fleeing figure he would have had to climb over the bed. It was a prospect he couldn't stomach.

"Just don't come in here. You don't want to see this. Oh, God almighty." With that, he turned, almost sagged, away from the carnage. Only the neurochemicals kept him from bringing the thousand-nuyen meal up the way it had gone down.

Serrin was still groggy from the drain of the spell; he had really let fly at the orks with all he had. As Geraint reemerged from the room, his face was ashen, but he waved away Francesca's frantic hands offering him slap patches for the girl inside.

"Forget it. There isn't an internal organ left where it used to be. We're too late. We're too damn late. Let's get out of here and call the police. That's all we can do now."

They descended the stairs, Geraint throwing some more money at the huddled forms of the dazed orks. Ace it, he thought; it wasn't their fault Serrin had to cream them. They might even have thought they were protecting someone.

When the three stepped out into the street again, they saw something totally unanticipated: a cloaked figure carrying a bag was veering crazily down the road toward a limo parked in the distance.

In the dark they could see no clear details. What puzzled Geraint most was how the man could be in this street if he'd gone out the back. Before he could fire his pistol, however, the first of Francesca's shots rang out. The cloaked figure disappeared into the opened rear door of the limo as two other figures moved out from the shadows, one with a snarling automatic weapon and the other gesticulating dramatically.

The mage, Serrin realized, almost too late. An invisible tidal wave of concussion slammed into their bodies.

The impact sent Geraint flying, Francesca managing to stay upright only by hanging on to the remains of a lamp post, her gun hanging uselessly from a hand that had lost all power of grip. Only Serrin managed to stay in some semblance of shape. His magical defense kept the worst of the manaball's effects away from them. Clutching at the best spell focus he had for combat, he dropped the defense that had saved them and let the combat mage and the street samurai have it with the works.

A huge ball of fire sprang into existence at the end of the road, illuminating the scene with a hellish inferno. Dimly, the lights of the limo could be seen speeding away, but the two figures were still standing there, now become screaming, flailing human torches. Serrin collapsed to the sidewalk.

As the car squealed around the corner and away, the scene fell into an eerie silence for a second or two, a stillness broken only by the crackle of flames licking at the two charred bodies in the distance. Francesca slapped patches desperately onto the elf, whose hand clutched instinctively for the healing spell focus.

Gone. Gave it away. Oh, drek. Serrin couldn't really focus his vision. Clouds swirled in his head; rocks hung heavy in his stomach.

Geraint fumbled in his bag and readied a subcutaneous as shouts began to ring out from the blackness of the streets. Francesca slapped patches on both herself and the noble while the elf's body jerked into life at Geraint's ministrations. From somewhere north of them, a whooping siren began to wail, getting closer by the second.

"Two assaulted orks, one maybe dead," Geraint said tersely. "I'm covered in blood and you just torched two people. We are *not* staying around to explain this one to the Metropolitan Police. Come on!" He and Francesca draped Serrin's arms around their shoulders, limping away into a side-alley just as the flashing lights of the police cars appeared in the distance.

Serrin was beginning to feel as if he, too, was on fire. He dropped his arms from around the shoulders of his friends, but he still gazed at them with wildly dilated pupils.

"Come on, let's blow these fraggin' bastards to hell

and back,'' he croaked as he reeled about. Francesca and Geraint exchanged frantic looks.

"What the hell did you pump him up with?"

"Too late to worry now. It's only got a couple of minutes, then he gets the shakes. If he's lucky. Run, you two, *run!*''

Speeding haphazardly through the dark back streets, praying they wouldn't fall headlong over some smashed-out wino or shattered slab of concrete, the three fled into the murderous night.

* * *

Rani was a few minutes early, but even with that he was late. She huddled in the corner of the warehouse, shrinking into its darkness. At least she knew the exits, should she need them, the huge front doorway through which she had come in and the small barricaded door at the back. That is, it might have been barricaded if the wood weren't all rotted. Still, it was an emergency exit, just in case. She also guessed that Smeng must have friends lurking about, though she didn't look for them.

It seemed like an hour or more passed before the other ork suddenly appeared beside her in the cool darkness. He put his arms around her and she gave him the coconut sweet wrapped in rice paper. He smiled tenderly and murmured, "You didn't have to do that."

"But I wanted to."

"Thank you." He took half of it in one mouthful and chewed happily. "Oh, that's good. Too good to eat all at once." He shoved the remainder into a jacket pocket and refastened the zipper. "Rani, you asked my help in getting vengeance. I can only do so much, but what you do get, it wasn't from me, right?"

"Of course," Rani breathed. Their voices, held low in whispers, still sounded to her ears as though they were being broadcast throughout the silent warehouse.

"All right, this Pershinkin, he has many, many contacts. And a lot of friends, too. He's not someone who you can pull into a dark doorway and interrogate, right?"

Rani remained silent. She had expected as much.

"But one night, a little someone sees something.

Maybe that someone hears something they shouldn't. Get my drift? Good. That someone overhears Pershinkin acting as a middleman. He is being asked to find some people to make a run to a place called—Longstanton?''

He pronounced it oddly, over-extending the middle syllable. Rani was glad. It meant Smeng wasn't the one who'd overheard the conversation; this sounded authentically secondhand. Somehow she didn't want him to have seen or heard anything personally, not to have been involved in this terrible thing, not even inadvertently.

"That where you went?" he asked.

"Yes." As simple as that.

"Let me tell you now, no one's seen Pershinkin all week. Not as far as any of my people know, anyway. But that's not so strange. The man is west of center a lot, so we hear tell. He talks to the suits and only comes back here to find heat, right?"

Again, it needed no more than a simple nod from her.

"Well, what I got for you is two more things. First, the men he meets. Two suits. One tall and thin, all sneers and hair slime; the other one a little shorter, losing his hair at the front, and he's got something classy, some kind of jewel in his front tooth, yeah? My little bird says he's a chiphead. He shakes a little, see? The suits disappeared into a flashy limo. Now, I can't tell you where all this took place. That might not be in the interests of my source, got it? But not so very far away, I'll tell you that. Hope that's some use to you." Smeng paused and glanced carefully around him for the twelfth time.

"Second thing is, it was a bum run. What I heard is exactly what you said happened. The suits said, 'Just get some suckers, a bunch of slints what can be relied on to rakk up.' Sorry, Rani. I don't want to hurt your feelings. But that's—"

At that moment they heard footsteps approaching. People were obviously heading toward them, splashing through pools of half-frozen water outside.

"I don't like this." He was backing away toward the secret door. "Let's take cover."

Rani was about to join him when the three figures appeared in the doorway. With her ork's low-light vision, she could make them out pretty clearly. Two humans, bedraggled, but the third one, ah, the third one.

She knew him. She couldn't ever forget him. Fire danced around his hands as his fatal power was unleashed again in her memory.

The sirens began to wail again, so close now.

"Here!" She called to them. They edged forward, unsure of themselves. They couldn't see her, and were craning their heads left and right trying to see who was waiting for them in the gloom.

"No, Rani, no! Baggies coming!" The huge Undercity ork was furious. "Not here! Come now!" He stood by the exit, ready to close the door behind him at any moment.

She couldn't desert them. "But he saved me. I know them!"

"No!" Smeng screamed at her. "They're not blood! I took chances for you, Rani. I can't take any more! Hear the sirens! Now! Come on!"

She looked around, desperately torn, but she would not move toward him. With a growl he slammed the door and she heard the sound of bolts being slammed home behind him. The three figures were staggering toward her, obviously in desperate trouble. The sirens were growing louder by the second. Running forward as unthreateningly as she could, she yelled, "Friend!" to reassure them, then grabbed the elf's hand. He registered surprise without recognition; she thought he was either drunk or in shock.

"This is a dead end." The voice of the man told her he was from another part of the city, another world entirely. It also expressed something close to despair. He was casting about frantically for a means of escape. She knew where to find it.

"Come with me. I'm a friend," Rani urged. They weren't going to stop and check. She got them out the back door and into the tiny cul-de-sac only moments before the first police car roared to a halt in front of the ramshackle building.

Somehow, against all odds they managed to drag themselves over the wall and to grab a few panting breaths behind it. There was no time for more than that, though.

They could hear people still moving inside the warehouse. Some of the walls separating the houses along the street were little more than rotted wood and others had gaping holes in the plascrete and wire. By the time they'd squeezed their way through a dozen or so, all except Rani were just too shattered to go any further. The back door of a house stood before them; lights were on inside.

"This is crazy even for us, but I think we're going to have to do it anyway. Smile and be nice to the people," Geraint said. He reached out a hand and tried the door, which opened to his investigative push. They entered the darkness of the room beyond as Rani checked what was going on behind him, staring into the night with her sensitive eyes. It smelled bad, but that wasn't really an obstacle. Not to begin with, anyway.

Geraint was about to use a flashtube when someone threw the lights. The room was bigger than he'd expected, somehow, but it wasn't the room's dimensions that concerned him. Distinctly more of a problem were the occupants.

"Well, gentlemen, what DO we have here?"

The guttural voice was full of sarcasm and hostility. It looked like seven, maybe eight, trolls, but they were so large Geraint expected another half-dozen to pop out from behind them at any moment. They seemed to cover the far side of the room without leaving any space for air. The single naked light bulb was all that lit the place, but at that instant it seemed to shine unbearably bright and harsh. Most of the trolls seemed to have guns, and one had a shotgun that looked like it could neatly blast all visitors to hell and back with one delicate squeeze of the trigger. At their feet lay some large plastic trays covered with opaque plasbags filled with soft substances Geraint didn't want to look at more than once.

He and the others retreated gingerly back against the doorway. The trolls were smirking, all weapons pointed at their surprise guests.

"Come in, why don't you?" one of the trolls ventured, but the four newcomers stood stiff and rigid. Deciding on a less polite approach, the one with the blackened snout barked out an order.

"Shut that rakkin' door or we'll blow you to buggery,'' he snarled. Trying desperately to still the shaking of her gun hand, Rani complied.

The four of them stood immobile with guns readied, Serrin managing to fumble the huge net-gun from his coat, shaking and shivering. His eyes registered the presence of forty trolls in front of him, but there were as many Geraints as he had hands on his fingers.

''Hur, hur, hur,'' one of the trolls sniggered, then spat violently onto the stained floor. He fingered a serrated knife with what was left of his left hand. Several of the others licked their lips. All looked as though they were slowly edging forward.

''Well, my, my. What have we here?''

It was Rani, cool and calm beyond even her own dreams, stepping forward to confront the brutes. ''We try a little run down here in the East End, then when we have to make tracks sharpish, we bust into just the kind of people we can talk to. Guns and money. Lovely. Nice to meet you.''

She had her Ceska pointed directly at the head of the troll who'd done most of the talking. Though the elf had the shakes real bad and the other man looked totally at a loss, Rani was glad to see that the woman also had her pistol pointed at the same target.

The trolls hesitated long enough.

Just.

21

For a second that stretched out for hours, both groups stood frozen, weapons readied and pointed at each other. The leader of the trolls had some respect for them now, Rani could see, and he was looking to her. He realized she was a local, not some cross-town rich kid who'd be easy to fool, easy to catch off guard in a fatal instant of vacillation. Still, he was drooling slightly, a stringy glob of mucus hanging from one corner of his mouth. The other gang members were looking to old black-snout now, not quite so arrogant but still eager for the fray. Rani prayed they weren't high on some of the crazier stuff around; if they were, reason would never get her group out of here alive.

"We're very grateful for your hospitality," she said as steadily as she could manage. "I imagine you'll want some reward for that. Guess we can come up with something for you."

The trolls chuckled inanely, gripping their weapons tighter. Black-snout leered at her.

"I'm rakking sure you can, girlie. Looks like you got some nice weapons there. Not the kinda gear to stop a troll, of course. Probably got some real money in that suit, slick kid, huh?" He slid his shotgun across to point at Geraint. "Poor little pixie there, he don't look too good to me. Don't think we'd get too many bullet tokens for his scrawny body. Rest of you worth a few nuyen, though. Hey, don't look so sad and dismal. You ain't gonna die! Different bits of you gonna be alive everywhere from Seattle to Tokyo!"

The trolls laughed among themselves, but none of them made a move. Yet.

Serrin's shaking suddenly stopped, but he hardly knew his own state. His mind was lucid and calm, but his skin was clammy and he felt as if he might simply keel over at any instant. Fixing his gaze on the troll with the shotgun seemed to help him focus his attention and stay on his feet.

"The guns we have might not stop you, but they could do some unpleasant damage," the elf said. "But I'll tell you one thing, brother, if I'm going to die here, first I'm going to pump some hellfire so heavy even your thick butt-skins will go up in smoke. I mean, what the fraggin' hell, what've I got to lose?"

Black-snout stared hard at Serrin, mentally gunning him down with his eyes but not daring to do more. He could see the strange stones the elf was clutching. Magic was the one real edge these intruders had. The weapons didn't frighten the trolls, but a suicide strike by a mage with a serious death wish was another matter entirely. It wouldn't be the first time one of his gang had ended up on the wrong end of a corporate combat mage. Many of them also had friends who'd suffered the same fate, and hadn't lived to discuss it. The atmosphere began to change.

Please keep me standing up long enough to get us out of this, Serrin prayed mentally as Geraint and Rani began the negotiating. Geraint was listening to the flow of Rani's clever comments, taking his cue from her as she told him implicitly what the trolls might accept for their release. Credsticks they wouldn't touch; they had no way of verifying them. Geraint's high-denomination sterling and nuyen notes did, however, speak to them in another language. Dumping slap patches and a pile of shiny equipment out of his bag, Geraint upped the ante even further.

Slowly the trolls began to move sideways, while Rani and the others did the same. It might have been hilarious had it not been so desperate, both groups circling around each other. Geraint covered their retreat through the far door with his heavy pistol. The trolls had one final challenge.

"Hey, ken-boy, why don't you leave the woman here?" one of them smirked, rubbing his greasy crotch. The low chuckle that rippled through the group was a most unpleasant sound, but Geraint didn't dare scratch the itch burning in his trigger finger. When the others reached the street, Geraint covered their final exit, then he backed out too. They still couldn't relax yet, though.

"Where the hell are we? Got to get to Aldgate, the Shaking Samurai," Geraint told Rani. She moved into action immediately, grabbing Serrin's hand and guiding them as they ran up the street.

The trolls had changed their minds, two of them firing from the upper floor of the house as the fleeing figures disappeared into the darkness. The group had almost reached the end of the road when Geraint drew up with a yelp of pain. He clutched the back of his leg just below the hip, but kept on going, limping around the corner as best he could. He'd taken a bullet, and when he took his hand away it was smeared with blood.

"They won't follow. They've heard the sirens by now," Rani tried to reassure them.

"Who are you?" Francesca gasped out at last, trying to conceal her disgust at the ork girl's ugliness.

Rani scowled. "This isn't the time for questions." She pointed at Geraint. "He's just been shot and elf-face is completely rakked. Look at his eyes. You got wheels?"

"Parked outside the Shaking Samurai. A troll's guarding it. Owe him money," Geraint managed to force out through the pain. "Ngh! I'm not going to get that far."

"I can go for the car, but you gotta give me something the troll will recognize."

"Give him this," he said, handing her all his remaining notes, "and tell him the gas won't be a problem if you touch the car. He'll remember that. Oh, and tell him this includes a bonus for the noses if he's managed to collect any." She looked at the nobleman as if he were mad. "He'll understand. Honest." He handed her the keys.

"Geraint, is this wise?" Francesca was alarmed. "It's our only way out of here. We could make it ourselves."

Serrin collapsed down to all fours and began to cough, great racking heaves that convulsed his body. Geraint hung on to his shot-up leg, looked at the elf, and back to Francesca.

"You want to walk it alone, Fran?"

"Got to get you safe while I get the car." Rani was staring urgently about her. "Yeah, got it. Can you make it a couple of streets? Three minutes?" With Francesca holding up Serrin's long, slim form, and Rani helping Geraint get along on one good leg, it took eight, but they made it.

"Through here," she said. "Saw it this afternoon. There may be some little street kids about, but they'll be scared off if you point a gun at them."

With Geraint's flashtube lighting the scene, they saw that it was an abandoned house whose ceiling had collapsed. A couple of rats scurried out of sight among the piles of rubble and excrement strewn over the floor. The stench was overwhelming, but compared to the danger on the street, the place seemed deliciously inviting. There was no one inside it.

"I'll be back as soon as I can." Rani was about to skip off into the night when Geraint called out to her.

"Oh, hey, you! The keys!" He took them back and showed her the plaque that slid out of the key-ring. "You need to put that into the green slot, right? This'll get you past the ID checks, but you'll still need the password sequence to activate the controls."

"Phew! What kind of car is this?" She was impressed.

"One that's hopefully in one piece. The password, er is,"—he gestured her closer to whisper in her ear—"Queen of Heaven."

Rani stood back from him and smiled. Her face broke into a wide grin and she felt almost euphoric. She imagined these people were heavy-duty shadowrunners and she was saving their lives. That made it an adventure, the very thing she'd always wanted.

"Hey, lady, you wanna know my name? Call me the Queen of Heaven!" She ran off giggling into the night.

Francesca turned to Geraint in the darkness. "You almighty fool! You've just handed the car keys to a complete, bloody lunatic. And a sodding ork on top of it."

"Like I said, you want to walk the East End alone at night?"

Again Francesca had no answer.

*   *   *

By the time the car came veering unsteadily along the road, Serrin had slipped into unconsciousness. Geraint's leg felt sore as hell, but the slap patch had staunched the bleeding in what looked to be only a flesh wound. He looked up quickly at the sound of a car door slamming and the crunch of boots over the frosty ground.

It was the ork girl. "Got it," she said. "I had to give that troll everything. He really strung me along even though he knew I was from you." She was angry, but obviously excited too. She grabbed at the elf's comatose body.

"Be careful with him," Geraint said quickly. "Fran, help her."

The American's nose registered her repulsion at the ork's distinctive body odor. The girl smelled strong, musky, and Francesca imagined that if not for the oil on her body she would probably have smelled even worse.

Between them, they picked Serrin up and deposited him in the back seat of the car. Francesca tucked herself into a corner with the elf's head in her lap.

Geraint took the driver's seat, and the Indian girl climbed in beside him. "Hey, we owe you." He held out the credsticks. "They're worth ten thou. I'm sure you'll get a good deal on them. But I don't feel right leaving you out here alone." He winced as he tried to press his foot against the pedal.

Rani waved away the proffered money and said she didn't want it. "Take me with you."

Geraint grinned as he used his hands to shuffle over into the car's passenger seat. "See how the other half lives, huh? Can you drive this for me?"

She looked unhappy. "Um, it was a bit difficult getting here. I'm not used to driving, I don't get the chance much. You really can't manage?"

He held her arm briefly to reassure her. "It's all right. Fran, you better act as chauffeur. We can put the walking wounded in the back." They changed places, and Francesca pointedly avoided looking at Rani as she placed her hands on the wheel. She needed directions, however, so she was forced to speak to her.

With Rani navigating, it was only minutes before they hit Gracechurch Street, heading west. Geraint was briefing Francesca on what to do when they got back to Chelsea. She would have to bring down a coat and a change of clothes for him, because he couldn't walk in wearing clothes covered with blood.

She followed the Embankment around as far as Geraint's street, driving smoothly down the ramp into the underground garage. It took fifteen minutes to get changed and emerge looking passably like occupants and guests of a nobleman's penthouse. Rani pulled the hood of the dark velvet cloak over her head as she emerged from the car, keeping her head down as if that would somehow prevent detection. She and Francesca draped Serrin's lifeless arms around their shoulders while Geraint limped along on his ebony walking stick. Then they were into the elevator at last, and then staggering into Geraint's flat.

Rani gazed speechless at the evidence of the meal

they'd eaten so many, many hours ago. Geraint tried to bow to her, bidding her welcome to his home, but his face betrayed the pain and impossibility of the gesture.

"Let me look at your leg. I know about cleaning wounds," she volunteered eagerly.

"You sure about that?" he said, alarmed. On the other hand, he didn't want to call Careline about this one. They had to notify the Lord Protector's minions automatically when called upon to treat bullet wounds, whether the injured party was a noble or not. And that would start a lot of awkward questions being asked.

"At least let me look," Rani urged.

He hobbled into the bathroom, showing her the medical kit that boggled her mind. Where she came from, people would kill for a tenth of what this man had in the kit alone.

Geraint had been lucky, as far as it went; the bullet had passed right through the big muscle at the back of his leg, doing no serious damage. Rani gave him a local and cleaned away the dried blood. Lying on his stomach, he watched her work in the big mirror at the end of the room. Her hands were hard-skinned, almost gnarled, and the last word anyone would have used to describe them was delicate, but her touch was gentle even though he was anesthetized.

Finally, the cumulative stress of the night caught up with him, his mind clouding and his vision beginning to blur. He had just managed to ask what her name was and to hear her reply when his muscles gave up the effort in a final bodily sigh and he passed out.

Rani left him on the floor, putting folded towels under his belly and calves, and laying a pillow from the huge bedroom under his head. The mage was lying comatose on a sofa, his breathing shallow, but he seemed peaceful enough. The woman hadn't even undressed before crashing out in the second bedroom.

Rani skipped around the room, very pleased with herself. Then, guiltily at first, but with a growing sense of delight, she began to stuff her mouth with truffles from the remains of the meal on the table.

If only Imran could see her now. . . .

22

Rani gazed in awe at the control systems in the penthouse. She longed to play with them, to find out what did what, but she feared setting off some alarm or rousing security, so she contented herself making coffee, raiding a fridge stocked to overflowing, and taking twenty minutes to figure out how to operate the juicer. After getting it to work without breaking it, she gulped down the tangy orange juice, licking her lips with a murmur, almost a growl, of pleasure.

"Help yourself!" He stood watching her from the kitchen doorway, weight on his right leg, elegant in a kimono that was finer than any sari she had ever seen. She put the glass down guiltily.

"No, I meant it." Geraint sniffed at the aroma of fresh coffee. "Oh, that smells good. Thank you." He limped to the breakfast table, poured himself a cup of strong black coffee and considered a cigarette. Not this morning, he thought. My body's taken enough of a beating.

In the living room beyond, Serrin groaned in his sleep and stirred. He'd still be groggy from the reaction to the drugs Geraint had administered.

"I don't know what you like," he said waving at the fridge, "but there's bacon, ham, eggs, cereals in the cupboard there, fruit and cheeses and, oh, let's see what else. . . ." He clambered up painfully to investigate the contents. He didn't feel much like eating, but thought he'd better force something down. He settled for some Jarlsberg and salami on rye while Rani began to assemble a sandwich on some grainy black bread, piling layer upon layer more out of curiosity than anything else. By the time she was done, the sandwich was an inch and a half high. She chewed a great chunk happily, and then looked warily askance at his expression.

"No," Geraint smiled. "I'm not laughing at you. Glad

to see you enjoy the food. I don't know what, um, ork people like." He didn't know what else to say.

Rani looked at him suspiciously, backing off a little.

"Don't take offense, please. It's just that my friends and acquaintances don't include many orks. Well, not really *any*, to be honest. You see, I'm a member of the House of Nobles, and as you may know, not many noble families have orks among them." Geraint knew he was digging an even deeper hole the more he talked, but the words came out faster than he thought.

She didn't know any of the details, but it was a well-known fact of life that the Sixth Age hadn't changed noble prejudices in Britain. When the first wave of unexplained genetic expression brought elves and dwarfs, the first of the metahumans, into the world, noble families got their fair share of pretty elven children but only the rare ugly little dwarf. Registered stillbirths and neo-natal deaths among dwarf babies had been astonishingly high among society's upper echelons. Then, when the transformations brought orks and trolls into their midst, British nobles took steps to make sure they stayed elegant, handsome, and socially acceptable. Most of the unfashionably ugly creatures proved to have alarmingly short lifespans, for having an ork in the family just wasn't done.

"Please forgive me. It isn't prejudice, or at least I hope not, it's just ignorance. You are very welcome here. We owe you our lives. I'm not going to forget that." Geraint smiled genuinely at her.

Rani knew he was sincere, and she wanted to stay and talk to the elf she'd seen that fateful night just over a week ago, but she was still unsure.

"She doesn't like me." The allusion to Francesca was obvious.

He sighed. "I'm sorry, but I suppose she's just not used to you either. She lives among the same kind of people I do. And she's, ah, well, she's a little vain about her own looks. But I know Francesca. When she's had time to think it through, she won't forget what she owes you."

"Doesn't mean she'll like me any better," Rani mumbled, hands in her lap, the remnants of the enormous sandwich left untouched on the table.

"Please," Geraint said almost pleadingly. "It's something like the way you had trouble with the controls in the kitchen, right? It didn't mean you were dumb because you couldn't figure them out right away. It just meant you aren't used to this kind of place. Well, it's the same with us—we're not used to you and your ways. Doesn't mean we don't like you just because we need a little time to get used to you." He wasn't entirely sure what he was saying, and he wasn't sure why she seemed to need their approval, but when the words came out they seemed to reassure her a little.

"I've seen him before." She pointed to the elf, who was groggily trying to sit up on the sofa. He looked to be losing the struggle.

"Yes?" He was casual, looking at Serrin more than listening to her. He assumed Serrin had done a little wandering around the Smoke before they had met, and perhaps she'd seen him somewhere on his jaunts.

Rani was about to explain when Francesca ambled into the kitchen. The Indian girl fell silent again, feeling awkward.

The woman almost seemed to ignore Rani, poured herself some coffee and rubbed her eyes. "God, I'm wiped out. What time is it?"

"Eleven-fifteen," Geraint told her. "Looks as if Serrin is trying to wake up, too. Let's get a coffee relay going and talk this all out."

* * *

Two pots of coffee later, they had all begun to perk up a little. Serrin still felt light-headed and unsteady when he tried to stand, which Geraint warned him was how he would feel most of the day. Francesca was more worried about Geraint's leg.

"Well, tomorrow I think I may have to ask you to drive me to a friendly contact of mine in Oxford. Get this dealt with." The wound was clean, bandaged, but even after a local shot, his whole leg throbbed with pain and stiffness.

Rani spoke up. "Why were you in my patch last night? You're strangers, but you must have known it wasn't safe.

The Harry Hooks or the other gangs, they'd have ripped you apart if they'd been around. You were lucky." Her directness caught the others off guard. They looked at each other for a second or two. How much could they trust her?

"Ah, well, Rani." Geraint began uncertainly. "We were . . . we were trying to prevent a murder."

"Why should you want to do that? They happen every day. Was it someone important?" She was very curious.

There was a long silence. "Rani, please don't be offended, but we aren't really sure how much we should tell you. We may be dealing with a string of related murders, and we haven't yet had a chance to talk about last night among ourselves. There may be another murder soon and we'll have to figure out what we can do. We're still not sure who we can talk to. . . ." Geraint's voice tapered off into an attempted apology for not trusting her enough to tell her more, but she was unabashed.

"Can I tell you about me? Trusting me might be easier if you know what I was doing."

"Sure. Fire away," Serrin said. If nothing else, it would give them time to think while she spoke.

Rani began by explaining the need to revenge the deaths in her family, the bungled sucker run in which several had been killed, and why her brother wasn't helping much. She didn't give any details, and was rather awkwardly beginning to explain her Undercity exploits.

"This bungled run," Serrin broke in. "When was it?" Something she'd said had his mind fretting.

In her urgency to explain, to prove herself trustworthy, Rani had forgotten all about the elf. She smiled in delight as she played her trump card. "You know already. After all, you were there too."

"*What?*"

"I saw you. Imran and I were running from troopers and a huge fire thing—"

"Fire elemental, yes." Serrin looked confused.

"Fire thing, it was coming after us. I saw you, and then it disappeared. We managed to get to our car and get away. The others weren't so lucky."

The girl was sitting forward on the edge of the armchair. Her gaze was fixed directly on the elf and her shoulders were hunched forward, the power of her ork muscles very apparent.

Of course, Geraint realized. Strength; here she is. He addressed himself to the mage.

"Serrin, do you remember that I said someone else was going to be a part of this?"

The elf struggled to remember. So much had happened to him since Geraint had foretold the struggle to come. But then, as if a storm-gray cloud had lifted from him, he perked up, and smiled. Yes, he remembered.

Rani, though, looked confused, not understanding Geraint's inference.

"Rani, I don't know how much of what I'm going to tell you now will make sense. We're still trying to sort it all ourselves. But it seems to me an amazing coincidence that Serrin's magic saved your skin last week and then you rescued us last night. I suppose in some sense that makes us quits."

She smiled sadly. That was what Smeng had said, and she had lost him. She didn't want to lose the excitement of being with these people, such different people in this different world.

"But I still feel we owe you an explanation," Geraint went on, "as far as we've actually got one. You've told us enough about yourself. Now it's our turn."

* * *

As the conversation unfolded, they began to realize that two different strands of events had been affecting their lives.

On the one hand, there were the murders, the living Ripper in the here and now of London, 2054. Geraint thought this affected only the three of them, so he kept his explanations short, deliberately eliminating any details of the brutal, gory scenes he and Francesca had witnessed. When he got to the fourth name, though, Rani's expression changed. Before, she'd been simply attentive. At the mention of Catherine Eddowes, she grew upset and then angry.

"I knew her, a little. She used to come into Beigel's Bake in the mornings, always had coffee and two cheese bagels. When I was little my dad used to tell me not to go near her because she was a bad woman. Because of what he said I was afraid of her, but when I got old enough to go down to the markets with my brother sometimes she used to buy me coffee and a treat. She didn't change after I, um, after I changed, you know? She was kind to me. Plenty of people weren't.'' Rani shifted uncomfortably in her chair, reliving some painful memories of late childhood.

"I saw her only a few weeks ago. She'd been knocked about, had a bad black eye and a bruise covering half her forearm. She looked miserable, and for the first time I could see she was getting old. Now some bastard's cut her up.'' She held her head in her hands for a few moments, then sat upright and reasserted her presence and strength. "I want to help find out who's doing this. I live in the East End. I know the patch and the people. I could help you.''

"You probably can, Rani,'' Geraint replied. "I hope so. But in the meantime, we still have to figure out what we're going to do next.''

Then they talked of the other business, less straightforward, difficult to comprehend. In some way, they had all been drawn into set-ups of one kind or another. Serrin couldn't figure out what had been going on with his employment, Francesca had blundered into something vicious in the Matrix, and Rani had been part of the most obvious set-up job of all. They had chased their tails thinking about this one before, and they still couldn't work out what, if anything, had been behind each of their misfortunes. But when Rani began talking about the man Pershinkin for the second time, the crucial detail she had omitted first time around gave them something extra.

"So the fat man with the jewel in the tooth and his thin accomplice disappeared into the limo and—''

"What? Say that again.'' Serrin couldn't believe what he had just heard her say. He grabbed the table for support and leaned forward toward her.

Rani was not sure what she was supposed to reiterate. "Two of them, the fat one and the thin one, they got—''

"No, no!'' he snapped impatiently. "What did you say about the fat guy?''

"Well, um, he was losing his hair. . . . and he had a jewel in his tooth. Sorry, that's all I was told."

"I don't suppose you got to hear which one?"

"Which what?"

It was becoming a comedy of errors, Serrin shouting, Rani confused, Geraint and Francesca totally bewildered. Finally, though, they heard her say that the fat man had a jewel fixed in a front tooth.

Serrin sat back with an expression as black as thunder. "Frag me with a baseball bat. That's fragging Smith!"

Geraint looked pained. "Please, Serrin, you're not in Seattle now, and there are ladies present. Watch your language."

The elf wasn't bothered about his language. Now he was suspicious as hell. "Smith. Smith and Jones, right. You know, the men who hired me? Smith was a fat guy, balding, chiphead, and he had a small ruby set in his right front tooth. Couldn't miss the damn thing."

Excited, Rani confirmed him. "Yes! Yes! Smeng, the ork who told me about them. He said these men were users—the fat man shook a lot, he said."

Serrin was nodding. "Didn't he, though? Well, my friends, this *is* getting interesting."

"So the same people hired Rani for a fake decoy run and—" Francesca said, trying to get a handle on the situation.

"More than that. Geraint, do you remember, I told you that security was actually looking right at them when they popped up? I bet you a thousand sterling to a brass button that Smith and Jones tipped off Fuchi. Maybe they were Fuchi."

"No, no, wait." Francesca stopped him from getting carried away. "How about this? Smith and Jones, we think, hired Rani and her family for a sucker run. They also hired you, but they didn't hire you to hit this guy—what's his name, Kuranita?"

Serrin nodded, his excitement diminished. "Yes, that's a real problem. They didn't actually hire us to do that." The connection seemed to be failing. Francesca reestablished it.

"No, but they did change your instructions. They specifically told you to attend the Cambridge seminar in the

Crescent Hotel. Maybe they knew you would see Kuranita, or at least hoped you would. Then they hoped you'd try to make a hit on him. Rani and her people were a decoy for you. They hoped you'd get a shot.''

Serrin and Geraint looked across at each other.

"I think she's got something," the Welshman said with a frown, trying not to contemplate what it meant.

"But they would only expect me to do that if they knew my past pretty well. I didn't exactly broadcast what I found out about him," Serrin replied thoughtfully.

"Still, someone might have noticed your inquiries. A really good corp, for one. Then you'd become an unpaid hitman.''

They pondered that for a while, until Geraint hit upon some objections to this explanation. "Two difficulties, although one isn't insoluble. First, they couldn't have been certain that Serrin would definitely see Kuranita.''

"They'd have had contingencies for that, surely. They'd have fed him the information somehow," Francesca said.

"Yes, I know. Which is why I say this problem isn't insoluble." Geraint paused for a moment to give what he was about to say an extra emphasis.

"Unfortunately, it doesn't make sense. We're suggesting that an unknown corp spends a fair bit to track down a fullish past history on Serrin, then lays a trap based on his maybe seeing Kuranita, and then maybe taking a shot at him, with a hired decoy to make sure the shot gets fired from an unexpected place. Right?''

"That sounds like it," Serrin agreed.

"So, with all this money and time and effort, and too many maybes, why the hell don't they just spend the same money and get some real assassins in? Let's face it, we're hardly expert hitmen, are we?''

That silenced them all for a while. It seemed an impossible confusion. Geraint, though, decided to do something while the others pursued their own thoughts.

"I think there's one thing I can work on right now. We've had murders on November the eighth, fifteenth, and twenty-second. Okay, so the first half of the double event was on the twenty-first, but it still looks to me as if the twenty-ninth is a fair bet for number five—if there's going to be a number five. And I really do think that there will. So excuse me while I begin to track down Mary Kelly. I'm afraid that we're going to come up with a fair few Mary Kellys. So I'll make a start.'' He walked to the cyberdeck.

Geraint sat absorbed in his frame programming as the others checked for any relevant reports on the trid news. Newstext had an item on mage warfare in the East End, two killed, but nothing on Catherine Eddowes. Serrin and Francesca were puzzled by that.

''They wouldn't get baggies involved if there was any chance of keeping it quiet,'' Rani explained. ''The pimps there handle any trouble themselves. They'd have barricaded the front doors and turned all the lights out as soon as they heard sirens. Customers wouldn't like getting ID'd by the baggies either. They'd have cleared it all up themselves. Probably even sold her corpse to the meatmen.''

Serrin didn't want to know any details about the meatmen. He remembered the trolls and their trays from the night before. ''We can hardly go back and interrogate the orks about what they've seen,'' he said. ''Not after what I did to them. On the other hand, maybe Rani could . . .''

They sat staring at the screen as Geraint hunched over his desk. The first fall of snow was dropping on those parts of London not covered by the ragged remnants of the disastrous city dome, destroyed by a corrosive years ago. On the street it turned swiftly into gray- and brown-slicked filth, but against the penthouse windows the soft flakes hung for a second, almost white, before they melted. Serrin went to turn the central heating up a notch or two. He was shivering again.

*   *   *

Sunday, November 22, 2054. Noon. London. They're going to try very hard to find Mary Kelly. They'll find a whole bunch of them, but there's only one who matters.

The monster's head is beginning to fill with that Mary Kelly. He sees her picture, watches the hologram, begins to understand that she is a shield for the woman he hates and fears. Why, these are her clothes! He lifts the linen and cotton in his hands and wads them up in his balled fists. They have her scent on them, cheap floral perfume, and her woman's smell. He watches the holograms dance; she is a skilled whore herself. The mania begins to burn in his brain, and his hands shred the clothing as the moans and groans fill his head. He is swiftly restrained, but the anger and hatred rage within him, his fear and terror.

The smiling man in the suit watches the vidscan.

Four down, one to go.

23

Plans were beginning to form as dusk fell. They had decided from the outset not to contact the Metropolitan Police; their own role in the events surrounding Catherine Eddowes' slaying made that impossible. Geraint needed time to analyze data on the fifty-four Mary Kellys he'd discovered in the capital. The programs wouldn't take longer than seconds to run. It was the programming that was going to take time. Before then, he would have to deal with his troublesome leg, and that meant a trip out of town.

There was another reason for that, too. Francesca had come up with the link to the British-based corporation, Transys Neuronet. It was into TN's London system that she had pursued the bizarre, murderous persona that had nearly killed her, and though she didn't want to meet the thing again she certainly wanted to find out more about it. Furthermore, Transys was the only corp with a facility of any size and importance in Cambridge that Serrin had *not* been paid to check out. They hadn't much more than suspicion, but it was enough to try some determined system invasion. Geraint and Francesca planned to deck into TN's London system for a start.

"They may have a file on any of us, and if they do, it would be damn good to read it. Maybe they hired you, Serrin, and you, Rani, for the Fuchi attack. Why they didn't get decent assassins in, I don't know. Neither do

I know what it was Francesca followed into their system. But I know enough to feel that it's got to be worth a look. It's going to be very dangerous, so one decker may not be enough.'' Geraint paused for a moment's thought.

"Francesca and I need to get out of town to penetrate their system," he continued. "But first we have to get in and analyze the structure, just have a look round, find where the personnel files are, the surveillance files, what they may have. You can bet your boots they'll have trace and report IC to check where we come from. Rani, that means that if we enter their Matrix system, they have ways of finding out who we are.''

He did his best to explain matters to the ork, who wasn't following any of this too easily. In all her life the most complicated deal she'd ever seen was a decker using puny Italian demitech to rip off a Radio Shack. And when she'd asked that decker questions, he'd told her to mind her own business. In words of very few syllables.

"So, we have to disguise our decks. That means a little reconfiguring. The Lord Protector's Office makes sure licensed decks have very identifiable internal ID codes. We have to change that by fooling around a little with the licenses, like putting fake plates on a car.'' Rani grinned, getting the gist immediately. "And we have to operate somewhere else. Oxford should do it. I can get my leg fixed there, too, no questions asked. Old college friend of mine.''

"Which college?" Francesca asked perkily.

"Didn't I ever tell you?'' he asked. She shook her head. "Peterhouse. My father's doing, I'm afraid.''

"I seem to remember someone telling me the only way to get in there was if you were Catholic, or gay, or both.''

He frowned at her. "Not these days. Hell, they've even started admitting women.''

Francesca let the jibe pass. Oxford and Cambridge were said to be great centers of learning, but the twenty-first century hadn't changed them much. She knew that from dating their chinless upper-class graduates.

"That may get us somewhere. At the same time, I can put the Kellys through the mincer.'' Geraint winced the moment the words were out, regretting the unfortunate expression. "If we get someone who looks plausible, we can give the police an anonymous tip.

"Something else. Serrin, your visa runs out at the end of the month, doesn't it?"

"Yep, 'fraid so."

"Wouldn't you like to go abroad for a couple of days? Look, I know it sounds weird, but here's the form. You want an extension to the visa, it takes six months for the Aliens section to get around to even considering it. No chance.

"However, due to one of those weird technicalities that makes British justice the envy of the world, the powers that be will automatically add the days to your visa if you come up with an amazingly good excuse for disappearing abroad, like an illness or death in your family. Maximum of seven extra days. If you make it three, it'll give us the extra time we need. After all, we're expecting another killing on the thirtieth. If you have to fly off on that date it's going to make anything we plan very difficult. Could you get a friend over the Pond to fax notification of a serious family illness to you?"

Serrin was bewildered, but he wasn't the first person to be startled by the intricacies of British immigration law. "Yeah, sure. For how long?"

"Say you go tomorrow, get back Wednesday evening? That'll give us enough time out of town and a margin of time after the thirtieth."

Suddenly, an old recollection stirred at the back of Serrin's mind. He'd thought at once of Manhattan, visiting acquaintances, maybe testing the waters for work when this madcap chase was over. He thought of a contact, then he remembered something about a crazy. He began to mentally plan a schedule for his time.

"Yeah, it's a good idea. I might even be able to get something for us over there. There are always people I can talk to." His face betrayed concentration as he chewed at his lower lip.

"Now, Rani." The noble turned to face her, realizing she'd been left out of things so far. "We'd like to find these men, Smith and Jones, the scum who've made fools out of Serrin here and cost your people their lives." He was aware that he had no leads on them, and that troubled him, but he needed to appeal to a common ground. "Can you do some things for us? I can give you money and some equipment if you need it."

"I've got a gun, and ammunition for it, and a good knife. I'm fast, I got wired reflexes. My brother paid for them, to protect me." She was almost asserting her self-esteem; he smiled and made it clear her competence wasn't in doubt. "Wish I had the Predator, though. Shouldn't have sold it, really." Then she had a flash of insight.

"Hey! You know, they gave my brother a gun, a Predator Mark II, and some armor-piercing ammo. Hard to get, a weapon like that. I sold it to Mohinder—he's street samurai. Hard man. Needed to get information from him. That was before I met the Undercity people and everything."

Serrin's eyes glinted. "Predator Mark II? They're not easy to get outside of corporate contacts. They all have IDs in the barrel mechanism and in internal nanochips. At least, the export models do."

Francesca leaped on that. "You mean, if we could get the thing back we might be able to check the ID? Find out where it comes from?"

"Maybe." Serrin was unsure. "Good corporate guys might be able to dosh the ID around, erase the barrel marker, maybe alter the chip. But if we had it in our hands, we could check it out, at the very least."

"Reckon you could buy it back, Rani?" Geraint's voice was urgent. "I can give you money."

She balked at the thought of trying to persuade Mohinder to part with the weapon so soon after selling it to him. But, what the heck, if she offered him double what she'd sold it for, it would be a big profit in a short time. "I can try. He gave me fifteen hundred for it, though. He'd want a lot more to part with it again."

"Not a problem. As I said, I can give you what you need. Also, maybe you could check out the area where Catherine Eddowes was killed. Look for anything, anything at all. Maybe pay some kids to do some sniffing around. Can you do that?" Her nod said money could buy that, too.

"And, last thing. In a week's time we might be in a

place where a fifth murder's going to be committed. We might need every advantage we can get. That means, for a start, muscle and firepower. Last night we ran up against an automatic weapon and a combat mage. Next time, who knows? What about those brothers you've mentioned? Can you get street samurai, spies, people we can trust? Again, I can pay. We're going to need them.''

Rani realized that getting the gun back from Mohinder could be easier than she thought. Especially if these people only wanted to check the ID. Pay Mohinder enough and he can have half of Spitalfields out on the street. She nodded determinedly at Geraint.

"Great. And for us, I'll set wheels in motion. Weapons and armor are no problem. Surveillance equipment I can rustle up. Slap patches are a little low, so I think I might renew my acquaintance with Edward while I'm in Oxford.''

He pronounced the name with a curious emphasis, deliberately inviting Francesca's puzzled query.

"Oh, Edward? Professor of biochemistry and neurobiotics. Boy genius. He's the man I talk to when I have a need for high-grade drugs.''

* * *

The Indian girl had never seen so much money in one place in her life. She was astonished that he trusted her with it, and said so.

"Rani, you had family die, yes?'' Geraint asked. They were in the hallway, out of earshot of the others.

She shrugged, as if to say, what's it to you?

"When I was a kid, my best friend died. I was an only child, and at the time I had no other friends, really. He was a nobleman's son, too. When he was twelve, he transformed. It happened while we were out fishing, him starting to scream and me thinking he was having a fit. I ran for help and when I got back with his father, he was beginning to change his form. I'd only seen pictures of orks, but I knew what was happening to him. We were out on the edge of the Dragon Lands, that's in Wales, west beyond London, Rani.'' He could see that she had no idea where the hell Wales was.

"A long way off. When we got him back to his father's castle, his home, he was almost fully changed. Less than six hours. I gather that's pretty fast, yes?" She nodded, remembering how long her own agonies had been.

"But he was okay, right? He was weak, and only barely conscious, but he was alive. They sent me home in a car and told me not to tell anyone what I'd seen. I never saw Daffyd again. They told me he was dead, but I always knew they'd killed him. Can't have orks in the family if you're a noble, you see.

"I didn't tell anyone. Well, I told my father and he told me to keep quiet about it or I'd be disinherited. Daffyd's family murdered him because of his change. For a long, long time I felt guilty for not telling anyone. Maybe the only reason I have everything I've got now is because I didn't speak up and tell the truth. Maybe, if we can help each other now, it will make up a little for what I didn't do back then. So, Rani, it's only money. What does that matter?"

She was defenseless against his brutal honesty. Somehow she knew that not even those other people in there, the elf mage and the smart American woman, they didn't know about what he'd just told her, and maybe never would. She was an Indian ork, lowest of the low, but here was a member of the British nobility almost begging her to be part of a forgiveness. She felt very strange indeed, thrilled but overawed.

"The car will be here. And here's my number," Geraint said, pushing a card into her hand. "Come back Wednesday evening. After seven, yes?" She nodded urgently. "Get them to bring you. I'll pay for it. They'll bring you. You can do that?"

Rani nodded again. She didn't know what she was getting into, but she knew she wanted to come back here again.

He closed the door behind her. Through the security camera he watched her walk down the hall. Serrin came up behind him, putting a hand on the nobleman's shoulder as he turned from the doorway.

"One thing, Geraint. I want to know who's responsible for sending me on a wild goose chase, nearly getting killed myself. Rani's got family to avenge. Fran's had a real bad time and I think those nightmares may start again. But what about you? Why are you investing all this money and effort?''

Geraint sighed and gave a wan smile. He might have said, because it's real, and I'm tired of nobles I despise, business deals marinated in cynicism, and too much easy living. But one confession was enough for one day. He decided to be facetious instead.

"Oh well, it's something to pass the time, I suppose." Evading Serrin's questioning expression he walked off to talk decking with Francesca.

Serrin booked the suborbital to New Jersey's Newark International. All he could get for the next day was a standby at six-fifteen, unless he was prepared to pay for Deluxe Ripoff Class. At least he had the long-duration residence permit, allowing him a few precious days in Manhattan each year. What the hell, he had a week left on it and Christmas was only a month away. Looking at the huddled pair eagerly discussing the technicalities of decking, he realized that for the first time in a while he had people in his life for whom he might actually want to buy Christmas presents.

24

The neon half-blinded the mage. It was two-thirty in Newark International, and all he wanted to do was get through Customs and Immigration and park himself in one of the coffin hotels around the airport complex. He needed to catch up on the sleep that rising at five in London had cost him.

"It's a kind of permanent temporary pass," he explained to the suspicious, gun-toting official who looked like he was missing his sleep as much as Serrin was. It didn't make him any too helpful. When the wanted to be, New York's finest could wield the old quadruplicate red-tape routine as well as any Brit. The guy had already scanned the pass twice and come up with approvals on the security checks, yet he still glared at the pass as if it were a rabid dog. Entry into Manhattan required one of at least a dozen different kinds of passes and permits. Serrin's was the kind the guard was least familiar with.

"Allows me twenty days' stay every year; there's a week left on it. Hey, I'm only going to be here two days." Serrin was beginning to lose his patience, though he knew he shouldn't. With an effort he calmed himself and was rewarded by finally being waved on his way. Having caught sight of a couple of Hispanics in the queue, the official suddenly seemed more eager to harass them than to detain the elf any longer. Serrin trudged wearily off into the monstrous concrete complex beyond.

As planned he went straight to bed to catch up on his sleep, but awoke feeling slightly worse, if anything. He had slept too long, nearly twelve hours altogether, albeit interrupted by the flight. His head felt thick and he shivered in the cold morning air. He was a bit light-headed from hunger, but Serrin didn't think he could face real food.

Well, he thought, I'm in Manhattan now. I don't have to eat real food if I don't want to. I can live off garbage like everyone else.

Getting through the access points and more checks with his pass, he then took a bus into the city, where he decided to stay at the opulent Hyatt. After the second shave of the day and a steaming hot shower, he began to feel more alive. While dressing he surveyed the contents of his suitcase, feeling some distaste at how tacky and ridiculous were the souvenirs he'd bought in the Heathrow shops. Smiling to himself, he picked up the druid doll dressed in a white robe with the blue insignia and carrying a gilt sickle. The only druid he'd ever seen didn't look much like this. She was for real.

He jump-started his body with a pot of coffee as thick and syrupy as he could get it in the hotel coffee shop, stuffed down a couple of bagels, and then did what he always did when he first hit Manhattan. He had some people to see, maybe a contact or two to check, but something else always came first.

Grand Central wasn't far from the Hyatt, one of the reasons he'd decided to stay there. Serrin had been barely

three feet tall the first time he'd sat amazed by the sheer
scale of the station, its endless spaces and swirling masses
of people. Something of that awe remained, always ready
to strike a chord in his emotions whenever he was there.
He sat down with a magazine and another cup of coffee
and just took in the scene.

There were suits, kids, fresh-faced youngsters from
out of town come to find out how long their wide-eyed
looks would last before the poison of the city destroyed
their dreams, a sprinkling of metahumans and Hispanics
mostly doomed to suffer indifference or outright hatred,
a couple of guys who were obviously racing to find out
which they could destroy first, their bodies with steroids
or their minds with essence—the usual panoply of folks.

It's been cleaned up, though, Serrin thought. Security
didn't take long to pounce on any wino or other wretched
soul with terminal despair who might still think he could
drift in here. Those for whom it all had become too much,
who would burst into tears, begging any stranger, "Got
a cigarette, oh, any damned brand," just to have something to say. Just to get a glance, a touch of a hand, a
chance word or two in reply.

Serrin hated Manhattan. Its soul was deader than any
city he'd ever known. It swept away its poor and hopeless, its disabled, handicapped, troubled people, its
blacks and Hispanics and Puerto Ricans into decayed
sumps of suburbs—if they were lucky. What about the
street shamans? he wondered. How could any totem
breathe life into a soul when the very essence of a place
was dead?

"A dollar for your thoughts." Looking over his shoulder at the woman who sat down beside him, he suddenly
broke into a broad, beaming smile.

"Barbara! What are you doing here?"

"I could ask you the same! I'm just finishing college."

"Hey, that's great!" He was genuinely delighted.
"And how is delightful Lafayette? And Judy?"

They had met in Serrin's birthplace, not long after he'd
been shot up bad in the Renraku business. For some reason, he'd decided to use a little of the money they'd paid
him to spend a few weeks in the place of his birth. Not
that he had any roots there; his parents had traveled too

widely and too often for that. It was just to see what the city was like.

"Oh, I moved from there not long after you went to Japan. Figured I couldn't stick around much longer. I met a good man in Syracuse, he looked after us real well. John and I were together five years, but after he got sick with cancer, I drifted around awhile before ending up here. Put myself through college. And Judy's doing real well. She sells some of her stuff in the Village. She's a really bright kid."

He was glad. Trying to get by as an unmarried mother with a half-caste child in Louisiana hadn't exactly been a bed of roses for her. The child had been clever, sensitive, vulnerable, and he had feared for her. Serrin hadn't been in much shape, physically or emotionally, to do much about it himself, but it was good to know Barbara had picked up the pieces.

He studied her as she sipped her coffee. Passing through her thirties had been good for her; she wasn't so painfully thin, the lines around her eyes and mouth looked like they came from laughter and smiles. At least, in fair measure. Her hands were the same as ever, great knuckled fingers more like a man's, well-suited to sculpting the pots, ceramics, and oil burners, all the little things she made.

"What about you?" She wanted his news, but he hardly knew where to begin.

"Well, I'm only in town a couple of days, but I always like to come here whenever I am," Serrin replied, gesturing around at the huge station. "Just like to sit and watch it all. Watch the world go by. I guess I've been doing that a lot, one way or another. Hey, I got something for Judy!" He reached into his pocket and brought out the little toy. He pressed the small control panel in its back and placed it on the ground.

It was a Beefeater, a toy soldier with black pants and a red jacket and the impossibly large, furry black hat of a real Tower of London guard. The toy jerked into life and began to march, high-stepping it along the floor while holding its ceremonial rifle over one shoulder, swinging the other arm along to the marching rhythm. After a dozen steps it swiveled in a perfect U-turn and marched all the way back again. Barbara burst into delighted laughter.

"Oh, that's priceless!" She picked up the hand-sized doll, giggling with pleasure. "Thank you. Jude'll love it."

"It has an optional feature. You can get it to sing *God Save the King* while it marches if you like. I guess Judy's too old for this stuff now, but it's genuine Olde England." He chuckled.

She grinned, clasped the toy and hugged him. "Got time for some conversation during your stay?"

"You betcha. Hey, you want to show me Judy's stuff?"

* * *

Most of the day had gone by the time they finally said their goodbyes, Serrin taking Barbara's number and promising to call. Judy had remembered him. She was fifteen now, painting cards and murals and even getting a commission for a couple of posters. She had her mind set on compgraphics and Matrix sculpting. She still had the same gifts and sensitivity Serrin remembered, but now she was worldly for a kid of fifteen. Somehow that disappointed him. It was as if Manhattan was already beginning to take her over. He hoped she would hang on to what she'd started out with. The disappointment made the goodbyes less difficult, though.

Thus it was after dark when he started making the calls from his hotel room. It was a long shot, and he had called Seattle, Philly, DeeCee, and half of California Free State by the time he roused Kerman.

The bleary-eyed face stared unhappily at him through the static. "You fraggin' pointy-eared SOB. What you wake me up for?"

"Wake you up? Are you kidding, it's five-fifty."

"Yeah, well it's only three-fifty here, you scumsucker. When did I ever get out of bed before five?"

Serrin grinned. "You missed a beautiful day. Here I am in the Rotten Apple, walking in the winter sunshine and admiring the poseurs and wannabees in the Village. And you just sleep your life away."

"Look, chummer, life starts at midnight. Spare me the
drek. What you want?"

"Kerman, I'm involved in something in Britain. Old
London town. Funny thing is, it rings a bell and I can't
place the connection. I had to get out of the Smoke for
a couple of days so I flew over to see if I could check
out a few things with some people. I didn't think of you
till the last moment, or I'd have come back just to see
your sweet smiling face in the flesh."

The man was yawning affectedly. "Yeah, yeah. What
do you want?"

"All right. What do you know about Jack the Ripper?"

Kerman was not amused. "What the frag should I
know? You're the one who's been in London. Didn't he
go a-merrily butchering over there a century or two ago?"

"Yeah. But it may be that someone's getting into some
very accurate re-creations. That's NFP, so keep it to
yourself for now, please. Funny thing is, I seem to remember some crazy Jack stories in Seattle two, three
years ago. I was only in and out of the city then, didn't
pay any attention, and missed the full version. You remember anything?"

Kerman rubbed his chin, avoiding the unpleasant spot
on it, and screwed up his face in concentration. "Yeah.
Got it. There was some madman serial killer around.
Nothing special in that, but I remember mutterings about
the Ripper. Story wasn't around long. There was a big
Mitsuhama/yakuza story that broke right after, if I re-
member right, and that pretty much took over. Look, can
I get back to you on this?"

There was a whining "Hun-ee, come back to bed"
from somewhere behind and to the right of Kerman,
clearly audible over the phone.

Serrin grinned at Kerman's wince of discomfort.
"Sure. But make it this evening. I haven't got long."

* * *

It was three and a half hours before the return call came.
Serrin was eager for it; tracking down the Manhattanites
on his list had yielded little more than some desultory

invitations for drinks and the usual litany of polite "how ya doin's."

"Pointy!" Shaven, bathed, and resplendent in a dinner jacket and bow tie, Kerman beamed at the elf over the telecom screen.

"Hi, there, chummer. Hey, you're looking good."

"Naturally. But no time to waste. Here's how it pans out. Know about Global Technologies?"

Serrin recalled the small skillsoft and simsense corporation in Seattle, but couldn't remember any details. "Yeah. What of it?"

"They're the only lead I could get. Rumor associates them with the Ripper thing, but who knows if that's just a little bit of street slander. If I believed ten percent of what I hear about Renraku, I'd have to believe they were run by baby-eating Satanists who drink nuclear waste for breakfast and piss it out in the water supply. But my source is good on this. For a little something, I could give you a name and address in Manhattan that might get you further. Can't make any cast-iron promises, but it's interesting."

Serrin groaned audibly. His credsticks were running low uncomfortably fast. "Hey, you sleazeball, what about that Atlantean business? Hell, you ripped me off big-time on that one. If we'd split it, we'd have made fifty thou apiece for that fake drek we sold 'em." The Atlantean Foundation probably still believed the "artifacts" were genuine. That scam had been a real joy.

"That's business, ear-features. Five thousand gets you a name and something to check out."

"What? You fraggin' vampire," Serrin squealed, and they got down to some serious haggling. By the time Serrin had cleared a credit transfer of three thousand, he got a name he should have remembered himself, and cursed his corrupted-disk memory.

It was past ten at night, but SoHo only really came alive around then anyway. He had never seen Her Ladyship, and the telecom got a pre-recorded from a troll who looked more machine than meat. Okay, what the hell, Serrin decided, the security rating's good. Let's give it a whirl.

25

Serrin found the place easily enough. The house looked like an architectural impossibility; narrow, seeming to lean a little on one side, its five stories looking like almost too many to stand upright. The ground-level floor was a florist's shop, but it was closed now. Didn't find too many fresh flowers in Manhattan these days. There wasn't much to indicate what went on in the floors above the shop. Serrin rang the ancient intercom by the side door. It buzzed into life.

"I'm here to see the Lady. Name's Serrin Shamandar. She doesn't know me personally, but I need some information and I can pay."

There was a long pause. "Just a minute," the distorted voice boomed. "I'll have to confer with Her Ladyship. She don't take many visitors."

The link clicked into silence.

It was ten minutes before the voice was back again.

"You may come in to discuss the possibility of an appointment, but be warned that we take serious precautions against any form of magical assensing or spell use. Any action suggesting active spell use will be construed as a hostile act and you will be dealt with accordingly."

Well, of course I know there are countermeasures, Serrin thought. Think I didn't try assensing already? He was about to voice a curt rejoinder when he realized he'd been listening to a pre-recorded message. The door swung open before him, and an array of cameras tracked his long and painful passage up the five flights to the top floor. Spirits, hadn't these people ever heard of elevators?

When he finally dragged himself up the last set, he was breathing hard. Before him was a heavy steel door; he touched the detector panel to trigger it into scanning mode and stood back. Within seconds, the door opened. Most serious runners in Manhattan knew of Her Ladyship, but few had ever seen her or set foot inside her domain. She never left this place, existing as an information sponge, soaking up everything and anything. Even top corporations came to her when desperate for a lead from her deranged mind. Her information was so vast and so valuable that no one dared harm her, for fear of what tidbit she might have stored away only to be revealed if she were killed. The place was said to be the weirdest cybercomplex outside of the really heavy corps. In Manhattan that had to be very weird indeed. Serrin was braced for the expected, but not to encounter anything like the troll.

Looking upward from the metahuman's enormous feet, which had to be at least size eighteen, Serrin didn't register anything too odd about the steel-reinforced boots or the heavy olive-green pants. It was only when the troll took a step forward that he heard the hiss of the hydraulics. Across his chest, looking for all the world like a row of military medals, a row of sensor panels and lights blinked a neon mantra.

Heaven only knows what's chipped into his autonomics and respiratory systems, the elf thought. The troll's arms looked as if they were made of liquid chrome, shiny and unbelievably flexible metal. It was a touch of absurdity that he had one fleshy hand and one of the same flowing metal.

But it was the metahuman's head that really startled Serrin. It wasn't the cybereyes that were strange, but the filamentous network of fine, intermeshed metallic strands and what looked like monofilament optical fibers radiating out from them and flowing around the troll's facial musculature and forehead. His mouth gleamed with metallic lips and his voice betrayed the existence of a fine voxsynth at work in his throat. The troll had no external ears, but concentric rings of carbonized steel and monofilament that suggested a level of chipping and cyberware that Serrin would never have dreamed existed.

All that was enough to startle the mage. What really scared him, though, was the gun in the metal hand. It looked like a taser, but was linked to a pack bulging with chiptech on the troll's hip. Once those hooks were in you, who knew what they might do to your body? Serrin was so scared he began to put his hands up.

"Just a standard precaution," the troll said in a husky voice. "If you have any weapons, please hand them over now." Serrin gave up his little hold-out, apologizing that he felt safer on the streets with it. The troll ignored him as he took the pistol away. It was a comical moment, a thin elf handing over a puny little hold-out to this gigantic troll arrayed in armor and defenses, but Serrin wouldn't see the humor in it for many hours.

"Please sit down."

Now that he had edged through the doorway Serrin could see a little more of his surroundings. The decor was a bizarre clash: oil paintings behind security glass—a Rembrandt, if he wasn't mistaken—and more anonymous Dutch landscape works, a cabinet stuffed with elven crystal work from Tir Tairngire, and a Ming vase on a pedestal. Truth be told Serrin didn't know whether it was a Ming vase or not. He'd tagged it that mentally because Ming was the only dynasty name he could remember. Interspersed with the art were surveillance vidcameras, sensor systems, sprinkler systems, and a pair of wall-mounted autofire crossbow pistols that swiveled to face his chest as he sat down in the room's only chair. None of it made him feel very safe and secure.

The troll wasn't saying anything. Serrin began to ask timidly about an appointment, but the troll put a hand up for silence and the elf obeyed. Time ticked by and Serrin began to squirm in his chair as an eyeball-shaped sensor swiveled smoothly out from the wall beside him on a long, flexible metal arm. It scanned his face and thorax and, despite his best leg-crossing efforts, showed a definite interest in the more private areas of his anatomy. It scanned down, then up at his face, before finally returning to its wall socket.

When nearly half an hour had elapsed, Serrin began to get up, very slowly, and addressed the troll, who had remained motionless the whole time.

"Um, it's getting very late and I really would be very grateful if—"

What happened next was utterly bizarre and confusing. The troll broke into an operatic aria, then got up, twirled

a pirouette, and spread his hands wide, grinning with
steel teeth. He flicked out a disturbingly large tongue and
pointed to the other door in the room, which opened
slowly. Serrin had no idea what the troll had been singing, but he thought it might have been Italian. Flipping
his tongue back like a frog, the troll clicked his teeth
when Serrin entered the darkened corridor beyond. This
is good luck, he thought. They say she rarely agrees to
see anyone, let alone lets them walk right in out of the
blue like this.

Coming to four doors, he decided to knock at the one
with a red light glowing above it. At his touch it swung
motionlessly open, inviting him into Her Ladyship's
sanctum. With a mixture of hope and trepidation, Serrin
walked through.

*   *   *

He gawked at the sight that greeted him on the other side
of that door. Wall to wall, endless viewscreens, trideo,
telecom, and satellite links, all downloading everything
imaginable. He saw commodity price lists, air travel
schedules and passenger IDs, corporate accountancy reports, a chat show with a nude female psychiatrist as
host, a wildlife documentary, a cartoon squirrel smash-
ing a cartoon dog on the head with a baseball bat, a film
on Inuit society, slo-mo replays of football touchdowns,
gruesome surgical operations in living color, shots from
space satellites, everything in humanity's full range of
information flow. He had to shield his eyes from the constant flicker and glare.

The other elf was alone in the room, a ghastly figure
in the center of a great netted web of fiber cabling,
pumps, pipes, feeders, and inputs of every imaginable
type. A multi-stranded feeder cable pumped an endless
supply of data into the middle of her forebrain. Meanwhile, fluids pulsed and pumped into myriad tubes, pipes,
and filters of an I/O port complex into her hindbrain. The
elf herself had only the vestiges of a body, shrunken and
virtually embalmed alive. Her muscles were wasted, fingers hopelessly knotted and shriveled, but the eyes were
alive, and they were real eyes. It was perhaps the only

part of Her Ladyship that betrayed any functioning vestiges of her original body.

Very slowly she lowered her eyelids, with their inch-long, heavily-mascaraed eyelashes, and the flow of information through the forebrain diminished just slightly. The screens in the room dimmed.

"Ah, one of my people. An elf come to see me." The voice was utterly flat and devoid of expression, so Serrin couldn't tell if it was mockery or an honest expression of welcome. The face gave nothing away because it did not move; the vocal synthesizer was in sensurround, so it couldn't be localized either. Between Her Ladyship's lifeless arms appeared a little green and blue hologram of Serrin, dancing a jerky, mannequin-like round. Spiraling about the figure was a four-colored double helix, his DNA code, and to one side of that a continuously scrolling update on his vital signs and physical parameters. To the other side the output of a quarkspin tomographic brain scan throbbed in vivid color. He felt very frightened now, completely in the power of this obscene creature. The DNA helix was seriously spooky; someone could use that for ritual sorcery against him. He wondered where she'd gotten the code.

"Serrin Shamandar. This will substantially add to my file on you, little elf mage." The hint of a smile seemed to play around those white lips. The eyes were unblinking, taking in his discomfort and enjoying it.

"You have a file on me?"

"I have a file, a pretty little file, on everything and everyone. We are all information. Look at you sparkle and shine."

The DNA helix sparked into a fireworks display of crackling energy. It had a peculiar beauty, with the blue and silver and radiant purple of the bondings. "Oh, you are a pretty one. Look at your Power," the voice said, as a stretch of the scrolling helix began to glow golden before his face. The figure before him began a slow, smooth, almost peristaltic rocking movement, to and fro. The eyes never left him.

"It is an honor, your Ladyship," Serrin said, beginning to feel that this creature was quite insane. He needed to tread very carefully.

"So you come to learn something, my pretty little
mage. Why come to me? Not many do. Or many do and
few are allowed within. Your scans amused me. You are
damaged, pretty one. I like that."

"I was given your name by a friend. He told me you
might know something about a corporation I am trying
to investigate."

The screens blazed into life again. "You come for
something as boring as that? A runner come for information on a corporation? You waste my time. I only dispense information, just a tiny little tidbit perhaps, if I am
asked something interesting. Look!"

The sensory overload was impossible. The screens ran
riot with fast strobing, and the sensurround amplification
assaulted his mind. He was forced to his knees with the
pain of it, desperately trying to shut it out. The avalanche
subsided.

"It is interesting, Lady. Please hear me," he managed
to force out between clamped teeth. He began to explain,
telling her of the murders and the coincidences between
lives drawn apart for many years. She liked that, and the
voxsynth purred at him.

"Oh yes, oh yes, pretty one. Your friend was right.
Years ago, little one, BTL chips. Jack the Ripper, oh yes,
I so enjoyed that."

Better-than-life chips; someone had chipped up a version of the Ripper. Of course.

"But they didn't get it right, no, no." She created a
dancing hologram of her images, putting his imagery behind her where it continued to dance in silence. "Pretty
little whores, slash! slash! slash! Hee hee hee hee . . ."
The voice trailed into psychotic laughter, and then, most
horribly, into a song, a child's lullaby.

Serrin didn't think even the word madness was ade-
quate here. Not even schizophrenic could have fulfilled
the task of describing this one. He didn't even want to
look at the hologram, with its mutilated bodies in lace
and chiffon.

"So he's back, he's back! Jack's back! Hee hee hee!"
Again the high-pitched laughter reverberated around him.
"Well, little one, is it pretty now? Have they done it well
this time?"

Serrin nodded grimly. He wanted desperately to find out who had made a Ripper BTL chip, and he decided to risk her ire by asking outright.

"Oh, well," she sounded fussy and mildly irritated. "Little people with big money in the shadows. Global Technologies made the chips. Little people used them. Hollywood people. Never know what they're doing, Hollywood people, always so self-absorbed, never attend to details. We're not stylish and we're not pretty," she half-sang in mockery.

For a split-second the withered form seemed to rock just a little further forward toward him. She gazed right though him with eyes the frequency of lasers. "Hollywood Simsense, little mage," she said simply. "Corporate warfare. But who was behind the Hollywood people? Who's bigger than all of the Global world?"

"Go now." The voice changed very abruptly. "I am bored now. I think I shall have a soiree." Abruptly the screens as one flipped channels to show an endless array of celebrities. Politicians, artists, simsense stars, religious leaders, writers, sportsmen and women; Serrin recognized almost all of them. Almost all were silent, but to Serrin's amazement the Russian president began reciting an old and especially obscene joke about a New York mayor and an actress. He looked quizzically at the expressionless elf.

"They shall say what it pleases me to have them say. You will go now. But, oh, before you go, pretty one, you shall dance for us all. We shall applaud most politely. Dance for us."

It felt as if he were being pushed and pulled throughout his body, and he lost all voluntary control. His mind went spinning across the possibilities: low-wave EM, quarkspin modulators, subliminals, photic driving . . . they couldn't do this to him. But he had no choice as he skipped and swayed across the nightmarish room.

Afterward, though, Serrin did not remember anything of that nightmare dance. When the troll dumped him outside the door, he had a mechanism and some names. Better-than-life chips. Global Technologies confirmed for him, and Hollywood Simsense. It was far more than he'd hoped for. Walking dazedly along the sidewalk, he real-

ized that he hadn't had to part with a single nuyen, and
he smiled. He even skipped a few steps, until his leg hurt
him and he settled for an ordinary walking pace.

Thank you, Lady.

It was after midnight when he got back to the Hyatt.
He just couldn't resist the home-grown taste of some
snacks from the Stuffer Shack on the way back. Real
synthetics. He had eaten too much good food back at
Geraint's in London and it had begun to upset his system.

There was only one message on the telecom. It was
one of his New York contacts getting back to him for a
meet at eight the following evening. Of all the people he
knew in this town, this was the one he'd hoped would
come through. If anyone could tell him who might be the
brains behind the BTL scene at Global Technologies and
Hollywood Simsense, it was Shrapenter.

Serrin made his return flight arrangements. What he'd
gotten was more than enough to take back with him.

26

Heading northeast, the Saab purred along the expressway.
It had been a good morning. While waiting for Francesca
to finish her software shopping and bag-packing, Geraint
happened on a glitch in currency transactions across the
major banking centers of three continents that netted him
four thousand nuyen for about fifty seconds' work. He'd
learned that he could usually put one over on the Swiss
satellite banking system by keeping his eyes on the South
American and smaller Far Eastern markets. Even a gain
no bigger than small change gave him that glorious feeling
of bucking the system.

He'd decided not to bring his Tarot deck with him. No
matter that he was a magical adept, the Oxford location
was daunting. Being a center of English druidic magic,
certain spots might be heavy with magical interference.
Background count, the scholars termed it—places where
powerful residues of emotion or repeated magical oper-

ations made most magical, or adept, work difficult. It was said that the druids knew how to harness the background count for their own purposes. Geraint deliberately avoided contact with most English druids, and wasn't about to do anything that might alert them to his presence and activities now. Most of all, though, he never knew what the Tarot might reveal, so how could he guess what someone magically snooping might detect?

Still waiting for Francesca, he'd meditated awhile at his desk, then shuffled the cards and spread them out for a reading. So engrossed and absorbed was he in his thoughts that he didn't hear her open the front door with the magkey, only becoming aware of her presence when she crept up on him.

"Do I cross your palm with silver?" she said with a grin. She got a frosty glare in return.

"Don't trivialize this, Fran. You know me well enough that I wouldn't use it if it didn't work."

That chastened her. Eager to placate him, she asked Geraint to tell her what the spread meant, pointing to the first card with its explosion of yellow-red plumes surrounding a crackling pillar of energy.

"Ace of Wands. I wanted to know where we stood at this point. It doesn't tell me very much. An ace is a starting point, wands are intuition, energies in a general sense. So the card says energies are unleashed, we are all expending energy in different directions. It's vague, but it fits; we're all in different places, and we're all chasing leads, not sure where we may end up."

"Who's the old geezer?" she asked, moving on to the next card. Geraint turned to her with the hint of reproach in his expression.

"The Hermit. Me, actually. I asked where *I* was in all this. He's rather solitary, introspective, detached from the world. I think he's telling me to back my own judgment and not depend too much on others. If we get into an argument, my dear, I'm afraid you're going to lose."

She laughed and tossed back her hair. "You're just saying that to intimidate me so I'll give you your own way. I know you."

"No, really. See," he said. "This is you." The card showed a green-cloaked figure seated atop a stone ped-

estal, waving a sword in the air in a defensive posture. "Princess of Swords. The card shows you're going to be very practical and down-to-earth, but you just might be missing something. Smart but not creative, the Princess. No offense meant, Fran. Bear with me." He moved to the fourth card lying on the desk.

"I asked how our part of things would go. I asked for two cards: one to show the most important problem we might face, a second to show the final outcome. In this context the Five of Coins says that something is unsettling and worrying. The foundations of what we're doing aren't quite right somehow. But the Six of Swords, that looks good. It says that our little trip will be successful, but we may encounter some unforeseen difficulty. It's all right, though," he continued, catching her look of uncertainty.

"I've just asked about Serrin. The Magician, of course. He's doing what he's good at. We've got no problems there. Since it's his own personal symbol in the deck, it also tells me this reading is working. I was just about to ask about Rani, how she's going to figure in what we decide to do next." He turned the next card face-up.

Francesca whistled in admiration. "Oh, that's a fabulous design." A great red and silver rod stood strong against an azure background, with a flaring sun at one end and a crescent moon encompassing a darker blue sphere at the other. Crisscrossed behind the rod stood eight arrows, red-shafted, with silver fletching and silver crescent moons for arrowheads.

Geraint nodded gravely. "Nine of Wands. Strength. Looks like she won't let us down."

"Strength? Isn't there another card called that? The one with the woman and the lion? Haven't I seen that?"

"Yes, but this card was given the same title by the original designer of the deck. Different meaning, too. Maybe he ran a bit short on names after a while. Nine of Wands says final success, a moment of glory." He felt a little uncertain. The card was a good omen, pure and simple; it was powerful, radiant, victorious.

Geraint felt a sudden twinge in the left side of his brain, urging him to see something else in that card, something related to him. His own response to it. He flipped up a final card.

The Hanged Man.

Ankh and wise serpent at his feet, the dancing, swaying figure was head-down on the card, an inversion that caught Francesca unawares, as it did most people the first time.

"Hmm. Looks like I have something to learn about her. I won't find out by making any effort, either. It'll come in its own good time." He drew the cards back into the deck, shuffled it once, then swathed the deck in its black silk.

"Time to go, Francesca. You ready?"

*   *   *

Geraint remembered the Hanged Man as they checked in at the Imperial, or rather the Hanged Man nagged at his own mind. He put it out of his consciousness as he limped to the elevator, Francesca taking the magkeys and walking imperiously before the baggage-trundling porter. No sooner had they arrived at their suite and shut the door than Geraint was tapping a number into the telecom.

"Russell? Great. We're here now." On the way here he'd used the car's portacom to make a provisional appointment. "When can you fit me in?"

The cheerful, fresh-faced man on the screen looked down at something on his desk and waved nonchalantly. "Let me see. Old chum, helped us with the Mitsuyama grants two years back, never comes up to a college feast with me, might have run off with my wife if I hadn't been such an attentive husband . . . oh, how about next March?"

"Russell, what do you mean? Amanda's far too good for me. And the last college feast I came to gave me food poisoning." Francesca glanced at Geraint joking at the face on the screen and decided to take a shower.

"Oh yes, nice little strain of salmonella that one. Half of Oxford was down with it for a week or two. Well, Geraint, how about seven this evening? Come round to the Radcliffe, old boy. I should still be sober then."

By the time Francesca had showered and changed,

Geraint had his evening arranged. Seven o'clock at Oxford's famous infirmary, nine o'clock at the research laboratories of the Biotechnology Department complex. That took care of both Geraint's leg and the pharmacological helpers he needed, and in that order. Francesca began setting up the Fuchi decks, attending to the most important part of their business.

They worked in virtual silence for half an hour, reconfiguring the decks to change the ID chips installed by the Lord Protector's officials. It wasn't desperately difficult, but it was delicate. Any mistake would set off an alert that would scream its way to the local Administrative Bureau, calling officialdom down on their heads in a matter of minutes. With all that done, they demolished the first pot of coffee.

The next pot was sunk as they planned the general tactics of their hit on Transys Neuronet's London system. Francesca had the SAN number, so they knew where to get in. In broad terms they also knew what they wanted to get at. The problem was figuring out how to deal with what stood in their way. After half an hour of discussion they'd sketched out a plan.

This was Francesca's specialty, so she took the reins. "We'll use evasion mode as long as possible and your smartframe to deal with any IC. If the system alerts, our reaction depends on where we are at the time. If we're into the storage systems, you switch to bod mode and fight like hell while I go to sensor mode and get as much as I can. I'll use a dumbframe to handle it if I can program it fast enough. That way we'll have a few extra seconds if we have to fight when we get close to what we're looking for. Stay together at all times and put the emphasis on system analysis while we're getting into the damn thing. I think my sleaze program is powerful enough to get us through the system's access and barrier defenses. We'll just have to use scrambling IC for the decrypt programs. Right?"

Francesca was in her element now, scribbling down notes at a furious pace, already high on the anticipation of the run. She had a look of utter determination on her face, a look that made Geraint ruefully reflect that he didn't see how his careful, cautious Hermit would be able to hold off her Princess of Swords if they had to change plans halfway through.

"Sounds good. The question now is, what do we want to do about our Matrix personas?"

It was a crucial question. They knew the Transys Neuronet system would have a sculptured Matrix, an individually designed set of icons and representations that would try to force its own reality on to them. Unfamiliarity with it would make their mental operations slower, unable to react in a split-second if necessary. That obviously gave their enemies within the system—both the IC and the corporate deckers—just the slightest edge in combat. What to do about it was the question.

"I don't think I want to use your filter, Geraint. I know it'll help, but I won't be able to get used to it fast enough. Trying to operate with an unfamiliar filter against a sculptured system would only double my handicap."

Geraint had a reality filter, which was what deckers laughingly called the powerful representational program. It allowed him to see any Matrix constructs through his own selected set of images, which consisted of knights, warriors, warhorses, the Wild Hunt, and the whole panoply of Welsh and Celtic heritage. The filter balanced some of the disadvantage of being in an unfamiliar system, giving *him* an edge that the sculptured system might not be able to overcome. It would be an interesting struggle between his filter system and the power of Transys Neuronet's system sculpture. Francesca, however, wouldn't have the same advantage.

"Well, we've got to have representations of each other within our own systems when we travel together, and we need ones that aren't out of sync with the Transys sculpture. That way, it's all smooth, and neither of us has a major disadvantage." He sighed. "Trouble is, even if that works I'll be seeing them differently from the way you do. You'll see black IC in their terms, probably, and I'll see it as a hostile knight or chimera or some such, if I'm lucky." Then something dawned on him.

"But hold on, Fran! You've been in their system, haven't you? What did it look like?"

She shook her head in reply. "I hardly saw anything apart from that thing. If I suffered any disorientation from being in a sculptured system, it was part of the general trauma. Hell, Geraint, make damn sure you protect me with your attacks and whatever you've got in that frame of yours. Are you sure we don't want my frame on attacking options?'' It was something they'd been arguing about in the car most of the journey. Francesca was understandably paranoid about meeting the murderous persona that had nearly killed her once before. Geraint disagreed with her.

''We've got enough punch. Anyway, the flatlining jackout options you've been working on really should handle that. The only way we could get total insurance now would be to wait for Serrin to get back or have a friend of mine here sit around to pull the jacks if we get toasted. Besides, I really don't want to risk anyone else knowing what we're up to, and it's too long to wait for Serrin. Or Rani. First sight of anything that looks like that thing of yours and we're out of there. Promise.''

They went over every last detail again and again, reviewing the possibilities for IC constructs opposing them, how to deal with hostile deckers, contingency arrangements, and finally they ran some simulations. Though it wasn't the real thing, it made them both sweat and showed that they could work together well enough. By the fourth run they'd gotten good. They jacked out together, full of smiles.

''Geraint, you really creamed that IC construct.''

''The Black Knight? What did he have up his sleeve?''

''I'll check. It's a quasi-random IC construct with, let's see, Red-4 node, killer, blaster, jammer. Oh, well, maybe if he'd had an acid program instead of a jammer, you wouldn't have fared so well.''

''My dear lady, I didn't even need the frame.'' Full tilt with a simple attack program had gone right through the Black Knight's shield and chain mail, skewering him. All Geraint needed was to ride over him to keep the IC suppressed.

They had one final, tricky decision to make. Should they head straight into the system to carry out their mission, or should they go in for an initial snoop first? The advantage of the former was that it preserved for them the element of surprise. The advantage of the latter strategy was that they'd know better what they were getting into, and would be able to configure their own personas accordingly.

Francesca was arguing hard for the second option. "Look, we both go in using evasion mode. Heavy on masking and deception. We just see what the sculpture is like. We don't go near IC, we invade almost nothing past the SAN. We analyze and download and look over it at our leisure. Our chances of triggering even a passive alert are minimal if we use the right operational modes." This made good sense and Geraint had to agree with her.

"We've done all we can," Francesca said. Tonight at eleven, then. "Absolutely no alcohol at all until afterward. Not even a sherry with your old college friends." She looked almost stern. "Come on, we've got an hour before I have to wheel you over to the infirmary. I'm hungry. We may not be able to drink, but we can sure get something decent to eat."

* * *

"Exactly what's in those vials?" She was suspicious, looking askance at Geraint as he gleefully pored over the small case of multicolored liquids and oily emulsions. He grinned conspiratorially. He was feeling great.

At the Radcliffe, he'd gotten deep laser treatment and growth stimulators, differentiation regulators, modulated hemostatic complexes, and a dozen other agents Francesca couldn't even remember the acronyms for, let alone their full names. All that mattered was that within an hour Geraint was walking on a leg that would be as good as new by the next morning, save for a need to avoid straining it for a few days. He had gladly downloaded charitable contributions to the hospital's welfare and research funds—all tax-deductible, of course.

Francesca had politely declined the lecherous attentions of Geraint's medical friend, whose hands had shown as much interest in her as in his patient. Somehow, in the guise of showing her what he was doing, the octopus seemed to get an arm around her waist or fingers fluttering along her arms. She had hidden her distaste and allowed her accumulated irritation to explode in anger at a smug and healthy-looking Geraint in the parking garage. He suffered the onslaught quietly and then they'd moved on to the research labs. It was the fruits of that visit he was reviewing with such glee now. Another charitable donation had been in order, of course, but that was the price one had to pay for cutting-edge experimental materials that got mysteriously used up in the cause of science. That, and another expensive dinner at Oxford's best restaurant for Professor Michaels the following evening.

"Oh, this is lovely, Fran. Perfect dopamine agent here, colloidal, and the slow gamma-aminobutyric acid modulators in the complex keep you from crashing afterward. Slight effect in the nigro-striatal ascending fibers, keep it to the D4 large neurons, but the major hit is in the ascending mesocortical, in the DA3 subcomplex, the vesicular . . ." He stopped in mid-flow as he saw she wasn't taking in a single word.

"Sorry, Fran. It's not jargon, really. What this stuff will do is the question. Some of it makes you smart, some of it makes you fast, some of it makes you alert, some of it keeps fatigue at bay, and if you keep the doses sensible, you won't have to pay for it later. I want to use the association cortex agents myself during our decking runs. It'll definitely boost my awareness of threat and the ability to respond to it. For those poor souls like you who can't whack this stuff straight into your brain," he said, fingering the cannula implant on his neck, "the options are more limited. Mind you, Edward did give me a peripheral that is absolutely guaranteed to enhance your enjoyment of, er, certain acts. He's been supplying me with that for years. Not that I ever, not with, I mean . . ."

"Not when you were bedding me?" She was half-amused and half-livid. Who wanted to think that desire and its consummation were the playthings of some academic pharmacologist?

"No." He smiled, ever so slightly apologetic. "Anyway, he gave it to me because I think he fancied you some."

She scowled; two lechers in one day. That was annoying.

"Forget it. We've got work to do. I need ten minutes."

He applied the yellow vial to the cannula, triple-clicked the security seals, and felt the steely rush begin to spread over his scalp. The slight edge of paranoia that followed was normal, and soon he could feel the sounds and colors and vividness of it all. She was already setting up the decks.

"All right, Viviane." He grinned at her lack of understanding. "In my reality, I'm Taliesin, and you're going to be Viviane. That way we both look like harmless folks in simple robes. We should be able to get away with that, no matter what form the system sculpture takes.

"Away to London!" he called delightedly, and they were off.

27

They woke in the separate bedrooms of their suite at much the same time, then glumly shared coffee and what claimed to be a continental breakfast from room service. In the end it had all been rather anticlimactic.

"Well, at least we know the details of the system sculpture system now," Geraint summed up. "I must admit that it surprised me. Very pastoral, nothing organic. Nothing that we encountered, that is. We got away fine as the wizard-bard and the priestess." He was trying to be optimistic, constructive.

"Yeah, but there was nothing in there. Nothing in the personnel files on Smith, Jones, Kuranita, Jack the Ripper, and none of us either. I'd say we drew a total blank, Geraint. Useless."

"Try to look on the bright side," he insisted. "You didn't get attacked by some homicidal maniac, and we got by their decker so sweet. He didn't even realize we were outsiders. So much for the defenses of the most dangerous cybercorp in the UK. Not so much as an active alert triggered."

"But where did it get us? We learned nothing." Francesca poked at the limp croissants. After all their bright hopes and expectations for the run, it had been as bad as this breakfast.

"Well, apart from what I've mentioned, we did learn something. And we should have seen it before! Look, remember the cards I showed you yesterday? Five of Coins. We're not getting the foundations right. But the outcome was the Six of Swords. Remember, we have to face some new element of the problem and deal with it."

"Okay, I buy that. It does fit. But how did we get the foundations wrong? Our plan worked. No one picked us up."

"But we didn't get what we wanted. We didn't find any sign that the database systems had any answers. That's how the foundations of the enterprise were flawed. We were in the wrong system."

She misunderstood him. "You mean we should have checked Fuchi instead because Transys is after them? But—"

"No, I don't mean that at all. It was the wrong Transys system. We're going to have to hit the central system. That's where the information will be. In the Edinburgh system, where their HQ is. If we're on to something big, that's the obvious place. We'll have to deck into the Edinburgh system."

Francesca was becoming frustrated. "But we don't even know the number of the SAN!"

"You telling me you can't hack that one? Fran, you're the best decker I know."

"Yeah, well, I suppose I can find it." Honest flattery usually worked for Geraint. "You sure about this?"

"Got a better idea?"

She looked deflated. The buzz, the thrill of yesterday was gone from her. Then she inhaled deeply, dumped the cold croissants into the trash, poured a third cup of coffee, and thumped her fist on the mahogany table.

"Okay, let's do it," she said. "If what I've heard about the TN system is true, it's going to be damn tricky. We've just got to hope that its sculpture is configured like the one we saw last night."

"Why would it be any different?" Geraint asked. "They're bound to be the same. It would be too expen-

sive any other way." They smiled at each other, clinking
their coffee cups together.

"Well, Master Bard, shall we sally forth and astound
the varlets with our wizardry once more?" She was play-
ful, her spirits improving.

"Viviane, my dear, I believe the hour of enchantments
is finally upon us." He spoke with mock grandeur. "And
I believe we should disguise our sorcerous purpose by
downloading a few tidbits elsewhere in the system, perchance from their research files, should we happen by a
helpless little SPU that reveals them to us. That way we
can also make a few sovereigns into the bargain. Cover
our tracks too. Verily, milady, let us sally forth anon."

They got up and went toward the gleaming cyberdecks
across the room.

"Ten minutes," Geraint said, then reached for the
cannula once more. "Mustn't forget the shot."

* * *

They stood outside the system access point, ready for the
verdant scene that would greet them upon entry. Geraint-
Taliesin stood with an almost fierce expression, a gri-
moire at his belt, a magical stave in his hand, and a harp
at his back. Meanwhile Viviane of Avalon readied herself
to pass through the mystic barrier and head for the SPU
beyond. It worried Geraint only slightly that the Viviane
icon was clad in a décolleté dress today. At the very
least it might distract any Black Knights who came their
way.

Viviane's mystic utterances dispelled the barrier program and then they were striding through into the green
pastures, sending animals scurrying hither and thither
across the sward. Data routing, obviously. Just what
would be expected.

Geraint saw the quicksand of the tar baby trap immediately, but he didn't need to alert Francesca-Viviane to
it. She skirted the edges of the pitfall and he followed,
treading in her steps exactly.

Heading through the peaceful woodland, the couple
came to another clearing; the first of the subprocessors.
Hiding behind the trees was a small gnome who skipped

out and asked them the simplest riddle imaginable. What pathetic access defense, Francesca thought. Kindly, she gave the gnome the answer, and the inquisitive pixies lurking behind the older oaks stayed put on their toad-stools as the gnome nodded his acceptance. A trace and report program, she guessed. It looked feeble, but that was part of the skill of it. It disarmed a decker's defenses to be faced with something that looked so pathetic. She was all too aware that the system had imposed its reality upon her perceptions, making it harder for her to give the right responses swiftly enough. Well, then, she just might have to leave some of the answering to Geraint-Taliesin. As they strolled across the clearing, she muttered to alert him. He nodded his head sagely, and they strode out hand in hand.

At the far edge of the clearing the fuachan leaped out at them when they tried to open the gate to the path beyond. One-legged, one-eyed, and one-handed, the mus-cular protogiants hefted their heavy clubs and posed their riddle.

"How may I circle the world in but a second?" The demand for the key, the password, was instant and direct. Access with a heavy edge. The clubs were poised to fall on their necks.

Francesca-Viviane produced a simple blank vellum scroll from the folds of her robe, and a quill appeared in her hand. Swiftly she drew a globe, held it up for the fuachan to see, then drew a line arcing from one side of the sphere to the other. "Like this!" she said and flour-ished the solution triumphantly.

The fuachan was about to make another challenge, but the playing of Geraint-Taliesin's harp soothed it. With that, the other fuachan laid down their clubs and ignored the visitors, hovering by the gate as the cloaked pair went on their way. Francesca breathed a sigh of relief and moved beyond the gate into a summery meadow ringed with trees. It was like a crossroads offering many possi-ble paths. Francesca-Viviane looked around with her witch-eyes to see where the paths might lead.

Her analyzing soon told her that there was only one datastore, an arcane library in the far distance, and a path to yet one more woodland. The rest of the paths led to

simple villages with working artisans, a sure sign they
were mere slave nodes in the system. The library needed
checking. She pointed it out to Geraint-Taliesin, who followed her soft footfalls across the grass.

The librarian stood with the card index clutched to his
chest, a mundane collection of works arrayed on the
shelves behind him. She reassured him that she had no
desire to steal or even borrow any of his tomes, analyzing
the contents of the index as he concealed it. There was
nothing here but records of system operations, and only
minor-league stuff at that. The books weren't even gilt-
edged. The librarian was suitably deceived and didn't
ring his handbell to summon assistance.

Geraint-Taliesin stood and observed the scene in silence, magical stave readied in case a phantom or sorcerous beast should unexpectedly swoop down upon
them. They left and made for the path to the woodlands
once again.

"That would have been too easy," she said to the old
man beside her. "Got to be further in than this."

The woodland path was a nasty decoy. Only at the last
moment did she see the slough begin to open up beneath
her feet, leaping back from the treacherous terrain just
in time.

Tar pit, yuk! Francesca thought. This is getting confusing. I can hang on to the Welsh-Celtic imagery Geraint's generating, but this is a definite whiff of old-time
John Bunyan. Whoever sculpted this sure has a sense of
humor. In the distance, she thought she heard an owl
hoot. Passive alert. Geraint would have heard it, too.
They'd missed something, obviously. If it was white IC,
no sweat. If it was gray, they were in trouble now. There
didn't seem to be anywhere to go, either.

Shifting into sensor mode, she saw the concealed path-
way between the trees when she returned to the woodland
they'd just left. As Francesca-Viviane urged the bard forward, his eyes flashed everywhere, looking for menace
underfoot and in the trees. Her intuition told her they
were getting hot now. She was right.

Passing below the tree canopy they beheld a castle—
moat, drawbridge, pennant-topped towers, and all. The

central processor. This had to be it. There was nowhere else to go.

As they approached the drawbridge, it lowered and a mighty knight mounted on his thunderous charger appeared before them. In the swirl of his flowing robes, it was almost impossible to perceive his outlines clearly. He wasn't armored, but the robes shimmered with magic. Geraint was becoming worried about the defenses the IC construct might have. It would be hard to focus an attack on him. Francesca-Viviane did her best to hide her form as her companion spoke his words of invocation. She didn't think it was time yet to join the fray.

In his own perception, Geraint called the great Eagles of the Hunt, and drew down the wise serpent to the battlements. The snake's honeyed words seemed to calm and transfix the guards preparing their weapons up on the castle's battlements. Suppressed an alert there, he thought. Now give me strength to defeat this mother. This is serious killer IC.

The Eagles tore at the helm, shoulders, and body of the knight, ripped with their talons at his destrier, and drew blood. As a ripple of intense blue light flowed from Taliesin's staff, the knight raised his shield to deflect it. The bolt flashed incandescent when it struck, reducing the shield to a corroded lump of burning wood. The knight dropped it and galloped forward, lance raised, tip pointed at the offending magician.

Do I attack or defend? Geraint thought wildly. My serpent-frame is occupying the other guards, so I can't use it to defend me. I live or die here. Another spell to destroy this errant knight.

The feathery flames hovered over the knight, then engulfed him as he rode on to the solid ground beyond the drawbridge. The mount faltered and the knight fell from his mount, but no call was heard atop the battlements. The serpent calmed the hearts of those within the castle.

"Haste, Taliesin!" Viviane called. They rushed across the drawbridge and entered the citadel. Within were many towers, a keep, servants scurrying to and fro. Two squires stared at them uncertainly; gray IC not yet activated, they guessed. The enchantress scanned the scene, her inquisitive frame-servants exploring the citadel.

Taliesin grew increasingly anxious, wondering how long the confusion would last. As Viviane pointed in triumph to the far limestone tower, a trumpet sounded. Great, he thought, they're on to us. Work swiftly, my priestess. We have little time left to us now.

Reaching the tower just as the dogs were unleashed in the courtyard, they slammed the door behind them with a crash. She led him up the winding stone staircase to the warded and barred door. He battered on it with his staff, screaming spells to dispel the magical protections. On the stairs, they heard footfalls and clanking sounds. Stuff the organic feel of this, Geraint's panicking brain was howling, these guys have got swords.

The door opened without a sound, revealing a room in which myriad crystals floated airily, each containing a picture and a scroll. Viviane's summoned sprites began to examine and read, analyzing the contents. They had taken one crystal and were looking for another when Nimue appeared before the bard's eyes.

She smiled seductively at him, her hands alive with gelatinous webs. Her voice soothed him, called to him, her eyes alive with poignant sorcery. She cast aside her flimsy gown and stood naked before him. Adrenaline raced through his body at the sight of her, his arousal distracting him from his true task. Feebly he murmured an incantation of self-defense as the succubus advanced on him. Her body brushed his, and he delighted in that instant. He could feel her breasts pressing against his body as she began to wind her arms around him.

"Tell me, darling, where you have been, that I may come with you and rest within your bower and be your lover. I want to bring you my delights," she purred, curling a leg around his, rubbing against him with her thigh, her tongue seeking his. He almost fainted.

"Sorcery! Succubus!"

Taliesin heard the words in time and turned to see Francesca's form changed into the fury of Morgan le Fay, in an instant changing again into the black bird. He changed his own form into that of a dove and escaped up into the airy cupola of the tower, circling around with the raven beside him. As one they dived beyond the furious, clutching maiden and sped down and out of the tower.

They were hunted. They heard the wolves and erinyes, the seductive words of sirens, but they closed their ears and flew through the air, over the rustling trees, across meadows stalked by enraged guardians, past gates and barriers. As they flew toward the exit to the Isles of the Sun, a great fireball came down at them from the heavens, and as they soared over the sea the fire engulfed them in a flash that blinded and disorientated them.

Yet they soared still, and their forms came home at last to the blessed place. Viviane carried with her a tattered bag, the spoils of their foray into the deadly castle. They landed amid a copse that smelled sweetly of lavender and apple blossom, and instantly jacked out.

* * *

"Oh, God." Geraint was coming down from the boosters. It seemed that Edward had significantly downplayed the drugs' after-effects. It was four in the afternoon and he had dark circles under his eyes. He looked like he hadn't slept for a week.

Francesca, however, was jubilant, alive with energy. "I'm not going to download this lot yet. Maybe that lady you were so engrossed in got a fix on your magical home, my Welsh bard. We've got to get out of here fast. They may have our location."

Geraint was seeing double, but they managed to pack their decks, adding them to their other luggage, and made it to the parking garage in seven minutes flat. He couldn't even remember the faked identity he'd used to check in.

"Mr. and Mrs. John Smith," Francesca sniggered as they closed the car doors. "The traditional alias of furtive lovers. But we've been doing something much better than that."

It was true, he reflected. Francesca really got off on a good run in a way that she never really did with sex. *Perhaps I should have used Edward's little recipe after all,* he thought idly.

"Now, you've got dinner tonight. I think we should drive to, um, let's see." She ruffled the pages of the road atlas. "Banbury. That's nice. Those old fakes, the druids, have got some stuff out there. Let's check in there. Ooh, and they've got a Holiday Inn too. Aren't we lucky?" She turned the key in the ignition and pulled away quickly.

"We did it. We got something. The spirits were smiling. Tonight I can get a good look-see at what Transys has got on us."

28

Arriving home, Rani had to face far stronger opposition than she had expected. Imran had shaken Sanjay out of his usual self-indulgence, and the two brothers confronted her angrily. She'd been out all night, she'd been seen on the street, talking to strange men—none of which she should be doing if she had any respect for the family's good name. She belonged in the safety of the home. They were worried about her. The streets were not safe. All the old arguments came pouring out. Finally, Imran forbade her to leave the house without his permission for the following week.

"Oh, so you can take care of business? And what have you been doing about our vengeance?" she spat out defiantly.

They argued long and hard, yelling at the tops of their voices until the old people trying to sleep upstairs started hammering on the floor. Even then, they ignored the complaint and just went on arguing.

When they finally sank into sullen silence, having reached no agreement, Rani felt only contempt for her brother. He was trying to compensate for his own inadequacy by belittling her, using every shred of emotional blackmail he could dig up. Anand, their father, would not have wished her to do what she was doing, he said. The family would be ashamed of her, being out all night and up to no good. Such conduct would be shameless from any Indian girl, but from an ork it could destroy any hope of a satisfactory arranged marriage. She had deserted her brothers and failed in her duties in the house. She was a Bad Girl.

When the argument flared again after midnight, Rani was in no mood for further antagonism. She turned on her heel, told Imran to rakk off and die, and stomped up the stairs to her room. When he banged on the door, demanding an apology, she jammed a chair underneath the door handle and merely told him again to rakk off.

In the morning she didn't bother with breakfast, but simply headed straight down the stairs with the bag she'd packed. She had a wad of notes, people to see, and business to conduct. She could eat on the hoof. When she got downstairs Sanjay was waiting for her.

"You heard Imran last night," he said, sorrowful eyes averted, but with his body determinedly barring her way to the front door. "You stay here."

"If you don't get out of my sodding way, I'll kick you so hard you'll never be able to rub any white trash again," she yelled. She advanced upon him. He just managed to avoid her knee striking home, but the kick numbed his leg enough to prevent him from stopping her from scrambling out the door.

Monday morning was freezing fog and a shopping list of missions. Precious hours were spent putting the word out for Mohinder, dispensing small change to get some local street kids to learn what they could by scurrying around Fenchurch Street, and then visiting the first Mary Kelly on her list.

The nobleman had found only four women by that name in Rani's patch, so she figured she could check them out personally. This one lived just off Brick Lane itself—or at least she once had. The squinting, rat-faced landlord told Rani that Mary Kelly didn't live here anymore, and his toothless grin said she'd have to dispense some money to learn anything else.

A handful of notes got her access to Mary Kelly's old room in this rancid dump of a flophouse, but the chamber yielded no sign of its former tenant. A vacant-eyed, anorexic trancer stared unseeingly at Rani from the single rickety chair in the almost lightless shoebox of a room. What she finally learned was that Mary Kelly Number

One had died on the streets a couple of months back, choked on her own vomit most likely. She had been a wino so hopeless that even this landlord had kicked her out onto the streets.

Rani got her first break in the middle of the afternoon, while sipping her coffee at Beigel's Bake. An ork contact who looked at her with the respect money brings told her quietly that the pimps had cleaned up a mess at their place and dumped some unidentified stuff into the river. One of them had bought enough disinfectant to swab down the public baths. Since Rani hadn't told the ork about the murder, she thought it very likely he was telling her the truth. As expected, the pimps had gotten rid of the evidence and virtually no one knew about the cruel midnight slaying. Life was cheap hereabouts, and nobody wanted the baggies knocking at their door. Especially if it was the door to a brothel.

The ork was eager in the way he talked, hoping for a good payoff. She looked at his disintegrating plastic shoes, the trousers with more patches than original cloth, and she remembered having seen him out shivering in the cold in his thin jacket and dirty, discolored vest. She gave him two hundred and fifty and he looked at her like she was some Indian goddess sent down from the heavens.

"This buys silence, right?" Rani said sternly. "Don't tell anyone about it. I've got others on the payroll who'll know who to box if you get so much as a touch of the gators about this. You know what I mean?" He shrank back in fear, pleading his trustworthiness over and over. She looked at him more kindly.

"Okay, Merreck, I'll trust you. Maybe I'll have something else you might be interested in a week or two from now. I'll know where to find you?"

He was pathetically eager, promising anything she could possibly want. Two-fifty was more than he'd see in a month. He shuffled out the door and dreamed of real American jeans. First, though, he'd get some hot food into his grumbling belly. A really fat, juicy burger stuffed full of onions and chemicals. The kids would also be getting their first decent meal in a week, so it wouldn't hurt if they had to wait a bit longer.

Rani realized the power money gave her and for a time she reveled in it. But she kept cool, knowing not to advertise her wealth. The notes were safely stashed in the locked money belt. Anyone who wanted them would have to kill her first.

Next she phoned Mohsin and arranged to visit London Hospital after work the next evening. She was on a roll, and needed to get her hands on some meaty hardware to keep that good feeling going.

Finally back home that night, having capped a fairly successful day by picking up a good lead on where Mohinder might be the next morning, she found a reception committee in all its splendor waiting for her. There was Imran and Sanjay, of course, and a handful of male cousins as well, all gathered in the front room. In the back room she could see the swirl of saris.

Oh, here we go, she thought. The men are going to put me in my place and then the women are going to tell me how good it is to be there. Stuff this!

Anger boiled up inside her as her cousin Dilip began a placatory speech to which she wasn't even listening. She was livid. How *dare* they? I'm growing up and I know what I want. Well, maybe I don't, but I like being on the streets. I like talking to the people in Beigel's, I like putting some money the way of street people who need it and who look at me with real respect. Rakk it all, I'm becoming a samurai, I know I am. I've got rich friends who trust me with their money. And I believe they like me. I remember what that funny-speaking nobleman said when I was leaving. If I was just a nobody, he wouldn't have told me about that. I mean something.

"Rakk off!" she shouted at the men before her. "I've got my own life. I'm not going to be a good little girl. Be like them?" She pointed to the back room. "Tied to the sink and allowed, honored, to pander to every wish of my menfolk when they care to come home? That is, when they aren't rubbing white girls like Sanjay does, or if they aren't spineless slints like my own brother, doing nothing to avenge dead family."

"As for you, Dilip, why don't you tell Kriss there how you cheated him on those chip deals last March? Kriss, those chips weren't worth half what you paid for them, and Dilip and Imran had a really good laugh about that. I wasn't supposed to hear because I was in the kitchen cooking supper like a good little girl. We women can't hear anything in the kitchen, right? They were too steaming to care anyway. So who are you to lecture me? Honor and duty? There isn't one of you who wouldn't kill the other to save sixpence, and you bloody well know it!''

The men were thunderstruck. Kriss looked at Dilip, who tried to avoid his gaze. Her revelation had set the men against each other, while Imran was looking away from everyone in shame. Silence descended on them. She seized the initiative and delivered a parting shot.

''You're pathetic! You make rakking pennies from little deals, and half the time you're swindling each other. Or like my brother, you're stupid enough to let people sell you as fools and dupes, and then have family die because of it. But the world isn't only losers like all of you. I'm eighteen years old. Old enough to get out of here and that's just what I'm gonna do before you make me toss my dinner.'' Rani turned and walked out, not daring to look behind her. When the men finally recovered their wits enough to chase after her, she was already far enough down the road to elude their pursuit.

Of course it was crazy. She knew already that the family would disown her—after they'd tracked her down and made some vain and insulting attempt to bring her back. They'd never succeed. Maybe she had no real skills, nothing she was especially good at, but she had youth and energy and a heart beating fast inside her chest. Tonight, that seemed plenty. The money would rent her a room for the duration. She was on her own now.

*   *   *

Rani finally tracked Mohinder down at Grits the next afternoon. She was edgy now, unhappy about what had happened with her family. Waking from her restless sleep in the cold light of dawn she realized that she might well have burned her bridges. But if she could control her fear, she'd be all right. Maybe it wouldn't show. Just don't be too eager, girl, don't give too much away.

"Like to do business with you, big man," she chirped as she approached his table.

Mohinder's chest puffed a little with pride. He chewed at his burger and eyed her coolly. "More business, huh? Well, what are you in for this time?" He sounded faintly amused.

Rani tried hard not to get riled. "A few things, actually. I know you don't come cheap, Mohinder, not someone with your reputation. So let me say straight off, I can pay you what you're worth." Flatter him, Rani, her common sense was insisting. He looked suitably happy. "First thing, you know that Predator I sold you?"

He gave her an almost friendly look. "No problems, girl. Lovely gun. Thank you for that one." He devoured the last chunk of the soyburger, which to Rani smelled like something had rotted to death inside the bun. Why didn't some slint come up with an artificial scent that wouldn't affect the greasy taste of those things? They could make a fortune.

"I can pay you double the price to get it back." She gazed at him without blinking. Her expression said, I want this and I can pay. I have money. No kidding today.

She saw some respect in the way his cybereyes gazed at her, but he shook his head. "Rani, you can't get Predators over here. I don't know where you got this one, but it's a precious thing. I haven't even sold it. I kept it for myself. I can sell you someting almost as good for your money, and I won't rip you off, but that Predator is too good to let go. Sorry." He slurped a great mouthful of scalding soykaf and almost had to spit it back into the cup.

She had her reply ready for the refusal. "Three times. I'll pay you three times what you gave me for it. That's my final offer." She really didn't want to go that far—it took out too much of her funds—but she knew how much the elf wanted to check out the gun.

"You're persistent, huh?" He smiled at her, not taking offense. "Honestly, Rani, no way. That gun's mine now. Not for sale. Just the sight of it can make people back down, you know? Big people. It gives me a real edge. And money can't buy that. Not the way a Predator II can when you're pointing it into the face of some snakeboy."

She had half-expected as much. She dared not push the request any further, for fear of losing the other things she wanted from him.

"All right, Mohinder, so be it. But I need to get my hands on some good weapons. I mean good, the best. If I can't get the Predator, I want the best pistol I can get by, say, Friday night. Best ammo, too. A crossbow wouldn't go amiss either. Say a couple of each.

"Also, I heard a news report that some baggies lost their stun batons in one of the Squeeze checkpoints south of the river last week. And, well, I would be terribly interested in any that may have found their way down here."

He laughed until he realized she was serious. "Where you getting the money for this, little gopi?" he scowled at her.

"Oh come on, Mohinder! I don't ask you where your dosh comes from, now do I? Hey, tell you what, I've got an even better proposition for you to think about. I'll be in the market for street samurai and willing hands for the weekend. Local work. You're the best, so I talk to you." Boy, was this man a sucker for flattery. She could see him virtually preening. Even his cybereyes seemed to be twinkling with pride.

Then, with some weird intuition, she took a complete leap in the dark. "I've also heard that you might be able to lay your hands on automatic weapons. Heavy duty. As I said, I can pay."

Mohinder grimaced angrily and grabbed the front of her jacket with hands the size of sledgehammers. "You heard what? Who tells you such things?"

She decided to brazen it out. "I'm nobody's little gopi now, Mohinder. I'm eighteen. I can go to jail for refusing to pay my poll tax just like any other adult now. And I've got friends with money, friends who, like me, want your services."

"Show me."

She couldn't refuse the challenge. Carefully unzipping one of her pockets, she showed him the first wad. Five thousand nuyen in notes. It was enough for an automatic weapon, more than enough by far. He whistled through his teeth and let go of her.

"Well, the Uzis are my banker, right? Don't know where you heard it. Don't know how you could have heard about it. If you speak a word, you're corpsemeat."

"Mohinder, I wouldn't be showing you five grand if I wasn't doing real business with you. I wouldn't show that to someone I didn't trust to deliver. And you can take it as proof that there is more where that came from."

He drummed his fingers on the table, pondering. She gave him the final bait.

"The weekend thing, that's for real too. I need as many good street samurai as you can muster. About six, but only people you trust. If you trust them, that's good enough for me. They get a couple of hundred in advance to show goodwill, five hundred each to keep the weekend free, and they'll get the balance on Friday night. Payment for any run required will be negotiated on Saturday. We don't expect trolls with wired reflexes and assault cannons, but these guys should be able to look after themselves. It won't be anything dumb; should be anti-personnel. If you can arrange it for me, you get an extra three hundred up front and a five hundred bonus for getting them all in order for the weekend."

Rani gave him her most winning smile. "Sound good?"

Mohinder stared at her in near-astonishment. "You spamming me, girl?"

"Look, if you go for this I'll give you the advances, two hundred for six guys and five hundred for you, right now. That buys me a group meeting on Friday night, wherever and whenever you feel comfortable. Got it?"

Mohinder recovered his professional manner rapidly. "Give me the money, little sister, and I'll make sure you get some real mean bastards. Meet me Friday night at eleven in the room over Rievenstein's deli. I'll have all the weapons you can pay for, and the meat too."

She slipped him the seventeen hundred under the table. Mohinder grinned as he remembered the intimately physical way he'd made their last transaction, but things were very different now. Now it was Rani who was calling the shots, and they both knew it.

* * *

Two more Mary Kellys turned out to be a complete waste of time. One had long ago gone back to Tir Nan Og. The other was a hopelessly hebephrenic invalid tended by her dejected family.

Rani had paid the tab at Mohsin's and got a bagful of goodies for her hard-haggled nuyen: a couple of medkits and some slap patches. She'd been lucky to get those, and they had cost her dearly. There was no time to get any cyberware. Besides, Geraint hadn't given her the money for that. Her bag was bulging and she was happy except for one problem still lurking on the horizon.

That problem was her family. She'd been ready to make the trip back to Chelsea when she'd spotted two cousins heading determinedly toward her flophouse. Sneaking out via the remains of the fire escape was a real risk, but she'd just made it. Hurriedly, she phoned Geraint and left a message, then scurried off along the streets to look for a safe place. She'd have to get away from the old neighborhood, away from the family determined to drag her back to her old life. Just hide out for tonight, girl. Get over there later. A few hours won't matter.

Rani did not know, could never have dreamed, what the next few hours would bring.

29

Wednesday afternoon was crisp and clear, the watery winter sunshine showing the M4 motorway in all its tawdry gray glory, a succession of roadworks, graffiti-covered overpasses, and potholes. Driving through the latest in a succession of ugly outlying suburban sprawl-zones, Geraint cursed imaginatively but anatomically impossibly. What set him off was another snarl of traffic fifteen miles beyond the outer orbital, a tailback from one of the ubiquitous road repairs that had the highway down to one lane of traffic in either direction. Francesca sat beside him with fingers flying, dumping notes into her laptop.

"An interesting yield, Geraint," she said without looking up. She had not heard his curse. "Serrin's going to positively adore what we got on Kuranita."

Geraint was in a foul mood, hands gripping the steering wheel tightly, staring grimly along the column of slow-moving traffic before him.

"That was the cleanest download," Francesca was saying. "We could have done with more on Smith and Jones, but at least now we know who's employing them. Finally."

"But that degrading IC," he said. "Sneaky bastards. I wasn't expecting anything like that. The file we got was only a fragment, but I'm confident the probability program can reconstruct it. We won't be too far off. And as you say, now we know who Smith and Jones are working for."

Geraint craned his head and sighed as the column of vehicles ahead of them stopped again. "No way of getting at them, though. Nothing to tell us where they are or what they might do next. Nothing on the Ripper, either." Geraint turned to read the expression on Francesca's face, but she seemed to be recovering well from her ordeal.

"They may have been too fast for that. That information might very well have been scrambled. Hey, we're moving again. . . ." Francesca broke off speaking as Geraint accelerated to more normal speed. The traffic had begun to flow normally, at last. Beyond the bottleneck, however, they hit another line of indicator cones fencing off another deep hole in the plascrete. Geraint wanted to pass up some of the other traffic, but was stymied by a series of cars in the fast lane. He vented his impatience in an uncharacteristic expression of anger.

"Move over, you tosser!" he exploded, then turned sheepishly to his companion. "Sorry, Fran. I'm just eager to get home again, and this traffic is really beginning to get to me. Wonder what Serrin and Rani have been up to."

"If they did as well as we did, they'll be . . . Geraint, what's wrong?"

It was a single shot, probably armor-piercing. The sound of the hit should have been lost among the honking

horns of the snarled traffic, but the Saab's internal security systems went active, alerting Geraint. From the flashing alert panels he saw that the bullet had only passed through the main chassis, hitting nothing important.

"Clazz, Fran, someone's just taken a shot at us!" They were passing under an expressway overpass when the car behind them veered crazily and swung into the next lane. Glancing into the rearview mirror, Geraint saw a shattered windscreen and a splash of red blur across the fragmented plasglass before the other car veered off and plunged into the embankment. He floored the gas pedal, sending the Saab screaming out from the other side of the bridge, lane-dodging to the sound of other drivers angrily sounding their horns in protest.

The grenade burst hit just to their rear, a spray of tarmac and stone splashing up over the hood of the Rolls traveling behind them. The windshield didn't break, but suddenly the driver could see nothing.

As the Saab raced away, Geraint saw the Rolls screech to a stop, creating a very messy pile-up among the cars trailing behind it. The Saab's systems had already alerted him to the second bullet hit. He kept his head down and his pedal to the metal. Taking the next exit he put some distance between them and the expressway.

Deciding to lie low, they took a room in a cheap motel, where Geraint accessed his telecom's answer message and reprogrammed it. No way was he going to risk returning to London tonight. Francesca was more philosophical; snipers on the freeway were almost an old California tradition. Geraint was definitely the more shaken up of the pair. In Britain such things didn't happen.

"I think we should try to meet Serrin at the airport when he arrives," he said.

Francesca looked at him sharply. "But we don't know when his plane gets in."

"It doesn't matter. We'll just be there to collect him when it does. He may be a target, too. Rani should be all right where she is."

Even so, Geraint called the code she'd given him. He got an angry-looking male Indian ork who refused to answer his urgent questions and then abruptly cut off the connection.

"Oh, great. Can't locate her. Let's hope she calls me as planned. She'll get the new message. Now for Serrin. Let's cover the angles." He began phoning again furiously.

* * *

By the time they got to Heathrow, Geraint had guards from Risk Minimizers PLC crawling all over his flat. He also had more private security waiting for them and Serrin at the airport, but he was still uncomfortable.

They didn't even get out of the car, but just sat and watched as a phalanx of bodyguards hustled the bewildered elf mage carefully and securely toward a waiting limo. When Geraint and Francesca emerged from the Saab, another crew of secguards ferried them with the same finesse over to the same limo. As the Saab was whisked away by the security team, the limo glided off into the late evening. Serrin turned to them, pure astonishment on his face.

"Don't worry," Geraint said smoothly. "It's just that somebody decided to make our car ride home a little more interesting by setting a sniper and a grenade launcher on us. We thought they might come after you too. Tried to get Rani earlier but no luck. She's supposed to be calling me at home, though, and I left her a warning. Security is scouring my flat right now, and we're not going back there until they've worked it over from top to bottom."

The nobleman was terse, edgy. His lifestyle didn't normally include being shot at while behind the wheel of his car. He used the portacom to access the telecom in his flat, and was relieved to pick up a message from Rani. She mumbled rather incoherently that she was on the run, but that they shouldn't worry, she'd get to them soon.

"Spirits, what have you two been stirring up?" Serrin was alarmed, his head full of fantasies about their decking exploits.

"Nothing really staggering, but it's beginning to fall into place. We got something on you and certain employees of the company. I think you'll like it," Francesca told him.

"The Savoy." Geraint's voice was authoritative as he triggered the intercom to the driver. Flicking it off again, he said simply, "The best place is somewhere very public, I think. And the Savoy has a fine security system indeed." He was already calling to register, listing the security services he required. They were confirmed within two minutes.

"That's better," he said to no one in particular, and relaxed very slightly. "We'll get better protection than the French president on his last visit. Let's hope we don't need it as much as he did."

* * *

He took the call at eight the following morning, exactly as arranged. Posted at his flat were ten security samurai and two combat mages. The electronics had also been reconfigured and the street was crawling with security. The residents of Cheyne Walk would wonder what on earth was going on in their peaceful oasis but, being Brits, they wouldn't pluck up the courage to complain to anyone. Geraint wanted to get to the flat to retrieve money, cards, equipment, clothing, but he wasn't planning to stay long.

"We need somewhere safe. If they're on to us we've got to go somewhere they wouldn't expect us to go." His voice was brittle.

"Geraint, look, it could just have been some crazies. We don't even know they were specifically after us." Francesca tried to calm him.

"Two shots, both into the chassis. They only just missed us. And a grenade? Come on, Francesca, grenades just don't fall into the hands of crazies. Only a handful ever leak away from the corporate security goons. It had to be a corp that came after us. It must have been that bloody succubus that let them trace us. I'm sorry, my friends." He wrung his hands in anger. "Look, it only needs one of us to get over to my place. I'll go in the limo. It won't take more than an hour to pick up what I need. Then we can figure out what to do next."

When the hotel desk notified Geraint that the limo had arrived, he left with the bodyguards. Serrin turned to

Francesca, eager to hear more of what had been happening.

She was glad to oblige. "After the run we analyzed what I'd downloaded. We didn't get everything we wanted, and some of the data in the files was degraded. I had to run a program to fill in the gaps, but it wasn't too bad. For starters, they've got a file on you, Serrin. It records your being employed by unspecified intermediaries to investigate security arrangements of various corporations in Cambridge. It's got some personal stuff about you, too, but nothing especially juicy." She looked mischievously at him and handed over the printout.

The elf scanned the pages. There wasn't much, but he was surprised to discover that Transys had been behind the Portland runs he'd done in '43, not long after he'd left Renraku. Interesting. The target was specified as a tiny subsidiary of Global Technologies.

"Oh, by the way," Francesca went on, "they did hire me for the Fuchi run. The file I got had nothing about them setting a spy on me—that thing that nearly killed me—but there's a strange, scrambled line of garbage I haven't been able to decrypt. So who knows?

"They had a file on Geraint, too. He read it, told me it contained nothing relevant, and kept it to himself. I guess he doesn't want me to know what they've got on his financial and political dealings." She smiled knowingly. "By the size of the datafile I think they've got quite a lot. Makes you wonder what he's been up to, the devil."

"As for Melvin Aloysius Smith, he's a corporate fixer. The data on him was seriously degraded, but it's clear that he and Peter Karl Jones have arranged at least a dozen missions together. They're tagged as having hired you, and also as commissioning the Fuchi raid in which Rani and her people took part. No apparent connection. Actually, I can't be absolutely certain about that. The target wasn't specified in the subfile entry, and, again, the data was very degraded. Let's just say that what I got is easily compatible with that supposition. They've hired some people for other runs, too, but nothing that seems to connect with anything we've got."

Serrin nodded as he scanned the hard copy. Based on

this evidence, Smith and Jones looked like very ordinary corporate fixers.

"No way of tracing them, though. There's a Brazilian address we can crosscheck against the address from that Registration Services agency, but it'll mean nothing. There's some coded garbage after that, which we still haven't been able to decrypt. If it's significantly degraded, we won't be able to decipher it at all."

She continued with her summary. "As for any entries on Jack the Ripper, well, nothing. Nothing except an obviously crashed, scrambled, empty file. Whatever was there was gone by the time we got to download. Still, that tells us they used to have a file on him."

"Oh, indeed, Francesca. I'm sure they did," Serrin nodded grimly. "Sorry, tell you later. You finish your part first."

"Okay." She drew in a deep breath. This was the big one. "They had a file as fat as a walrus on Kuranita. Hey, he was a heavy samurai in his day. Before his little accident in Jo'burg he worked for quite a few corps, according to the info we got. Transys, oh so helpfully, attached probabilities for active employers to the list. In some cases, they knew for sure. That's when they hired him themselves. There's a certain episode from about twenty years ago I think you should see."

She had highlighted the hard copy. His hands shook as he read the matter-of-fact text. It gave the date, time, place, the fee paid, everything that was simple fact. There were no reasons given. Just a scattering of phrases such as "eliminating counter-research personnel," the dehumanized language of executives who assassinate by memorandum.

"My parents." His face was pale. "They hired the fragging bastard to kill my parents." There wasn't anything else to say. If that one crucial entry was accurate, it gave him one damned good reason for wanting to hit Transys Neuronet with everything he could muster.

*   *   *

Serrin took a few minutes to compose himself before telling Francesca what he'd learned during his jaunt across the Atlantic. He didn't bother with the details of Her Ladyship, just dismissed her as weird but reliable.

"I got the names: Global Technologies and Hollywood Simsense. Then I got really lucky. I've got a Johnson in New York, a man I stashed one big favor with some years back. He owes me big-time, so I cashed in. He sweated when I asked him, which meant he already knew about it. Took him close to all day to get back to me, but he came through and now we're quits.

"Global developed a combination of skillsoft and BTL technologies, apparently planning to sell them to the military. Story is that their researchers cooked up a bunch of really sick personalities, complete with their skills and memories, and the Ripper was one of them. He got out onto the streets when the goon implanted with the personality chip was unleashed after some corporate infighting between Global and Hollywood. Anyway, the two companies virtually brought each other down and the Ripper disappeared. Nobody's quite sure what happened in the end. Odds are the military, somewhere or other, has the technology now. Nice thought, huh?"

Francesca shuddered involuntarily, all of a sudden feeling very cold.

"Just one extra flourish," Serrin concluded. "When Hollywood Simsense stole the chips, they had a sleeping financial partner. The partner might have woken up and gobbled them alive, according to my source. You'll never guess who the partner was."

"Transys Neuronet, perchance?"

"Give the lady a radioactive coconut! They could have had access to those chips for long enough to know all there is to know about them. Transys could have taken the design and been testing it all this time. They've had more than two years to do it. This time, they could be making sure they get it right."

The telecom on the bedside table beeped. They were almost afraid to answer it, and Francesca used the descrambler Geraint had given her from the security firm. The screen showed Geraint in his flat, smiling on the other end of the line. They could also see a very scared-looking Rani almost pinioned between a burly pair of security guards.

"Got here to find our young friend having her collar squeezed by my highly efficient security people. Fortunately, their guns were mostly set with tranq shots. Well, mostly. Anyway, we're both safe and we'll be back before lunch."

"Where are we going to stay?" Francesca was beginning to run out of clean, smart clothes, and it mattered.

"Talk to you about that when we return. Not over the phone," he said in mildly reproachful tones before disappearing with a smile as wide as the Cheshire cat's.

It was nearly an hour before Geraint and Rani traipsed into the hotel suite escorted by a pair of hulking security men. They had only one bag apiece, certainly less than Francesca had expected. She had imagined the nobleman would turn up with whole valises stuffed full of the contents of his wall safe. When the security guards retired to a discreet distance, Geraint explained.

"The Savoy wouldn't like me arriving with certain items, even if they were officially licensed. Think about it; would you allow people to bring serious weapons into a top-class, heavy-security hotel if you were running it?"

She could see the sense in that. "So what's the plan?"

"Well, Rani needs to be in the Smoke tomorrow night. She's got contacts to firm up and some advances to dispense. She's also got a little family trouble. So, we'll take the limo, pick up the bags I left at my flat, collect whatever you need, and then we take a plane westward." Serrin and Francesca looked at each other, surprised.

"Time to visit the old ancestral home, I think. As it happens, Transys Neuronet has a facility of sorts just down the road, but if we head for my northern keep we should be as safe as anywhere else in the country. Besides, ever since I told young Rani about it, she's been really eager to go. You see, she's never actually seen a field with a cow in it. Can you believe that?"

30

Cwmbran was a pleasant South Wales town, but they didn't get much opportunity to see it. The Lear-Cessna dumped the group close to the grounds of the forbidding, moated castle keep, and they'd scurried straight in under cover of darkness.

All the way there, Geraint had apologized for the state of the castle; his father brought Japanese and American contacts here, and they liked their authenticity faked. Even with every regulatory system installed, a real castle keep would have been cold, damp, and uncomfortable. This one had been built barely thirty years ago to be as comfortable as possible, right down to the four-poster beds.

Rani didn't care what the noble was apologizing about; it was all very real to her. She walked along slowly, wide-eyed, reaching out hesitantly to touch the stone walls. It wasn't simsense, this was the real thing. She felt so good, she just had to hug Geraint.

"This is banging!" she cried out in unabashed joy.

He smiled broadly and put an arm around her, leading her to the dining hall. On the walls of the long room were Welsh heraldic shields, above the fireplace hung a great stuffed boar's head, and the almost endless table was set with silver and crystal and had real wooden chairs. To the ork it seemed like a scene from a fairy tale vid.

Serrin, too, was delighted by it all. "Well, Geraint, you're a class act. It's no less than I would have expected."

Even the worldly and cosmopolitan Francesca was plainly impressed. It was a pleasure for Geraint to dim the lights and light the candles.

"Sorry, folks. Not much in the way of wine tonight," Geraint apologized later just as a liveried servant appeared to serve a silver bowl of mulligatawny. Rani slurped at the peppery soup, pleased at its almost-familiar taste. Suddenly self-conscious she looked up guiltily, wondering if ork table manners were out of place here.

Geraint burst out laughing in his seat at the head of the table, but his face was kind and she knew he wasn't laughing at her. "God, Rani, it's really good to eat with someone who really enjoys their food and doesn't put on any fancy airs and graces. I tell you, it's a bloody relief. There's more than we can possibly get through in that bowl, so go to it. Keep room for the trout, though. Pierre does fish to perfection."

Trout. She had eaten them, of course, but she imagined that Geraint's would be a far cry from those spawned in the huge depolluting sewage farms clustered around the Smoke. Perhaps these fish would even taste of something. A liveried butler was heaping up real wood in the fireplace, then setting it alight. Good grief, they were burning wood here?

"Oxide converter in the chimney, ladies and gentleman, so we can actually have a real fire tonight," Geraint explained. "Don't do that too often. Anyway, as I say, not too much alcohol. We've got work to do after this, and plans to make. It's all beginning to swim into some sort of focus now."

* * *

Friday morning saw Geraint walking with Rani across the meadows within the castle grounds. The abundance of nature so entranced her that he wished it were spring so that she could see, smell, and gather the daffodils, daisies, buttercups, and other flowers that grew hereabouts. It had taken a dozen years of detox before the first of these had blossomed once more in the land.

The cows had really frightened her at first. She'd seen them on trid, of course, but in person they seemed so much bigger than expected, and a whole herd of them was quite scary. It had taken a real effort of will for Rani to walk up and actually touch one. At the hesitant touch of her hand, the Jersey mooed pleasingly. The ork jumped back in alarm, but quickly recovered her poise enough to go back and caress the animal as it chewed on the sparse winter grass. That something so simple could bring an expression of such delight to her face touched Geraint. Too long in that penthouse, Master Geraint, he chided himself silently.

As they strolled down to the farmhouse, he talked over the night's decisions with her. He hoped he wouldn't seem patronizing, but he wanted to be sure she understood everything.

"Well, Rani, we're up to fifty-six Mary Kellys now, but we can discard seventeen of them, plus the four you checked. It's too dangerous for us to go back to London, so it was a good move to have private investigation firms doing the spadework. Every hour of today should bring us more information. We can narrow down the candidates without going anywhere near the threat of danger."

She nodded. "But what about the others you found in my patch?"

"Yes, three more. If you plan to get back to your contacts tonight, well, that gives you Saturday to check them out. This time we've got to get to the girl before the murderers do."

"The police are really no help?" She actually wanted him to say no. If he'd said yes, it would have made everything an anticlimax, brought an end to all this enjoyment. The police had never done much to protect East Enders in her part of the streets of London, but she'd always believed that powerful rich people controlled the forces of law and order with ease.

Geraint sighed. "Because of what happened to us the night we met you, going to them would be too much of a risk. Despite all my connections we could still end up in jail ourselves. I gave them the best anonymous tip I could, using a special ID code that should alert them that the information comes from a source to be taken seriously—nobleman, politician, or one of their own. But they won't do anything about it. Not in time, anyway. And they won't even be able to check out some of the evidence. For one thing, they've got nothing on Catherine Eddowes. Without evidence they won't act purely on the basis of a tip. But at least we've tried."

Walking down the stony path toward the thatched farm

buildings, Rani nodded sadly. That was the one murder that had touched her own heart.

"Smith and Jones, those men, we can't get at them?" She wanted them badly. The way she saw it, they were the ones who had killed her family.

"No way of knowing their whereabouts. They might be acting as fixers right now, and we wouldn't, couldn't, know where. Not much we can do about them, curse it. I've got my investigators checking them out, but it's unlikely we'll get anything soon. When we do, Rani, you'll be the first to know. I promise you that." Geraint knew what it meant to her.

"The people behind it all. That company, Transys?" She wasn't sure, even now, if she remembered the name right.

"Oh yes. We know that they hired Serrin for something pointless, we know they were behind hiring you, we know they hired Francesca. Whether those things are connected, we *don't* know. And the problem is that we can't find out in time. Their computer system won't let us back in."

He didn't bother trying to explain all the details of the midnight run he and Francesca had attempted late last night; the alerts were constant, the IC impossible to deal with, and the corp had installed an algorithmic node rerouting system that they'd utterly failed to decrypt. They'd gotten out of the system very, very quickly. No more fun and games for a bard and a priestess in Edinburgh now.

"We also think that, for some reason, they're using brainchipping technology to re-create the Ripper. We've got no proof, though. We only know they were once associated with another corp that tried something similar a few years back. We found a file on the subject, but we couldn't get at the information in it.

"We don't have much that's concrete, but it's still plenty to go on, especially after Francesca was attacked by that Ripper construct in the Matrix. Transys has to be playing around with this. There isn't any clear link between the Ripper and what Transys has been doing with us, though," he concluded. That was the sore point for Geraint. He ached to find some connection, some link that would tie it all together, but for the moment nothing presented itself.

"It surprised me that the American knew something about the Squeeze," Rani said as they reached the bottom of the hill. Geraint knew that disparaging references to"the American" had to mean Francesca; it was as plain as the points of Serrin's ears that Rani resented the other woman's beauty and condescending attitude.

"Yes, me too," Geraint agreed. "But she did some work for British Industrial a while back; you know, the people in Angel Towers?" The corporate arcology adjoining the notorious, strife-torn South London districts known as the Squeeze was an all-too-familiar London landmark. Peter the Panda, the ghastly, fifty-foot-tall purple neon corporate logo, shone far and wide.

"Seems she has a contact in British Industrial she can use. He knows folks in the Squeeze. British Industrial gets their labor there."

"Don't I know it." Rani thought of the busloads of hopeless, underpaid slave laborers, desperate to earn even a subsistence, that the corporation brought in every day. She'd seen their desperate faces behind armored plexiglass. The hell of the Squeeze, its mutated and wretched people, caged in the armored buses, selling themselves for peanuts. She could relate to that.

"You want to see Transys Neuronet?" He was suddenly emboldened. "They're not far away, or at least their weirdest place isn't. The land belongs to the Earl of Cardiff, but I can easily get permission for a quick sightseeing tour. While Francesca and Serrin deal with the computer downloads, we'll take a copter and show you something really off the wall. Can't risk flying directly over their heads, but we'll get close enough for a good look. What do you say?"

* * *

As they sat down to high tea Geraint continued talking about this and that, but Rani wasn't really listening. Her head was full of the amazements of Caerleon. Nothing he could have said had prepared her for the sights of the place.

Caerleon, once a Roman town, was more than two thousand years old. The muddy, glistening banks of the River Usk bisected the old from the new town, and from the copter she could see the incredible amphitheater and Roman bullring, with its concentric stone circles ringing the field of battle. Clustered around it were a complex of shiny, flat-roofed buildings, the Transys corporate complex, wrapped up delicately within a web of triple security fences and a whole army of private security.

It was the Knights of Rage that had really amazed her. Resplendent in their black, brown, green, and gold apparel, the dreadlocked blacks stood in knots around the perimeter of the fencing. They raised their crooked staves as one to greet their copter, and the almost simultaneous gesture affected her somehow, bringing tears to her eyes. She had no idea what kept them here, no idea of what this bizarre juxtaposition of high technology and primal instinct meant, at least no conscious idea. Something simpler than that had tugged at her emotions.

Geraint had given her a little time, sensitive to her emotions, before adding, "The dragon . . . we won't see him, of course. Virtually no one ever has."

"A dragon?" Her voice was approaching a squeal. She knew of them only as mythic beasts. She had heard that they existed after the Awakening, but she had never seen one, and she'd never heard anyone else claim to have had.

"Celedyr. One of the three Welsh great dragons. This is the land of the dragon, Rani. It's our national symbol, it's on our flag. Celedyr is here, somewhere below the surface of the earth. You know, some people say they can see the ground itself form into waves when it moves."

"So there's a dragon, and this corporation, and these Knights of Rage from the Squeeze, altogether? What brings them together?"

"Ah, Rani, if I knew that I'd be a wise man, indeed. The Earl just collects the hefty rent and doesn't ask awkward questions. That's all I can tell you." With that they'd turned around in a gentle arc and flown back to the keep. On the trip back, Rani contemplated all that she had seen and heard, her mind almost approaching information overload.

* * *

Almost as soon as they returned to the castle, Geraint called the group together for a final briefing. "Let's go over what we've got," he said. "On the Ripper front, we believe there's going to be a fifth and final murder on Saturday night or Sunday morning, probably in the early hours. It is a horrific assumption, but it follows the logic of all the previous murders.

"The information we've been getting on Mary Kelly is down to fifteen remaining possibles. Between now and the weekend, more data will keep coming in, and we'll reduce that number further. In the end, we'll have to contact the likeliest possible candidate and have my security people cover the others. I've fed data on the fifteen into the upgraded program Francesca's written, using all the leads on the original Ripper we could get, from every A to Z in the libraries. We have to keep plugging away on that."

"And we all agree to put our own personal beefs with Transys on the back burner for the moment," Serrin put in.

The nobleman nodded, looking around at each one in turn. "That is for one very simple reason. We'll have time to pursue revenge or justice with Transys later, but we have good reason to think the final Ripper murder may be only thirty-six hours away. That's the priority for now. Let's not get distracted."

Geraint turned at a signal from the console. "Rani, the copter's here. You have enough money?"

"You bet." She held the moneybelt tight around her waist.

"Good. If you need more the credstick's been linked to any branch of Coutts' to dispense cash at the addresses I've listed, and it will only work with your retina scan. We'll be back in London by ten tomorrow, but it would be great if you could call us here tonight to let us know about your street samurai." Geraint smiled at her look of eager anticipation. "And Rani, good luck!"

She walked out of the room, down the hall, and out of the keep. She strode across to the waiting helicopter, its blades still whirring. All right, Mohinder, she thought.

Let's see the meat you've got for me. This weekend is the real life.

31

Mohinder sat with four of his samurai in the dusty, cobweb-strung upstairs room. Rani was sure that she'd seen a couple of them on the streets before, but she'd never known their names until now.

The one-eyed man with the combat axe and the Bond and Carrington Elite, especially, had an unforgettably familiar face. The way the missing eye had been gouged out wasn't a pretty sight. He shook with a fine tremor that suggested either brain damage or heavy drug use, but his speech was controlled and coherent enough.

The little Sicilian, Scirea, too; she had certainly seen him scurrying in the shadows. Cybereyes, hand razors, boosted reflexes, sure as hell. He had his bandolier of throwing knives, the bulge of a pistol in his pocket, and body armor, too. With all that she was sure he was probably worth what he was getting paid:

In addition to these two were an immense, bone-headed troll and a muscle-bound dwarf.

After the brief introduction, Mohinder quickly got down to business. "Tell us about the deal," he said. His granite-faced expression told her not to waste their time and that she would pay for it with her life if it was a double-cross.

"I have friends who are trying to prevent someone being murdered, Saturday night or early Sunday morning." There was a low guffaw from the group.

"Sure do, baby. I thought that's what we were being paid for, to dust someone." The dwarf sniggered as he picked at his over-long fingernails with a knife.

"No. We need to stop the murder or catch the assassins. Hopefully both."

"Sounds easy," Scirea said. "All we got to do is sit tight and ambush them when they come."

"Not as easy as that. We're still trying to trace the woman who might be the killer's target. That's why it's contingency payment. The basic five hundred hires you to sit tight for the whole weekend. Maybe we won't find the woman in time. If not, you get good pay for doing nothing more than chewing the fat and playing poker for a few days. If we do find the one you need to protect, you get paid extra for that part of the run. Fifteen hundred apiece."

"Fifteen hundred nuyen? Makes two thousand total?" Scirea was incredulous.

Well, knock me down with a cricket bat, he knows how to add, Rani thought, but kept the scorn off her face. It was true that she was the one calling the shots here, but that didn't mean she had no need for a certain finesse. "My friends are rich people."

"So why don't they just hire security?"

"They have. At least, we have that ready if the target is somewhere like the West End. But a team like you is better suited to a job down here. You know this patch as well as I do, far better than any hired security goons. Plus, we got a little extra in the way of weapons and contacts, yeah? Down here you're the best there is, everyone knows that."

Scirea was smiling now, a grin that would have been equally at home on the face of a rabid werewolf. The deal made sense and the pay was good. It didn't sound like a shag job. Besides who'd send an ugly little gopi to try to sucker hardened killers like them?

"Which reminds me, Mohinder," Rani continued. "That bag you got looks good. You got something for me?"

He showed her the Uzi, the heavy Imperial pistol, the boxes of ammunition. The crossbow and the other bits and pieces didn't count for a lot compared with the power of the automatic and the heavy pistol. "Eight."

"What?" Rani lost her cool for a moment; Mohinder was pushing his luck. "Come on. For that price I could get a *pair* of Uzis and a fresh elf's head into the bargain." She knew that the haggling was going to be tough. In front of four of his own, Mohinder wouldn't want to look bad by giving away too much. To make it worse, two more men arrived just then, one of them even smuggling in a grenade launcher, by the look of it. Rani consoled herself with the thought that even if she ended up having to pay through the nose for the hardware, she couldn't complain about the meat and muscle here. Mohinder had pulled out all the stops.

After a heated debate they eventually settled on a price of sixty-five hundred nuyen, far more than the equipment was worth, but everyone was happy enough with the final deal. Rani gave Mohinder one of the scrambled telecom codes, showed him the one she'd kept for herself, and told him of the third, which Geraint had. When they heard that it was a noble lord on the other end of the third line, the whole group began to look at her with new respect. That she had just handed out more than ten thousand nuyen bought her even more. She stood up as tall as she could among the hulking bodies in the room.

"Okay, you guys just keep together. Like I say, it's tomorrow we expect the drek to hit the fan. Now I'm out of here; I've got some other work to do."

Just two more Mary Kellys on the list. She might get around to the first tonight, but it was getting a little late and Rani decided not to take any chances alone on the street, not even with a heavy pistol in her jacket and a Uzi in her carryall. It would have to wait until the morning.

* * *

The others had agonized long and hard over the question of where to stay once they got back in London. They needed total privacy and protection, but couldn't risk having a security firm around while plotting their moves. Despite the certain knowledge that their enemies knew the exact location of Geraint's flat, it seemed the only viable choice. He settled for the discreet security outside and the new bulletproof glass and security systems inside. Not much short of assault cannons could get to them now, and the licensed security mages outside gave them as much protection as anyone could hope for against subtler infiltrations. For good measure Serrin also placed watchers around the building.

By noon, the computers were overheating, the telecoms beeping, and the data downloading.

"Right. London Security is posted at the second-level targets, the possibles. We're down to eleven left to trace and, ah"—Geraint paused as another download came up on the screens—"make that ten. Mary Christine Kelly of Acacia Avenue, Neasden, is currently visiting her aged mother in a charming suburban crumpler somewhere in deepest, darkest Kent. Anyway, she's a nice person. Goes to church every week, member of the Universal Brotherhood, according to this. Well, well. I think we can knock her off the list."

"A crumpler? What's that?" Serrin wasn't entirely familiar with the more arcane Britspeak.

"A place where old folks go to crumple quietly. Their sympathetic young relatives prefer them somewhere out of sight."

"By God, Geraint, look at this stuff. Where do you get this kind of detailed information about people? It's damn scary." Francesca was astonished at the sheer depth of data she was trawling.

"Francesca, dearest, it's not for nothing that I'm a nobleman with friends in government and the corps, that I'm familiar with common and semi-restricted databases, and also an occasional employer of security services. One of the mixed blessings of living in our over-regulated society is that so much information is stored somewhere or other on almost everybody. The government sells a lot of it to various commercial concerns to raise money for the Exchequer. For a fee, those same concerns will allow access to the information. You'd be surprised what all kinds of people know about you. For example, only this morning I learned about the plastic surgery you had at Guy's. Frankly, I think your nose looked cute the way it was." He smiled broadly at Francesca's half-angry, half-startled look.

By tea time, they'd whittled the list of potential targets down to a much more manageable four. Three looked possible: two women with convictions for prostitution, and a tea-leaf reader from Tir Nan Og whose files referred to the high proportion of male clients among her clients.

"She's way out in SX, though, pretty suburban. Really doesn't seem the right district. You know, apart from Annie, these murders have all taken place in the right locations, more or less. Right districts, at the very least. None of these three would fit that pattern, but it's the best we have. I'm going to run the semantics package on them to see what that does."

"What?" Serrin hadn't a clue to what command Geraint was planning to give the bewildering array of electronic hardware now.

"Francesca and I went back over the four murders and used a template system to compare everything we could find on the original Ripper killings. Fran did most of the work, actually, bless her." Serrin could sense her smile from where he was sitting, though she was facing the screens.

"We banged in all the known past history of the victims, place names, locations, all the incidental details. Then we compared it to other people with the same names in London. The four names came out as the likeliest possible targets by virtue of the factors we included in the analysis. They were all prostitutes, the districts they lived in and where they were killed were similar, and there were some odd curves thrown out. Like, the original Annie Chapman's body was found in Hanbury Street, while Fran's friend of the same name was found slain in her flat in Hanbury Court, part of a building of another name. That was weird."

"It's almost as if someone else did a similar comparison to choose the right victims." Serrin was pondering what he'd just heard. "As if the women were selected by computer."

"That occurred to me, too. If Transys is testing a personality chip with these killings, it wouldn't be out of character for them at all. They're famous for the meticulousness of their tests. But the one remaining problem is the Mary Kellys we'll never be able to find."

Francesca was bent over one of the multiple screen arrays, but she'd been listening. "The Squeeze download, such as it is, is a pure shambles. It's almost impossible to keep tabs on people. There are five Mary Kellys there, but the data is all marked incomplete, too dated, too many unknowns. If they're going to hit one of them, we'll never be able to stop them.''

Serrin sat bolt upright. ''But then, someone living in the Squeeze wouldn't be the target! Think about it. Even if you had spies checking around in that place, it would be desperately hard to make sure your victim was in the right place at the right time, right?''

''He's got something there,'' Geraint conceded. ''No one finds it easy to monitor what goes on in the Squeeze. After the genetic manipulation disaster that the corps tried when the Squeeze was first formed, the people there hate corporations of any stripe. A corporate spy would have a very short life span among them.''

''Don't I know it,'' Francesca sighed. ''That's why the data I'm getting from my British Industrial source is such drek. Even they can't get more than fragmentary data, and they're right on the spot.''

''So let's take a chance,'' Geraint suggested. ''Let's say that the difficulties inherent in the Squeeze mean they wouldn't select a target there. That leaves us our two hookers and the tea-leaf reader. They're the only realistic targets we have left since Rani called. The last two East Enders don't fit at all. We take the top probability target, stake it out, and leave my security people with the other two.''

''The police?'' Serrin offered the suggestion, but only as a matter of formality.

''Waste of time. They'll consider it a wild goose chase. Frankly, London Security will handle it better.''

''We could kidnap the three of them, as it were. Place them under our protection somewhere. Bring them here.'' Again, Serrin was fishing for solutions.

''No way. We want to get the killers, and that means we need to use the targets as bait. It sounds bloody cold and callous, but I'm also thinking about the four women they've already killed. They deserve their murderers being brought to justice. With the security we can provide, the trap will be a deadly one unless they bring a coachload of troll samurai and enough mages to light up the whole of St. Paul's for a week.''

By ten-thirty they'd been able to select the most likely target after all the additional data had been downloaded

and analyzed by Francesca's program. Geraint closed
down the screens one by one.

"Well, Abbey Wood it is. Mary Nicola Kelly. The
telecom trick was a nice touch, Fran. Well done."

"I'm surprised it was so easy to sell her the idea that
she'd won a random lottery prize."

"Oh, but the way you told her to gather family or
friends around was brilliant. She was obviously delighted, but they'll get a very different visit from the one
they're expecting. I think we should bring them some
champagne."

The telecom beeped, bringing the call that would
change everything.

* * *

Paying off the last of her Fenchurch Street contacts, Rani
had gotten luckier than she could ever have believed possible. With all the excitement of the last few days, and
especially the visit to Wales, she'd almost forgotten about
him, but there he was, ducking away into New London
Street.

Of all people, Pershinkin.

She trailed him cautiously to the derelict house. A pair
of orks emerged soon afterward, smiling and stuffing
wads of money into their pockets. Another pair of dupes,
huh? This time, my friend, she promised herself, it's going to be very different.

He was alone, she was determined, and he didn't hear
her until she had her knife around his throat from behind.
He was kneeling, just about to finish packing his case,
and he made the cardinal mistake of having his back to
the doorway.

By God, man, over-confidence is a real failing, Rani
thought grimly. And one you're going to pay for dearly.

"Hello, scumbag," she said. "You spammed my *family*. My rakking family, you wanker."

Pershinkin froze as he felt the cold metal cutting into
his skin, hardly daring to breathe while his eyes flashed
from side to side trying to get a glimpse of the woman
hissing death into his right ear.

"The run out to Cambridge, remember? Poor Imran?

'Just get some suckers,' wasn't it? Well, looks to me like you're the sucker now. Prepare to die, sleazeball.'' Revenge was sweet but Rani had already waited so long for this moment that she wanted him to beg for his life first.

He obliged her. "Look, I didn't know! I didn't know! It wasn't me! It was the people who hired me. I'm only the man in the middle,'' he whined. "You gotta believe me.'' He was scared now, very scared indeed.

"Won't do you any good, ratface. You're going to die anyway. Better say your prayers.''

"No! Wait!'' he whimpered. "Look, the men who gave me the job, I've got a meeting with them tomorrow night. I swear it. It's true, it's true! If I tell you where we're to meet, you can show up instead. Was them who hired your family to get killed. What have I got against you? Why would I harm you?''

She hadn't expected that. "Tell me where and when, you stinking slime. Now!''

He was too afraid to negotiate, his wits too scrambled to realize he couldn't just give it all away. He stammered out the place and the time of the meeting in a voice wracked with sobs.

Then Rani tightened her grip on the knot of straggly hair at the back of his head and drew the blade in an arc across his throat from ear to ear. She didn't give herself time to regret what she was doing. When she finally released her hold, the body slumped forward onto the grimy floor like a heavy sack of laundry.

She wouldn't tell the others about this one. Not yet. It was family honor. She'd tell them after she'd dealt with Smith and Jones.

* * *

It was well past ten o'clock when Rani got back to the men. She'd found her Mary Kellys at last, and a complete waste of time they'd been, too.

Once in the musty-smelling upstairs room she dumped herself into the vacant chair next to Mohinder. The men were becoming restless now. Yes, they'd been paid well, whether or not they had to work this weekend or not, but the adrenaline was pumping. And a few other good chemicals, Rani judged, from the stimulant patches and broken vials she saw lying among the pizza boxes and burger bags littering the room.

"You look tired, little sister." Mohinder grinned at her, knocking back another of an endless series of coffees. "Have a burger," he said, handing her one. "Regal Burgers' very best, with the chili and black bean sauce. Lovely grub."

She declined the offer with a shudder. "Thanks anyway."

"What you been up to?"

Rani sighed in apparent fatigue. "Hunting for someone called Mary Kelly. She's the person we think is going to be killed, a prostitute. I been running around trying to find anyone who fits the picture." She made herself sound laconic and weary, not wanting to mention anything about Pershinkin. Mohinder might not be at all pleased about that.

"You don't say?" Mohinder's expression changed totally. "And you couldn't find her?"

"Between me and my friends we've found scores of Mary Kellys, but they're all dead ends. No one fits the bill."

The samurai twisted in his chair and called to the men. "Hey, Scirea! You know Typhoid?"

Scirea grinned. "Sure do. Crazy blooming decker. Bit of a trancer, head full of drek with too many rags she shot up and some of that tanking stuff. She used to work for me. Wasn't bad when she was younger. Used to take payment in kind sometimes."

The men around him sniggered unpleasantly. Rani realized they were talking about one of the women Scirea's family pimped for. She was disgusted by them as they laughed again.

Meanwhile, though, Mohinder was tapping a number into his telecom. A vacant-faced girl appeared on the screen. She had hair dyed black, mascara that looked like she'd put it on with a spoon, black lipgloss, and an expression somewhere between hopelessness and complete despair.

Rani's mind triggered a memory: the Toadslab restaurant. After she'd sold Mohinder the Predator. Her.

"Yeah." The woman's voice was virtually robotic.

"Typhoid? What you doing right now?" Mohinder was grinning like a crocodile.

"Mohinder? Hey, guy, thanks for the little loan, y'know. Pay you back soon as I can." Her expression, and all of her vacant hand-waving, did nothing to suggest that it would be too soon.

"Typhoid, baby, tell me something simple. What's your real name? I mean, we all call you Typhoid Mary, but what's the real thing?"

She was suspicious. Panda eyes narrowed sharply through her chemically assisted fog. "What you want to know for? You freelancing for the poll-tax hunters?"

"Come on, honey, you know me better than that. Tell you what, we'll forget those few nuyen. Just speak your name to Mohinder."

That persuaded her like nothing else ever could. She spoke the words slowly, in a childlike voice, as if remembering what she'd been called in a dim and distant past when someone actually cared about her.

"Kelly," said Typhoid Mary. "Mary Jane Kelly."

* * *

Geraint whooped in delight. "My God, even the second name is right. Mary Jane Kelly, a young hooker in White-chapel. This is it! This is bloody it!"

Serrin and Francesca grinned back at him. All the tension of the day evaporated from the room like a puddle on a sunny day.

"She isn't in any register because of the tax evasion, and if she's a decker she can make enough to stay out of sight and pay people to lie about her. This has to be the one. No time to run the analysis programs and we don't have the additional data, but we're ready now. They're on their way to protect her, Rani says. Greatorex Street, Whitechapel. If they plan to kill her tomorrow, we'll be there almost an hour in advance. Come on, people, this is it. At last."

32

The Saab screeched into Greatorex Street at eleven minutes past the hour. They'd been delayed by a random police patrol, in which a pair of blasé officers had tested the alcohol levels of Geraint's breath. To everyone's fury, they'd had to sit for more than ten minutes behind a line of five other cars stopped for the same reason. The only good thing about the delay was that it gave them time to pay the samurai in the car.

Heading down the right road at last, they could see two figures standing under the streetlight outside the address Rani had given them. Geraint picked out the Indian girl easily; the other he didn't know. Serrin was leaping out of the passenger door almost before Geraint had parked the car.

"She took off!" Rani was calling out. "We told her someone was out to hurt her and she should stay put until we got here. Said we would only be a few minutes, but she got crazy and she's bloody gone and left," Rani yelled breathlessly.

Serrin turned and slammed his fist into the roof of the car.

"It was my fault," Mohinder said calmly. "I shouldn't have warned her. Should have come over without saying why. But she's so unpredictable she might have gone out anyway." He grinned at the elf. "Hello, pixie. I won't shake hands." The retractables flashed from his fingers.

"I sent my people out to look and talk to folks, and made a couple of calls," Mohinder continued as Geraint and Francesca joined the listening throng. "There're a couple of places she might go, and a bar or two where we might find her. She doesn't have many places to go to ground. We'll get her. You can bet on it."

"But how long will that take?" the nobleman demanded.

Serrin stifled Geraint's impatience. "Look, Geraint, if

we can't find her, then neither can they. And we've got local people to give us an edge in the search.''

"Unless the killers already had the place staked out with spies of their own,'' Francesca muttered. She looked up at the elf in a moment of understanding, and he switched his perceptions immediately, probing for a mage in the area. He had to be there. Serrin found him for an instant, before the masking shut him out. He got a strong impression of movement, receding into the distance, and that gave him a fix.

"Just to the southwest. He must be in a car. They're heading just south of west. It's got to be them.''

"Bury Street.'' Mohinder was emphatic. "She knows old Jen, the owner of a flophouse there. Takes her food and stuff sometimes. She used to work near there when she was still on the streets, I remember. If she's gone that way, that's where she'll be. For sure.''

They were already piling into the car as Scirea and the dwarf joined them from the shadows. Mohinder was phoning his other samurai, telling them where to meet up. There was no time to drive around to pick them up now.

"Didn't know you could get seven people into one of these things,'' Francesca grumbled.

"Honey, you can't. Come sit on my lap,'' Mohinder suggested, licking his lips.

She scowled and opted for Rani's instead.

* * *

The group of samurai whipped out of the darkness of an alleyway as the Saab hurtled down the road. The fire from their automatic weapons ripped into the car, but Geraint had installed a strobe blast that augmented the headlights. He flicked the anti-strobing window modulators as everyone inside the Saab ducked their heads and the back windows wound down. The windscreen could take one good burst for sure; after that it was down to luck and a prayer.

Then Geraint stopped the car on a dime. Because of the stroboscopic lighting one of the samurai couldn't get out of the way in time, his cybereye mods become useless. From the impact Geraint guessed that he'd knocked the guy down, but he probably wasn't out. The second samurai had taken an expertly directed burst from Rani's Uzi as the car hurtled toward him, and the gaping holes in his body armor showed that ballistic had been no protection against the volley of bullets.

Though Serrin had a protective barrier spell running, the column of fire he saw shimmering down the street told him he wasn't going to be able to keep sustaining the spell because he'd need his concentration somewhere else.

The third samurai was changing a clip, ready to pump lead into the back-seat passengers as they got out of the car, but he never got the chance. Scirea had his sleeves rolled up as the car entered the street, and the tube strapped to his forearm delivered a small metal globe straight into the samurai's torso. It must be some kind of grenade, Rani thought, but she couldn't guess what sort or how it was fired. The demitech worked, though. The samurai reeled back, sticky flame burning and licking across his clothes and body. His screams were like needles in her ears.

They poured out of the car, reflexes boosted to maximum one way or another. Others were working on pure unaugmented adrenaline, but they were all afire.

Serrin moved to the side of the road, into shadow, concentrating on combating the raging elemental bearing down upon them. Here we go again, he thought gloomily. Why do I seem to spend so much of my life trying to deal with these fraggers? Francesca moved to his side, covering him with her pistol.

On the side nearest the house they sought, Scirea backed up to the wall, pistol readied, a grenade in his left hand. He lobbed it down the street ahead of them, and a wall of smoke began to rise where it landed, some twenty yards away.

Good thinking, Geraint thought grimly. If that's where their mage is, they may have other back-up there. They've probably got the equipment to see through the smoke, but maybe not all of them can. There were so many possibilities.

Mohinder had dispatched the injured samurai with one

sweep of his hand razors across the man's throat, but now his cybereyes were scanning the doorway, a machine pistol in one hand and the Predator in the other. Geraint was just behind him as Mohinder sprayed an armor-piercing clip through the closed door. Perhaps it was a scream they heard from inside, but it was impossible to tell beneath the rattle of the guns. A spurt of automatic fire burst into the road from a middle window of the three-story house, then all hell let loose at the far end of the street. Wild fire was streaming through the smoke, and everyone was grateful for the ballistic body armor they wore for protection. Ricochets pinged off the surface of the street.

"Get inside!" Geraint screamed, but that wouldn't do for all of them. Francesca and the dwarf were returning fire into the open window of the house, the dwarf switching his attentions from the north end of the road where he'd been watching for any sneak strike from their rear. He seemed to move with effort into position to shoot back, and Francesca saw that his armor was shredded from bullets.

He's been hit, she realized, with a sickening chill through her body. Then she saw the hint of a figure behind the flash of the automatic weapon, and she took extra care with her aim. If that slint was firing at the dwarf, it gave her a little edge. She got lucky; three close-timed Colt shots were enough to stop the chatter of the other man's gun.

The dwarf was urgently plastering patches on his side, but Francesca screamed at him to take cover. It was brave of him, trying to get to her to protect her, but he could hardly walk and she knew he was gravely hurt. Two men with pistols, one also hefting a ridiculous-looking axe, were running toward them from the end of the street. Francesca was leveling her gun again, but the dwarf croaked the word "Friends" to reassure her. Thank heavens the cavalry is here, she thought.

The elemental came roaring through the smoke just as Mohinder crashed the door open enough for Scirea to lob a grenade through it. The Italian reeled back as he took a chestful of shots, then collapsed lifelessly onto the ground like a puppet whose strings were suddenly cut.

Mohinder waved Geraint and Rani back as the grenade blast exploded in the room, sending shards of glass and splinters of wood flying everywhere. It was a minor miracle none of Geraint's team was blinded by the stuff, but somehow they'd all managed to turn their faces away just in time. Mohinder was the first in after a Uzi sweep by Rani had cleared whatever might still be alive in there.

Serrin was struggling desperately. He clutched at another spell focus and poured himself into denying its force, grinding it down, forcing it away into banishment.

Francesca was emptying her gun into the smoke, hoping for the best. She had a horrible feeling some amorphous forms were beginning to storm through from behind the blinding brilliance of the flame pillar. Just then, one of the reinforcements dropped to his knees as the axeman waved comically and toppled over backward. People were coming out of the smoke, but the kneeling man's launched grenade turned the ones in the front to mincemeat. Frag me, she thought as her stomach lurched sickeningly, this is one heavy-duty business.

Automatic fire ripped through plaswood floorboards as the heavy gunners fired through the ceiling. Geraint screamed at them to stop, they were trying to prevent Mary Kelly being killed.

"Too late for that, term," Mohinder yelled at the top of his voice as he slammed a new clip into the machine pistol. Rani moved to cover him as he headed up the stairs to the landing. They seemed to be working well together, each covering the other at just right moment. A troll slumped in the stairwell was playing possum, feigning death, but that couldn't save him. Just to be sure, Mohinder emptied the rest of the Predator's clip into the body. The troll twitched to death in a blood-spattered spasm.

Reaching the top of the stairs, Mohinder kicked down the last door on the top floor. Rani darted out from behind him to empty the last of her magazine into the elf by the window before he could complete his spell. That left two of them standing over the hideous, eviscerated body, staring at the three people in the doorway. For the tiniest instant, they were frozen as if in an old still photo: one bloodied corpse between them on the filthy mattress

and an elf off to the side, with an expression of fatal surprise on his face and a half-dozen holes in his torso.

The cloaked man was middle-aged, flabby-faced, a bushy, positively Victorian mustache wavering above full, fleshy lips. His hands were still twitching, the fingers and hand razors covered in gore. The black bag lying on its side by his feet had disgorged its collection of surgical scalpels, scissors, saws, and retractors across the floor; now they were abstract, shining slivers glinting amid pools of deep crimson gore.

The samurai next to him was a surprise: neatly be-suited, almost all machine. Yet he stood still, the ghost of a smile playing over his features until the burst from Geraint's heavy pistol ripped away his jacket. Some flesh remained, but not much. He slumped to the floor very slowly, his legs collapsing under him, pistol falling from the lifeless hand.

The three assailants edged around the monster by the mattress.

"Got you, you rakking bastard," Geraint yelled in an ecstasy of victory as the man backed up against the far wall. His face was expressionless, already dead. His teeth and jaw ground together and he collapsed in a heap.

"Drek! Bloody suicide implant," Mohinder roared.

They were all fumbling at the medkit but it was too late.

"Mohinder, get back outside and cover the others," Geraint ordered. "We can't do anything else here," He was searching furiously for any ID on the bodies. The Ripper was beyond any medkit now.

But Mohinder waved Rani outside instead. Scanning the scene, he saw something bizarre happening to the Ripper's body. It was beginning to decompose before their very eyes, at an impossibly rapid rate. The flesh lost definition and form, deliquescing into a heap of shapeless tissue. Geraint was astounded, staggering back from the horribly degrading corpse. For an instant he almost didn't notice that the scanner he'd brought in was indicating that this monster had no headware chips.

"Oh God," he moaned softly. "How are we ever go-ing to prove what happened here?" His mind was racing. "The police—"

Mohinder jerked back from him. "No way, term. No police. They'll be here in a tick, but none of my people are gonna wait around to greet them."

Geraint nodded numbly, thinking there was wisdom in the samurai's words. It would be difficult, if not impossible, to explain his presence at this gory scene tonight. It was time to grab up the evidence and run for it.

When they got outside, they found three of their own dead. The troll from Mohinder's group had never arrived and Scirea they knew about, but the dwarf had bought it while unleashing one final burst of shots at the samurai who'd come running out of the smoke. Rani had arrived at the door of the house just in time to cut the last one down as she fired at his flank. Of the reinforcements, the axeman had breathed his last and the grenade expert had made off into the night as soon as the shooting stopped.

Can't blame him, Francesca thought. He's done his job. Saved my life, too. Go on home, man. You've earned it.

Serrin was unconscious, having succumbed to the drain of dispelling the elemental. Francesca had taken a ricochet in her calf, but she smiled wanly at Geraint's concern. "My turn to visit your doctor, I guess." She was also aware that the ballistic armor over most of her lower body was shot to ribbons. She was lucky that all she got was a leg wound, and she knew it—but that didn't stop it from hurting plenty.

Mohinder and Geraint ran back upstairs to frantically search the samurai while an exhausted Rani helped Serrin and Francesca into the back seat of the Saab. They didn't have to worry about the opposition, but the all-too-predictable sirens were beginning to wail in the distance.

Coming back down again, Geraint thought the flophouse looked like something out of a war flick: six dead bodies littered the blood-soaked street, a couple more sprawled in the distance, and the house was equally full of corpses.

No, Geraint thought, I don't think we want to be here when the police arrive.

* * *

"He'll live," Francesca reassured them. Serrin's breathing was shallow but regular, and it was obvious that he would come around eventually. Her own wound was still bleeding even after the application of a trauma patch, but the additional hemostatics seemed to be doing the job slowly. It would leave a nasty stain in Geraint's car, though.

Oh, well, time to get another one anyway, Geraint thought, scowling through his fatigue. In the meantime this one would need a spray of paint. He was sure the Saab had taken damage from the automatics, damage that would be somewhat hard to explain.

"We got a little bit of ID from those goons," he told the others as they rode along. "It might be enough. The pistols will be licensed and that should do it. The tissue samples I took from the samurai and the mage upstairs may help, too, but it's a damn nuisance my portacam got shot up. I never even noticed it. If I could have gotten pictures of the Ripper and his victim, we'd have been home free."

Mohinder turned to him and smiled his reptile's grin. "Null perspiration," he said, his eyes squinting slyly.

"What do you mean?" Geraint asked.

The samurai stared at Geraint with his unblinking cybereyes. "I got a video link, man. It's all in here," he said, tapping his skull. "Got a minute's worth. All it takes is a downloader link and then it's on your screen, term."

Geraint relaxed back into the plush driver's seat and smiled broadly. "Mohinder, you just earned yourself one hell of a bonus. It's enough. More than enough.

"We've got them."

33

By four that morning most of the follow-up was complete. They were all still pumped up from the rage of battle, and Francesca's calf wound had responded well to the slap patch Geraint had taken from his safe.

Serrin was still groggy when he finally came to, but so ravenously hungry that he devoured two huge bacon and egg sandwiches. He felt a lot better, but the whole business surprised him. Drain didn't usually affect him that way. Most times, he felt like the walking dead for at least a day or two after serious draining.

"We should have the tissue sample results by about six," Geraint was saying. "The mage will be licensed, surely, and we'll get a match with the official sample archive. That I can pull. Yes, Francesca, another Cambridge pal. The old college tie's a wonderful thing." He smiled broadly, the knots of tension within him easing as they completed each step on the way to finally resolving the whole sad affair.

"Added to that, we'll be able to check the gun licenses through a contact in the Home Office. That should pin something down, too. They wiped the internal chip IDs, but overlooked the ID on one of the pistol barrels. That really was most careless. Between the mage and the gun, I think we have Transys on the rack now. Add in all the other stuff, and they're going to take a beating. We've done it."

"Enough to give to the police?" Francesca asked.

"Rakk the police," he muttered, almost to himself. "No, I've been thinking about it. There's a young lady from OzNet. . . . We'll give the story to her. Maybe OzNet's only a plazzy little trid channel, but when they splash this story, the rest of the media will sit up and take notice." He was tapping out her telecom code already.

"Then we'll supply duplicate data to the police. They'll be able to DNA-type the elf—that is, if they suspect he's a mage. We did take his spell focuses away with us so it might not be quite so obvious. But they'll be so slow with their inquiries that—oh, hello? Christine? Hi, it's Geraint. Yes, the Welsh—yes, Cambridge, yes. I know it's an ungodly hour of the morning, but I've a huge story for you. Exclusive, yes. We'll have the last of the evidence ready for you around six this morning. If you want to make a name for yourself, girl, be here just after then. You're guaranteed a promotion for this one."

He gave her his address, then rang off. "Time to get it all assembled in a nice, clean order," he said. "That chip must have been something really strange. I couldn't scan it at all. It's a pity, but I don't think we really had the time to cut off the head and bring it with us."

"Geraint, please!" Francesca was appalled.

"Sorry, I didn't mean to . . . Oh, what the hell, we left a whole streetful of bloody bodies and now we're worrying about niceties of language? Pah."

Mohinder had downloaded his video recording well before the results from the lab came through. He took the fat cash payment and stuffed the twenty thousand into his pocket, grinning broadly. Then he told Geraint where he might find him should he ever need help again. He even bowed to Rani on the way out.

"Got to hand it to you, girl," Mohinder said. "You've come up in the world. Guess we might not see each other again for a while?" He wondered where she might be when all this was done.

"Oh, I'll be around and about, Mohinder. I won't forget tonight." They hugged, friends, maybe even equals.

"Hey," he said, in a parting shot, "wasn't that as much fun as you can have with your clothes on?" Rani giggled; she'd seen that trid show, too. Mohinder closed the door behind him carefully.

* * *

The telecom beeped at a quarter to six. It was Geraint's contact in the genetics lab at Imperial College.

"Morning, Geraint. Thanks for the charitable donation. We'll put that toward the metagene research project. You're most generous."

"You're welcome, Richard. Now, tell me what you got."

"Well, a courier is on the way with formal confirmation of the data and samples, but in summary, here's how it goes. The metahuman was a magician, licensed to a corporation. But first, is this line safe?"

"You can speak freely. I've got more precautions against bugging than you can imagine. Retroactive phasing scramblers. And more," Geraint breezed.

"Good. His name is Pieren Featherbrook, age thirty, lives in—"

"Yes, yes." Geraint was impatient. "That'll be in the data you've sent over. Who did he work for?"

"Transys Neuronet." It was a moment of absolute, exquisite beauty.

Geraint was delighted. "Thanks, Richard. That just about ties it up." He paused for a small gloat of pleasure. Oh boy, have we got them now.

"The other one, well, that was a problem. And *very* strange. Tissue was almost completely degraded by a fungal mycotoxic agent, but we had just enough. Can't make any ID from the link we have with officialdom, for which help many thanks, but there's something very weird indeed."

"Like what?"

"Like, there's a ninety-nine point nine hundred ninety-seven percent chance this guy is a member of the Royal Family."

"*What?*" Geraint spluttered. He couldn't believe his ears. This was completely beyond belief.

"Yes, really. I know it sounds bizarre, but it all checks out. He has the GA2 gene, which is a real marker, has been for generations, and the F52-A3-gamma linkages on chromosome 16 are a cert too. There's other stuff, but it's all in the specs. No doubt about it in my mind. He's a Royal." The academic paused, wondering. "How did you get this? I know you're titled and all, but I didn't realize you had friends in such high places."

"Well, you know how it is," Geraint said modestly, trying to accommodate this new revelation. "Richard, I think we should have lunch somewhere disgustingly expensive fairly soon. My treat."

Francesca was already at work on the console. She'd done some checking on the original Ripper stories, and she knew where the archive was. On the left-hand screen was the image of the Ripper's face from 2054, scanned in from Mohinder's vid record. Hacking through the photo archive in the optical storage systems, she used the matching program to lift out the Ripper, 1888 version. The image lit up on the right screen. A perfect match.

The template matching program was registering a probability as close to one hundred percent that no differences existed between the two. They all stared at the evidence flickering electronically before their eyes.

"Prince Albert Victor Christian Edward Windsor, Duke of Clarence. By God." Geraint could hardly speak. In the background came the sound of the doorbell ringing. "No wonder my scanner couldn't find a chip. It was a rakking *clone!*"

* * *

OzNet had checked the core facts, then cleared the first bulletin for transmission at seven-thirty. By nine o'clock, they'd even found a witness to the dumping of Catherine Eddowes' remains, and had people starting to dredge the river. Every media station in the country was going bananas for a piece of story.

"The series of Ripper slayings we have documented were carried out by a clone of the original Ripper, the Duke of Clarence. Investigations by the Metropolitan Police are said to be focused on the theft of bone samples from his grave, and we anticipate a bulletin on that shortly. When we hear it, you'll hear it, here on OzNet, the station that brings you *all* the big stories first." The news blonde couldn't hide her delight in getting something meaty to read for a change.

"The evidence incriminating the British corporation of Transys Neuronet is now overwhelming. The body of a licensed Transys mage was found at the site of today's fifth slaying." Mohinder's grainy cybereye recording showed the room with the elf, the samurai, and the Ripper, and then the backscreen cut to a profile of just the elf. "Pieren Featherbrook has been a registered employee of the Transys hermetic security division since March 2046. Identification of weapons carried by security personnel at the site of the slaying shows they were licensed to Transys Neuronet, and OzNet researchers have found still further links."

In Geraint's apartment they all edged forward on their seats. They'd had no advance warning of this. Photographs of two dead samurai came up next to grainy, older pictures of the same men.

"How did they get those shots of the guys we killed?" Francesca whispered. Serrin hushed her as the news-reader continued.

". . . identified as Transys employees currently engaged in corporate security, as these Transys archive photographs show. Confession statements made by the owners of the house where Catherine Eddowes was slain reveal that they received retainers from current Transys employees, although these witnesses are still under police interrogation."

My word, Geraint thought, they've dug up all this in three hours. This is really impressive. I'll have to make sure these guys get special attention the next time a broadcasting bill comes to Parliament. We'd never have been able to come up with all this dirt.

But there were more hammer blows to come.

"The human cloning technology in these gruesome murder re-enactments is believed linked to research experiments in progress at Transys Neuronet's laboratory at Longstanton, near Cambridge. Officials from the Lord Protector's Office raided the installation just under an hour ago based on information supplied by OzNet, *the* station for news and views. Applications for a number of patents connected to biotech research may be evidence of increasing emphasis on cloning studies at Longstanton." Some archive footage of grumpy-looking security personnel filmed within the complex from long range helped the message along a little.

"That's what the druid meant," Serrin put in. "She said they were blaspheming creation."

The report ended with the promise of a re-run of an historical documentary on the Victorian Ripper, together with a series of "No comments" from spokesmen for the Royals and for Transys. Serrin flicked the tube dead.

"Oh." It was a long, long sigh from all of them. They hadn't slept all night, and their bodies were as stiff as iron rods.

"We got them, Serrin," Francesca said. "The guys who tried to use you got a lot more than they bargained for. You also just wiped out the corp that killed your parents. They'll sink without a trace after this.''

''Didn't get Kuranita, though.''

''Well, I guess you can't have everything. But revenge is sweet. Rani, you just paid off the people that baited three of your own family into a death trap. You got what you wanted, too.'' The Indian girl nodded silently, keeping her own counsel. She still had Smith and Jones to box.

''And me, well, I got who killed Annie and damn near killed me. That Ripper construct in the Matrix must have been part of their experiments in personality encoding. Doesn't matter. Stuff the details. We got the bastards. Maybe I'll even be done with those nightmares now. All I have to worry about is my leg.''

Geraint smiled again. ''No problem. We'll get you up to Oxford this afternoon after you get some sleep. You saw how good my doc was.''

''Yeah, as long as my leg is all he touches. I definitely wouldn't want to take anything more than a local anesthetic in his clinic.'' She laughed, then relaxed back into the cool of the analgesics Geraint had given her to mellow out the trauma of coming down from the night's highs.

''And what did you get, Geraint?'' Serrin was eager to know why the nobleman had done all this. It had cost him a lot, and he'd used up plenty of favors and risked his own life.

''What did I get? Let's just say the satisfaction of a job well done. Life lived. Wrongs righted.'' He changed the subject. ''Ladies and gentleman, I suggest we avail ourselves of something cold with a lot of bubbles in it, and then get some desperately needed sleep. We won. Let's celebrate.''

* * *

They slept well into the afternoon. When they woke again, Francesca set out for an overnight stay at Oxford, the wound bad enough to require a night's rest at the Radcliffe. Rani said she had to take care of some business in the East End. I'm sure she does, Geraint thought, what with another bunch of her samurai killed.

"I want you back here, though. From what you say, your family's disowned you and you don't really have anywhere to go." She shrugged, but he could see she was disappointed at losing the excitement of being with them. He didn't want this to be goodbye. "Look, I don't know if you'd be interested, but did you like Wales? You seemed to."

She smiled a little wanly at the memory. It had been another world entirely, just like the life of this nobleman.

"We can always use security people there. You wouldn't have to stay if you didn't like it or if you got homesick. Try it for a couple of months perhaps? Then you'll have some money, maybe your family will be cooled down a little. Would you like—"

Her spontaneous, crushing hug told him she would. But with the best will in the world, the embrace of an ork who had been sweating inside body armor during an unwashed thirty hours or so wasn't entirely agreeable to him. He was somewhat glad when she backed off.

"When you've concluded your business, come back here. We'll work out the details. Take care, Queen of Heaven."

Serrin was the last to go. Geraint had expected him to stay, looking forward to a slow, lazy evening winding down, but the elf had something on his mind.

"I'm leaving England Tuesday night," he said sadly. "First I've got to go back and find that druid. I want to let her know that the Transys place will be closed down now. Oh hell, I just want to see her again."

Geraint looked at the elf. The dark rings under his eyes said Serrin was still exhausted, but the nobleman didn't insist that he stay until morning. Maybe Serrin had found something that would give him more peace than lazing in a Chelsea penthouse.

"Sure you can find her again?"

"Why else do I specialize in detection? But don't worry, I'll take a mobile telecom and stay in touch. Let you know I'm all right. And I'll be back here Tuesday morning anyway. This time we won't lose each other for so many years."

Geraint was surprised at how frail his friend felt when they embraced in goodbye. He needed recuperation and maybe he needed it with someone who wasn't part of these weeks of blood-soaked murder and mayhem. An escape from all that.

So, Geraint sat alone into the evening. He had no taste for champagne or food, barely any appetite for coffee. He aimlessly flicked from channel to channel on the tube, seeing the Ripper-clone story dominating the news over and over again. But he wasn't really listening, and as night fell around him, he settled into a state of fatigued reverie.

It was just around nine when the constant, gentle urging from his Sight sent him to the Tarot. He needed two cards: one for those he had defeated and one for himself.

Ten of Swords.

Ruin. Ah yes, the end of the road for Transys Neuronet. And now one for himself. Maybe the victory of the Seven of Wands or the completion of the Ten? Judgment? Justice? But it was none of those. In utter horror he stared at the card he'd turned face-up. The telecom began to beep, nagging at his attention.

The Moon.

Illusion, false perception. The jackal-headed guardians stared in mockery at him from the image, the four-legged servants at their feet smiling in the darkness. The figures clenched their ankhs as if to say, you see nothing. These are our insights. They do not belong to you.

It had been five years since Geraint had seen the Moon in that way. Last time it had been when he'd trusted a friend who swindled him out of nearly half a million.

The urgency of the telecom's continuing summons jarred him out of his confused self-absorption.

It was Rani, grinning from ear to ear. "Geraint, I tied up a last piece of business," she panted somewhat breathlessly. "You know I told you about the man Pershinkin?"

He had to struggle to remember. "Yes, um, the man; yes, the man who hired your family."

"I killed him. I didn't tell you about it and sometimes it seems like it happened in a dream, but I did it. Before he died, though, he told me he had a meeting set up with

Smith and Jones. Told me when and where. So I staked it out.''

The slightest ache began in his stomach, as if he were in an elevator starting its descent. ''What happened? You killed them?''

She looked content, but also crestfallen. ''Well, no. When they turned up at the place Pershinkin had said, a whole swarm of street samurai suddenly appeared out of nowhere and gunned them down. They dragged the bodies into a limo and buggered off sharpish.

''But they're as dead as the scumbags we fought last night. Didn't kill them myself, but they got what was coming to them. I got my own honor by killing Pershinkin. How about that? Anyway, see you tomorrow. I got friends to see and some celebrations waiting for me. Call you later on if they get really good. You could even pop round and join us! See ya!'' The screen went dead on her smile.

Oh no, no, no.

It just went over and over in his mind. Smith and Jones were Transys men through and through. The corp wouldn't have killed them because they might squeal. Not now. Everything was already busted wide open. Sending a whole gang of samurai to kill them didn't make sense, unless, unless . . . He just couldn't see it.

It was almost like automatic writing, the way he downloaded the analysis programs and began examining the stock markets. Transys had crashed out of sight. Well, of course. But there were buyers. A whole string of them, all across the world. Everyone chipping in for tiny amounts. Little piranhas taking a single mouthful each from the corpse of a dying shark.

It took a little while to engage the global program. All his adult life he'd been updating, refining, cross-indexing this beast, fitting it out with its range of probability functions and estimators. He upgraded it for the last week of dealings, not having had time to do his usual updates.

Transys wouldn't have killed their own people unless those weren't their own people.

And now they weren't in any position to kill anybody. Decision-making would be completely frozen; the entire board of Transys had resigned.

Someone else killed Smith and Jones.

Someone else who was swimming into focus on his screens right now. He could see the shadows behind what he thought to be real. He could see who was behind these little fish. He could see the ancient predator lurking in the waters. He saw him at the bottom of the Moon, at the base of the card, armored and clawed.

"My God," Geraint thought, " we've been horribly, terribly wrong."

That was when they knocked on his door.

34

The Rolls Royce Phaeton purred comfortably along the M825, the great orbital highway ringing inner London. Geraint hadn't much choice about whether to get in it or not. The unsmiling gentlemen with guns had decided it for him. Once inside, he came face to face with two smartly suited middle-aged men in the enormous rear portion of the car.

The two looked similar, with their winter tans, their straight white teeth, graphite-black hair, and heavy shades. The first thing they told him was that they weren't going to kill him. For some reason, he believed it. He was happy to believe them.

"Frankly, we would prefer to," one of them said as the car weaved northward up Edgware Road toward the orbital. "However, someone might start asking awkward questions if you were to disappear. Your little kylie at OzNet has been rather indiscreet, I'm sorry to say. Now other people know about you and, well, you're going to be something of a celebrity. The Man Who Stalked the Ripper. Better be ready for the journalists tomorrow, my Lord." The title was uttered with a sneer. "Not to mention the Met police."

"Would you care for some?" The speaker's colleague was already opening the wafer-thin case with its rows of small gray chips.

"No thank you," Geraint said. "My mother told me never to accept drugs from murderers."

"Suit yourself." The man exhaled his pleasure as the chip began to work on his nervous system. He leaned back, relaxed. "Well, after we monitored you making those transaction checks we knew you'd get the right answer pretty quickly. You'd have found out eventually, of course, but by then it would have been yesterday's news. Hence the need for our little talk now.

"In case you were wondering, we'll have our people remove all the surveillance instruments from your flat whenever it's convenient for you. You see, we really *aren't* going to kill you."

"Your what? But I had the place—"

"Well, of course you did, dear boy, of course you did. I must confess that Risk Minimizers is a very good client of ours. Very rarely do we ask them for a favor. On this occasion, however, we had to cash in."

Geraint was dumbfounded. Wasn't there anyone left he could trust?

"So, would you like the big picture first or the details? It'll make life easier to give you the big picture, I think. Then you can ask us any questions, if you're so inclined." The man was behaving like a teacher explaining something very simple to a willfully dim-witted child.

As they headed through Wood Green, Geraint learned about the attempts to buy out Transys. The corp was secretive, tightly controlled, and not an easy nut to crack.

"We had some people on the inside, obviously. Disaffected elements who weren't happy with the way the company was going, bright people who saw research opportunities going astray. Then, of course, we had a sleeper or two in Transys."

"Like Smith and Jones?" Geraint's voice was little more than a croak.

"Oh, those berks. Yes, they were ours. Pity about them, really, but it did tie up a loose end."

So that's what murder is, Geraint thought. Tying up loose ends. I'm stuck in the back of the most expensive limo on earth with a pair of complete psychopaths.

"We had hoped to break into the corp last year after they lost that wacko star decker of theirs in the Edinburgh business. Quicksilver, wasn't it? Unfortunately, the new chairman of the board was a tough fellow, not someone who'd let us exercise the control we wanted. So we decided it was time for Plan B. Was it Plan B?'' he inquired casually of the other suit.

"Hmm. Plan C, I think.'' His fellow added nothing else by way of explanation.

"Well, there you have it. Plan C it was. The good old ploy of discrediting a company, shooting its stock value to drek, and then buying it up for nothing. Trouble is, with Transys it proved very difficult indeed. They're infuriatingly moral for a megacorporation, you know. The bad stuff they get up to, well, it's small potatoes like dumping hazardous drug stocks on the third world. You know the score, I'm sure. Dodgy experiments on kiddies in what's left of Bangladesh, that sort of monkeying around. Problem is, nobody in the civilized world gives a toss, quite honestly.''

The civilized world, oh yes, Geraint thought grimly. That's the one you people belong to, right?

"That wouldn't be scandal enough for the media. It had to be something closer to home. So, we really had to engineer it ourselves. Fortunately, one of the less scrupulous Brazilian subsidiaries of Transys was beginning to get somewhere with cloning technology. One renegade émigré scientist did some excellent work. Cloning from early fetal cell tissue isn't too hard, but trying to clone from adult DNA samples, well, that's another flaskful of enzymes entirely. The mad boffin, as our wonderful free press will no doubt dub him, made some startling advances in that department.''

"From what we heard, he sounded like a real Mengele,'' the other man commented laconically, before lapsing back into silence.

The first man flicked the intercom to the ork chauffeur. "Let's take a drive around the orbital, my good man. Thank you.'' He closed the link. "Rakkin' baldrick.'' The two men exchanged grins that evidenced their vast debt to cosmetic dentistry.

The main mouthpiece resumed his explanation as Geraint sat patiently. "After a while, however, that lab boy got rather crazy and became something of a security risk, so we terminated him and changed the data a bit. When the Transys head people got to it, it looked like a crock. Then we had to sit on it for a while, another couple of years before we could get the Cambridge sideline opened up, nice and quiet. Purely experimental biotech, no pressure, no snooping from the high-ups in Transys when the turds hit the tumble dryer over the Quicksilver business.

"By then, our people there had the cloning down to a fine art—except for one problem. Clones developed from adult DNA samples turned out to be mentally unstable, hopelessly so. Seems there's something in the morphologic fields of the brain during development that doesn't go quite right. The forced growth and development of a complete clone imposes too much strain on those delicate neural circuits. Ain't it a shame? The good thing is that the old data will prove that Transys has been playing with cloning for quite a while. We arranged for the story to be released to the media around five this afternoon. Last nail in the coffin for Transys."

He lit a cigarette. "Care for one? Very soothing gamma-yohimbine extract. Relaxes the body, really mellows an edge."

Geraint accepted the cigarette. Why not? He wasn't having much input into all this.

"But we always believe that a problem should be seen as an opportunity. That's our motto, you know. So, we thought: why don't we clone someone who's a complete nutter? Then, if he's completely deranged we can pin it on Transys. The friendly company that has been cloning madmen. That would do the trick." He exhaled a perfect smoke ring.

"Dear Jack was just the ticket. Everyone's heard of Jack the Ripper. Top news ratings guaranteed, Transys shafted good and proper. After that, it was really down to the details. There was an extra advantage when Transys got involved in the Global-Hollywood business with that pathetic Ripper chip affair. We were delighted when the elf found out about that, though it was unexpected. That jaunt back to Manhattan threw us a curve, but we had contingencies for feeding that information to you. Anyway, we needed truly independent exposure of the horror of it all, this terrible new Ripper stalking London's streets again.

"So we picked the right people."

"The four of us." Geraint had questions, but he wanted to hear out his enemies first.

"Good God, no. Not that little slag of a baldrick." He spat out the insulting term for an ork like it was poison. "That was pure coincidence. That you met her again after Smith and Jones spammed her over the Fuchi job was a chance in a million. Wouldn't have made any difference if you hadn't. Again, we had contingencies planned. We had one or two more people up our sleeve that we never needed to bring into the frame, in the end."

"So you started with—who?"

"Well, we have a file on you so thick you could wipe your arse on the pages for a month and still have clean hands. We knew your links to Shamandar and the Young woman. You had a good range of skills and contacts between you. You are resourceful and smart. You were a good choice. You worked out great."

"How did it start?" Geraint was not sure he could take much more of this.

"Well, the Kuranita thing was just to get you all thinking. We thought the mage would start sooner asking what the rakk was going on. It was so bloody obvious that Transys wasn't on his list, but he didn't seem to see it. So we changed his instructions to stay at a place where we knew he'd see Kuranita. If he hadn't, we'd have made sure he found out somehow. We knew he'd do something, and we knew you'd help him.

"We fed you the information about Kuranita's visit to the Fuchi installation. We hired those Indian idiots as a decoy and warned Fuchi to expect them. They're good clients of ours, Fuchi. The real Kuranita didn't turn up at Longstanton at all, of course. But we wanted you to get away in the confusion, so we alerted Fuchi to the attack by the other group. We'd given the Indians a tactical briefing. We knew there was no way you would be so stupid as to make a frontal attack. All of that stuff was just to shake you up, like I said, because the elf wasn't asking the right questions at that stage. Oh, and it also earned us a loyalty bonus from Fuchi for tipping them off. You know how it is; never pass up a chance to make money.''

''The murders?''

''Well, of course, the first one nobody would even notice. The second we'd park right on your doorstep. Wasn't that convenient? Part of the reason we selected you, of course. If we'd had an Annie Chapman closer to another of your friends, we'd have roped them in somehow. We had contingencies.''

I don't doubt it, Geraint thought.

As if reading his mind, the man leaned forward slightly to emphasize a point. ''It cost us a fair bit, you know. We actually had to pay Elizabeth Stride to change her name by deed poll a year ago, just to fit in with the series. She was humble Jane Dews before. But perhaps you know that already.''

That's one thing I didn't check, Geraint reflected. Name changes. Clazz, I should have had the sense to find that one out.

''After the second murder, we knew you'd be hooked. We paid Ms. Young to make the Fuchi runs, and our experimental construct worked pretty well.''

Geraint interrupted him. ''But I thought Fuchi was a good customer of yours.''

''Well, they are, but so are all manner of people. That's business.'' He shrugged almost innocently. ''Anyway, the Transys London system is very lax because they've been concentrating all their resources on the Scottish HQ. It was so easy to get our little Jack-in-the-Matrix into that subsystem. Actually, our purpose was merely for Young to see the IC complex, not necessarily to be harmed by it. Annie Chapman's murder would have been enough. She was involved then, just like the elf was after seeing Kuranita. With her history, she'd have to be. Got her psychiatric reports after that San Francisco business, you know.

''So, with the mage in, and the decker in, you had·to be. You were all old friends, and our file says you and Ms. Young haven't exactly been cool toward each other in the past.'' He smirked unpleasantly.

''But how could you know about Catherine Eddowes? How could you know that I—''

"Ah, well now, you'll learn a little more about that later. That one helped to drag you in a bit further, didn't it? We didn't actually expect you to arrive there, you know, not so fast. Our security was a bit on the light side for that one. That's when we realized you were better than we'd thought.

"So, we shipped Mary Kelly out of sight for a while. Here's something you'll love: she was the main decker who worked on the Ripper construct for us. Isn't that lovely? Of course, she didn't know it was a Ripper. Whacked her full of hypnoconditioning and neuroactives and she just did it by automatic configurings right out of her nightmares. Totally amnesic afterward. She was putty in our hands. Dozy bitch."

Geraint leaned back, wearily. He'd never dreamed any of this might have been going on. He was tired, depressed, defeated. Still the explanations kept coming.

"The fact that there were lots of Mary Kellys you could check was both a good thing and a bad thing for us. Good because you'd be occupied tracking them down for the whole damn week, bad because it made it harder for us to point you at the right bloody one. We took a while to figure that one out, I can tell you. Meanwhile, we simply suppressed all the data regarding our little Typhoid Mary, got her out of sight, let you waste a week—or most of it—with the others and then, presto! Up she pops. And when she did, you knew for sure it had to be the right one, because the others were hopeless, let's face it."

"But she wasn't out of sight. Rani said—"

"Ah yes. Saw her in that disgusting baldrick foodhole. Unfortunate that. Our man shouldn't have let her out. She was drugged to the eyeballs and kept under surveillance up to the last minute. Mohinder staged that very well."

"Mohinder?" Another defeat. Another snake. Another thing he simply hadn't seen.

"Great fellow, huh? Quite a moralist too. Refused point-blank to box any of you after the run. Won't kill anyone who's paid him money in good faith, how about that? So we didn't compromise his morals. Actually, you know, I think he wanted to jump that smelly little Indian girly's bones. Rather him than me, I must say.

"He had quite a key role; he knew where the security

was in Kelly's hidey-hole and he had the vidlink to make sure you got the evidence. Needless to say, I'm afraid Mr. Mohinder is somewhere at the bottom of the Thames by now. We really *couldn't* risk letting him live. He won't be missed, I'm sure. He didn't know exactly who he was working for, obviously, but we really couldn't take any chances.''

''You could have killed us all with the meat and muscle you had in that final battle,'' Geraint said.

''No, not really. Mohinder knew what the opposition might be. You were well up to the job. Anyway, to let you in on a little secret, we did wire some very nice glitches into the weapons our folks carried. Buggered up their aiming completely within a hundred yards or so of your car. Very simple little telemetry toy. Practice with the gun out of range, works as sweet as anything. Put it next to your Saab, you couldn't shoot your granny off a commode ten yards away. So our people looked fierce, but they were pussycats. Really. The mage with the elemental actually got a bullet in the back of the head from a cover sniper of ours. We wanted the scene for show, not to turn you into noble toastie.'' He sniggered.

''Most of the rest is incidental detail. We had the police under our thumb, obviously. We had certain contacts make sure Swanson got panicky messages from Annie Chapman's nobleman clients. I think you overlooked that one. The killing wasn't publicized, so how did those people get in touch with the police so fast? But, then, poor old PC Plod's daughter has been a very naughty girl herself. We have the photographs to prove it. Poor old sod would fall apart if it got out. So he was only too happy to keep it quiet and on the back burner.''

''But, the media. You couldn't have known that we wouldn't go to the media.'' The two men exchanged glances behind their shades.

''Yes, I must give you that one, my lord. That was the one calculated risk we took. We decided you almost certainly would not do so initially, because you had escalating levels of personal involvement and your own curiosity would make you want to investigate on your own. Once you'd gone to the media, you'd have lost that chance. That's one of the reasons we tossed Kuranita into the pot, as I've said. It gave the mage very personal reasons to be involved. Same with Ms. Young and her dead friend, not to mention the Ripper construct in the Matrix. That also served to make you confused; there was so much that didn't seem connected, right?''

Geraint had to nod in agreement.

"And you, you're conservative by nature. So you'd want time to try to piece it all together. Our top shrink said you wouldn't blow the whistle until you'd gotten a high level of personal satisfaction from your own involvement, all of you, and he was right. Guess we should slip him a bonus for that. When you did finally go to the media, it couldn't have suited us better.

"Thank you, Lord Llanfrechfa."

Signed, sealed, delivered. The logic of it was inexorable. There was almost nothing left to say, apart from a couple of final queries.

"But why a Ripper? Why the hell would anyone believe that Transys would want to clone him, rather than their own executives, for example?''

"Because they're a megacorporation, and our glorious British public knows that megacorporations are bastards. And research scientists are mad boffins, right? Oh, there are theoretical reasons, too. Such as, it is important to know that it is possible to successfully clone even an old and degraded sample of DNA. Working that out is easiest if you try to clone someone with known and extreme behavioral patterns, right? You can test the validity of your experiment best when you can more easily appraise the outcome. Then again, the Brazilian scientist was obsessive; he had a personal thing about serial killers. Sick, sad man. It's just what he wanted to do, and then Transys took the experiment over, as it were. We've established all that in the data we had leaked to the press."

"The Duke of Clarence? He was really the original Ripper?''

The suits burst into peals of amused laughter.

"Good God, almost certainly not! No one has any idea who the original Ripper was, well, not really. We cloned him because we wanted a Royal involvement. You'll find out more about that later, too. He was the one Royal possible in the frame. The clone was conditioned to become a Ripper, sir. A whole year of dream conditioning, psychodrama, subliminals, neuroactives, sadistic surrogates, you name it, we pumped him full of it. We patterned his innate psychosis, or rather, our insiders at Cambridge did. Stuffed him full of the original scenes, stories, and rumors. Boy, did he have a downer on whores when we were through with him.'' The men shook their heads and sighed quietly.

"Well, we're going to take you home now. Very soon, there'll be a huge gaggle of reptiles from the media outside your front door. Wouldn't be surprised if they started bribing your security and getting up to all sorts of shameful mischief to get a story. Tomorrow, you'll have to give them the full monty on how you caught the Ripper.

"Incidentally, I'm sure I hardly need point out that you don't have a thing on us. We spent seventeen million nuyen and almost three years on this, and you won't find anything. You're smart enough to have tracked the purchasing of Transys shares to us, but that could just be insider knowledge. It would only prove we have someone inside Transys, that's all. The Cambridge lab was stripped out in midweek. There is nothing left to show that the project ever existed. Trust me on this.''

His face was grim and Geraint knew it was true. People who could go to such lengths really wouldn't have left anything to chance.

"And, sir, you wouldn't want to hurt your friends. Mr. Shamandar thinks he has avenged his parents, doesn't he? It would be tragic for him to learn, as he certainly would, that the datafile you got at was, ah, slightly modified. It would pain him deeply to know that he has just delivered Transys to the company that *really* paid for his parents' death.

"As I say, Fuchi is a good client of ours. When Kuranita was unable to continue working as a samurai, we were happy to pass him along. Most people thought he was a freelancer. We knew better.'' He smiled warmly. "Oh, neural implants can buy such loyalty. You never betray a company that can turn your brain to soggy mush in five seconds flat. Those mycotoxins are lovely agents, don't you think?'' The second man grinned his agreement.

"Then again, Ms. Young feels she has avenged her friend Annie Chapman. Wouldn't it cut her to the quick to learn that she has done nothing of the kind? That she's just handed a billion-nuyen company over to the people who really killed Annie Chapman? From what I read in her psychiatric files, well, she just might suffer some kind of permanent breakdown if she learned that. I don't think that's something you'd want to risk with your ex-lover, I really don't.

"I admit our files on the gopi are a bit thin, but she'd feel the same about her family, no doubt about that. Rather like the elf. Isn't it convenient, all these dead families lying around the place? People are so sentimental about their kin. Such a terrible weakness. And I believe honor is very important to the baldricks down there. Consider how she'd feel if she learned the truth. Only eighteen, too, I gather."

Bastards, Geraint agonized. That's the real killer. I can't do this to the others. I can't tell them the truth, I can't. I'll have to live with this all my life. He looked at the two of them, with their self-satisfied smiles. "Why the hell are you telling me all this?" he said.

"Why?" The mouthpiece seemed slightly startled. "I'd have thought that was obvious. Now you know what lines not to cross, what rocks should not be turned over. You can't hide behind ignorance, sir. You now know too much."

"Doesn't that make me a threat?"

"Of a sort, but your own complicity guarantees your silence. That, and the complicity of your friends. Speak about it, and not only will you be implicated in what's occurred, but your friends will too."

Geraint took this in, but when he got out of the car, he shook the man's hand. Somehow, he felt that he had to accept his defeat that way.

"By the way, might I know who I have been speaking to?"

To his surprise, it was the man who'd remained quiet for almost all of the journey who leaned forward and shook his hand. The mouthpiece had done all the talking, but the other man was the real puppeteer.

"Paul Bernal the Third, my Lord. Be seeing you."

The limo swept off into the distance. Paul Bernal III, Geraint thought. The new Deputy Chairman of Hildebrandt-Kleinfort-Bernal, the most ruthless financial corporation in the City of London. The shadow lurking in the sea of little fish. The great predator.

King of Swords.

* * *

Geraint had only just been smuggled back into his flat by a posse of twitchy Cheyne Walk security men when his doorbell rang. He ignored it for a while, but it just kept on ringing, so he slouched to the door to shout at the intruder to rakk off. A reptile already. He just couldn't face the media tonight.

But it wasn't the media, nor was it a visitor he could ever have expected.

"Must speak with you, old fellow. Political crisis. Very important indeed." The flatulent Earl of Manchester ignored Geraint's pleas to be left alone and bustled in, parking his gross frame in an armchair. Wearily, Geraint closed the door behind him and poured two large brandies.

"Please, sir, make this quick. I'm not feeling very well tonight," Geraint said as he handed him a glass. The Earl looked at him most appraisingly.

"Well, old feller, this Ripper business of yours has been causing a bit of a stir, I must say. Duke of Clarence, you know, he's related to the Gordon-Windsor side of the Royal Family."

Related to the pretender to the throne. After the Royal Schism of 2025, it had been a long-running internecine war between the Windsor-Hanoverians of George VIII's circle and the rival Gordon-Windsor bloodline. The appearance of the Ripper would drive a stake through the heart of the rivals to the throne. Or, at least, set them back a long way. Utterly idiotic and illogical, but a smear was a smear. Geraint took a large swig of brandy, but did not taste it.

"Well, that's all well and good for the King in one

way. Rival fellow a cad and a bounder, hands steeped in gore, all that kind of thing. But, old chap, it does make people wonder about royalty generally, you see. Anything that weakens the family weakens the King.''

Now Geraint saw it in all its glory.

He knew Hildebrandt-Kleinfort-Bernal was one of the corporations behind King George VIII. The Ripper gave them a perfect double strike. On the one hand, the scandal struck a possibly decisive blow against the rival to their man. On the other, it weakened the King himself, even if only slightly, and made him more dependent than ever on his political and corporate backers. What a payoff HKB had bought for their seventeen million.

''Now's the time for all good men to rally to King and country, old boy. I can tell you, there'll be something in this for you. And there's a little personal thank you, too.''

Geraint experienced a fleeting moment of something close to depersonalization. He knew he was going to have to listen to words he would later dread having heard, but right now he felt almost completely uninvolved in what was happening.

''I want to thank you for keeping young Lawrence's name out of all this with that Eddowes woman. I know what you did there, old boy. Damn decent of you.

''I can't tell you how glad I am you're keeping quiet about this.''

It was a thunderbolt, the slow emphasis of the final sentence. What it meant was so simple: keep your mouth shut.

He remembered the words of the man in the back of the limo: *You'll learn a little more about that later.* For a second, Geraint wondered whether Lawrence had possibly been sent to the woman, and even arranged for him to come there deliberately. It would be part of the plan, increasing the chances of Geraint becoming involved in the Ripper killings when he knew one of the victims. That would mean the Earl would have been in on it. He made a mental note to check Manchester's stock holdings in HKB.

''Well, my boy, I have to say that the Prime Minister will be making some minor modifications to the Cabinet tomorrow afternoon. Consensus of opinion is that Farquahar isn't too sound at the Foreign Office. I'm delighted to say that you can expect to be named Junior Minister of State at the Foreign Office at five tomorrow afternoon. How does that suit you, eh? We need a man we can trust there to keep an eye on the Foreign Secretary, my dear boy. We need one of our own. That is, unless you'd prefer something a little less onerous at the Treasury?''

Geraint hardly knew what it was he mumbled, but the Earl took it as acceptance of the Foreign Office offer and saw himself out. Staring blankly across the room, Geraint saw the vellum and red ribbon sitting on his table. Wearily he pulled himself up and went to investigate, already knowing exactly what he would find. Reading the header, he discovered that he had been owner of ten thousand HKB shares for three months. He had little doubt that his own financial transactions would have been retroactively altered to show when, and how, he'd bought them.

How did it go again?
We need one of our own.

* * *

The telecom messages kept piling up until well after midnight. There were journalists, tridstars, media agencies offering their brokering services, image consultants, a couple of psychics, wackos, even some faces he would have known, if he had looked at them.

Francesca called twice from Oxford to say she was recuperating and wanting to arrange dinner for the next day.

Serrin called twice from Cambridge, saying he had found what he'd gone there to find, and wishing Geraint success and happy dreams. He'd see him Tuesday.

Rani called a couple of times too, drunk and flushed, saying that she couldn't track down Mohinder, but apart from that, everything was great and she loved Wales and he was the best thing that had happened to her and she'd be around tomorrow and where was he?

The man sat at his desk in the electronic twilight. Screens flickered around him. As the telecom poured out its endless stream of calls and cries and messages, he sat with his cards, turning them over and over and over.

INNER LONDON

YOU'VE READ THE FICTION, NOW PLAY THE GAME!

S·E·C·O·N·D E·D·I·T·I·O·N

WELCOME TO THE FUTURE.

Magic has returned to the world. Man now shares the earth with creatures of myth and legend. Dragons soar the skies. Elves, dwarves, trolls and orks walk the streets.

Play **Shadowrun** and **you'll** walk the streets of 2053. When the mega-corporations want something done but don't want to dirty their hands, it's a shadowrun they need, and they'll come to you. Officially you don't exist, but the demand for your services is high. You might be a decker, sliding through the visualized databases of giant corporations, spiriting away the only thing of real value—information. Perhaps you are a street samurai, an enforcer whose combat skills make you the ultimate urban predator. Or a magician wielding the magical energies that surround the Earth.

That's exactly the kind of firepower you'll need to make a shadowrun...

AVAILABLE AT FINE BOOKSTORES AND GAME STORES EVERYWHERE!